Take Me As I Am

JM Dragon & Erin O'Reilly

Take Me As I Am

JM Dragon & Erin O'Reilly

Affinity
eBook Press
NZ
2016

Take Me As I Am
© by JM Dragon & Erin O'Reilly 2016

Affinity E-Book Press NZ LTD
Canterbury, New Zealand

1st Edition

ISBN: 978-0-908351-54-1

All rights reserved.

No part of this e-Book may be reproduced in any form without the express permission of the author and publisher. Please note that piracy of copyrighted materials violate the author's rights and is Illegal.

This is a work of fiction. Names, character, places, and incidents are the product of the author's imagination or are used fictitiously and any resemblance to actual persons living or dead, businesses, companies, events, or locales is entirely coincidental

Editor: Nat Burns
Proof Editor: Alexis Smith
Cover Design: Irish Dragon Designs

Acknowledgments

It is always exciting to work together on a story for we always feel we bring out the best in each other. We hope you will enjoy the read.

Nancy, thank you for the feedback, as always spot on the mark. Lisa, thanks for your observations and sorry it kept you up late…well we're not really since it made us smile.

Thanks to Natty for her wonderful edit and Alexis for her attention to detail on the final proof.

As always thank you to our many readers who continue to follow this marvellous journey we travel with the written word.

Dedication

For all our Affinity family members. You all rock.

Table of Contents

Chapter One	1
Chapter Two	7
Chapter Three	12
Chapter Four	15
Chapter Five	24
Chapter Six	38
Chapter Seven	45
Chapter Eight	60
Chapter Nine	71
Chapter Ten	85
Chapter Eleven	103
Chapter Twelve	110
Chapter Thirteen	122
Chapter Fourteen	133
Chapter Fifteen	148
Chapter Sixteen	160
Chapter Seventeen	170
Chapter Eighteen	177
Chapter Nineteen	184
Chapter Twenty	197
Chapter Twenty-one	211
Chapter Twenty-two	221
Chapter Twenty-three	229
Chapter Twenty-four	239
Chapter Twenty-five	257
Chapter Twenty-six	269
Chapter Twenty-seven	280
Chapter Twenty-eight	289
Chapter Twenty-nine	298
Chapter Thirty	308
Chapter Thirty-one	323
Jo Lackerly's Songbook	335

Also by JM Dragon

Do Dreams Come True?
The One
Letting Go
Circus
Falling Into Fate
The Fixit Girl
In Name Only
Death is Only the Beginning
Lonely Angel
Echo's Crusade
A Window in Time
Waterfalls, Rainbows and Secrets
The Dragon's Halloween Collection
Incantations – A Collaboration
Affinity's Christmas Collection 2010
Christmas Collection 2011
Christmas Collection 2012
Christmas Collection 2014

Define Destiny Series
Define Destiny
Haunting Shadows
In Pursuit of Dreams
Actions and Consequences
All Our Tomorrows
Two Steps Forward One Back
A World of Change

When Hell Meets Heaven
Fatal Hesitation

by JM Dragon & Erin O'Reilly
Against All Odds
Earthbound
Echoes of the Past
Paradox of Love
Quest For Love
The End Game
Requiem
New Beginnings
Atonement

Also by Erin O'Reilly
Return to Me
If I Were a Boy
Through the Darkness
Deception
Fearless
'55 Ford
Fractured
Revelations
Wolf at the Door
Sandcastles

Writing with JM Dragon
Earthbound
When Hell Meets Heaven Series
New Beginnings
Atonement

Take Me As I Am

Chapter One

"Get the fuck out of my car now, you useless bitch," Jed bellowed before forcibly pushing her hard against the handle of the door.

Joanna Lackerly, wincing in pain, scowled in hatred at the man who was yelling at her. "Screw you, Jed. I hope your sorry ass rots in hell," she muttered loudly.

"Bitch, you'll rot in hell way before me. I guarantee it." He revved up the engine of the car. "Now, get the hell out of my car."

"I hope I do get there before you. That way I get to be the welcome party," Jo responded sarcastically.

She pushed open the door and hastily placed her pride and joy—her guitar and case—on the concrete sidewalk. Without getting out, she reached in the backseat for her suitcase and swung it over the seat before placing it next to the guitar case. She wouldn't put it past the bastard to speed off, leaving her with nothing but the clothes on her back. As she cleared the car by a mere two inches, he sped off at a pace that left a cloud of dust.

Jo brushed herself off and looked around the small town that she was now stuck in. She was alone in the middle of the sidewalk with only her guitar and a strong voice to help her make a living. She assumed she would find a bar that needed or wanted her brand of entertainment. But she'd learned long ago that life held no guarantees and finding work in one-horse towns usually meant she had to consider something less savory in order to make money. She hadn't done that in a while and hoped she wouldn't have to ever again.

She looked toward the shabby entrance of the motel, situated at the end of what seemed the town's only street, aptly named Main Street. "Danvers Motel. Can this get any better?" Jo picked up her belongings and began walking in that direction.

From the outside, the motel looked like the typical run down place she stayed in wherever she went. The creaking door, with dingy, peeling gray paint opened to a neat looking lobby, which was in total contrast to the outside facade. She could smell the fresh scent of cut flowers—carnations—and smiled as she saw several vases scattered around the room full of different colored carnations. It looked quite cozy and rather unusual.

Bet this is gonna cost me, she thought.

There were two well-worn but clean and comfortable looking easy chairs next to a coffee table with several magazines neatly spread on its polished surface. To the left of the motel desk was a long table with a coffeepot full of what appeared, by the smell of it, freshly brewed coffee. Jo was sorely tempted to pick up one of the china mugs situated in neat rows next to the machine. There was also, what was clearly fresh milk and cream next to them. Alongside that was a carafe that, she could tell by the faint, fragrant aroma, held a fresh brew of tea. The place was so out of the ordinary that she was certain her imagination was playing tricks on her.

Shaking her head, she heard voices getting closer, the door marked private opened, and Jo saw the back of a small woman with short blonde hair waving her arms as she spoke to an elderly woman.

"Daisy, it isn't my decision anymore, it's the bank's. What do you want me to do?" If the tone of the blonde's voice was anything to go by, she was distressed.

"I want you to go and tell that good for nothing George Andrews that you need more time. If your papa were alive, this wouldn't be happening."

The old woman, who was shouting in a passively aggressive voice, looked toward the opening and Jo could feel the eyes boring into her.

"I...oh, I know that, but if it hadn't been for Papa in the first place, none of this would have been happening," the blonde said.

"Little girl, keep them thoughts to yourself and go see what that tall stranger wants." The older woman gave her a pat on the head and turned on her heel slowly before walking away.

The blonde turned green eyes on Jo as if startled by a stranger being in the lobby.

"Oh, no, why does this always happen when there's a potential customer about?" she muttered, loudly enough for Jo to hear. She walked toward the reception desk, swallowed a couple of times, and then smiled politely. "Hello. What can I do for you?"

Jo looked at the considerably shorter woman and gave her a thorough examination. "I need a room, nothing fancy. What are the rates?" Jo once again felt the urge to take up the coffee invitation to her right hand side.

"Twenty-five a night is the cheapest room I have. It's very basic with a twin bed and a small bathroom. There's a small television but no cable or internet."

Jo quickly added up what she had on hand and thought she had enough money to see her through to the end of the week without a job. She nodded. "I don't need much. I'll take it."

"Would you sign the register for me? And how would you like to pay Ms....?"

Jo arched an eyebrow in the other woman's direction and saw the faint blush appear on her face. "Lackerly, Joanna Lackerly. I'll pay with cash."

"Well, Ms. Lackerly, I'm pleased to have you stay with us. Your room is number five."

Jo signed the register and looked at the coffee, which was causing her nose to twitch in response to its aroma. "Is the coffee and tea a perk of staying here?"

"No. We charge fifty cents a cup."

Thea Danvers smiled as she took in Joanna's worn clothes that were relatively clean, but probably could do with replacing. The midnight black hair that was hanging loosely around her shoulders could do with a trim and a washing since it looked rather lank. The most captivating feature of the woman was her deep, dark blue eyes. She wondered what had brought Joanna Lackerly to Danvers but politeness stopped her, at least for now, from being too inquisitive.

Thea looked at the rather dour expression on the face before her. "Would you like coffee, Ms. Lackerly?" She looked at the woman and watched as she ran her tongue across her lips.

"No. Not right now. Maybe later. Where do I pay if no one is here?"

"There's a jar behind the cups. We go by an honor system here," Thea said briskly. She removed some keys from under the counter of the reception desk and jangled them. "If you follow me, I will show you to your room."

Thea hadn't wanted to sound too friendly and offer the woman a free cup of coffee. She'd learned that being friendly wasn't what the customers wanted, although in the case of the men that stayed there, they would prefer the personal touch—a little more personal than Thea was ever going to offer.

Thea stopped at the door marked five and placed the key inside the lock and heard the snick as the lock was released on the turn of the key. "I hope you will be comfortable, Ms. Lackerly," she said handing a key to the woman behind her.

Thea had felt the woman's light breath on the back of her neck. When she turned, she noticed that the blue eyes were searching her face before the dark head nodded and accepted the key. She moved aside to allow the woman to move by her.

"Enjoy your stay," Thea said with a smile before quickly moving back down the corridor.

†

Jo had followed the woman down a small corridor lined with motel rooms.

Damn. I could have used some coffee but I need to watch my pennies until I can find a job.

She had noticed when she looked at the brochure on the reception desk that there were ten rooms. The place was certainly well looked after and the decoration was tasteful. All the furnishings along the corridor looked old and worn, but seemed remarkably expensive in style. She speculated that someone bought them at a house sale or something.

She opened the door to her room and took a step inside. Her eyes widened considerably at the sight and she turned back to the corridor. "You've made a mistake," she cried out. The blonde was no longer there.

Not really knowing what else to do, she went back inside, put down her things, and glanced around the room. The decoration was in pale blues and lilacs and it was so light and airy that it made her feel welcomed, as if she were coming home. She could smell fresh cut flowers and saw lilacs on the small table next to the window. Outside she saw what looked like a small patch of grass along with numerous flowers in several stages of growth.

The bed was a king-sized monster draped at the headboard with filmy translucent satin of the deepest royal blue with matching bed linen. There was a small television on a shelf, which made viewing easy from the bed or from the easy chair that was next to the table. The dresser had a large mirror and the local newspaper with a few flyers indicating what was available in the area rested on the dresser, along with a basket of fruit.

When she opened another door, she was amazed at the bathroom. It was a Victorian style bath with an overhead shower and a lilac shower curtain. Several toiletries were in a basket on the sink along with fresh smelling towels. Jo shivered at the thought of feeling soft clean towels after a long luxurious bath filled to the brim with bubbles.

It had to be a mistake for the woman clearly said the room had a single bed. She was there for now and decided that she could treat herself to one night of luxury before moving to a cheaper room. *Thank you, God.*

After putting the plug in the bathtub and turning on the taps, she watched the water immediately steam and begin filling the tub. She smiled in satisfaction. It had been a long time since she'd felt hot, hot water. Most places she stayed had lukewarm water at best. Jo grinned when she saw bottles of aromatherapy bubble bath on a glass shelf positioned above the washbasin. For the first time in ages, she laughed genuinely as she saw the names of the two products—Sensual and Exciting. It was a hell of a combination. Selecting the one marked sensual, she poured it liberally into the flow of water and watched in pleasure as the bubbles rose.

"I wonder if I can get work around here. If it turns out that this is what I get for twenty-five dollars a night, I would stay here forever."

She stripped off her clothes, which she knew needed laundering badly, as did all the other clothes in her bag. *Do I even have clean underwear?* It was a depressing thought. Nevertheless, she wouldn't let the opportunity of having her body clean pass her by even if she couldn't quite manage to extend that to her clothes. That was a task for later. Right now, she was going to soak in that old bathtub, which had her name written all over it.

Jo lowered her lean body into the hot water and bubbles as the strangely familiar aroma surrounded her. A decadent purr escaped her lips as she settled down into the depths and closed her eyes to everything. Everything that is, but the pleasure of the next half-hour or more.

Chapter Two

Thea looked around the small lobby and placed a couple more old issues of *Time* magazine on the coffee table. Danvers wasn't a bad place. She had been born and raised in Danvers yet something was missing in her life. If she knew what that was, then maybe she'd know how to find it, or at least where to look. Sighing heavily, she failed to notice the door open and a portly, well-dressed man enter by the side door. When she heard the door close, she looked up.

George Andrews was watching her from his position at the door. To Thea it was more like a leer than a glance. No matter how many times she told him she had no interest in him, he kept coming around, insinuating that it was only a matter of time before she'd give in to him. Even though he practically owned her motel, she vowed that she'd never capitulate to the disgusting man's overtures.

He mopped his sweaty face with a less than clean handkerchief and smiled at her. She noticed his eyes resting on her breasts and reflexively put her hand to her neck, pulling the collar tight, all the while chastising herself for leaving three buttons undone. Her stomach roiled at his devilish smile when his eyes met hers.

"My dear Thea, surely you can get Daisy to do the menial tasks of putting out the literature. She's certainly capable of that, at least," he said sarcastically.

Disconcerted by his very presence, Thea shivered. What the hell did he want now? "Mr. Andrews, how I allocate tasks in *my* motel is *my* concern, not yours. I'm sure you have far better things to do than worry about how my staff spends their time."

Andrews's eyes raked across her body again and she shivered. "Thea, my dear, please after all these years, we can dispense with the mister and you can call me George."

Thea knew he was a snake in the grass with a slimy attitude. How her father ever let the man dupe him into believing he was a friend, astounded her. Now she was paying the price.

"Mr. Andrews, what brings you here today? Doesn't the bank need you? It is still open at this time, isn't it?"

Thea had almost given in and said his first name. She had decided that as far as the business and this town were concerned, she wasn't completely dead yet. The town named after her great grandfather was a decent place to live despite the likes of George Andrews.

He gave her a speculative look and shook his head, but kept his smile in place. "I thought I would pay a social call and check on how you're doing. As you know, the bank has invested heavily in the motel."

Thea heard the sarcastic tone and wished she could say the place was full, but it wasn't. All she had was a woman who looked like nothing more than a drifter and who had only been prepared to pay the lowest possible rate. Not that she had been given a downgraded room. She hadn't. To hell with Andrews. "Actually I have a customer and she's going to be long term and is paying the best rates," Thea said in a defiant tone.

George gave her a shrewd look as if he was trying to determine if she were lying to him. It was no secret that there hadn't been anyone new in town for weeks.

She held his eyes with a steady gaze.

"Who is it?"

Thea looked at his ruddy complexion and his pugnacious features. He had the look of a boxer who had been in too many fights. He was also overweight for his height and his fat stomach came out to meet you before his hand did. "She's a traveler."

Andrews looked at her suspiciously. "What kind of traveler?"

Thea continued to hold her gaze steady. "Ms. Lackerly wasn't all that talkative about her personal life. She implied that she would be staying a time." Thea had her hands behind her back with fingers crossed as she spoke the words. She didn't want to lie exactly, but stretching the truth under the current circumstances was necessary.

George shrugged. "I see. So, how long will that be?"

"How would I know? She didn't say," Thea responded quickly.

"You're right then, she isn't talkative." His tone was malicious.

"No. No, she isn't. There again, would you be, in a strange town?" Thea crossed her fingers twofold at her blatant lies.

Andrews nodded and gave her another long look. "Perhaps not," he conceded.

"So, Mr. Andrews, I have things to do. Do you want me for something in particular?" Thea countered in an amiable tone, forcing a smile.

"No. No, I will let you carry on. Thea, would you consider going to the dance on Saturday night with me?" The man's ruddy complexion became redder still.

Thea didn't like to hurt anybody's feelings, but she seriously didn't want to go with him. "Sorry, but I have other plans."

Andrews once again glanced at her speculatively. "No problem. I will be here soon to see you again." He gave her another long look and then disappeared out the side door.

Thea watched his retreating back and let out a sigh of relief. God, what was she going to do if he took control of the motel? She had nothing to fall back on and no qualifications.

Her eyes tracked toward the corridor where her new resident resided, hoping that she'd stay at least long enough to give her claim credence. Only time and a miracle would tell.

†

When George left the motel, he turned and looked at the shabby building before he let an evil grin cross his lips. For a brief moment, he wondered if she was telling him the truth about the new customer. Why would she lie? It certainly would not solve her problems. Was she really otherwise engaged the night of the dance? He had to concede that he would not know otherwise until she turned up at the function with someone else. He could wait. He had waited ten years, so what were a couple more months? The bitch was going to pay up eventually and when she did, it was going to be on his terms.

It was all her father's fault. Daniel Danvers had gambled away the last of the Danvers property years before and he'd taken full advantage of the situation. Had it not been for Daniel's sincere love for his daughter, he would have gambled her away, too, just as he'd attempted to do with his wife. A wicked smile came to his lips as he recalled the look of horror on Danvers' face at the suggestion that he trade his daughter for his debt. Had the man lived a little longer he would have relented, of that George was sure. The stupid bastard died in a bizarre car accident. The mystery surrounding the accident was such that the insurance company still hadn't paid off on his death policy. That put George in the driver's seat as far as Thea was concerned. He'd do whatever was necessary to ensure that the payout never materialized.

He recalled her trim and enticing figure that always caused him to sweat even more than usual. The olive green shirt she wore was not in itself revealing, but the number of buttons open at the neck gave him a very tempting view of pale flesh. She would be his—there was no doubt about that. He held the note on the motel, which meant she was dependent on him and soon she'd have no other option than to accept his proposal. With that thought, he smiled before heading back to his bank.

Chapter Three

Jo felt decidedly better than she had two hours earlier. In fact, she was glad Jed was gone. He'd been nothing but a fucking pain and he sucked in bed and not in a good way, either. His one merit was the ability to talk bar owners into giving her a chance to sing. Only problem with that was Jed usually took umbrage when anyone made a play for her, ending in wrecking more than one bar with the ensuing fight. In the end, a sheriff would usually escort them out of town rather than them leaving of their own accord.

Now she was on the sidewalk gazing up at a sign of what must be the only bar in the small town. With swift steps, she was at the entrance of John-Henry's Tavern within seconds. As she placed her hand on the wooden door she noticed it needed a paint job. "This whole town could do with a makeover," she muttered.

She opened the door and sauntered in, her guitar case slung over her back as if she didn't have a care in the world. The bartender looked at her in speculation before he grinned.

Good start.

"Hi." Jo gave a wide smile.

"Hi, yourself. New in town?" he asked in a friendly, open manner.

"Yeah. Wonder if you have any openings for entertainers hereabouts?" Jo looked him straight in the eye. She'd know before he said the words if he wasn't interested. Eyes always had that kind of way of letting her know things like that. The man returned her eye contact and she could see that his brown ones had a serious expression in them. He was clearly weighing her merit.

"What kinda entertainment?" He nodded at her guitar. "Do you play that only or sing, too?"

Jo gave him a keen glance. "I sing some and play this some, too."

"Wanna let me hear you and decide if my customers will like what they hear?"

"Sure, why not?" Jo reached behind her and set free the clasp that held the guitar's harness in place. It dropped into her securely waiting hands, deftly removing the casing.

"The people hereabouts like country music."

"Country it is, then. Have a request?" Jo strummed absently on the strings of her beloved guitar. It had cost her a fortune way back when she was playing in a club in her hometown and making real money, not just enough to live.

"Surprise me." The bartender settled his elbows on the bar's smooth clean surface and waited.

A soft strum of the strings brought about an intro and Jo started to sing.... *"I'm a traveling girl. I travel the world to find you...."*

Jo finished the soft ballad, glanced up, shaking the dark hair out of her eyes, and gave the man a small smile. Sucking in a breath, she waited for his verdict.

"Lady, I can't pay you much, but the package you have to offer, I'd be a fool to let pass. How about fifty dollars a night and all the drinks you want are free," he offered.

Jo didn't give much away, but she was happy. It meant she could afford to stay at the motel, have a decent meal, and still have change. It was better than sharing with Jed and she could sleep on her own if she wanted to. "Works for me."

"John-Henry Bascome." The man held out his hand.

"You're the owner?"

The man nodded.

"Joanna Lackerly. My friends call me Jo."

"Jo, it is then."

"When do you want me to start?" Jo asked.

John-Henry raised an eyebrow. "Be here at seven this evening. I'll expect my money's worth. If you need a place to stay, I'd recommend the Danvers Motel. Might not look much from the outside, but believe me, it's worth going inside."

Jo heard the warmth behind the words about the motel. "Already been there and you're right, it's not what I expected from the outside."

"No. Well, sometimes nothing is exactly what it appears to the outside world," he replied.

"Yeah, I guess. I'll see you later, boss." Jo replaced her guitar in the case before slinging it over her shoulder with practiced ease and clipping it in place. "See you at seven sharp."

Jo turned to leave, deciding that she needed to get some of her stuff cleaned if she was going to be performing in a few hours. Walking out of the bar and into the afternoon sun, she glanced around for the nearest coin-operated laundry and crossed her fingers that they had one. She didn't see one initially and surmised she'd have to go looking for it. With the size of this town, it wouldn't take that long.

†

John-Henry watched the woman leave. She was certainly beautiful and could play the guitar and sing as well as she looked. He was impressed and had no doubt that his customers would appreciate her style of entertainment. In his time he'd come across far too many men and women who had called themselves entertainers. This woman surely had a voice that was appealing.

"Wonder why she isn't in some fancy town making money off her talent." It really didn't matter to him since the folks around there would be in for a treat for however long she wanted to play to them. He went back to polishing the surface of the sparkling bar top, whistling an out of tune song that the woman had just played.

"Catchy tune. Wonder why I've never heard that one before."

Chapter Four

Thea gazed across the small yard out behind the motel. It brought tears to her eyes as she contemplated losing this one final family possession. Her family had been some of the earliest settlers in the area and had been the largest landowners for a thousand miles. Death, gambling, and silly forays into unsuitable investments during the past couple of generations had left Thea and her father as the only Danvers left alive in the area. And they'd had nothing but the ranch, the motel, and the local bar. Her father had succumbed to the gambling fever that was a common trait in the family line and first lost the bar and then the ranch to the bank. Unless she could come up with the mortgage payments, the bank would have the motel, as well. That meant that George Andrews would have full control of everything she held dear.

Her father's death hadn't helped at all. They told her that he'd been drinking heavily the evening he'd left town to visit a sick friend—at least that's what his friends said. Her father hadn't had a sick friend that she was aware of, and his car crashing into the ravine ten miles from town had been senseless and totally unlike her father. Whatever condition he was in, he would never have hit the ravine—it was just too far away from the road.

When the autopsy revealed a high alcohol level in his system and interviews revealed his financial troubles, the insurance people became suspicious. The insurance company hadn't paid out his death benefit, claiming that the circumstances had been suspicious and that there was a suicide clause. If it had been her father's decision to end his life and leave her with the insurance money, it had backfired in a big way.

She heard the entrance door to the motel open and walked quickly back into the lobby. Thea saw the back of the woman, Joanna Lackerly, who was staying in room five as she reached for a cup and poured herself some coffee.

"Have you settled into your room, Ms. Lackerly?" Thea asked.

She couldn't help the smirk that crossed her face as she saw what appeared to be a guilty start from the otherwise poised woman.

When the steel blue eyes captured hers, Thea was puzzled at the feeling of familiarity.

Ms. Lackerly nodded. "Call me Jo, please."

Thea saw the nod and inclined her head in acknowledgement. "Will you be staying in town long, Jo?"

"I might be here longer than the end of the week like I originally planned." She pushed a strand of dark hair away from her eyes before sipping the coffee. "I put the money in the jar."

Thea smiled. "I think since you are going to be staying longer, the coffee will be on the house from now on."

"Thank you. I must say this is great tasting and very refreshing. I've just spent the past few hours at what must be the smallest laundromat on earth."

Thea laughed. "Does it still have only one machine that works?"

"Yes, and there was some guy there that kept telling me the story of his life."

"That would be David Mahoney." Thea grinned. "I think he is the only one in town who uses the laundromat."

"And now me." Jo laughed.

"Is there a reason you might be staying longer?" Thea asked. "It's not like Danvers is a bustling hub."

"I've a job at John-Henry's Tavern. If it works out, I can stay longer. If not...."

Thea frowned. John-Henry rarely employed strangers and she wondered exactly what the woman's role in the bar would be. *What does it matter to me anyway? She is a drifter and can do what she wants.*

"John-Henry is a good man. He wouldn't have employed you if he didn't think you'd work out. What exactly do you do? If you don't mind me asking." Thea was genuinely interested.

"I sing and play the guitar. An entertainer of sorts, I'd guess you'd call it." Jo once again sipped her coffee.

"Are you good?"

"Depends on your taste."

"I like country music. Cissy Lenard style, although I do have eclectic tastes in other music." Thea was frustrated talking to the woman since she didn't answer anything with any clarity.

"Then I could sing a few that you'd like, I guess."

"What do you prefer to sing?" Thea persisted. For some reason she wanted to know what the other woman preferred.

"My own compositions. I need to do a few things if you don't mind, Ms—?"

"You write your own songs? You must be very talented." Thea saw a change of stance from mild interest to boredom. When she raised an eyebrow, Thea realized she hadn't answered the question.

"Oh, sorry. My name is Danvers, Thea Danvers. I own the motel." Thea could feel her cheeks heat from her oversight. The woman turned away and Thea was immediately disappointed that she wasn't going to get an answer.

"I have many talents. You would have to hear them and decide for yourself if they were any good." The woman said before heading toward her room.

Thea, surprised by the rejoinder, smiled slowly as she watched the retreating woman. "Perhaps I will. Perhaps I will," she whispered.

Her eyes once again strayed to the yard and the colors that presented themselves there. Her tears this time stayed away. She might be poles apart from the woman she now had as a customer, but perhaps her luck was turning. If her new tenant was paying and became a long-term resident, who knew what else might change in her favor. Idly thumbing through the guest register, she saw the bold and precise signature and knew that the woman probably reflected that style.

†

John-Henry watched his new singer enter the bar and saw heads turn at her appearance. She was dressed in faded denims that had seen better days or maybe were just fashionable. She was wearing a denim shirt that had studs everywhere and on the back of the shirt, he could make out the name JO. The shirt itself was open to reveal a cleavage that would keep the male customers happy even if she couldn't carry a tune in a bucket. The plus was that she could sing and just maybe she would bring in more customers. If she failed tonight, it will only cost him fifty dollars and free booze. He didn't think she'd fail, her voice was too good for that.

†

Jo was pleasantly surprised to find that the bar was busy. The customers appeared to be local ranch hands and others that she surmised were professionals of some sort. There was a distinct lack of women, but that was usual in small town bars. She looked at John-Henry then at the crowd before putting a hand behind her neck to ensure that her hair was secure in a band.

"I cleared an area for you over there," John-Henry pointed to a raised area with a stool on it.

Jo went toward the area. As she moved, she could feel the eyes on her. It was always the same—men leering, along with the requisite wolf whistles that followed. She sat on the stool, lifted her guitar plugged it into a nearby amplifier, and began strumming. After sucking in a deep breath, she sang.

†

When Thea entered the bar shortly before nine, she was amazed at the excited buzz coming from the normally reserved patrons. The guitar sounds amplified by a speaker system playing an upbeat tune and she felt the excitement of the evening and the music start to pound in her body.

Thea moved to a stool at the end of the bar, away from the mass of people that were surrounding her new motel guest. She looked at the way the woman casually played to the audience, clearly knowing exactly what would excite them. A chanting of 'Jo' sounded throughout the room.

"Ms. Danvers, nice to see you," John-Henry said. "Haven't seen you in here in a long time," he added.

Thea turned her attention to the softly spoken man and smiled. She liked him. He had always been civil with her. She'd found out recently that he'd paid more than it was worth for the bar deed and had been subsidizing her father's drinking habits for some time prior to his death. "The last time was when you called me to come get my father. It's good to see you, John-Henry. Quite a crowd you have tonight."

"Yes, it is. What can I get you?"

"I'll have whatever lite beer you have on tap." Thea gave him a dazzling smile as he went on his way to fetch her drink.

Thea turned her attention back to the woman who was making the men in the room whistle and shout. They seemed to be enjoying themselves. The music changed tempo and a tune she'd never heard had her shifting her glance toward the woman sitting on a stool on the small stage.

The steel blue eyes she'd seen that afternoon were staring directly at her and Thea was sure they peered into her soul. She caught her breath. The eyes were seemingly asking her a question. Mesmerized, Thea didn't notice John-Henry placing a frosty mug in front of her. She listened intently to the words of the song....

"Innocently I loved; it was real for me, another notch for you..."

To Thea, the song was plaintive in tone and sung with a melancholy that gave it a truth beyond the words. Not a country song exactly, but the crowd was lapping it up. She tried and failed to catch the other woman's eyes again when a slurred voice at her side caught her unaware, diverting her attention.

"Msss Da..anvers you wanna dance?"

Politeness being an overriding character trait of hers, Thea gave the man a wary smile and shook her head. "No. Thanks anyway." She quickly grasped the mug and drank from it thirstily. She hoped her actions would put the man off.

"Ah, a lady after my own heart." He belched. "John-Henry, look here!" He waved his hand. "Ship us refills, will yah?" the young man shouted arrogantly.

"That's okay. Please, I only came in for one drink. I need to go." Thea desperately looked around for a means of escape. The man was rather tall and bulky. She had seen him around, but she didn't know his name and now didn't want to. He was no gentleman.

"Little lady, I'm buying." He placed a heavy hand on her shoulder and effectively stopped her flight.

"Really, I don't want another drink. Please, if you wouldn't mind taking your hand off my shoulder. I need to go." Thea wasn't used to this situation and never wanted to become used to it. Her eyes darted around uncertainly for some help. The only one who could help her was John-Henry and he was engrossed in trying to stop a fight that had started at the other end of the bar.

"I say you do. If Tony Reed says he's buying, that's reason enough." He placed his other hand on her opposite shoulder and tugged her closer to him.

Thea smelled the whisky and the memory of picking up her drunken father invaded her thoughts. All she wanted to do was to escape.

"The lady said she didn't want a drink, so beat it," a low, carefully controlled voice said.

The voice came from somewhere behind Thea and its nuance was so neutral she didn't know if it was a man or woman.

"Y...ou her keep...er," the man slurred.

Thea heard the hesitation in the man's voice and wondered who it was that was coming to her rescue.

"Yeah. Going to make an issue of it?" The voice had taken on a vicious quality that made the smile on the man's face turn to a scowl.

Releasing Thea's shoulders, the man moved menacingly toward the person who had spoken in her defense.

Thea, jumping from the stool, moved so that she could see her defender and her mouth dropped open. She came face to face with the singer who it would appear was invading not only her thoughts, but her life, too.

"I'd like to see you stop me." The man lunged forward with a fist and was easily side stepped and he cannoned instead into a post with his face planted flat against the surface.

The singer laughed cruelly as the man staggered away from the post with a bleeding nose. "Wanna have another go?" she taunted.

"You bitch! I'm gonna make you pay for this. See if I don't." Reed snarled at her and was about to pounce again when one of his friends intervened.

"Tony, leave it. Andrews would kill you if you...," his voice trailed off, and he gave the women a furtive glance as he dragged the man away without another word.

The singer turned to Thea and gave her a quizzical look. "You all right?"

Thea had to laugh, for the situation was laughable. Here she was, in a bar she'd not set foot in unless her father had been inside, being manhandled, then saved, by a tall woman, who she'd met only hours before and had scarcely passed the time of day with.

"Yes, thank you. I... that is... I'm not...." Thea gave her an apologetic glance and then turned her eyes to the shining toecap of her black shoes.

"No problem, Ms. Danvers. Maybe next time, you should bring a protector," Jo said.

Thea heard the amusement and could feel her face turn hotter than she suspected that it had been.

Does she think I'm funny?

"Thank you for your help. I'll leave now."

Thea finally gained her composure and with as much decorum as she could manage, quickly exited the bar with the image of the amused gaze of her motel guest firmly emblazoned on her mind.

†

"Thanks."

Jo spun round to her new boss, who was grinning at her. "For what?"

"Well, it would have been a little grim for Ms. Danvers, had you not stepped in to help her out. She's not exactly the most experienced person around here," John-Henry said.

"I noticed. I told her to get herself a protector next time." Jo sat on the stool that Thea had vacated.

John-Henry laughed, a deep belly laugh, and indicated the cooler. "What's your pleasure?"

"I'll have a Stella."

He put the bottle down next to her. "She needs a keeper, too. She left without paying for her beer."

Jo looked at the half-empty bottle of beer close to her left hand and smiled wryly at it. "That's okay. I'll pay. It seems like I got the job by accident this evening."

The man looked at her with a deeply concentrated expression and then smiled. "Looks like it. She could do with someone like you to protect her around here."

"Why would that be? He was only some drunk out for a good time. She probably won't come back here." Jo was interested, regardless of her usual *make no friends in strange places* attitude that she maintained.

"Tell you what, after we close up here, I'll tell you a short story. Now, drink your beer and go slay'em, girl."

Jo couldn't help what she knew was a startled expression on her face. She wasn't sure she'd heard right.

A story? Fucking hell, I haven't had a bedtime story since I was eight years old.

Back then, she had never listened.

It had better be some story if it's going to waste my sleep time.

Taking a long drink from the bottle, her lips twitched in a small smile as she placed it next to the mug the blonde left behind. She smirked, recalling the embarrassment as she'd left the bar. In one fluid movement, she slid gracefully off the stool and headed back toward the makeshift podium while the crowd cheered her name.

Chapter Five

Jo couldn't be certain, but she felt sure she heard faint sobs coming from the room next to hers. One thing she'd always been grateful for was her acute hearing. It had proved excellent for, not only her chosen career path, but also, for when situations got a little crazy and she needed to bolt out of town.

Now that she was wide-awake and listening intently, she heard the muffled sounds of crying once again—she was positive this time around. With a quick motion, she pulled the pillow over her head, trying to shut out the sounds. They persisted and she thumped the pillow in annoyance. Jo had been staying in the motel for more than three weeks now and knew that the owner occupied the room next to hers. Although she'd seen her occasionally in those ensuing weeks, they had barely passed more than polite short sentences after the situation in the bar. The owner appeared to be avoiding her and it hadn't been a problem. They had nothing in common.

Jo gave up any chance of sleeping until the woman stopped crying and crawled out of bed to make an instant coffee. It was easier than setting up the small percolator she'd bought the week before. Ten minutes later the crying had increased in volume.

She usually equated impulsive decisions only to when she landed herself with another partner but this time it was different. She picked up her shirt, partially buttoned it, and slipped on her boxer shorts that she had discarded earlier—sleeping in the nude was a given in her book. After silently opening her door, she moved to room seven, the one she knew Thea Danvers occupied. She knocked decisively. At first, she wasn't sure if the woman heard her, but then she heard a shuffle within the confines of the four walls before she heard a small voice.

"Who is it?"

"Ms. Danvers, it's Jo. I heard noises, just checking to make sure you're okay." Jo wasn't sure what to say without causing the woman any embarrassment.

The door opened partially and it seemed to Jo that they were both uncomfortable.

"Thanks for asking, but I'm fine."

Jo hadn't missed the red swollen eyes, indicating that the woman had been crying for some time. The green eyes staring at her were welling with tears as they stood looking at one another. That woeful childish expression was Jo's undoing. She moved a fraction closer, put out a finger, and gently lifted Thea's chin and looked into her eyes.

"Pardon me for saying so, but you don't look fine. Can I help? Sometimes talking to a stranger releases the tension." Jo waited as she saw the expression on the face change to astonishment.

"I appreciate your concern, Ms. Lackerly, but there's nothing you can do. Thank you for your offer."

"Suit yourself, but can I ask you to keep the noise down, then. Some of us paying guests want to get some sleep." Jo knew her words were harsh as she retreated to her room before slamming the door.

"So much for good intentions," she grumbled. "Fucking great. Try to help someone and she throws it in my face. That's the last time I'm going to come to the aid of that frigid bitch."

Jo discarded her shirt, sank down on the bed, and looked up at the cream-colored ceiling.

The door to her room burst open and in marched a furious Thea Danvers striding quickly toward her. "What do you mean 'keep the noise down'?"

Thea had obviously lost touch with reality during her angry outburst and Jo felt a wicked streak rear as she looked at the woman standing inches from her. "Ms. Danvers, didn't anyone ever tell you it's polite to knock?"

Jo watched the realization of her actions cross Danvers' face and she smirked in satisfaction. She noted the woman's eyes grow large as she stared at her semi-nakedness.

"I usually invite people to my bedroom when I'm in this state of undress. Not have them forced on me," Jo added.

She watched in fascination as the pink shade she'd seen in the bar now turned a beetroot red.

"I'm…I'm sorry…truly, I'm sorry. I…I don't know what could have possibly gotten into me." Thea put a hand to her mouth, as if trying to stifle a sob that threatened to engulf her.

Jo watched once again, the multitude of emotions that passed across the other woman's face, and knew now was not the time to push the younger woman. "Hey, sit down, Ms. Danvers. I'll make you coffee. How do you take it?"

Thea sank gratefully onto the side of the bed and gave her a watery smile of thanks. "White, no sugar."

"Coming up."

Jo set to work on providing the coffee and once she handed the woman a cup filled with the hot liquid she sank down opposite her on the bed and drank from her own cup. She realized that the woman opposite her wouldn't look her straight in the eye before recalling her state of undress and a grin replaced the smile.

†

Thea kept her eyes averted. The ample breasts of her guest sent a shiver down her back. The woman didn't seem to be embarrassed that a virtual stranger was seeing her half undressed.

Silence descended on them as they sipped from their respective coffee for a few minutes. Thea finally broke the silence. "I received some bad news, I'm sorry if my…my crying woke you up. I apologize." Thea continued to avert her eyes.

"I'm a light sleeper. If the cat was crying outside the window, I'd be awake. It's the curse of having acute hearing."

"Thank you. I'm sincerely sorry for breaking into your room."

Thea couldn't believe she had actually done it, but she had, obviously, for it wasn't a dream. She was sitting on the edge of Jo's bed, and that proved it was reality. Thea felt a tug at her heart but didn't want to open it up to her. There was something about her that she knew was familiar, but she didn't know if it was good or bad. It was disconcerting to say the least.

"Well, I wouldn't call it breaking into the room. Let us say you thought there was a fire that needed to be taken care of." The singer moved closer and smiled. "What do you say? Shall we call it that?"

Thea was breathless and couldn't take her eyes from the ones that had captured hers. Her heart raced within the confines of her chest, feeling the heat of the woman so close to her. "Why are you being nice to me?"

"Let's say until you find another protector, looks like I'm still on the payroll and it's part of the contract to be nice."

The engaging smile from the woman astounded Thea with its intensity and she returned the smile with a dazzling one of her own.

"Who says I need a protector?" Thea challenged half-heartedly.

"I do."

"I can't afford to pay you," Thea tentatively answered.

"Who says I want payment?"

"I'm sorry. I didn't mean to offend you. Most would, and do," Thea said bitterly.

"Not this time. It's free, Ms. Danvers, so take it while you can." She shrugged. "Why look a gift horse in the mouth?"

"In that case you better call me Thea." She held out her hand.

The singer looked at her outstretched hand and smiled. "Beautiful name, is there a story behind it?"

"Do you mind if I call you Joanna? It's a beautiful name too." Thea felt the heat stain her cheeks again. Joanna certainly did have a strange effect on her and it definitely wasn't unwelcome. Joanna seemed perplexed. This time Thea couldn't help but watch the well-formed breasts move, with nipples that had grown in their smooth brown background due to the coolness of the room. It made her mouth salivate at the thought of her lips sucking them in. Her body was going out of control and she panicked, needing to leave the room immediately. She hadn't had thoughts like this since her crush on Jennifer Coulson in high school.

"My mother is the only one who calls me Joanna. I haven't heard it in a while," Joanna said finally.

"Okay, I will leave you now and…and perhaps tomorrow you would maybe join me for breakfast? I will tell you about my name then," Thea asked. She moved away from the bed and placed the coffee cup next to the small machine.

"I guess…what time is breakfast? I don't usually…well, I work late…" Joanna was looking at her quizzically as she trailed off.

Thea, who had partially opened the door, heard the hesitation from the usually confident woman. "As I've disturbed you, how about I say ten-thirty?" Thea said quietly without turning back.

"Sure, I'll see you at breakfast. Do you have any particular place in mind?"

"How about I meet you in the lobby and we take it from there?" Thea said as she exited the room and turned so that the door effectively shielded her from the woman's half-naked form.

"Works for me. Thea, will you be able to sleep now?"

Thea looked back into the room and gave Joanna a bright smile. "Yes."

"I'm glad." Joanna said quietly.

"Goodnight, Joanna." Thea closed the door to the room and went to her own room. Emotions were crashing like waves within her mind and body and she didn't know what to make of it.

"Goodnight, Thea."

†

Jo sank down onto the bed and contemplated the ceiling once again. This time her mind was full of the woman, as it was previously, but the thoughts this time were remarkably different. When she was close to Thea, she felt as though she was burning and that feeling was disconcerting. She'd noted the heightened color that stained Thea's cheeks when she looked pointedly at Jo's breast. It gave Thea a cute look and made something in Jo feel even more protective of her. It was a feeling that she was not familiar with, but it was oddly soothing to her. She grinned, remembering seeing the same look on the faces of other women who had looked openly at her, wanting to know her better. At times she let them.

Jo chuckled as Thea had looked like she was being chased by a raging bull when she made her hasty exit. It was amusing that she refused to look at her once she got to the door except to look back and say goodbye. Jo looked down at her breasts and grinned.

Perhaps I will tease her about that in the morning at breakfast.

She nixed the idea. Thea seemed fragile and probably hadn't ever seen another woman's breasts before. Perhaps she'd open up a bit more at breakfast.

"A protector? Who the hell would see me as a protector?" she mused. Now, I'm having breakfast—more like brunch—with her. I wonder if my hormones are telling me to settle down at last."

Jo chuckled at the thought of the alien concept. Staying in one place was definitely not her style. As sleep gradually claimed her, her mind drifted to a scene, comprising a figure waiting for her. "I wonder what it must be like to come home to someone who loves me, every day for the rest of my life," she mumbled as sleep took her.

†

Thea paced up and down the lobby. It was nearly eleven. She wasn't sure if Joanna had overslept, forgotten her, or decided against the invitation. What should she do? Should she go and knock on the door and ask? Maybe she should go out and work in the garden?

She stopped pacing and stared at the empty corridor that housed her guest's room, shaking her head. She gave a bitter laugh to the empty lobby. "Why would she want to spend any time with me anyway? She is obviously popular with the men in town and that isn't surprising. After all she is a very beautiful woman."

Her stomach was grumbling and Thea felt a little sick. Normally she had eaten by eight in the morning, but she'd been far too nervous about this breakfast date that she had been unable to eat anything and had only managed one cup of coffee.

Finally making a decision, she retrieved a coffee from the lobby's coffee urn and went to a door marked *private*, which led to her office and the outer door to the yard. After putting the coffee cup on the small table close by a wrought iron chair, she sat down with a heavy sigh and looked around the yard. It was full of blooming flowers and the sounds of birds singing. It created an area for her to relax and enjoy some peace in a place away from her problems. Closing her eyes, she tried to rid herself of the hurt she felt at the rejection, for that was exactly how it felt.

Jo skidded to a halt in the lobby and was disappointed that Thea wasn't around.

"Shit, I'm too late," she murmured.

She couldn't help but feel angry with herself. She had awakened around ten and decided to snooze ten minutes more. That ten minutes had turned out to be forty-five and a quick shower and dragging on clothes still hadn't made up any time, for it was now eleven fifteen.

The enticing aroma of the always freshly brewed coffee in the lobby made her wonder why Thea would provide the service. To the best of her knowledge, she was the only person staying at the motel. There had been less than five overnighters in the place in the three weeks she'd been a resident there. Coffee appeared to be a luxury that Thea could well do without if the circumstances that John-Henry had briefly explained to her the first night she performed at the bar were anything to go by. She moved to the coffee machine and poured coffee into a cup and added sugar.

While sipping from the cup and relishing the taste of her first drink of the day, her eyes caught the blonde head of Thea sitting outside in the yard. It looked like she was also drinking coffee. Jo looked around for the door that led to the yard and became frustrated not seeing one. She decided that her only option was to knock on the glass pane that overlooked the yard. Jo rapped sharply on the pane of glass, hoping that Thea would hear her. No luck.

"Knowing my luck, if I hit it any harder it will break," she muttered.

†

Thea, feeling deeply melancholy about her aborted breakfast with Joanna was contemplating what to do next. The singer had certainly gotten under her skin and in a big way. It brought memories of her life to the forefront.

Her early upbringing had been reasonably stable and happy. Her mother had left her father when she was ten years old. She ran off with a 'salesman' as her father always called him. Her father had loved her dearly and he'd tried to make up for his only parent status. He sent her to private school until she was fourteen and finances became tough. Going to a university wasn't an option even though she had the grades. His gambling and drinking had brought about his ruin by then and they had quickly lost everything but the motel.

When her father died, there was a hefty mortgage on the motel. Her one hope had been—as calculating as it sounded—the insurance money from the life insurance policy that her father had taken out. Yesterday the insurance company informed her that they would *not* pay the claim since there was strong evidence that her father committed suicide. Now what would she do? She couldn't counter the claim since she had no money.

The sound of rapping on the glass of the lobby brought her head sharply around. For Thea it was like the sunshine coming out after a rather gloomy dark start. She was staring into the eyes of the most improbable protector you could possibly hope to have. It brought her heavy heart soaring. She rapidly moved out of her chair, went back through the exit of her private office, and into the lobby.

"You're here," she gushed.

†

Jo had watched the sadness on the blonde's face leave as soon as they locked glances. It was a profound feeling of relief that went through her chest at the sweet smile Thea gave her. Her eyes followed the blonde as she left the yard and within seconds appeared in front of her.

"Hey, I'm sorry I'm late. I overslept." Well that had been a partial truth anyway. She didn't exactly want to look stupid by saying she'd been lazy and decided to go back to sleep.

"That's okay. That's fine. I kinda wondered if that was the case. I did keep you awake after all," Thea said happily.

"I guess." Jo smiled before drinking the remains of her coffee. "Yours is the best coffee I've ever had."

"Thank you. Would you still accept my invitation to eat? It might be more like lunch now, but I'm sure that's more in keeping with your routine anyway."

Jo looked at the nervous woman in front of her closely. Something that was familiar was drawing her to the woman. She wasn't exactly sure why, but it wasn't an unpleasant feeling. It was as if she'd always felt a protective mode concerning Thea. It was weird, because she certainly hadn't met Thea before. What was even stranger was her offer to protect another human being.

Take Me As I Am

"Lead the way, Thea. I could eat a horse." Jo smiled engagingly and watched in fascination, as the blonde seemed to lose her nervousness and gain confidence at those few words.

"Lucy's Diner is three doors down. How about there?" Thea turned anxious eyes toward Joanna.

"Great idea. I go there every day. I think Lucy knows all my likes and dislikes in the food area by now." Jo chuckled and went to stand next to Thea.

"Let's go then. I can't have you starving to death. You are my only paying guest." Thea chuckled.

Jo noticed Thea turn a faint shade of pink as she held open the door that led to the outer street. Wow, not only was she being protective now she was being chivalrous also.

What am I coming to? Inwardly she laughed.

†

As they walked amiably to the diner, Thea saw several locals, mainly men, looking in their direction. One of them seemed to be especially interested in watching their progress to the diner. As they entered, Thea saw him out of the corner of her eye as he moved with speed toward the bank. She sighed heavily.

That's all I need. Another visit from George Andrews. It would only give me indigestion.

"You okay?"

Thea gave her a weak smile. "I'm good…" she paused for a moment. "I saw someone I'd rather not see today…ever actually."

"Good thing that you are with your protector then." Joanna gave her a warm smile. "Smells good in here, as always."

"Yes, it does and I'm famished." Thea pointed to a booth in the corner. "Let's sit there."

Joanna nodded and guided Thea to the empty table.

†

Lucy Evans, a plump motherly woman, was the sole owner of the diner ever since her husband Kent died of a heart attack ten years earlier. They never had children, so everyone who used the diner frequently became a member of her family. She watched as the newest member of that family came into the diner with one of the oldest members.

When Jo had appeared in her establishment three weeks earlier, Lucy'd sized up the younger woman as arrogant with the self-confidence to match. Normally that type of person didn't do well in towns like Danvers. John-Henry had hired her to sing and from what she heard from others, the woman was certainly good at that. In a town starved of young women, she certainly did offer a stunning sight. Within a week, Jo's eating habits had been deciphered and during the following weeks, they had developed a friendly rapport.

Now, the woman who had all the young men champing at the bit to take her out on a date was talking amiably with Thea Danvers, the motel owner. They obviously would know one another since the motel was the only place for out-of-towners to stay. What surprised Lucy the most was that the two women *were* socializing. In all the years, she had known Thea, she'd never seen her socialize with anyone. It was common knowledge that the banker George Andrews had staked a claim on her and warned off the other men in town.

Obviously no one told Jo that.

She beamed at the two of them as she headed for a table. "Hi, girls. What can I get you today?"

"Hi backatcha, Luce. I'm having an early lunch with Ms. Danvers here," Jo said.

Lucy saw Jo's hand resting on Thea's shoulder and gave her a friendly smile.

"Well, I have the steak special that'd I'd recommend, but if you girls need something lighter, well, I can...."

"No. No, that sounds good to me," Thea jumped into the conversation.

"Then count me in also," Jo said.

"How do you want the steak, Thea?" Lucy asked. It was rare she came into her diner. When she did, she always sat away from prying eyes and scribbled in a notebook as she ate two helpings of apple pie and drank coffee.

"Well done for me, Lucy."

"Well done it will be then. I don't need to ask you, Jo. Medium rare about cover it?"

"Yep, that about covers it. If you need me to help with the serving, give me a holler." Jo grinned at her.

"Comin' right up."

†

Thea was astonished at the friendliness that emanated between the two women. She was surprised, but happily so when she felt Joanna's hand rest with what seemed a natural occurrence on her shoulder.

"You know this is the same table I sit at every time I come in here," Joanna said.

"Why this table?" Thea asked, intrigued.

Joanna seemed to be scanning the occupants of the room.

Thea looked, too. There were four men eating. She didn't know any of them by name.

"Ah, well, I like to see everyone in the room. I don't like surprises, but I also like my privacy and this affords both."

"That's exactly why I sit here when I come in for a meal." Thea grinned at Joanna.

"Great minds, then."

"Can I ask you a question?" Thea asked tentatively.

"Sure. I can always refuse to answer if I don't like the question." Steel blue eyes captured her.

Thea cleared her throat. "How old are you? When did you become a singer? Where are you originally from? Have you any family? Have you ever—"

A slim finger rested on Thea's lips and she looked into twinkling eyes.

"I thought you said *a* question, not twenty?" Joanna laughed softly.

"Sorry, I guess I got carried away." Thea could feel her face heat up and she looked away.

"Yep, you sure did." Joanna's finger traced a pattern on the cotton tablecloth. "No need to be sorry." A gentle smiled filled her face. "You know, you're cute when you blush."

Thea could feel her face get hotter.

"I'm thirty-five. I've been singing since I could talk. Probably before then, if you listen to my mother. I was born and raised in a suburb of New York City and both my parents are living and I have a younger brother. I'm single, never been married and never likely to be either with my track record," Joanna answered in a lighthearted tone.

Thea grinned. "Thanks."

"No problem. Now it's your turn. I'm still waiting for why you're named Thea."

Thea chuckled. "It will sound crazy but I'm kind of named after a silent movie actress who was quite famous in her time. Theda Bara. They got rid of the d and here I am."

"Wow. Okay, I'm going to go all nerdy on you now. Wasn't she in the early movie version of Cleopatra?"

Thea nodded vigorously. "Do you like…no, too many questions already unanswered." She looked away suddenly conscious of being alone with Joanna. "I'm twenty-nine, my parents split up when I was ten. My father's dead and my mother remarried and ironically, she lives somewhere in New York too. I'm an only child. I can't sing to save my life. I'm single and have never married either." Thea was surprised at her light tone, which reflected the ease with which she could talk to Joanna.

"That gets the preliminaries out of the way at least. So what do you do for fun around here?"

"Fun? Fun. Hmmm. Well, I…I suppose I write." Thea looked down at her hands.

"Write about what exactly?"

Thea looked at the table, picked up a napkin absently, and twisted it. "Poetry and short stories. Nothing very good. I tinker at it more than anything else."

"In that case, would you allow me to read some of it so I can be the judge of the quality?" Joanna asked.

Thea moved her head in neither a positive nor a negative way. She didn't know what to say. This was all foreign to her.

Joanna's hand reached out and stopped her shredding the paper napkin. "Can I take that as a yes?"

Thea felt the warmth and surprising comfort in the hand on hers and it felt right. "Yes."

"How about I buy lunch tomorrow and you can bring something along for me to read? What do you say?"

Green eyes tangled with blue and a message passed between them that Thea didn't understand—but felt it was nonthreatening in its content. "Okay. I'll look forward to that."

"So will I." Joanna grinned.

Lucy chose that moment to deliver their meal. "Here you go, ladies. Enjoy."

"Thank you," Thea said. "It smells and looks wonderful."

For the next hour, she chatted with Joanna as old friends did, or what she thought old friends did. She had never had a friend before. When they left the diner, it was clear to her that, no matter what happened next, she had found a friend—a good friend. In her heart, she knew that Joanna felt the same way.

Chapter Six

George Andrews sat down heavily on the worn, but comfortable sofa in what a stranger would find as a surprisingly elegant motel. He knew that with a lick of paint on the outside and a little renovation inside, it would be a fantastic place. Just that small attention to detail would bring more people into town to stay rather than pass it by. The motel in the next town twenty miles away was poor inside by comparison but it didn't look like it was suffering from depression on the outside.

Some of the locals wanted to help Thea paint the place when her father had died but he'd blocked all attempts by using devious but effective methods. Once he had some of his friends indicate that the bank might call in all the loans if anyone helped Thea and the offers stopped. He smirked, remembering the faces of John-Henry and Lucy, two who had spearheaded the motion to help Thea. At first, others had agreed, only to gradually decline helping without explanation. He couldn't touch either of them from the bank angle, but he sure could make it difficult for others in the town if they helped.

Thea was his. No one and nothing would get in his way to have her. What aggravated him further was when he saw her eating with that whore singer from the bar. Why John-Henry had employed a drifter was beyond him. No way would he let that bitch get in his way either. Thea would marry him and soon. Now that the insurance company had refused payment, it was only a matter of weeks before she acquiesced.

The door to the motel opened and he heard the harsher tones of the drifter before he heard the tinkling laughter of the woman he was waiting for. That annoyed him even more. What did that bitch say to make his woman laugh?

"Who told you all those jokes?" Thea had her face turned to Joanna.

George scowled as he watched them.

†

Jo had seen the fat man in the lobby's expression aimed in her direction. From experience with others in the past, she knew exactly what it meant. She looked at Thea and seriously doubted that she understood the feral look of possession. She smiled gently at Thea and shook her head. "That would be telling, now, wouldn't it?"

"Oh, please, Joanna?"

Thea's pleading green eyes made Jo want nothing more than to answer her. She knew who the man was, since both John-Henry and Lucy had pointed him out as the *bastard banker*.

"You have a visitor." Jo pointed to the man and watched as Thea turned. Her smile froze. Instantly, Thea's posture became apprehensive.

"Mr. Andrews, what a surprise," Thea said politely.

Jo looked at the man, who rolled out of the comfortable chair before moving slowly in their direction. "Thea, my dear, I need to speak to you. Privately." The last word resonated around the lobby as his voice moved up a tempo.

Thea looked at her with pleading eyes. They planned to have coffee in the yard together but Jo knew that her friend had little choice but to comply with the man's request. Jo watched Thea's body sag and she instantly wanted to protect her from the horrible man. She had no choice, knowing that to interfere would only make matters worse for Thea.

"Go ahead. We can take a raincheck on the coffee."

Thea let out an audible sigh, her eyes still begging for a reason and it called to Jo. She turned away, only to make a swift decision and place her hand on Thea's shoulder. She bent and whispered into the blonde's ear. When she saw the smile she wanted, she left her to the bastard banker.

†

Thea watched Joanna's receding back and smiled gently at the sight. Joanna's words had made her feel safe and happier about the situation she was facing. All she said was *remember you have a protector*. The simple words soothed her troubled spirits when she saw George Andrews. In her heart, she felt that everything was going to be okay. If Joanna Lackerly was around, she knew she was safe and protected.

What else was missing? Love was the resounding answer.

"Mr. Andrews, please step into my office." Thea closed her eyes briefly before heading for her workplace.

†

George watched a nervous Thea shuffling paper on her desk. He grinned at the rush he always received when he sat in judgment of someone wanting his approval for a loan. It was a regular occurrence, but to consider actually making a proposal of marriage in that environment had him aroused.

"Thea, I think it's time you considered your options in light of the fact that you will receive no further financial backing from any other party," George said brusquely.

"I don't understand." Thea gave him a startled glance.

George shifted in his chair and gave her a shrewd glance. "Thea, I know that the insurance company has refused to pay out on your father's death policy. That was, I'm sure, your final source of finance that could have saved the motel from the bank foreclosing."

"How would you possibly know that, Mr. Andrews? I was only informed yesterday," Thea said angrily.

George cleared his throat and wiped the perspiration from his face. "That, my dear young lady, is my secret. You should know that word travels fast in this town. So, Thea, how will you pay back the bank now?"

"How long do I have before you begin foreclosing on the motel?"

"No time. You are months overdue and had it not been for my good graces, you should have been thrown out months ago." He mopped his forehead with a stained white handkerchief. "There is a solution to all this, of course." George focused on her full breasts and his eyes remained there.

Thea snorted softly in disgust. "What solution would that be, exactly?"

"Why, my dear, you know of course that I have always thought you a very beautiful woman. I have often asked you out on a date, to which you have always refused. Considering the circumstances, I propose, yes, that's the correct word," he looked at her directly, "I propose that if you marry me, the debt will be paid and you may keep the motel in the family, so to speak."

"If I refuse?"

†

George came unexpectedly quickly around the desk and invaded Thea's personal space.

Thea could smell the faint cologne, he used, which in itself wasn't unpleasant, but with his perspiring body odor, it was repugnant. It made her stomach churn and the meal she'd enjoyed with Joanna threatened to erupt. *Joanna.* Just the thought of her new friend and protector was the lifeline she needed. A sense of strength filled her as she recalled the earlier words of support.

"Thea, I can throw you out of here with the click of my fingers. After all, other than that drifter you have staying here, would it matter if the place closed for good? I think not. What would you do then? You have no money, nowhere to stay and no means to earn a living. Except…well, my dear, I would imagine my proposal is a far better a fate than selling your body." Andrews sneered as his eyes leered at her breasts again.

"I would never do that! I need time to think about it." Thea fought the urge to cry. She needed time to think and come up with a plan.

"As you wish. Join me for a drink and dinner at the bar this evening. I will expect you at eight. It would be in your best interest not to disappoint me." George reached out a sweaty palm to caress her cheek.

She flinched at the gesture and noticed the predatory look on his face. "I will meet you at eight this evening and will give you an answer." Thea swallowed hard to control her anger, fear, and revulsion.

George walked out of the room without another word.

Thea, feeling emotionally drained, got up and went to the door that led onto the yard outside. Her mind was in turmoil.

So, it has finally come to this.

The only asset left of the Danvers heritage hinged on her decision to marry George Andrews. Her mind and heart rejected the proposal as archaic and outdated, but her sense of family heritage was pleading with her to consider the possibility. *Keep it in the family line* rebounded in her head. One day she might have children to pass it on to—yeah, right.

Hot tears began cascading down her cheeks at the abhorrent thought. It wasn't the children, but who the father might be that was repugnant to her. She simply did not see herself as the mother of George Andrews' children, nor did she see herself as his wife. For that matter, she did not see herself as the wife to any man. None had ever touched her heart. She knew that they would have to reach her heart for her to consider marriage and children. They would have to reach her soul.

†

Jo stared out of the window onto the small yard with its cascade of color and brimming pots and troughs of flowers in every imaginable shape and size. Her mother had had *green* fingers and was always growing something in their apartment. The thought made Jo smile as the memories of far off events that rarely if ever invaded her thoughts before tumbling around in her head. She couldn't stop the trace of a smile they brought along with it.

While she gazed at the yard, she noticed Thea quickly make her way through the grass. After looking at her personal domain for a few minutes, she sank heavily into the chair in the center of the lawn. Her new friend, who less than an hour ago had been bubbly and happy, sharing jokes and stories without a care in the world, was now a different woman. Once the bastard banker turned up, the beautiful smile immediately disappeared from Thea's expressive face.

From her vantage point, Jo saw Thea begin to cry. Her face had the haunted look of someone who had the whole world on her shoulders and no one to share the burden. Damn, why did she feel so protective of this woman? What was it about Thea that called to her without words? As she stood there watching Thea cry, helplessness filled her and she was unable to make the move to invade Thea's privacy and ask why. Jo thought back to the previous night and her attempt to do just that. *This is different.* Thea had opened up to her and accepted her offer to protect her.

If that fucking bastard excuse for a man has laid a finger on Thea, I will see him in hell.

Jo was Thea's protector, but certainly not her keeper. That wasn't part of the deal—or was it? She knew that sometimes events that appeared simple to the eye could have the most far-reaching results on a person even if nothing happened until after the event took effect. This, she knew, was such an event. She felt her heartbeat react with a fierce thumping in her chest. Thea was a piece of the puzzle that was missing from her life. She was the person that Jo had been looking for all her life. Of that she had no doubt.

Thea asked nothing of her, other than to be around so they could share things together. No pressure. No recriminations. She only offered companionship, along with a bond that would take them into the future together.

Jo saw the tracks of tears on Thea's pale features along with noting her trembling lips. Thea was barely suppressing sobs. A short time ago those lips had tugged into a broad smile at her jokes. Despite the distance, Jo could feel the profound sadness that surrounded Thea and it made her heart sick on her behalf.

Not really knowing what to do, she picked up her guitar, which she had been idly strumming earlier and again took up that posture, her fingers feeling the frets with the expertise of years of practice. A tune sounded in the room as she quietly hummed along with it until unconsciously she started to sing along with the notes that emitted from the instrument... *"You will not be defeated, my love..."*

The phrases ended on Jo's lips as her eyes strayed repeatedly to Thea crying. With the final words, the picture that had been faint suddenly gained clarity and with a heavy sigh, she sank down into the depths of the bed, contemplating exactly what it meant to the rest of her life.

Chapter Seven

Jo hadn't seen Thea since she'd fled the yard minutes after she had made a decision to go see if she could help. By then it had been too late, and she only encountered the old woman that had been with Thea that first day she'd arrived at the motel.

"You want something?" Daisy asked gruffly.

Jo looked at the small, wiry figure in front of her and wanted to laugh at the distinctly antagonistic stance the older woman was taking.

"I was looking for Thea," Jo saw the raised eyebrows at presumably the familiar use of Thea's name. "Um…Ms. Danvers.

"Miss Danvers is not to be disturbed by anyone!"

"I was hoping that I was better than just anyone." Jo fixed the older woman with a scowl.

"What makes you think that, stranger?"

She certainly wasn't about to explain herself to the hired help.

"Doesn't matter. I'll catch up with Th…Ms. Danvers later."

Perhaps after her set was finished. If John-Henry didn't regale her with old stories of his music traveling days as a roadie for once, she'd knock on Thea's door and speak with her then.

"She won't be in later. She has a date."

Jo, taken aback by the statement, was speechless for a short time shaking her head at the thought. Her eyes screwed up and she glared at the woman who was watching her intently. "Well, in that event, I will catch up with her tomorrow."

Jo turned away her mind reeling at the thought that Thea was going out on a date. *Why and with who?*

"You give up easy, stranger."

Astounded at the remark, Jo stopped in her tracks. "I don't know what you mean."

"You're not interested in who she's going out on a date with? I'd think you would if you are a friend like you imply."

"Sure...sure, I'm her friend. Who?" Jo's mind and body were suddenly on high alert and she wanted to run to the room to work out why. Her reaction didn't make any sense.

"George Andrews. Do you know who he is?"

"Yeah, the fucking bastard banker." The venom that was behind every word Jo said made the room crackle with intensity.

"I wouldn't go so far as to call him that but...in the eyes of the beholder, they say." The woman had a tight smile.

"I thought he was just a banker, not a suitor?" Jo glanced at the woman who looked as though she wanted to laugh.

"George Andrews has wanted that little girl since she was out of school. He will get her if she can't find a fitting suitor who can go up against him soon. I'm Daisy, by the way."

"Thea can do better than that sorry ass," Jo replied.

"Ahh, yes, she could. Unfortunately, not everyone has George's...assets, shall we say." Daisy waved a hand. "Never mind. I'm just an old lady who's probably saying more than I should."

"What assets exactly? I wouldn't consider him much of a catch. He's a slob who isn't worthy of Thea." Jo searched Daisy's face for an answer.

Daisy let out a long sigh. "You have lots of money?"

"Who me?" At the nod from the woman, Jo smiled wryly. "No, otherwise I wouldn't be stuck in this town, now, would I?" Jo turned away intent on heading to her room.

"Like I say, you give up easily."

The woman's words rang in her ears, but Jo refused to return the challenge and walked away.

Fucking money. So Thea only goes for the ones with money.

She looked so sweet and innocent, but it looked like she was just another gold digger.

†

Daisy Kendall watched the woman retreat and by her very stance, it was clear that the conversation had rattled her in a very profound way. *Wonder why?* She saw the disappointed expression cross the beautiful features of the woman when she'd mentioned George Andrews. There was no mistaking that the stranger was very attractive, but it needed more than a pretty face and body to make a beautiful person. Thea was the epitome of both a lovely personality and stunning looks. She had natural beauty. Yet, her daddy hadn't contributed to the woman's effervescent attitude and her wayward mother hadn't helped any, either.

Thea hadn't mentioned that she knew the only guest of the motel with any familiarity. As far as Daisy knew, they hadn't even passed more than a civil word, yet it was clear from the stranger's conversation that they had some sort of relationship. She needed to talk to Thea and soon.

If George Andrews has his way, Thea will be married to him by the weekend.

"Seems like we have a dilemma in this town and something involving George Andrews can get nasty really quick."

Daisy heard a door slam and she had an inkling she knew why—the stranger did care about Thea and her frustration was showing. She brushed her hands together and lifted the pass through on the counter. She was on a mission and the first person to speak to was Lucy. Together they might come up with a solution to help Thea.

†

It was a Friday evening and the bar teemed with customers. Once John-Henry had hired Jo, the place was full every weekend and even on some of the evenings during the week that traditionally had been slow. He was grossing a healthy sum. He was glad he'd listened to the woman sing, rather than pass her off as another hopeless drifter. She was very good and he wondered why she didn't try out in a much larger community—he believed she would do well. He grinned, thinking of the idea that he had set in motion. Now, all he had to do was wait for a phone call.

Just at that moment, the door to the bar opened and Jo walked in. She was by far the tallest woman in the room and very possibly the most beautiful with her classic looks. Only Thea outshined her in the beauty department, according to him. Thea Danvers was class personified. He glanced at a table in the corner where Thea sat pensively eating with the asshole banker. He shook his head at the melancholy thought of what her father had let his daughter suffer in the past few months. Perhaps she would suffer for the rest of her life if she ended up with Andrews. After speaking with Daisy and Lucy earlier, they had agreed there was no other solution at hand.

"How you doing tonight, Jo?" John-Henry asked with a smile. Jo was scowling and he quickly lost his smile.

"No problem with me," Jo replied stiffly.

John-Henry had been impressed with this woman's sense of dry humor. However, something told him that tonight she wasn't in any good kind of humor—totally the opposite. He glanced to where her eyes were focusing. If looks could kill, Andrews would be a dead man for sure.

Looks like what Daisy said was true.

"You got a problem with that corner?" John-Henry asked.

Steel blue eyes turned to his and he tried not to flinch.

"No. Why do you ask?"

"Just wondered why you seemed so interested, that's all." He wiped at an imaginary beer stain, feeling the blue eyes boring into his neck.

"You told me that Thea didn't like Andrews, that he had caused her nothing but trouble. Yet there she is happily having dinner with him. I'd call that a date," Jo snapped.

John-Henry paused in his inspection of the gleaming bar surface and considered what the woman before him had said. It made him smile at her attitude along, with the feeling behind the words.

It sounded like green-eyed jealousy.

"Yeah, that's true. Andrews has gone out of his way to make sure Thea doesn't get any help from anyone around here with her property."

"Did you offer to help her?" The sound of an accusation laced Jo's words.

"Sure did. So did Lucy at the diner. We don't have the cash to help her and neither one of us is young enough to offer any physical help in the restoration of her place. Help of any kind petered out once Andrews' front men threatened folks."

John-Henry looked around to see if anyone was listening to his conversation. No one was. He wasn't about to let his own dislike of Andrews and his ways become common knowledge in town.

"Maybe she doesn't have a choice," he whispered.

†

Jo considered the words and then turned her gaze back to the corner table. She was looking directly into the black beady eyes of George Andrews. He was giving her what seemed like a taunting glance, telling her that Thea was his property and to keep away.

Jo shrugged at the glance and returned a glare with her answer.

She's no one's property, so fuck you.

The man turned away in what looked like disgust. She knew her message had hit its target.

"I need to leave early tonight, John-Henry. Okay with you?"

"Sure, but don't let the customers know or there'll be a riot. And I can do without that, you know." He gave her a wide grin and she returned a tight smile.

"They will get their money's worth, I promise you that." Jo picked up her guitar and walked to the small stage for her first set. A resounding clap of hands from the young men standing close had her giving them an appreciative nod.

†

Thea Danvers turned her head and saw Joanna walk onto the stage. The singer was stunning as she strode confidently toward a stool and amazingly settled her tall frame on it without it toppling. She started strumming a few chords. Her long hair was falling across her face and Thea's fingers itched to move it away from her eyes.

"Your only guest appears to have charmed most of the men in this town," George remarked.

Thea gave him a distracted look and then turned her eyes to the audience that had enclosed the woman. "Yes, it does appear they all like her," she replied softly.

"My dear, you have my company now. What more could you want but that?" George replied flippantly.

Thea found swallowing hard as she tried to digest what the man opposite her had said. He was right. There really was no contest. What she wanted was to be standing, watching the woman who was about to start singing and not looking at his satisfied ugly, pudgy, smug face. "I'd like to listen to Ms. Lackerly sing, Mr. Andrews. If you don't mind, of course," Thea replied.

George snorted and gave her a shrewd glance and nodded. "Yes, good idea, my dear. I hear she's quite tolerable."

"I hear she's very good." Thea turned away to watch Joanna and listen as she began her intro to the first song.

The echoes of the guitar rang out in the room and her clear voice began a loving ballad... *"Someone once said that a friend was worth a fortune if they remain a friend through the good and bad,"* Joanna strummed the strings. *"Well, this song is about that very thing. When you said you would be there for me, I believed you."*

Thea watched and listened, as Joanna's eyes never strayed from her. The tender words of the song had touched her in a way that made tears brim in her eyes. Entranced by the sultry voice of her friend, she wondered what she was doing opposite George. She didn't like him in the slightest as a person, never mind as a potential husband. God, she felt like laughing at the absurdity of her fate. She had always known her father had a keen sense of humor, but did he have to continue it even after his death?

"My, dear Thea, I asked you a question earlier, which I'm sure you recall. It was after all a very simple question that needs a very simple answer."

Thea had made a decision as she left the motel that evening and it had been all cut and dried. Yet, now. Now. She didn't know what to say. It really wasn't that clear, after all.

"Yes, it does require a simple answer." Thea's voice held a desolation that would have tugged at most people's heartstrings.

"Well, I'm waiting?" He leaned his hefty body toward her.

Thea felt as if her whole life was hanging by a thread. Time ticked by and the sounds of the up-tempo music did nothing to relieve the eerie silence that surrounded the table where she sat. She felt like a trapped animal that had no chance of escaping. She gulped and closed her eyes before she finally answered the question. "As this is primarily to do with a business proposition, would the marriage be a business situation, also?" Thea asked grimly.

George gave her a crooked smile, as his small, indented eyes studied her body with a calculated look. "If you wish to view it like that, Thea, then yes. Yes, in many ways, you could consider it so. You get to keep your precious motel and I...I get to have a wife in my bed. A willing wife." His gaze was evil. "Not a frigid one, I might add."

Thea turned her attention back to her new friend, who was singing and moving among the men who certainly relished the attention. "Will the deeds be in my name only?"

George shifted a little in his chair. "But of course, my dear, of course."

Releasing a heavy sigh, she turned to him with dull eyes. "You have a deal, Mr. Andrews." Her voice was flat and devoid of any emotion as she squelched the need to vomit at the revulsion she was feeling.

"Thank you, Thea, and since you will soon be my wife I insist you to call me George. Whatever would people think if you still called me Mr. Andrews now that we are engaged?"

Thea considered the remark and shook her head giving him a small smile, her thoughts very clear on that particular question. "They would think I didn't much care for you, Mr. Andrews." She inclined her head. "As you say, *George*." Just saying his name made her want to vomit.

George called his entourage with the crook of a finger. It so happened to be the very man that had tried to buy her a drink a few weeks ago.

"Tony, find Bascome and get him to bring the champagne and two glasses. We have an engagement to celebrate. Ah, and, Tony, have Bascome give everyone a free drink in the place…the rounds are on me…especially the singer…most definitely the singer. Better still…get Bascome to invite her to our table to celebrate our good fortune once she's done."

Thea watched the man retreat.

"My dear, I'm sure your new *friend* will want to toast your happiness. Won't she?" He gave her a keen glance and sneered.

Thea kept her head down. She didn't want Joanna to hear about this from anyone but her and now thanks to the banker that was out of the question. Her heart felt as if it was breaking for she knew Joanna wouldn't understand. No, she wouldn't and if she analyzed her own thoughts, she didn't understand it either. *My God, what have I done?*

George placed his hand on Thea's and gave her a satisfied smile.

With a swift movement, she slid her hand across the table and into her lap, trying to tap down the panic she was now feeling.

†

John-Henry couldn't believe his ears. Thea had given in to Andrews's intimidation and crushed her spirit. He had done that to many others, but not like this. He was damn sure that was the only reason that Thea relented. Anger filled him at his inability to help Thea, so she didn't have to stoop to marrying the bastard. He retrieved the ice-cold champagne and the two flute glasses and placed them on a silver tray that he had polished for special occasions. He supposed this warranted it, but it definitely wasn't right, at all.

"Hey, John-Henry, get a move on. The boss will be roasting my nuts if you keep him waiting. If he does that, I sure won't let you forget it either." Tony slammed his fist on the polished bar.

"Keep your hair on, Tony. Andrews will want it presented just so, if I know him. Waiting that extra couple of minutes isn't going to change things any, is it?" John-Henry looked at the smug expression on Andrews face and the averted face of the young woman who had finally said yes to his proposal.

Damn shame.

"Oh. Get on with it will ya? Can't understand why he bothers so much with the frigid bitch. Let's face it, she isn't exactly the warmest woman in town, don't know anyone who has ever dated her, never mind got in her knickers. She and that singer you have make a fine pair if you ask me. She's about as accommodating as an icicle, too." Tony turned his narrow gaze to Jo.

John-Henry couldn't help the small smile at the comment. Never a truer word said. "Could be, but then again icicles under the right temperature are known to thaw. It depends who offers the right temperature, I guess."

Tony scowled. "Come on, John-Henry, I haven't got all day. Oh, and talking of icicle lady, the boss said to get her to come to the table for a drink with them after she's done. Boss doesn't take kindly to *no* as an answer. You might tell her that."

He picked up the tray and sauntered back toward George, leaving John-Henry disconcerted by the request.

Jo leisurely walked to the bar and sat down on a stool vacated by an eager ranch hand. She gave a smile that didn't reach her eyes and sat down heavily upon it. "I'll have a beer and then I'm out of here, John-Henry, as we agreed.

John-Henry nodded. "Let me get these, give me a minute," he said indicating the drinks he was serving. When he came back to her, he was feeling a bit sheepish and tugged at his chin. He didn't know exactly how Jo would react when she heard the news but he had a good idea. "Sure, it's okay with me, Jo," he said and hesitated. "But I've had a personal request for your company."

Jo raised her eyebrows. "I don't *do* personal requests for anyone. Thought you knew that."

"Yeah, sorry. Wrong choice of words." John-Henry sucked in a breath. "Andrews the banker would like you to join him and Ms. Danvers to celebrate with a glass of champagne." John-Henry watched Jo's eyes cloud before shifting their gaze to the corner table.

"As I said, I don't do personal requests…for anyone." Jo moved from her stool.

"You never asked what they were celebrating."

Okay, here it comes.

John-Henry held his breath and watched Jo raise her eyebrow again.

"Okay. What are they celebrating?"

"Andrews and Ms. Danvers have just become engaged this very evening." He waited for her reaction.

†

Jo couldn't believe her ears. True, earlier in her set she saw Thea deep in conversation with the man. The sight brought a decidedly ugly hatred to her gut but this this couldn't be true. It felt that someone had punched her in the diaphragm making it difficult to breathe.

No way. No fucking way was Thea engaged to that bastard. She doesn't even like him.

Jo could feel her breathing become ragged and everywhere she looked it felt like the walls were closing in on her. She needed to get away as quickly as possible but she needed to know why first. "Pull the other one, John-Henry. What would she want to marry him for?"

"I explained what the situation was to you earlier. Remember?" The man said softly. "She might not have a choice in the matter."

"Yeah, yeah sure." Jo gave him a strange vacant look.

"He doesn't take kindly to people saying *no* to him you know," John-Henry said gently.

Jo looked around in a disinterested fashion and her eyes met the young man who had gallantly offered her the stool. He couldn't be more than a boy really.

He's barely out of diapers in the adult world. He'll do.

"Hey, want to join me in celebrating a friend's engagement?" Jo flashed her impossibly long lashes at the man and grinned when he beamed at her. She knew that all the men in town had been angling to be with her and it was his lucky night to be on the receiving end.

"Sure…sure," he stuttered, looking at her with what looked like devotion.

Jesus, do men only ever think with their dicks?

Jo snaked a long arm around his shoulders and placed a warm kiss on his surprised lips before leading him toward the corner table. Jo had practiced at keeping men attentive and the wolf whistles that accompanied her and the young man as they made a very public display of kissing on the way through the other customers, made for a very interesting sight.

†

"I see your new *friend* is proving the old saying about how free and easy these singers are with their favors." George had a smug *I told you so* expression on his pudgy face.

Thea turned to see where he was looking and her heart stuck in her mouth as she saw Joanna kissing a man as they made their way toward the table. It was a very passionate kiss and she didn't know how to answer the question. She wanted to refute the situation as ridiculous.

Jo and the man—a boy really—arrived at the table where Thea was sitting. Joanna's blue eyes were cold when she looked at her and even colder when she looked at George.

"According to John-Henry, you wanted to buy me a drink."

"Yes, that's right. As you and my future bride appear to be friends, I thought you might want to toast our good news."

Thea watched to see if her friend's expression changed. It did.

Joanna gave out a howl of laughter before smiling sickly sweet at George. Her hand clutched the boy she still held. "Whatever gave you that idea? Ms. Danvers and I are merely acquaintances as we share the same building at night," Jo said sarcastically.

"Well, in that case, what's your poison?" Andrews asked.

Thea cringed at the situation. Her heart pounded at what she suspected was that Joanna felt betrayed. *Why didn't I tell her when I had the chance? Daisy told me that she was looking for me. Now everything good in my life is crashing around me.*

"If I tell you that, I'd be dead tomorrow, now, wouldn't I," Joanna spit out.

"If you say so, but I was merely asking what drink you would like to have to celebrate our engagement. Isn't that so, darling? Now, what will it be?"

Thea refused to look at either of them. She was too ashamed to look at Joanna and couldn't stand the distaste she felt when looking at George. She cringed at George's words and wanted to do nothing more than crawl into a ball and hide away somewhere safe. Shame filled her. She had finally given in to the pressure of the man she detested and now she let down the only person who had backed her up and wanted nothing in return. It wasn't fair. What had she ever done in her life to make her go through this? It really was unjust.

"Yes, Mr. An…George, that's correct." Her voice sounded very small to her ears. She doubted that anyone heard her.

"Sorry, but," Joanna asked the young man at her side. "What's your name?" It was loud enough for them to hear.

The boy whispered back and Joanna grinned and gave him a swift kiss on the mouth. "Sam and I have other business. Maybe another time." Joanna turned quickly, pulling the startled Sam with her heading out of the bar.

George turned to Thea. "Told you so, my dear. The woman didn't even know his name. She will probably not even wait to get to a bed before she has her way with him."

Thea tried desperately to staunch the tears and failed as they slid down her cheeks. She needed to find a way to stop the sinking feeling in her heart and picking up the champagne glass, she swallowed it all in one gulp.

Maybe if I get drunk, I will feel better. Probably not but it is worth a try.

†

Jo sank heavily down on her bed half an hour later and tried to understand why she cared so much about Thea's engagement. It wasn't as if they were good friends. Right? Hardly more than strangers really, but—she thought the woman had more backbone. She remembered how Thea looked sitting there next to the gloating banker. A woman who had just accepted an offer of marriage shouldn't look sad.

Why? Is she marrying for money?

Jo thought back to John-Henry's words—*maybe she doesn't have a choice.*

It was then that she realized that Thea was marrying the bastard to keep her family's motel.

What a fuckin' waste. Why didn't she just go somewhere else and not marry someone she didn't love and from the looks of it, didn't even like much. Who would? He was a troll.

Jo managed to divert Sam, the boy she had used as a ruse to get out of the bar, who probably thought he was in for a night with her, with hollow promises of later. She wouldn't be going through with any of them. He'd been a nice kid though, and he was too wet behind the ears to know any different. The only education he was going to get was about fickle women.

What she really needed about now was a stiff drink. She'd been keeping a bottle of scotch in the bottom of the wardrobe for such an occasion. She was pleased with herself that she hadn't hit the bottle before now. Things had been going well—too well. After pulling out the bottle, she twisted off the cap and immediately wrinkled her nose at the aroma. She actually hated the smell, but once you got past the first drink, it grew on you.

After her fifth shot of the scotch, she heard the soft footfalls of the woman she had been thinking non-stop about since arriving back in her room. The steps slowed and Jo was sure that Thea was going to knock on the door and explain what was going on. After all, she had offered her services as protector and she was damn sure Thea needed protecting from Andrews.

The steps proceeded onward the few short yards to her room. She listened as a door creaked open. Jo closed her eyes at the sound of the door metaphorically shutting on any conversation between the two of them.

Damn woman is playing with me and she doesn't even know it.

She reached for her half-empty glass, filled it to the brim before swallowing it in one go. The scotch, having the desired dulling effect burned her throat. Jo refilled the glass and looked at the bottle in her hand—three-quarters empty. With the next glass, she was bound to sleep.

It was time to leave this hick town and its residents. Or was it one resident in particular? "What does it matter? It is time to leave," she murmured before passing out.

Chapter Eight

Jo had a hangover. Not a run of the mill hangover either. It was a hell of a good one and to cap it all, she looked like she had a hangover, too. Her eyes were bloodshot and as the sunlight streamed in from another glorious day, her eyelids closed at the explosion of pain it caused. The headache that twisted inside her head made her nauseous.

Normally when she'd tied one on, there was a good excuse. It usually meant she wasn't sleeping alone. She was sure Freud would probably have something to say about that. Today, she tentatively turned, looked at the empty space beside her, and felt the enormous relief of not having to share morning platitudes with a stranger. Her ears went into bat mode as she failed to pick up any sound from the bathroom. *Thank you, God.* Jo settled her pounding head against the pillow.

Her eyes traced to the small bedside table before she squinted at the small travel clock. To her amazement, it was barely eight-o-clock in the morning. Then she grimaced, wondering if it was the next morning or if she'd slept and lost a day. In the past when drugs were part of her life, it had happened. Not in recent times though.

A debate went on in her head as she considered the pros and cons of getting out of bed and eventually decided that it was a good idea. Maybe decent coffee and a good breakfast would make her feel more human. Her stomach instantly began doing flying cartwheels as the thought registered.

Take Me As I Am

With small steps, she gingerly made her way to the bathroom. She turned on the shower, and deposited herself unceremoniously under the water. It did, however, have the requisite effect of making her feel a little better. After stepping out of the shower and drying off, she rummaged around for a clean pair of jeans and a shirt.

With a sickly feeling in her stomach like a lead weight, she left her room and went toward the lobby. As she did, the reason for her overindulgence came back to her full force. She reeled at the sense of loss she felt. The last thing she wanted to do was to run into the woman who had caused her to lose herself in the bottle. Usually only men had that effect on her, although there had been a woman or two. She exited the building and slowly made her way toward the diner. At least Lucy would make sure she ate the right things to make her feel better. That is what she hoped.

†

Thea sat at her desk and looked at the numerous bills that had arrived that morning. Although she was looking at the paper, she couldn't, no matter how hard she tried, read any of the contents. She sat back in her chair, closing her eyes. Her thoughts wandered to the guest in room five. Joanna. She had thought they might become friends. Joanna had promised her protection. Yet, she had thrown that protection to the winds and possibly the tender developing friendship, as well, last evening. It should have been so easy to tell Joanna that she had no choice in the matter. Her increasing debts for the motel would have brought about bankruptcy and then what would she have done?

Thea had no immediate family—at least none that had bothered with her in years. When had been the last time her mother had sent a note or even acknowledged her existence? Far too long, there had been no hope from that slim chance of her mother coming back into her life. The only person who had helped in recent years was Joanna. It was clear she had no means beyond her singing and that only brought enough for her to live on. How could she have helped financially, even if she wanted to? As her thoughts continued to picture the smiling face of her friend from their lunch yesterday, it was entirely too painful to imagine not having Joanna's friendship.

What am I to do?

Hearing a sound from the lobby, Thea moved swiftly to the door leading to the lobby and stood behind it, not venturing outside. She really didn't know what to say to Joanna the past evening, and still couldn't think of what to say now. Oh, how she had wanted to knock on Joanna's door and talk to her, but she had feared that she would disturb her and the young man she had taken out of the bar with her.

Nothing in this life is ever easy.

From her vantage point, she could discreetly watch Joanna and saw that the woman didn't look her usual confident self—she looked extremely tired. Then again, it was the first time since Joanna moved into the motel that she'd ventured out of her room before mid-day. She smiled, recalling the day before when Joanna just made it for their breakfast date.

Thea was about to take her courage in her hands and face the woman when Joanna swiftly left the building. The swinging door was the only evidence that she had been there at all.

With a heavy heart, Thea went back to her desk and contemplated what would happen next.

†

Lucy watched Jo slowly make her way toward the door of the diner. Normally, the woman walked in with a buoyant step but not today. As Jo walked closer to the counter, she turned bleary eyes to Lucy and gave her a tired, defeated look.

"No need to ask if you're feeling fine this morning." Lucy couldn't help the smile that tugged her lips at the scowl she received at her observation.

Take Me As I Am

"If you're so clever, what do you recommend as a cure? I'd pretty much accept anything at this moment if you can stop the queasy feeling in my stomach," Jo said pathetically.

"What was your poison?" Lucy pointed to a stool at the counter. "Sit there."

"Seems a popular expression around these parts and quite frankly Scotch feels like poison about now." Jo seated herself at the stool.

"Hmmm, didn't your mamma ever tell you to beware the after effects of the hard liquor?" Lucy tried to keep the woman's interest for her face was turning some rather interesting colors.

"I always knew better." Jo gave a wry glance.

"Yeah, I bet you did. I bet you were a handful for her, too?" Lucy smirked and saw the nod indicating that she was right about that.

Lucy went into the kitchen and a few minutes later came back with an interesting looking drink and placed it on the counter in front of the woman. "There you go. It'll have you right in no time. My husband always swore it was the best hangover cure ever."

Lucy chuckled as she watched Jo tentatively pick up the glass. When Jo turned up her nose at the smell, Lucy laughed loudly. "Hey, I never said it smelled good, did I?"

Jo pulled another face before quickly swallowing the mixture, her features contorted in revulsion.

"Jesus, Lucy, have you ever tried that?" Jo rocked back on the stool. "My stomach is wondering what is hitting it."

"Can't say I have, but it sure took your mind off feeling sick I would say." Lucy smiled and turned to see who was entering the diner. Most of her regulars had already been and gone. Thea was hesitating at the doorway before going all the way into the diner.

Lucy looked at the pained expression on the blonde's face as she looked at Jo's back. So Daisy was right. There is something between these two. She wondered just how deep it went?

"Thea, it's not often you come here this early in a morning." Lucy smiled, beckoning Thea to the counter.

Lucy saw Jo stiffen when she said Thea's name.

Thea moved closer to the counter. "That's true but...I...well, I wanted to..." Her eyes flashed toward Jo seated silently at the counter with her back turned the other way.

Lucy decided that a standoff between the two women just wouldn't do. "Well, it's mighty nice to see you this fine morning. Isn't that so, Jo?"

The prompting from Lucy made Thea give her a grateful smile as Jo scowled.

"Sure. It's a fine morning," Jo replied finally.

"Would you mind if I sat next to you," Thea said in a tentative tone.

Jo never looked up. "It's a free seat. Sit where you like."

Lucy gave Thea a smile of encouragement. "So, what can I get you two ladies?"

Thea discreetly looked to her left.

Jo didn't look up from her contemplation of the glass that she held.

"I'll have bacon, hash browns, and scrambled eggs, please, Lucy," Thea said.

Jo shifted in her chair and turn toward Thea. "Toast for me as dry as you can get it and keep the coffee coming."

Lucy watched as Thea turned to stare at Jo and their eyes locked. "I'll be back soon with your orders. Why don't you two take a table?"

Lucy went into the kitchen smiling.

†

Thea twisted her hands in front of her and Joanna looked back down at the empty glass held securely in her hands.

"I guess I'll go and sit at a table." Thea swallowed hard. "Would you...that is...Joanna, would you care to share a table with me?" There. It was out and it was up to her friend.

Joanna concentrated on the glass in front of her. "Same as yesterday?"

Thea's heart beat again, feeling a deep sense of relief at the rejoinder. Perhaps not all was lost. "Yeah, that would be good." Thea slipped from the chair and moved toward the table. Everything had been so different between them when they shared the table the day before. Maybe today they could recapture that.

Jo moved from her position to join Thea at the table. "I'm leaving at the end of the week. Thought you'd want to know for the room," Jo said.

"You're leaving?" Thea repeated the words that brought all her hopes of a renewal of the tentative friendship come crashing in a heap at her feet. Joanna's voice was so barren that it was hard to associate it with the singer who could make the most implausible song sound wonderful.

"Yes."

"Why?"

"It's time to move on." Joanna shot a look in the direction of the kitchen. "Lucy certainly is taking her time with a simple matter of dry toast."

"I thought you liked it here?" Thea's eyes looked to the averted profile of the beautiful woman. She couldn't help the desolation in her voice.

"What does it matter to you? Surely you'll be far too busy with your future to care if I stay or go. Besides, what makes you think I like this small, backwater town? It's just like all the others I've experienced in the past. Why would this one be any different? It's a means to an end, Ms. Danvers. Only a means to an end." Jo's tone was cold, sarcastic.

Thea looked away and tried to recover from the pain she felt at the words, especially Jo saying 'Ms. Danvers'. It was obvious that Joanna really hadn't cared about her at all. It was just her own loneliness and need reaching out to a figment of her imagination.

"What a fool I was to think that there was anyone in the world who did care for me other than as a prize," she mumbled.

"Well, I wish you luck and a safe journey, Ms. Lackerly." Thea scraped back the chair and moved away from the table to escape as fast as possible. Her eyes filling with tears did not help in her navigation to the door. She couldn't see where she was going.

Lucy edged out of the kitchen just as Thea made her tearful getaway.

"No. No. Thea, please, don't leave." Joanna shot out of her chair and managed to grasp Thea's arm as she was about to open the door.

Thea, eyes brimming with tears gazed at Joanna and saw a warmer expression. "Why? Why shouldn't I? You don't want my company." Her voice broke and she sobbed at the thought.

"I do. I do. Please, Thea, let's have breakfast and you can tell me about your new protector. What do you say?"

Thea's depression disappeared with lightning speed as she looked into Joanna's beautiful face. "I really could do with breakfast."

"Good, come on then. Let's sit. Lucy is bringing our breakfast." Joanna tugged at Thea's arm and they went back to the table.

Lucy breezed from around the counter, placed two large platters in front of them, and smiled. "There you go, girls. Something tells me you need this meal."

"Hey, Luc, I didn't order this." Joanna said. Her plate was loaded with eggs, bacon, hash browns, and tomatoes.

"I know you didn't, but dry toast? Really, Jo, look at you. I doubt that a bitsy piece of toast is going to solve what ails you, my girl. So eat and enjoy." Lucy laughed and walked away.

"She's right, you know," Thea said softly. Their eyes briefly meet before looking back at the food.

"Mmm... not so sure I can eat it," Jo grumbled. She picked up her fork and poked at the bacon.

Thea watched, realizing that for some reason their roles had reversed. Thea felt very protective of Joanna. It was absurd. "I think it's dead, Joanna."

Joanna looked up and smiled ruefully before nodding. "It's always best to check," she said before placing a small forkful into her mouth.

Thea, finally feeling at ease, placed a more generous portion on her fork and began her meal in earnest.

Jo was feeling somewhat less queasy as she finally gave up on her breakfast, which she had tried but failed to do justice to, only managing to eat about a third of it. Now, Thea on the other hand, was entirely different. She was even mopping up the juices of the tomatoes with her toast. She had asked Lucy to provide more toast, which the owner had happily brought.

Bringing her steaming coffee cup to her lips, she sipped at the beverage and watched the younger woman eagerly decimate the final remnants on her plate. It was touch and go that Jo didn't offer her own wasted meal to Thea. The thought itself brought about a chuckle that she couldn't suppress.

Green eyes glanced up shyly and gave her a sheepish shrug. After placing the juice soaked final piece of toast in her mouth, she sat back and placed a satisfied hand on her belly.

"You obviously enjoyed that?" Jo smiled with indulgent warmth.

"Oh, yes. Lucy is a good cook and I was hungry. I haven't eaten much since lunch yesterday." Thea reached for her coffee cup.

"How come you never get fat eating all that? You're such a tiny thing. If I did that on a regular basis I'd never get in my jeans," Jo mused.

"I guess it must be my metabolism. I've never had a problem with eating whatever food I wanted. You don't look like you have a problem either." Thea stared at Jo over her coffee cup before looking away.

"That's because I travel around a lot and don't have the luxury of eating this well most of the time. I confess this month has given me some extra pounds." Jo looked down at her hands.

Lucy brought more toast for Thea and gave Jo a disparaging stare after looking at the plate of partially eaten food. "You want me to take that away?"

"Well, unless Thea here will help me out. I'm not going to eat it, Lucy."

"Sorry. I'm all full up right now." Thea chuckled. "Another time, perhaps."

Lucy clucked her disapproval. "Such a waste," she muttered collecting the plates.

"So, tell me about your new fiancé?" Jo didn't particularly want to know, but she did.

Thea now looked uncomfortable and stared over Joanna's shoulder and sighed heavily. "I've known George forever, I guess. He's been hoping that I would take up his offer of marriage for some time now. He's the local banker and has a solid background. I could do worse." Thea drank heavily from her coffee cup, frowning as she did.

"I was always under the impression that you married for love and not because someone has a *solid background*. Correct me if I'm wrong?" Jo couldn't help the caustic tone that accompanied the words.

"Is that why you're not married?"

"No, no that's not the reason." Jo laughed and tapped her fingers impatiently on the table.

"Do you mind telling me what the reason is?" Thea asked.

Steel blue eyes flicked across the blonde woman's features and saw the sincerity in her expression. "No one ever asked me."

"Really? I find that astonishing. You are so beautiful and talented. All the men in the town are raving about you. Surely you know that?"

"Ah, Thea, remember one thing about men, they think with a part of their anatomy that doesn't see the light of day unless it needs to pee. Lust is about the only way to describe what the men here are generally feeling when they look at me." Jo had a wry expression when she spoke. "Why are you marrying Andrews?" she asked directly.

"I know I don't have to explain myself to you but I want you to know my reasons even if you don't approve." Thea sucked in a deep breath. "My father left me heavy debts and the motel is mortgaged to the hilt. The insurance company has refused to pay out on my father's life insurance policy. I have no choice in the matter." Thea's voice was calm and flat.

"Why not just leave town and start again? Why marry someone you don't love or even like."

Thea looked down at the table and at the toast that was growing cold. "I do not have your talents for singing or anything else other than running a motel. It would appear that I'm not that good at that either."

"Perhaps not as a singer, but I'm sure you are talented in other things." Jo blew out an exasperated breath. "What's wrong with the way you run the motel? Surely you can get work elsewhere."

"No. I can't, Joanna. I've never left this place. It's the last part of my family heritage." Thea's eyes now glistened with tears of frustration at her own choices.

"Thea, you're an intelligent woman and don't need to stoop to this type of life. Who is going to benefit if you stay on at the motel? That asshole banker Andrews? You're better than that."

"Don't you see? My forefathers founded the town and I owe it to the family line."

Jo knew about family heritage. She had been born into a Greek family that believed the Greek gods themselves still had the power to affect their lives. It had annoyed her when she was young. Now, Thea was telling her the same philosophy using different words.

"I'm leaving early Saturday morning. Come with me?"

Jo shook her head. *Did I really just say that?*

By the look on Thea's face, she couldn't believe it either. She wiped a hand across her eyes before staring back at Joanna with a shocked expression.

"Go with you," Thea whispered.

Jo knew she was being stupid and ridiculous, but she didn't care. From the first moment she met Thea, she knew it was important to protect her and the only way to do that was to take her with her on her travels. "Yes." Her response was stark and full of so many possibilities, both good and bad.

Thea slowly got out of her chair, put out a hand, and touched Joanna's shoulder. "I...I need to go. I'll see you later." She moved hastily out of the diner and this time Jo let her.

Not much later, Lucy came out of the kitchen, went to the table, and looked pointedly at the space that Thea had vacated. "I guess you get the check or is she coming back?" Lucy asked quietly.

Jo, trying to process what had just happened, looked up and frowned. "No, I don't think she'll be back." Jo moved out of her chair and held onto the back as she felt a wave of nausea overtake her.

Lucy put an arm around her and led her gently, but swiftly to the bathroom. Jo had known her breakfast wasn't going to stay around long.

Chapter Nine

Thea had walked back to the motel and her office without really knowing how she did so or how long it took to get there. All she remembered were the last words from her friend and protector. Joanna.

I'm leaving on Saturday morning early, come with me?
"Go with her? My God, it is like something out of a movie," she whispered.

She was certain if she closed her eyes for any length of time the words would disappear and perhaps the woman who had voiced them also.

She stared unseeingly out the window onto the colorful flowers that adorned the yard. This garden was her pride and joy. In many senses her escape from dreary reality. She watched the breeze ruffle the leaves of the flowers. The butterflies that frequented her yard were flitting from one flower to another and appeared to sunbathe on the green leaves in the harsh glare of the full sun, their pretty wings held together in defiance of the sun's rays. All she wanted to do now was sleep, hoping that when she awoke, all would be well with her world. She would be free to make her own choices and have none of the weight of family heritage and debts weighing her down.

The door to her office opened and Daisy tentatively walked inside, a look of horror on her face. "Thea, Thea, darling, are you all right?" Daisy walked briskly to Thea and wrapped her ample arms around her.

"I...I don't know what to do, Daisy. I really don't know what to do. What should I do?" Thea could feel heartfelt fear heavily weighing down on her as she melted into Daisy's arms. The woman had been there when she was a baby and had become a mother figure when her own mother abandoned her.

"Oh, my dear, please, it's going to be all right. When has your Daisy ever been wrong?" Daisy pulled Thea into her arms tighter in a comforting hug, rocking her gently. Thea wasn't happy, hadn't been in a long while, and Daisy thought she deserved happiness.

"It's not. It's not, Daisy. How can she ask me that question, it's far too late." Thea let her tears flow.

Daisy had watched the interaction between Thea who she considered a daughter and the tall stranger, who was nothing like Thea in both background and manners. It was hard to associate the two together. But it was obvious to anyone who cared to notice that their relationship was a strong bond. What type of relationship exactly was developing could be cause for speculation. Whatever it was, it had set in stone and neither one of them looked happy about the events currently taking shape around them.

"Why not tell me what she asked you and perhaps I can help?" Daisy gently tipped up the tear-stained face and smiled encouragingly at her.

Thea gulped several times and then gave a weak watery smile and nodded. "She's leaving and asked me to go with her," Thea said tearfully. "What shall I do, Daisy?"

Daisy gave her a rueful glance and smiled gently back at the face she loved. She was such a sweet child and it was heartbreaking to see her troubled so. "What does your heart tell you to do, child?"

"My mind tells me I must marry George Andrews. My roots tell me I must marry George Andrews. My financial situation tells me I must marry George Andrews." Thea spoke as if she was speaking to herself rather than the woman at her side.

"But what does your heart tell you, Thea?" Daisy prompted her again.

"My heart tells me to accept Joanna's offer and leave with her and forget everything I have grown up with and feel comfortable with. To be a free spirit just like Joanna and travel and find my true path in life." Thea lifted her head and looked at Daisy with a wrinkled forehead. "Can it be that simple, Daisy?"

"Yes, it can." Daisy grinned at the flowery description, but she could see the happiness the words brought to Thea's face. It transformed it. Anyone who thought Joanna was bad for Thea, her expression alone would convince them that she was the opposite. "I think you have your answer, my child. I think the earlier you tell George the better. Don't you think so?" Daisy coaxed the younger woman to look at her directly.

"I could just leave with Joanna and let him find out that way." Thea sighed heavily at the unwelcome prospect of telling George she wasn't going to marry him.

Daisy raised an eyebrow at the comment. "I never had you down as a coward, Thea."

"True, I have more of a backbone than that."

"Perhaps you should tell your friend that you're going with her. When she walked in here a few minutes ago she looked deathly pale to me." Daisy had watched the woman slowly come into the motel entrance, glance quickly around, and grimace at the coffee happily brewing. That was a first. She then turned the color of Thea's eyes and headed for her room.

Thea turned concerned eyes toward the older woman. "Did Joanna look ill or just upset?"

Daisy patted her arm and smiled briefly. "Why not go and check on your friend and see for yourself. Then clear up the matter of your broken engagement."

Daisy chuckled as Thea rushed out of the room. "Well, I know what type of relationship those two could end up in by the way Thea ran out of here. The whole situation is quite romantic if it didn't have George Andrews sitting in the middle of it."

†

Thea could feel a sense of peace as if her soul had escaped its chains and was soaring free to meet whatever challenges the world threw in her path as she rapped gently on the door of room five. She waited impatiently for Joanna to open it but nothing happened. She knocked again tempted to barge in as she had once before. *God, was it only two days ago?* For her it seemed like a lifetime and that she had known Joanna forever.

Thea knocked again and shouted, "Joanna." With each passing moment, she was becoming increasingly frustrated. Perhaps Daisy had been wrong and Joanna had only come into the motel briefly and left again.

Is she gone for good or is she just doing laundry? Maybe she is visiting John-Henry, or maybe she's with that man from last night.

Her last thought galvanized her into action she placed her passkey in the door, and opened it quietly before stepping inside.

"Joanna? Joanna, are you here?" she asked from the doorway. When she heard a low moan, her heart rate increased. Was Joanna ill? She walked swiftly forward before seeing her friend spread-eagled on the king-sized bed. Her shirt was off and she was only wearing brief panties. She was lying on her stomach and the smooth back that came into view was like looking at creamy, blemish-free silk. Thea wondered what it would feel like to touch Joanna. Shaking her head from the thoughts that seemed to invade her mind when she was in close proximity to Joanna, she knelt at the front of the bed as close as possible to Joanna's head.

"Joanna, are you sick? Do you need a doctor?"

Joanna peered blearily and groaned a little louder but still didn't say anything.

Thea was now very concerned. Joanna appeared drawn, pale, and the bloodshot eyes didn't help. Thea had noticed them earlier, but hadn't thought it fit to mention that in light of the tentative conversation between them.

"I'll get a doctor, Joanna. Please let me cover you up, you're shaking." Thea tugged at the edge of the sheet under Joanna and was surprised at how easily the sheet came free in her hands.

The movement of the sheet and Thea's words seemed to finally penetrate Joanna's sub-conscious because she turned her head toward her coming within inches of contact.

"Thea, it's okay. I'm okay. I have a hangover." Joanna held her head and gave Thea a tight smile.

Thea gazed into the bloodshot eyes. "Hangover? You have a hangover?"

Joanna gave her another feeble smile. "Yeah, I kinda tied one over on myself last night. Sorry you thought I was sick."

Thea couldn't believe it. So possibly, all that Joanna had said earlier was probably not any more real than just something to forget once the hangover was gone. "I see. Well, I guess I'll leave you to your hangover then." Thea was feeling like a fool.

"Thea, what is it?" Joanna moved closer.

Thea stiffened when Joanna's naked breasts brushed up against the fabric of her cotton shirt. Breathing had suddenly become increasingly difficult. She was annoyed at herself, at Joanna, and now her body that was once again showing signs of uncontrollable feelings.

What's going on with me? I need her as a friend, not a romantic interest. Besides she wouldn't entertain that idea...she likes men.

Thea closed her eyes to ward of the chaotic thoughts that trespassed on her mind and body. The beautiful woman pressed with unconcerned ease against her body increased the tempo of her heart.

Could she hear that?

"I thought you were sick and needed the doctor. I'm very sorry for disturbing you. I seem to make a habit of invading your privacy without permission." The words tumbled past Thea's lips unabated.

She wanted to hear Joanna once again ask her to go with her on her travels, but she dared not ask and tempt the fates. While she didn't know if Joanna had been genuine in her request, she still had hope and that would give her the strength to see George and terminate their business deal. That's all it was could ever be for she didn't like men that way.

"You never disturb me, Thea. Thank you for your concern. I appreciate it," Joanna murmured.

Thea smiled at her shyly. "I guess I'll go and get on with things then. Are you sure you don't need anything?" Their eyes locked for several seconds and it seemed to Thea that an undecipherable message passed between them.

"Yeah, I need to sleep it off, that's all. I'll catch up with you later. Would you have dinner with me early? Around six," Joanna whispered.

Thea heard the gentle question and it brought her senses out of hiding and soaring like an eagle in the sky. "Sure. I have some business to take care of this morning and then I'm free the rest of the day. If you want, we can have coffee any time."

Joanna grimaced. "Business?"

"Yes, business." Thea looked away and attempted to move from the vicinity of Joanna. However, the woman seemed to get a new lease of life. She quickly put a hand out and grasped Thea's chin turning her face back so that they were mere inches away from one another.

"Do you need a protector for this business?" Joanna asked in earnest.

Thea smiled at the warmth flowing through Joanna's fingers as she unconsciously smoothed the planes of Thea's face with the tips. "Are you offering your services as protector to me again?" Thea couldn't help the heat that traveled into her cheeks at the soft caresses.

"I guess I am. Would you like to take me up on the offer?"

"How about you sleep and take me to dinner later." Thea grinned. "I'll be fine."

Joanna smiled as a tinge of color resurfaced and she withdrew her fingers. "Yeah. Okay. If you're sure."

"I am."

"Then I'll catch up with you later. I have laundry to do anyway. Can't have me going around naked, can we?" she replied jovially.

Thea chuckled at the thought and turned away quickly, *Naked indeed.*

She never seems to be in all her clothes whenever I'm around.

Then again, her bedroom was her domain and she probably didn't expect visitors. "No, that we can't. See you later and if you need me, just call." Thea moved away from the bed and the beautiful woman sprawled out on it.

"I will. Oh and, Thea?"

"Yes?" Thea had her hand on the door and waited for the question before she opened it.

"I meant what I said earlier. Will you come with me when I leave?" Joanna looked up at the ceiling.

Thea couldn't help the smile that crossed her face. She wanted to go back and hug Joanna, but it wasn't the time or place. That might be misconstrued in her current state of dress. "Yes," she said in a quiet but decisive tone before proceeding out the door.

†

Jo continued to stare at the ceiling. She was stunned.

Did she say yes?

Had Thea really said yes? Thea had said yes.

With that clear picture in her mind, Jo closed her eyes and although still feeling drained, tired with a sledgehammer working on her temples, she closed her eyes. A quiet joy filled her as sleep claimed her. Her dreamscape of green eyes that had once seemed to glow from a faceless person now had a visage and it was very welcoming to behold.

†

Thea had never felt this alive in all her twenty-nine years and it was all to do with her lone guest at the motel—Joanna. She was eternally grateful to whoever was looking out for her to have the woman enter her life at this stage. It could have been too late had she turned up a few weeks later.

With a determined walk, she went toward the bank, unable to stop the happy grin plastered on her face. She entered the bank and smiled at the teller who gave her a quizzical look. It was rare that she ever set foot in the bank. George always visited her personally to deal with her account.

"Ms. Danvers, it's wonderful to see you. Congratulations on your engagement to Mr. Andrews. I hope you will be very happy," Ted Wassle, the teller, said.

Thea sneered inwardly knowing that everyone in town knew that George Andrews used his business rather than his personal attributes to get that result. "Thank you, Mr. Wassle. I wonder perhaps if Mr. Andrews is in and if he could spare me a few minutes." Thea smiled at the teller, who had worked in the bank for as long as she could remember.

"Sure thing, Ms. Danvers. He will certainly make time for you without a doubt. Please take a seat. I'm sure he will be with you shortly." The teller immediately went to a door-marked private, knocked, and waited.

Within two minutes Ted was back behind his counter and George was ushering Thea into his opulent office. It was obvious that there had been no expense spared with the furniture or the various pieces of office equipment.

"My dear, this is an unexpected, but pleasant surprise." He bent close to her and kissed her cheek.

Thea had successfully turned her head to evade the lip-to-lip encounter, but couldn't stop the impact on her cheek. She moved away to stand at the window that looked out across the town and wiped her cheek with the back of her hand.

"George, I need to speak to you about our agreement." Thea turned to face the rotund man whose face never ever seemed to be anything but streaming with perspiration.

George eyed Thea with suspicion.

While standing by the window she knew she was fidgeting nervously. This was a monumental moment in her life.

"What is it? Do you need money for the preparations for our wedding? Never mind that, my dear, I have everything in hand and everything will be ready for a week from Saturday when we will be married."

Thea couldn't believe her ears. The man had everything in hand? Everything! Obviously, he had been so confident that she would say yes that he went ahead and planned the affair.

"No, George, that isn't why I am here." Thea gave him a quizzical look. Why had he been so sure of her saying yes? She hoped for the insurance payout yet the man was at her door immediately when she found they declined to pay. He didn't know about that beforehand. Did he? Did he have a hand in the final decision?

"Then, Thea, please tell me what's on your mind?" George seated himself in a large plush office chair that would have been more at home in a house than an office.

Thea looked at her motel from the window. At least for the moment it was hers until she had her say. After that, it would belong to the bank and the man seated in the room with her. It would be the last of her family heritage before her release to a new life. Thea cleared her throat to gain a controlled and confident tone. "George, I'm sorry, but I've been thinking about it and I can't marry you."

"Thea, my dear, its just a few nervous jitters. I'm not giving you much time to get used to the idea and I appreciate that. Perhaps if we postpone the wedding until the following...week, then you will have gotten used to it?"

Thea's stomach roiled at the very thought of marrying the man in front of her. She had a better offer—it might not be permanent—but it was a solution. One that she couldn't refuse. Her heart would wither and die if she did.

"No, Mr. Andrews, it's not nerves and delaying the wedding won't help at all. I'm not going to marry you." Thea's voice raised a fraction as jitters were starting to move to the surface of her emotions.

Perhaps I should've brought Joanna with me as my protector.

The mere thought of Joanna eased her fears. She looked at the man who was now bristling with anger, his face turning bright red.

"I don't accept that, Thea. You will marry me and that's final." His whole body shook with rage.

His angry and arrogant assumption that she had no choice in the matter made Thea's anger surface. "Go to hell, George. I'm not marrying you and that's final."

"If you don't marry me, I will instigate the foreclosure clause your father agreed to and that means you will lose the motel immediately," he snarled.

"I know," Thea acknowledged. She had already cleared all her personal belongings out of the hotel.

"Just like that. You're giving up something you have nurtured and cherished for years. I don't believe it. Who's put you up to it?" George exploded.

Unable to stop herself, Thea shivered at the harshness of the tone. She could see by the sneer on his face he had seen it and was taking pleasure in her discomfiture. "No one put me up to it. I decided that marrying you wouldn't make me happy and if I had to lose the motel, so be it," Thea said in a mildly aggressive tone.

"It was Bascome, wasn't it?"

"No one in this town put me up to it so you can leave them alone."

"You're lying to me. It was probably both John-Henry and Lucy, they tried to help you out once before but I put the dampener on their good Samaritan-ship," he spat. "You know I'm going to find out sooner or later, so tell me," he shouted.

"It hasn't anything to do with either of them. I told you it was my idea and that's the end of it. Serve whatever papers you need to and I will sign the mortgage deed to the bank. Goodbye,

Take Me As I Am

Mr. Andrews." Thea turned for the door. A sweaty hand on her bare arm stopped her.

"There's no way I'm letting you leave here until I know who talked you out of marrying me?"

"It wasn't anyone. Let go of me, Mr. Andrews, I'm leaving." His vice-like grip on her arm hurt, but she refused to give him the satisfaction of knowing that.

George didn't take his hand from her arm as he stared at her with what looked like comprehension on his face. "Get out of my sight, you worthless piece of trash. But remember this, Thea." He voice shook with rage. "I do not take rejection well, so beware." He spit at her and his spittle made a small track down her face.

Not giving him the satisfaction of letting him know that the words had scared her and letting him see her revulsion of his action, Thea rushed out the door. Within thirty seconds, she was breathing in the morning air. Her hand shakily went to her left cheek and she wiped at the moisture in disgust. She certainly needed another shower.

†

Livid, George stomped around his office cursing and swearing while occasionally slapping his hand against his desktop. There was no doubt that the whore drifter who sang in the bar was the culprit. Thea hadn't said it, but she had given it away in that comment about it not being anyone from the town. How could it have been? He had the town sewn up except for the bar and diner owners. Thea was his and she was going to regret ever having met that drifter. He'd see to it that she was a drifter again. That was a promise.

He sucked in a calming breath, walked briskly to his desk, and placed a call. "I have a job for you and I want it done this afternoon. There better not be any mistakes as to who sent you. I want the bitch to know exactly who and why," George said caustically. "Let me know when it's done." He slammed the phone down.

"Revenge they say is sweet and for a spurned lover to get his revenge surely that must be even sweeter," he said to the audience of an empty room.

†

Jo pushed herself off the bed and picked up her laundry lethargically. She'd been up about half an hour, had coffee, and showered. That was as near normal as she could be at three in the afternoon. Her stomach felt hollow and sore, but she guessed that was with the retching she'd done after breakfast. At least the pounding in her head was gone. She had a set in a few hours at the bar and planned to let John-Henry know she was leaving in two days.

As she was walking out of the room, she was happily humming a tune that she'd been working on as she made her way to the small laundry. After settling herself in the empty laundromat, she put her things into piles and calculated that she would be there at least two hours. The vending machine that hadn't worked the last time she was there had a steady light that wasn't flickering this time around. She selected an iced tea and waited for it to drop down. Her keen sense of hearing alerted her to the fact that someone else had entered the building.

Tony Reed brought his bulk squarely into Jo's personal space and stood toe to toe with her.

"You want something?" Jo asked confidently. It was the idiot she had saved Thea from that night at the bar. He was about her height but the breadth of his shoulders and body could be mistaken as threatening. Men never intimidated her and she wasn't going to start with this sack of muscle without a brain.

"Yeah. You." Reed's voice was full of pent up anger.

"Well, sorry I can't oblige." Jo turned away to pull her tea from the bottom of the machine.

"No one turns their back on me. Do you hear me?" The man put out his hand and wrenched her back round to face him.

Jo was surprised at his action, "What the fuck is wrong with you, asshole? Is it because I blew you off the other night?"

He gave her a nasty look before putting both hands on her shoulders and slamming her against the machine.

Jo felt the shock wave of metal to her body on impact. "Jesus! What is wrong with you?"

"My boss says, *hello bitch.*" He again pushed her against the machine.

Jo felt her teeth rattle. Once she recovered from the jolt, she glared at the man. "Who the hell is your boss?"

Tony sneered and pushed his face virtually nose to nose with Jo. "Oh, I'm going to tell you that, bitch, but first I want you to feel his message." He punched her in the face.

After the stars subsided, Jo could feel moisture trickling from her nose.

Shit. I think he broke my nose.

"He wants me to tell you that leaving town within the next hour might be beneficial to your health," he snarled. "He also said that you take with you only what you came with. No extra baggage. Comprehend?" Again, he brought his fist up and smashed it in her face.

Jo was reeling from the second impact, her left eye taking the main thrust.

No baggage. So this is about Thea. There would be only one man interested in that.

"Tell Andrews to go fuck himself, because it's still a free country and it's not my choice to make." Jo spoke in a voice that held no hesitation. No way in hell was she going to let this idiot get the better of her.

The jackass looked at her in surprise before positioning himself so he could hit her again.

Jo saw the pose and reacted automatically by lifting her leg .She raised her knee and placed it as hard as she could between his legs. His howl of pain made her grin. She'd hit the target.

He staggered. "You bitch. I'm going to get you for that." He moved unsteadily in her direction.

Jo smiled devilishly. Kickboxing was one of her many talents and moving a fraction forward, she took the stupid brute down.

He was on the floor, writhing in agony and looking up at eyes that held no mercy.

"You know if I wasn't a lady, I would kick the shit out of you until you begged for mercy. As it is, I'm a lady and if I hear or see you, or any of Andrews's goons anywhere near Ms. Danvers, or me, I will suddenly forget that the lady ever existed. Comprehend?"

"Yeah. Yeah, I understand you."

"Good. Now get the fuck out of here. I want to do my laundry in peace." Jo picked up her iced tea, sat in a chair, and looked at the two machines where her clothes were turning in the drum as if nothing had happened.

Jo watched him slowly pick himself up off the floor before creeping out of the building like a dog going home to lick his wounds.

As soon as she was alone, Jo put a hand to her nose and saw the deep red blood that covered her fingers. She then tentatively touched her left eye and could feel the swelling on the eyelid. "I guess I look a sorry sight."

With purposeful slow moves, she got out of the seat and immediately felt areas of her body protest. She probably bruised her back when he threw her against the machine. Guess I'm going to be leaving town earlier than expected. I'm good but not against an army. I bet Andrews will send in the cavalry. Now, how to explain to Thea what was happening? She hoped that when Thea saw her face, she didn't panic and change her mind. That would only favor Andrews, and no way was she going to let that bastard win.

Chapter Ten

Thea hoped to see Joanna, but so far, she hadn't turned up. A prickling at the base of her neck told her that there was a problem.

What is it? Why do I always have a feeling she's in as much trouble as I am here?

Joanna had shown she was capable of handling herself and Thea couldn't think of anyone who'd want to cause her trouble.

All her personal possessions were at Daisy's house for safekeeping. She had two battered suitcases packed with her clothes, toiletries and two of the journals of her writing to take with her when she left. Her other journals were safe with Daisy. Marrying George would have been the biggest mistake of her life. Although profoundly sad that she was going to be leaving so soon, Daisy was also happy that she had made the right decision.

She walked out into the afternoon sun beating down on her beloved yard full of flowers. As she strolled among them for what she surmised was the last time, her heart was heavy but full of hope. So caught up in the sights around her she didn't hear the person come up silently behind her until a hand settled on her shoulder. Startled, she turned.

"Joanna, you scared the life out of me." Thea was gasping for breath at the unexpected visitor.

"Sorry I frightened you but—" Jo never finished the sentence. A terrified Thea took her by the hand and led her to a chair in the yard.

"My God, Joanna, what happened to you? You look like you've had a collision with a truck!"

"Well, I guess you could call it that. Thea, I need to stop the nosebleed and I think an icepack on the left eye would help. Are you going to help me out here?" Joanna stuffed what was once presumably a white handkerchief under her nose to stem the flow.

"I'll go get the icepack. Do you think your nose is broken? Shall I call the doctor?" Thea gently pulled back from Joanna and tenderly pushed away the loose bangs that fell on her friend's face.

"Need to get a haircut, don't I?" Joanna smiled.

Thea smiled back and shook her head. "No. No, please don't. You have beautiful hair. Maybe if you just tied it back, that would help."

Joanna grinned. "Okay. For you anything. So the icepack?"

"Sorry. Be back in a minute. Do you want the doctor to come take a look?" Thea asked over her shoulder as she went toward her office.

"No, I think it's gonna be fine. I just need to stop it from bleeding." Joanna pulled the blood soaked handkerchief away for scrutiny.

Thea returned within minutes with an icepack and a cold compress and placed them on Joanna's injuries.

"Thanks." Joanna tilted her head back.

"You're welcome." Thea dragged the chair that was the other side of the table a little closer to Joanna and sat there silently for several minutes.

"What are you thinking?" Joanna mumbled.

Thea was surprised at the question, but smiled at the possibilities of the answer as she watched the beautiful woman at her side. "Oh, this and that, but mainly about you." Thea held her breath hoping she hadn't said too much.

"Me? What's to think about concerning me?" The cold compress fell down Jo's face when she moved suddenly.

Thea quickly captured the compress before it fell on the ground. She firmly tilted back Joanna's head and put it against her eye. "Yes, you. I was wondering why you want me to go with you."

Joanna was so silent and unmoving that Thea wondered if she had heard the question.

"I didn't want you to think that the only option left open to you was marrying that *bastard*," Joanna spit out.

Thea reeled at the vehemence of the final word. "We really need to work on your vocabulary when we travel together, Joanna," Thea said primly.

Joanna chuckled.

"Thank you for looking out for me, Joanna." Thea couldn't stop the tenderness she was feeling.

"Well, I *am* your protector. I know an improbable one, but hey, it works." Joanna's voice sounded nasal.

"Yes, it does work. When we travel, what exactly will I do? I don't exactly have the many skills you possess." Thea could feel her confidence waver.

"Thea, you can do whatever you want, when you want, if you want. I will be there to make sure no one takes advantage of your good nature. That's what a protector does. The rest, as they say, is up to you."

"Who looks out for you?" Thea smiled, feeling the woman next to her shift uncomfortably in her chair.

"Me? Me. Well, I guess…I guess… .No one has ever asked that before?" Joanna admitted. "No one has bothered about me for years. I've pretty much fended for myself. That's just the way of it."

"Would you mind if I did?" Thea's voice was barely above a whisper.

"If you did what?" Joanna looked at her in confusion.

"Look out for you on our journeys?" Thea held her breath in anticipation of an answer.

"Our journeys? Yeah, sure, Thea, anything you say." Joanna chuckled "I can just see you defending me in a dispute." She grinned. "Cute. Really cute."

Thea could feel the heat on her cheeks at the remark. "Thank you. So do you think the nose has stopped bleeding?"

Joanna, gingerly moving in the chair, released the compress from her nose and the bloodstained handkerchief, and waited for a few moments. Nothing. "Yeah. I think it has. Thanks, Thea. Whatever would I have done without you?"

"I'm sure you would have managed."

"No, no. I think your caring skills cured all that ails me." Joanna dropped her voice a notch and turned her gaze to Thea who was only inches from her.

What could she say to a comment like that? "You flatter me."

"Flatter you, Thea? No, I was speaking the truth."

"What is your favorite flower, Joanna?" Thea asked to get the conversation from the previous heavy overtones.

"My favorite flower?" Jo looked astonished.

"Yes. Your favorite flower? Even you must surely have a favorite." Thea smiled at the chagrined look she received.

Joanna stared at the blonde before smiling. "Well, I'm not really into flowers but I do like the way eucalyptus smells."

"Eucalyptus?" Thea smiled. "That's a tree but ok, do you know its meaning?"

Joanna shook her head.

"Protector. It is beautiful in a very discreet way."

"Well, I don't know about that, but I like it anyway. What about yourself? Which flower is your favorite?"

"Mine? Well, I love lots of them as you can see, but if I had to choose...the carnation. Yes, it'd be the carnation." Thea turned toward her friend.

"Nice choice. It's always good to know that kind of information." Joanna's gaze turned to the numerous flowers in the yard.

Thea continued to glance in her friend's direction. "Yes, it certainly is good to have that information about someone."

Joanna smiled and nodded. "It is indeed."

"How about a cup of coffee while I tell you my news?" Thea's reward was a grateful smile from Joanna, who was now looking a little better—but only just.

†

"So, you broke off the engagement." Jo realized that was the reason for the man attacking her. "I bet he didn't take that well."

Thea shook her head. "That is an understatement. He was furious. I've moved all my things to Daisy's and I think you should see if John-Henry will let you store your things at his place."

Jo frowned. "Do you think he'll try something like burn the place down?" Jo already knew the answer to that one.

"I wouldn't put it past him. He said he'd foreclose immediately so it is possible he'd lock us out and we couldn't get back in."

"I'm sorry." Jo reached out and took Thea's hand.

"Nothing to be sorry for, Joanna. It was always going to come down to this and thanks to you I have a way out of marrying that man."

Jo could feel Thea shiver. "Are you cold?"

Thea smiled. "No. I was thinking about being married to George."

"I need to speak to John-Henry and tell him I'm leaving," Jo said.

"He won't be happy."

"I know and to be honest, I've really liked working there. It's time for us to move on, don't you think."

"Oh, yes."

†

George paced his office floor. He saw the tread his shoes made on the smooth beige carpet and scowled at the marks. Where was Reed? He should be back by now. The words spun in his mind and not for the first time in the past ten minutes.

A soft knock on the door brought his attention from the marks on the floor to the paneled wooden door. "Come in," he barked.

Ted Wesley tentatively poked his head around the door.

"What is it, Ted?" Andrews asked savagely.

"Tony is here and he wants to know if you can see him immediately."

"Show him in now. Oh, I don't want to be disturbed until Reed is gone. Do you understand?"

"Yes, I understand, Mr. Andrews. I'll show him in immediately."

Within a minute Tony entered the office, closing the door behind him.

"Where the hell have you been, Reed?" George saw the large bulk of muscle before him shift uncomfortably around at the words.

"Well, it was like this...."

"All I want to know is have you convinced the bitch to leave town now and without my fiancée?" George interrupted. He walked to be within a foot of the much taller man.

"Boss, it was like this. She wasn't easy to convince." Reed's tone was defensive.

George eyed him with suspicion. "What does that mean, exactly?"

Reed took a step back. "I made your point known as you instructed. I thought she was on the rails, when suddenly she jumped me and did some fancy footwork with her legs and then I was the one of the floor. It was kind of embarrassing." Reed stroked his stubbly chin.

"Hell, man, you let a woman…a woman get the better of you? What kind of man are you to let that happen?" George was furious and the look he gave Reed implied what he thought as nothing else could. "You're a complete waste of my time."

"She might be a woman, boss, but she sure knows how to defend herself. Her feet are lethal weapons. Not sure I'll father a child in the next year or so," Reed reluctantly admitted.

"What condition is she in if you worked her over first?" George demanded.

Tony smiled. "Well, she might have a broken nose. I know she's going to have at least one black eye. She won't be a pretty picture for a week or two that's certain. It won't be a nice look for her audience."

"Does she know I'm behind it?" George's mind was now full of other solutions to the irritating problem of the whore drifter.

"Yes, she figured it out before I had a chance to tell her," Reed admitted.

"Mmm. Considering the circumstances, that might work to my disadvantage if she reports the assault." George moved toward his desk, picked up the phone, and punched in a number. He turned to Tony. "You can go. I'll let you know what I want you to do next."

Reed turned to go.

"Keep quiet about this little episode. Wouldn't be good for your reputation if it got out that you could be bested by a woman, now, would it?" George sneered.

Reed nodded and bent his head as he left the room.

"Sheriff Smith, what can I do for you?" George heard a male voice say.

"Ah, Sheriff, it's George at the bank. I have a situation I need you to handle for me, if you wouldn't mind." George smirked knowing that Smith was one of the most gullible people in town and his wife had expensive tastes. He owed the bank big time.

"What's that, George?"

"It's like this, Sheriff...." George continued the conversation, a satisfied sneer on his face.

†

Jo was laughing at something Jerry, the young bartender was saying. John-Henry had gone to take a call and she wanted to explain her situation to the man herself so she waited, patiently nursing a beer, for him to return. She'd asked Thea to join her, but her friend declined so she could close the motel and make sure she had everything she wanted. Once Joanna finished speaking with John-Henry, she'd pick Thea up at Daisy's house.

While drumming her fingers on the bar, Jo smiled recalling the concern Thea had shown about her injuries. They would get along fine while traveling. It had been a pleasant shock for her when Thea said she wanted to look out for her, too. At least it had made them both laugh at the absurdity of the situation—each as improbable a protector as the other. Jo didn't understand what was happening with Thea, but it didn't matter. They were going to be traveling together for a while and they would find out what that connection was. After all, according to her father, each soul matched another and if you were lucky in life, you connected at some time and were ever the richer for it. Lost in her thoughts, Jo failed to notice John-Henry's return.

"Penny for them?" John-Henry asked quietly.

Jo looked up from her quiet contemplation and grinned happily. "Oh, I was just thinking about a friend."

"Then it must be a very special friend by the expression you had when I walked back in here." John-Henry smiled.

"Yes. Yes, I actually think it is a very special friendship."

"Anyone I know?"

"Now, that would be telling and I'm not saying…just yet anyway." Jo chuckled before sipping on her beer.

"Well, tell you what. I'll trade your information for mine. How is that?"

"How do you know I want your information?" Jo asked.

"Tell you what else. I'll go first." The older man pulled a beer for himself, came round to her side of the bar, and sat next to Jo.

"Sounds good to me."

Take Me As I Am

"I just received a call from a friend of mine in Nashville," John-Henry said.

"So? Nashville is a thousand miles away. What's that to do with me?" Jo picked up her beer bottle and rubbed a fingernail on the label.

"If you let me finish, Jo, perhaps you will get to know how it affects you." John-Henry smiled and Jo nodded. "When you came here I was impressed by your singing talents obviously, or I wouldn't have asked you to entertain the customers. However, what I didn't tell you is that after that first week I started to record some of your sessions. You see, my friend is a record producer in Nashville, a small label called Trigon Records. He works with raw talented singers and songwriters."

Jo knitted her eyebrows. "Yeah, so."

"I took the liberty of sending him a tape of yours and he just called back."

Jo was watching him with mild interest but inside her stomach churned.

"And?"

"And," he grinned. "You're not fooling me for one minute I can tell you're interested." He took a long slow swallow of his beer. "He wants you to get yourself there as soon as you can because he wants to hear you live. If he likes what he sees…well…I guess that's up to you and him."

Jo felt speechless. This was like a dream come true. She'd had the odd skirmish with record companies back in New York with her original band, but it had never taken off. This sounded too good to be true. Danvers was a hick town yet she managed to find not only a friend she could rely on, but also the chance at a dream. How did she get this lucky?

"John-Henry, why?" Jo watched the older man shake his head.

"Why not?" he asked.

"That's not an answer and you know it?" Jo laughed.

"True, but then again, why should there always be an answer to every question? Some things you just have to take on faith," John-Henry answered.

"I guess what I'm going to say next won't come as a shock, then. I need to leave, John-Henry. I was going to stay until the end of the week but circumstances have forced my hand and I need to get out of town either later today or early in the morning," Jo explained quietly.

"Does this haste to leave town have anything to do with the marks on your face?" He lifted her chin and looked closely at the half-shut left eyelid.

"Could be." Jo shrugged. "I'm taking a friend with me when I leave."

"Wouldn't be the newly engaged Thea Danvers would it?" John-Henry's eyes were tracking to the corner table where Thea had become engaged to George.

"Yes. That would be the friend and it's the newly broken engaged Thea Danvers that will be accompanying me." Jo grinned at the older man who smiled at her and winked.

"I guess you must be more of an attraction."

Jo blushed at the inference but managed to control it. "No, hardly think so, but I suspect she enjoys the company more."

Both of them laughed and drank from their respective beers.

"So, who do I see in Nashville?" Jo asked.

"Forgot to tell you that, didn't I? Jack Wicklow. He's one of the finest people I know even if he's in the recording industry." John-Henry laughed.

Jo looked at him skeptically. "Guess I'll find out, won't I? When's the next bus out of here heading that way? Tonight? Tomorrow?" Jo took another long sip of the warming beer.

"Early tomorrow morning. Five a.m. to be exact. Think you can manage that?"

"Yeah, sure. Can I stow my things here? Thea thinks the bastard banker might lock us out."

"Not a problem."

"Since the bus comes so early, I can only do one set. That's assuming you want me, that is?" Jo glanced at him knowing the answer.

"I want a last session from you and the customers are going to be devastated," he said. John-Henry lightly tapped her on the shoulder and nodded toward the entrance where Sheriff Smith was coming in.

Jo had seen the expression on sheriff's faces numerous times in other towns. He was going to ask her to leave town. Probably just as well she was already leaving.

†

Thea looked out of the window of the room that faced the small neat drive leading up to Daisy's single story home. Had anyone told her twenty-four hours ago, that she would be leaving her home, her motel, and contemplating the drifting life with a virtual stranger, she would have laughed in their faces. Facts spoke for themselves and there she stood, waiting for Joanna to escort her back to what was now the bank's motel for her final night. She considered the motel her home along with the town founded by her ancestors.

The nerves she felt only hours earlier when she had felt totally bereft of hope in the future were now those of excitement at the prospect of what lay ahead. It wasn't what she had expected but it was far better than existing in a marriage of convenience and being miserable.

Joanna had said she wouldn't be more than half hour, but already an hour had passed. After what she termed a disagreement with *something* and the injuries she had sustained, Thea worried that the *something* might come looking for her again.

As she watched for Joanna to appear, she gasped and held her hand to her mouth. The portly figure of George was striding, if you could call it that—rolling might be the better adjective—up the drive toward the house.

Damn, the sooner I'm out of this town the better.

Thea rushed out of the room toward the kitchen where Daisy, who had shown her nothing but love and understanding from her childhood, was. Daisy insisted she listen to her heart. She had, and now that man coming to Daisy's home was the outcome.

"Daisy, George is about to make his presence known," Thea said quietly. She hadn't wanted to startle her while she was placing a roast in the oven.

Daisy stood to her five-foot stature and smiled in compassion. "Thea, don't worry. I'll get rid of the silly man." She chuckled while moving toward the front door. "He surely can't take *no* for an answer, can he?"

Thea waited behind the kitchen door for Daisy to get rid of the intruder. There was no doubt about it—that is exactly how she viewed the man now—an intruder. She listened to the conversation.

†

Daisy opened the door and looked at the man whose face held determination. "What can I do for you, George?"

"It's Mr. Andrews to you and I want to see Thea. Don't tell me she's not here, because I know she is and I have news that she might be interested in," he said in a condescending tone.

"I can't believe that there is anything you have to say to Miss Danvers that would possibly be of interest to her," Daisy said.

"Well, at least you didn't bother to deny she was here," George bit out. "I demand to see my fiancée immediately."

Daisy laughed. "George, why would I bother? You have spies everywhere. If you want to know anyone's whereabouts, you will know. You have known Miss Danvers whereabouts for years and everyone knows it. There are names for people like you and I'm sorely surprised her daddy didn't use them on you."

"Tell Thea I want to talk about her friend. It will be in both their interests."

"I will do nothing of the kind. Why should she believe you or anything you might have to say? You don't intimidate me, or Thea for that matter, so go away."

"If Thea doesn't come and talk to me, her friend might end up in jail. I'm sure she wouldn't want that if she could prevent it. What do you think about that?" George said.

†

Thea was convinced that it was a ploy of George's to get her to talk to him but if it meant there was any danger of Joanna being jailed and she could prevent it well then it wasn't an issue. Hadn't she said she would protect Joanna?

"I'm here, Mr. Andrews. You had better come inside." Thea moved around the door into the small hall and gave Daisy a weak but grateful smile.

"You sure, Thea? I don't mind telling this sorry excuse for a man to get out of here," Daisy retorted.

"I'll be okay."

Daisy moved aside.

"Don't think I'll let you get away with that remark. You'll pay. Count on it," George whispered.

"Mr. Andrews, don't you dare," Thea threatened.

With a scowl followed by a nod, George tagged along behind Thea to the small sitting room and the door closed behind them.

Thea walked to the window and waited for the man to say whatever he came for. The sooner he did, the faster he would be out of her sight. She never wanted to see him again for rest of her life.

"My dear, surely I'm not that abhorrent to you. After all, it was less than a day since you agreed to marry me and we shared our first kiss to seal the promise."

Thea flinched at the memory. "Say what you have to say and then please leave. I have things to do before I leave town." Thea refused to rise to the bait.

"I wanted to clarify the situation between us, Thea. I know you have a nervous disposition and I'm sure that now you have realized that your rather hasty words this morning should be retracted."

His arrogance surprised Thea. "You said that Ms. Lackerly may be in trouble and I could help. That's the only clarification that I need, Mr. Andrews." Thea could feel her simmering anger reaching a level that was ready to boil. She hadn't been happy to know that for years he knew her whereabouts. To her, that was a total invasion of her privacy along with stalking, which was illegal.

George smirked. "Ms. Lackerly was in an altercation with an employee of mine. I have convinced him to agree not to press charges for assault." He paused. "For the moment, that is."

Thea raised her eyebrows. *So that's how Joanna received her injuries. George sent one of his goons to make their mark on her.*

"Who exactly would that be?" To stop her fingers from moving in agitation, Thea threaded them together in front of her.

"You met him at our engagement. Tony Reed."

Thea virtually choked on the laugh that bubbled up at the name. "That's preposterous. Who in this town would believe that?" she asked. "Everyone in town knows he fights with anyone at the drop of a hat. Who would believe that Joanna would attack him?"

George looked down at the tip of his highly polished shoes, smiled, and then looked her directly in the eyes. "Sheriff Smith, for one. He's seeing your *friend* as we speak. I can, of course stop any of this from escalating if you would work with me on the problem."

Thea couldn't believe her ears. This was ridiculous. Tony and Joanna had an altercation at the bar, but Joanna would never assault the man. Would she? What did she really know about her new friend? Not a great deal. However, she knew that Joanna wouldn't have picked the fight. She knew it in her heart.

"What exactly do you want from me, Mr. Andrews?" she asked absently.

"I want you to tell your friend that you're staying in town and tell her to leave without you." George smiled sweetly. "The earlier, the better."

Thea turned back to face the window, seeing the afternoon sunlight gradually disappearing round the house. "That's all?" Thea asked in a stronger voice.

"Well, my dear, I want you to reconsider your earlier words," he said in a sickly, reassuring voice. "We can work on that after your friend leaves town."

Thea heard his tone but didn't believe it for one minute. Still there was a question of the sheriff arresting Joanna and locking her in jail. It looked like George could fabricate enough of a case to do that. Sheriff Smith was a nice man, but everyone in town knew he was in George's back pocket. Joanna didn't have a chance.

"I need to speak to Ms. Lackerly and tell her myself." Thea's voice sounded desolate even to her ears.

"Oh, no. I don't think so, Thea. That woman might convince you otherwise," George blustered.

Angry green eyes focused on him and Thea inwardly grinned when he opened then shut his mouth. "If you want me to co-operate, Mr. Andrews, I suggest you let me see Joanna, and we meet alone." Thea spoke with quiet authority. She fixed her face with a look that let Andrews know she wasn't going to give in to any external influence from him at this point.

"As you wish, my dear." George turned toward the door to leave.

Thea continued to look out the window and said nothing more. What was there to say? She heard the door click shut and the low mumble of voices as Daisy probably showed him out of the house. She watched the banker walk from the drive to his waiting car and the drive all of three hundred yards to the bank.

Her mind was so preoccupied that she failed to hear the door open.

"Are you okay?" Daisy asked.

"I don't know."

Somewhere in the house, a timer began ringing.

"Oh, my popovers are ready. We'll talk at dinner when your friend gets here."

Thea sighed. George gave in to her too easily and that meant he'd have his spies monitoring her conversation with Joanna. She closed her eyes and shook her head as a lone tear trickled down her cheek. Once her protector was gone—and Joanna would be gone, that was certain—she knew George Andrews would make her pay for rejecting him.

†

"No! No, damn you, Thea. What has made you change your mind about coming with me?" Jo couldn't believe her ears. They had just enjoyed a wonderful home cooked meal and just as she was about to impart her good news, Thea told her she couldn't go.

"Joanna, surely it is my prerogative to change my mind," Thea countered.

"Give me credit for some intelligence, Thea. Two hours ago, we were practically out of this town and now all of a sudden you want to stay? Give me one good fuckin' reason." Jo was angry at her reaction to Thea's rejection. "Was it a prerogative or coercion that made you change your mind, Thea? That is what I want to know? Who has been here? Andrews? Reed? Or that stupid sheriff you call the law in this town?" Jo wasn't going to mention either Reed or the sheriff, but her emotions got the better of her and she spewed it out.

Thea's startled eyes turned to look at her. "Why do you mention Reed and what's this about the sheriff?" Thea's voice was full of innocence.

"Nothing, nothing that concerns you, Thea. A misunderstanding, that's all." Jo, not wanting Thea to see her lie, shrugged before shifting her eyes away.

"A misunderstanding, you say? So tell me. Perhaps I can help clear up the misunderstanding."

"What does it matter? I'm out of here in the morning and you're coming with me. That's the only thing there is a misunderstanding about at the moment," Jo replied decisively.

"If you don't trust me enough to tell me what the problem is with our sheriff then how do I know that going with you won't cause me trouble?" Thea pointed out.

Jo glanced at her friend and was hurt at the accusation that she might be in trouble and that it would affect the younger woman. "I do trust you, Thea. However, on this one, I want you to let it go and I'll explain everything once we are out of this fuc… this town."

"I see. Don't you need to go to the bar for your final night? John-Henry would be upset if you're late." Thea turned away.

Jo heard the words—Thea didn't trust her. Why would she? What did she know of her? Except for once in her life, she was trying to be helpful and as usual, it was backfiring.

Fuck this town. To hell with you, too, Thea. Stay in this crummy town and marry that asshole banker.

Jo bit back the words she wanted to say.

"Yeah, I do. Can't let down the only person in town who still wants me, now, can I?" Jo turned on her heel and left.

†

Thea, unable to stop the threatening tears, watched as Joanna left, knowing that she was the cause of her anger and despondency. Her heart was hammering, knowing that it was the end of her dreams. When Joanna mentioned the sheriff, she realized that the banker's words were true. Joanna was in trouble and she was the only one who could help her friend. Of that, she was convinced. Thea would sacrifice her own happiness to keep Joanna safe.

She heard the door slam. "I still want you, Joanna. I still want you," Thea whispered into the gradually dimming light in the room.

Take Me As I Am

Chapter Eleven

Jo was playing to the crowd with every ounce of energy she possessed and indeed anyone who had watched her perform in the bar would think that. The frenzied performance was the best that she had ever done and it showed John-Henry that his faith in her as a performer was spot on. She was a wonderful entertainer and deserved to achieve credit for her talent. He hoped it would work out for her and Thea.

As she finished her final session in the bar, Jo moved forward through the wolf whistles and calls for encore toward the bar.

"That was magnificent, Jo. What was firing in you tonight? You'd better have some left for that live performance in Nashville. I guarantee you will be on all the billboards in a year." John-Henry laughed watching Jo sit on a stool opposite him.

"I have lots of pent up energy that I needed to release. It was much better than going out and crashing heads with that goon of Andrews." Jo's voice sounded hollow even to her.

John-Henry had listened intently to the sheriff and his questions regarding a possible assault on George Andrews' bodyguard. Jo's description of what happened was fitting.

"Wise move. I thought Thea would have been here with you tonight?"

"No. She is otherwise pre-occupied, probably with the banker," Jo said.

John-Henry raised his craggy eyebrows in surprise. "I thought you said the engagement was broken?"

"Ah, well, it appears that I might have been wrong on that count." Jo shook her head. "So very wrong."

"Does that mean you leave on your own in the morning?"

"Yeah, sure does. I was thinking I might as well finish out the night. If it's okay with you, I'll sit it out on the porch until the bus arrives in the morning. Any objection?" Jo asked.

"You don't want a decent night's rest and a shower before you travel?" John-Henry asked.

"I hardly think I'm going to be making any friends on the bus that will care about my personal habits, do you?" Jo gave him a wry look and then drank heavily from the beer he placed automatically in front of her.

"Well, let's hope not, because after your performance it's certain you might have a stale aroma about you." He smiled and stroked his chin contemplating the information Jo had given him.

Jo looked at the crowd, drained her bottle, placed it carefully on the bar, walked back to the podium, and talked to the crowd around her.

"Since this is my last night, I thought I'd stick around till closing. I've got one more song I want to sing and then I'll take requests."

John-Henry listened to the impassioned words and could tell Jo was hurting when she began her song. It was then he saw Thea standing near the entrance and listening to Jo sing the last song of her own repertoire… "What made you change your mind?"

When the song ended, John-Henry watched as Thea quickly exited the bar in tears.

†

Thea was crying softly on the porch and hadn't heard the soft footfalls of Daisy as she opened the screened door and walked out with coffee for them both. It was heart wrenching for her to see the child in pain. Whatever the trouble was, it wasn't going to end like this. It wasn't an option. Not for the gentle young woman who had done nothing in this life except love her father and want to help him through his woes. It had been a difficult time for her during the past five years, after the drinking and gambling took control of her father.

Now there was a little hope for her. Thea had seen something in Joanna Lackerly that brought a torch to light the flame of hope within the dear woman. By all that was holy, she wasn't going to see it extinguished by the arrogant son of a bitch, George Andrews.

"Thea, darling, please, drink this. It will make you feel better." Daisy passed a coffee cup to the crying woman.

Thea looked up at her with red-rimmed eyes and gave her a slight smile as she gratefully accepted the cup. "I'm not sure it will make me feel better, but thanks, Daisy."

"Once you take a drink and tell me what's going on, then perhaps with the coffee and the talk we can find a solution. What do you say?" Daisy grinned engagingly.

It was then that Daisy listened as Thea began her story. She learned why the banker had come to visit and later Joanna's lack of trust in her.

"She wouldn't tell me exactly what was going on or if anything that George said was true. If she'd only trusted me with the information, maybe we might have worked something out. All I could see was how hurt she was by my words and I let her go without a word of support."

"So you decide that it's in Joanna's best interest for you to stay here and fend off Andrews. Is that it?" Daisy asked gently.

Thea blew her nose on her tissue that was sopping wet with her tears and weakly nodded. "Yes, so it would keep her out of trouble with the sheriff."

Daisy chuckled. "If Joanna had anything to worry about on that score, do you think she would still be singing in the bar? Sheriff Smith might be in debt to Andrews but he knows the law.

He's very black and white in those circumstances, Thea, and you know it." Daisy was certain that if they had anything substantial on the woman she would be in jail. She also knew that certain parties could get emotions running high and things could get out of hand easily and then perhaps Joanna might have a problem.

"I can't take the chance that she might end up in jail."

"Darling, the only thing that is going to be trouble for Joanna is when you travel with her and she has to keep *you* out of trouble." Daisy laughed at the affronted look she received.

"I'm not going with her, Daisy. I won't see her beaten again and I never want to see her suffer in any way because of me," Thea said vigorously.

"Don't you think she's going to suffer more if she doesn't know the truth?" Daisy countered.

"What truth is that? She wouldn't understand my reasons."

"Love. That's the truth. I've never known anyone that didn't understand that type of reason."

"I can't tell Joanna I love her, Daisy." Thea looked as if she were agitated while trying to puzzle out the negative and positive issues in her head.

"Why not? She obviously cares about you or she wouldn't have asked you to go with her. Would she?" Daisy had a knowing smile on her face.

"Because—"

"Because you're afraid. My child, we are all afraid of reaching out for something that might be taken away, or never given back with equal measure. Darling, it's worth taking that step if there's a chance in a million that your love is returned." Daisy wanted Thea to understand that she had choices.

"I could lose her, or even worse, she could end up in jail if I try to leave with her," Thea whispered.

"Thea, answer one thing and only one thing, for that's all that will matter in the end. Would you be happier going with her and taking your chances together than staying here knowing that you have no chances left? You know where that will lead." Daisy stroked Thea's bangs away from her eyes and saw the answer without words.

"I'll leave you to ponder that thought, my child. Don't forget to lock the door, whatever you decide." Daisy got up and walked toward the screen door when Thea suddenly engulfed her in a warm hug.

"I love you, Daisy." Thea whispered tearfully into Daisy's neck.

Daisy shifted and hugged Thea back. "Yes, I know you do and I love you too. So drink your coffee and stop crying before this old woman joins you."

†

Thea smiled tenderly at the retreating back of the woman who had at least given her things to think about, even if she hadn't made a decision. After walking back to her chair, she looked toward the town. The faint strains of music floated down the street from the bar just as her mind drifted to the problems at hand.

†

Jo sat on the steps leading to the bar, her guitar by her side and her few personal possessions in the haversack at her feet in the dust. She gingerly placed her hand on her left eye and grimaced at the pain it caused. She smiled ruefully, for that pain was nothing to what she felt at leaving without Thea by her side.

The sunrise was beautiful, with gentle swirls of golden light heralding the dawn of a new day along with the fresh possibilities that lay ahead. Jo gave it a cursory glance and sighed. She waited patiently for the bus that would pass through town and take her away, part of the way to her destination—Nashville.

She'd said her good-byes to John-Henry, who had been sad to see her go but made her promise to call him if she needed any help. There was also the promise of free tickets if she made it in Nashville. Jo had laughed at his optimism. It had cheered her up and made her think of something other than her melancholy thoughts of Thea.

Lucy had surprised her at the end of the night with a short visit to say goodbye. She brought freshly made sandwiches and snacks for the journey. Jo had to wipe a tear away at that gesture. No matter how happy she felt at leaving, she would miss some good people. Once she boarded the bus, she would be leaving the nondescript town with a heavy heart. Definitely a first for her.

In the distance, on the horizon, she could see a dust cloud approaching the end of Main Street. With one last glance at the motel, she wondered if Thea had gone back there for the night. Maybe even for the rest of her life. She shook the thought away while pulling her tall frame up from the steps before stepping down onto the road, away from the building. Her arm rose to signal the approaching vehicle and picking up her bags and guitar case she looked around her and gave a wry smile.

Hell, a month ago I was cursing having that argument with Jed that brought me here. Now, I'm wondering why it is causing me so much more heartache to leave. Her attention returned to the approaching bus, her heart too heavy to contemplate what she was about to give up.

"Could you use company on the journey?" Thea placed two battered suitcases down. Jo's back stiffened at the sound of the voice she had never expected to hear ever again. It was like music to her starved heart. "Who says I'm going on a journey?" Jo answered with happy confidence.

"Isn't that why you're waiting for the bus," Thea replied.

"Yeah, yeah, it is. Don't know how long the journey will last though. Sure you're up for it?" Jo still hadn't dared turn around. She felt sure it was a trick of the early morning and she was talking to herself. The oncoming bus was about to stop any second to pick her up. No, to pick them up, she prayed.

"Yes, I'm up for it. For however long it lasts, Joanna. Even if it's a lifetime."

Jo heard a breath sucking in—it was hers. She turned around with a wide infectious grin that Thea returned in equal measure.

"Well, I'm not sure getting to Nashville will take a lifetime, but let's go, shall we?"

Thea laughed and picked up her bags as the driver opened the bottom doors for them to stow their belongings.

"You know, Thea, you're going to have to ditch the suitcases. We need to travel light."

Jo smirked at Thea's distressed glance at her cases. "That's fine for now, Thea. We'll work it out. Never fear."

"You know that no one told Tony that I wasn't staying at the motel. I saw him asleep in his truck parked in front of the building. I think he was on guard duty." Thea grinned. "I don't think I want to be him when good old George finds out I've gone."

"Come on, let's take our seats." Jo grinned at the news. "Serves 'em both right. The bus will be long gone before they know you're not there."

"Joanna, may I ask you a personal question?" Thea wrinkled her nose as she slid into a seat.

Joanna sat next to Thea and smiled. "Sure. Ask away."

"You don't always travel without getting a shower do you? I think that in the future you need to break that habit if you do."

Jo laughed so loud that the two other passengers on the bus looked in her direction. "Well, you see, it was like this, Thea…" Joanna settled down next to her friend as the bus speedily left the town.

Chapter Twelve

"Thea, are you home?" Jo flung her backpack onto the side table, causing it to totter. She quickly grabbed hold of the vase of fresh flowers threatening to fall. It was a pleasure to come home to a clean house where she didn't have to do anything.

Jo smiled recalling her days at the motel with Thea—a month she never would forget. In that time, they formed a solid friendship and thanks to John-Henry had the opportunity of a potential singing contract in Nashville…

They had arrived in Nashville three months earlier with little more than the shirts on their backs and even less money in their pockets. Now hard work, even stacking shelves in a local supermarket would see them through. There was no way Thea was going to end up in the gutter.

Keeping an eye on the inexperienced woman had become second nature.

At times, she wondered how the timid and innocent Thea managed to worm her way into her heart so rapidly. Jo's life had demanded that she survive in any way she could and she had few experiences left to challenge her but not so for Thea.

John-Henry's friend Jack Wicklow was true to his word. After listening to Jo sing in person, he advanced her enough money to rent a modest apartment along with money for other necessities. He'd told her that he knew she was going to make it big and it was only the first installment.

It made her heart flutter and her belly warm knowing that she would always be able to look out for Thea and keep her safe. Thea looked after the domestic needs of their lives. Jo found she had the amazing talent of taking anywhere and making it a home. The once dingy apartment was now a colorful, clean place that Jo was proud to call home.

The thing called friendship was turning out to be very satisfying.

"Thea, you home?" Jo called again as she walked into the kitchen. She was surprised that there were no succulent smells wafting through the room. It was empty. Spotless and tidy, but empty.

Jo looked out the small kitchen window, wondering if ever she would make the big time and have the luxury of a beautiful view one day. She snatched a cookie from the plate that Thea had around for visitors. Or so she said. There was always a fresh batch for Jo to snaffle and she suspected Thea made them for her since visitors were practically nonexistent except for the neighbor above them.

As she was munching on the delicious chocolate cookie, she walked into the living area surprised that Thea wasn't there either. She was either asleep or out somewhere. It was only four-thirty in the afternoon so it was doubtful she was taking a nap.

Once she'd settled on the sofa, stretching her long denim clad legs on the cushions she picked up the remote and turned the television on, using it as background noise while she relaxed from the long studio session. It had been a very busy day and she was tired. In the past three months, she had been practicing for long hours and although she knew it was for her benefit, her lack of a social life was getting to her.

Even Thea had given up on them having time to tour the city together. Thea had made a friend in one of the neighbors and now had someone to go out with and explore the town. Jo didn't really mind, for she was happy with her music and that was what paid the bills. She reasoned that it was a great way for Thea to stretch her wings and find out what she wanted to do with the rest of her life. The unsettling feeling in her stomach made her wonder if she was all that happy with Thea's newfound friendship.

Jo yawned. *Thea won't be long, she never goes far*, she told herself before letting the peace of the apartment lull her to sleep.

†

Thea smiled engagingly at her new friend, Alice Richards, who lived in the apartment above them. Alice didn't mind the odd late session that Joanna indulged in when she was working on a new song and would often come around from time to time to see a live performance. Joanna, ever the showgirl, seemed to bask in the attention. Joanna was a star to her and there was no doubt to the whole world one day—she just knew it.

"Alice, how's it been today?"

Alice worked in a law firm as an underwriter. It wasn't the most sensational job in the world but it had its compensations and paid the rent. The woman seemed quite happy with her lot in life although she admitted that she wouldn't mind settling down one day and was envious of Thea's relationship with Joanna. Thea did have to explain that they weren't a couple in *that* sense although she longed for that to be true. She knew Joanna liked her but not to the same degree that Thea did. With each passing day she was more certain she loved Joanna and her dream was that they would be a couple.

"Great. What about yourself?" Alice asked.

"Oh, you know me. I'm enjoying getting around the city. After living in a small town all my life, it's a novelty."

"A novelty you will find will wear off in time. I hope it doesn't tarnish for you too soon." Alice grinned as they walked toward the small apartment building in a mid-priced area of the city. "Who knows, you could be living with a star one day."

Thea's shining eyes looked up at one particular set of windows and smiled. Joanna was a star and without her, Thea wouldn't be free from the entanglements that would have emotionally killed her. "Oh, I think there's a great chance of that in the future."

As they climbed the steps to the apartment, a wolf whistle stopped them. Thea turned and saw a group of young men on motorcycles leering at them. She dropped her eyes fractionally. Joanna always tried to make her more assertive in handling what she termed the *riffraff element of humanity who tried to feed off the innocent in this world.*

"Hey, beautiful, wanna come for a ride?" asked the guy on the lead motorcycle. The girl already sitting behind him scowled.

Alice turned to face them. "No."

"Oh, I wasn't talking to you, red. I'm waiting for your friend's answer." His voice dropped seductively as his eyes roamed Thea's body. His taunts reminded her that she had seen enough of this kind of baiting for a lifetime.

I thought I left this behind in Danvers.

"No, thanks." Thea tugged on Alice's sleeve. "Let's go. Joanna will be waiting and it's already after five," she whispered.

The biker quickly dismounted his bike and ran up the stairs between them and the entrance to the building before they knew it.

"Want to whisper in my ear, beautiful," he said playfully.

The man was quite handsome in a tough way. His stubble had the effect of giving him an extra dimension to his masculinity. Thea remembered Joanna telling her that the look was raw sexuality. It might be to Joanna but certainly didn't ring any of her bells.

"No, thanks. Perhaps another time."

The young man smiled broadly showing gleaming white teeth. He lifted his hand and passed a fleeting finger across her cheek before grinning. "I'll hold you to that."

He vaulted down the stairs and mounted his bike before roaring away.

"Wow. Thea, you handled that well."

"I didn't do anything. Come on let's go. Joanna will be home." Thea looked at her friend and smiled. "Want to drop in for supper in an hour?"

Alice shook her head. "Sorry, I have my night class in an hour. Can I have a raincheck?"

"Sure. You know you are welcome anytime."

†

Thea unlocked the door and walked into the apartment hearing the low hum of the television. She sniffed the air. It lacked any smell that told her that Joanna had started dinner. Not that she expected it since it wasn't her field. They had tried it a couple of times but the singer couldn't add cooking on her many skills set.

"Hi, Joanna, have you had a busy day?" Thea picked up the knapsack on the side table and opened the closet door where they kept coats and shoes placing it on a hook inside. When she didn't hear any response, she went into the living area and saw Joanna asleep on the sofa. It wasn't an uncommon sight. During the past six weeks, Joanna was up early and working late into the night.

With quiet steps, she moved closer and marveled at the smooth features that belied the lines that crossed under Joanna's eyes and brow when she was wide-awake. It was as if, in sleep, she didn't have a care in the world. Awake, she carried a burden that Thea didn't understand. Joanna never spoke about anything from her past so how could she know.

They had been friends now for four months. In that time, they had opened up some, but now that Joanna was so busy, their time for intimate conversations was scarce. Thea knew she couldn't complain for she hadn't found work yet and Joanna was the one who kept a roof over their heads and food on the table.

Should I wake her?

It took all of a second to say no. Instead, she headed for the kitchen to begin their meal. She grinned knowing that as soon as Joanna smelled the cooking, she would be awake and sitting at the table. If there was one thing Thea had learned early in their relationship, she could make Joanna very happy and content with a decent meal.

Everything was going well in their world and she was happy. Very happy. Her fervent hope was that it would stay like this for some time to come and just keep getting better.

†

"Hi, Jack, how's tricks?" Jo asked.

Jack tossed his gray head to one side, looking at the beautiful woman who had sauntered into the smallest recording studio at Trigon Records. She looked as if she owned the place and if he admitted it, she did once she started to sing. Jo was a natural. She had a presence about her that defied her lack of star power. However, that didn't mean she wasn't going to become a star. If he had his way, she would be taking the whole country by storm in the next six months.

"Tricks are fine, Jo, how about yourself?"

"Good. I think we need to do "Needing You" again. It lacked something yesterday."

Jo was always to the point. It was another thing Jack liked about her. She had done nothing but work, work, and work harder still, every hour he allowed her in the studio. He suspected she did the same at home.

"Andy's helping Shawn with his backing track but I'll get him here after lunch to do your track again. Do you ever think of anything but music?"

"Not lately. I promised John-Henry that I would give it my best shot. Plus it pays the bills."

Jack watched the woman as she picked up the lyric sheet to the next recording they were going to practice. Her eyes were running over the words that she had written for the hundredth time, doing what she did best. She had a wonderful raw talent that rarely came into the right place at the right time. He felt that was now and he was going to see it happen. It wouldn't do his record company any harm either if she became the next overnight sensation.

"You go practice the songs for a while then I'd like you to join me and one of my business associates for lunch." He saw the quick flash in her blue eyes. "It's nothing sinister, Jo. He's from New York. Believe me, I don't want any distractions to the deal I'm making. What do you say?"

Jo tossed her long raven hair to the side and grinned. "So far everything John-Henry told me about you being a decent record producer has been accurate so, okay you got yourself a date. Andy can wait until after lunch."

Jack smiled as he watched her pick up her guitar strumming a few chords as she prepared for the morning session.

†

It was eleven in the morning and Thea had done all the basic chores for the day. There was nothing left to do but to prepare dinner. She was going to make Joanna her favorite meal, or at least one of them. Joanna had a funny habit of saying every meal that she cooked was wonderful…and her favorite.

A smile crossed her face as she recalled Joanna's face while enthusing about her session the day before. She had been excited about one of the songs she had been working on and had said she had finally figured out the arrangement. Not that she knew what Joanna was talking about, but the look of rapt concentration and excitement convinced her that this was a good thing.

Maybe tonight Joanna might come home early and they could talk for a change. The more she lived with her, the more Thea realized that they were still strangers, but at the same time, they fit together perfectly. Would Joanna ever think that way or would fame and fortune split them up? It was something that preyed on her mind but she refused to let it rule her life.

It was a beautiful day and Thea decided to go on another open topped tour bus ride of the city. She picked up her purse and jacket before locking the apartment door. As she stepped out the door, she smiled—it was a good day. She just knew it.

While walking along the sidewalk her thoughts drifted to Joanna and her preoccupation with her work. Her biggest fear was that once Joanna made it big—there was no doubts about that—she wouldn't want Thea around. Her stomach churned at the idea as it did every time she thought of their future together.

"Hi."

Thea swiveled her head toward the voice and was amazed to see the biker, who had asked her to go for a ride. *Is he stalking me?*

"Hi," she said hesitantly. When his blue eyes captured hers, she couldn't help but smile. He probably was still in college and she had no doubt that she was older than he was.

"Want to take me up on the raincheck?" he asked. He nodded toward the highly polished silver gray motorcycle.

Thea laughed softly and shook her head. "Sorry. I'm going to have a tour of the city on one of the open topped buses."

The young man rubbed the stubble on his chin. "Are you meeting someone or could I accompany you? I've never been on an open top before."

Thea glanced into his face, saw sincerity there, and grinned. What harm could it do? It's a public place and she'd like the company. "Okay, what about your machine?"

"Where are you going to catch the bus?"

"Two blocks north. I haven't seen the north part of town yet."

"A good choice. That's where the heart of Nashville really is. Tell you what, how about I give you a ride to the terminal and I'll park my bike there."

Choices, choices what should I do? He was a stranger and Joanna had warned her about strangers taking advantage. *Once I'm on the bike, he can take me any place.* The feeling that told her

Joanna was a friend it told her that the young man wasn't going to hurt her. "I've never been on a bike before."

Blue eyes lit up and his grin made the man even more handsome than before. "First time for everything." He held out his hand and shook hers. "Calum Rowlands, at your service."

Thea chuckled and took his hand. "I'm Thea Danvers."

Thea was surprised that she was giggling like a teenager as she walked with him to the bike. He handed her a helmet. "Has the machine a name?"

Calum strode to the bike and held out his hand to help her mount the rear seat. "Absolutely. Rebel Rouser."

Thea laughed and settled in behind Calum and clutched his jacket instinctively as he revved up the engine. She would decide if Rebel Rouser was a fitting name later.

"Thea Danvers, welcome to my world." Calum grinned. "You might want to put your arms around me instead of gripping my jacket. It'd be safer." Then the motorcycle roared forward.

Unable to answer, Thea sucked in a shocked breath as they set off at what felt like was a hundred miles an hour.

†

"Jo, I'd like you to meet Lee Weston. Lee, this is Jo Lackerly, my rising star." Jack grinned as he introduced them at the meeting table in his office. It had been set for an informal buffet.

"Hi. Nice to meet you, Lee." Joanna was pleasantly surprised to see a very handsome, well turned out man, who was probably her age, smile slowly at her in a genuine welcome. He stood and held out his hand.

"Hello, Ms. Lackerly."

The quiet but politely cultured English voice resonated in her ears. It was one accent she was quite happy to listen to all day. "Jo, please."

"Jo it is, then. Jack has told me a lot about you." He motioned for her to sit opposite him.

Jo scowled at Jack as she sat opposite the man. "The conversation must have been short then, since Jack knows squat about me."

Gray serious eyes glimmered with laughter and Lee chuckled. "You're right. Jack doesn't know that much about you personally but professionally he's done nothing but rave about your talent. Perhaps we can right that personal information at lunch and then if we haven't finished, would you care to join me for dinner later? At a restaurant of your choice, of course."

Jo eyed him for a moment trying to determine if he was one of those charming handsome men who thought every woman older than fifteen fell for him. "Sure, why not. Jack will call the best in town for us later, won't you, Jack?"

The door to the office suite opened and two servers from a nearby restaurant brought in the lunch and placed loaded platters in front of them.

"Yep, I will." Jack motioned for a server to pour the light sparkling white wine and nodded approvingly as Jo declined.

"So, Lee, what brings you into town and why here?" Jo asked.

†

"You have some mustard on your chin," Calum said.

Thea laughed and wiped her chin before continuing to munch on her second hot dog

"Where do you put all that food?"

"I've always had a big appetite. My dad used to say he couldn't take me any place where there was food, unless he hit the bank first." Thea turned to look at one of the plaques on one of the older buildings that they were passing.

"Yep, my pop says exactly the same. Even now." Calum smirked before biting into his second burger.

"Are you a Nashville boy, Calum?" Thea continued to walk along the sidewalk.

"Nope, I was born in Hawaii. My mother is a native of the island and Dad met her while stationed there in the army. They moved around for several years until we settled here about ten years ago."

Thea heard the affection in Calum's voice when he spoke about his mother but there was a slight aggressive tone when he mentioned his father. It didn't sound like a major disagreement though.

"What about you? Where are you from? Obviously you're not from Nashville or Tennessee."

"I grew up in Danvers, a small town in the Midwest." Thea answered. "My family basically owned the town a century or two ago. After my dad died, I was the only Danvers left in town. I tried to keep my motel going so I could continue the family legacy but it failed in the end. I left there three months ago."

"You tried to save your family name, quite at opposite ends to me then." Calum turned to face Thea as they stopped at a curb to wait for the traffic to stop.

"What do you mean?"

"My dad wanted me to go into the family business. Had my life mapped out for me for the next ten years and I decided that I wasn't going to do that. I wanted to live a little first. Needless to say, my dad is disappointed in me."

Thea sighed, wondering if anyone ever had a straightforward upbringing with parents who didn't expect them to follow in their footsteps. Her father hadn't been any better. He found it hard to loosen the apron strings and in the end, the lack of funds had been his final undoing.

"Do you still live with your parents?" Thea thought it might be time to discuss the age difference. Calum looked like he belonged in college.

"I was in college for three years. I finished last fall and came home to the high expectations from my dad. I live with my folks until I can get a job and rent a place for myself."

He must be around twenty-two. That makes me six years older. Why is he bothering with me?

Take Me As I Am

"I never went to college. The motel was struggling and Dad needed me home."

Calum nodded. "Sorry to hear that."

Thea saw his genuine compassion in the depths of his gray eyes. "What did you study?"

"Oh, this and that." For the first time, Calum wasn't forthcoming. He changed the subject by pointing to another burger bar. "Want to try out a super whopper?"

A trait she'd learned quickly living with Joanna was to know when to quit asking questions. "Of course. I love food."

Calum grabbed her hand, pulling her along gently toward the new eating establishment.

Chapter Thirteen

"I heard you sing today. You're very good." Lee Weston ran a finger down the side of his ice-cold beer glass to wipe away the moisture that had settled there.

When Jo decided a steak and beer were what she needed after a heavy session in the studio, Lee hadn't minded at all. Since arriving from England and becoming a vice president in the Trigon Corporation, he didn't have time to do much socializing. His new assignment was beginning to look like it offered everything, especially the woman who was dining with him.

"Thanks. Jack was talking of doing three or four venues a week around the country for the next three months until the first record comes out."

Lee heard the hesitation in her comment. "The live appearances will complement the record release. You need to have a public following."

He looked at her. "You don't sound so sure about that?"

"I know why I have to go on tour, but I was just settling in here and after spending ten years non-stop on the road. It is kinda nice to do that."

Lee, after resting his beer on the table, placed a hand on Jo's hand that was idly tugging at the checked tablecloth. Blue eyes flashed at him and she pulled away her hand. He shrugged and settled back in his chair. "Once this tour is finished, maybe you can settle back on your laurels but now you need to do what Jack tells you. He has the experience in this field."

"I do listen to him. Do I get to take an entourage?"

Lee considered the question seriously even though he wanted to laugh. "You better ask Jack. He's the man with all the answers. Better yet, get your manager to make it part of the deal."

Jo looked up sharply at the reply. *Manager?* She didn't have one, never had except the odd boyfriend who thought they were. "Yeah, I guess I'll get my manager to do just that."

She smiled at the Lee who seemed to be different from other men she'd met. Maybe all men aren't a waste of space after all. Some of them did have good points and she was warming to the man opposite her.

†

Thea paced the length of the small apartment for the hundredth time, not knowing what to do. Joanna hadn't come home, it was nine-thirty, and worry filled her. She wanted to call the studio but didn't want to appear that she was checking up on her. Joanna always called if she was going to be late at the studio.

"What if she's been injured and lying alone someplace, without any help?" Worry continued to fill her stomach with acid. "Where are you, Joanna?"

With quick movements, she picked up the remote, switched on the television, and tuned to the local news station. Maybe there was a major traffic jam or something that stopped Joanna from calling or getting home. She didn't care what it was just as long as her friend was okay.

On a Friday, Joanna would sometimes come home early and they went to the local bar and shot some pool. So far, she hadn't beaten her friend at the game but one day she would, even if Joanna didn't believe it, she did.

Her mind strayed to the day with Calum. He had been both witty and a gentleman and they had shared some family stories that seemed to help each of them in their own way. He had suggested that they meet up again tomorrow evening for a movie and he'd get the popcorn. She'd declined.

The churning in her stomach usually didn't indicate good things and she tried to stop her mind from conjuring up grisly situations involving Joanna. Her nerves were rattled and her call to Alice went unanswered. She needed to get her mind off Joanna and all the horrible things she was imagining was happening with her. "How can I keep my mind free of Joanna? I can't. I love her."

Standing close to the window, she looked down on the street below hoping to see Joanna striding along toward the apartment. Was that too much to ask for? Her face broke into a wonderful smile as she saw the woman who had occupied her thoughts for several anxious hours step out of a cab.

"It must have been traffic."

Thea's smile died as she saw a man quickly come around from the other side of the cab and enclose Joanna in an embrace before they kissed.

"Who is that she's kissing? She can't kiss anyone. She just can't." With tears smarting in her eyes, she dragged herself away from the window. Joanna had never mentioned being involved with a man. Why should she?

Thea despondently dropped down onto the sofa and dried her tears. There was no way she was going to let Joanna see that it mattered to her that she was seeing a man. How could she? Joanna didn't know how much she loved her.

The door to the apartment opened and Thea watched as Joanna dropped her backpack onto the small table. The word 'shit' followed by the sound of breaking glass echoed in the small space. From her vantage point, she saw Joanna on her knees trying to pick up the broken pieces of the vase that had adorned the small table. Thea's tender heart swelled as she saw the dark head bent at the task while several curses floated out of Joanna's mouth as she tried unsuccessfully to retrieve the broken vase.

"Leave it, Joanna. You'll cut yourself." Thea's heart stopped for a second and then beat erratically as Joanna's sheepish smile tugged at her heartstrings. She could smell alcohol and she gave her friend a closer look.

†

On her haunches, Jo looked at Thea and wondered why her heart tumbled in a nosedive as she stared into the expressive face. Thea wasn't happy with her but she was trying to hide it. Jo always knew and that surprised her but this time the quizzical expression on Thea's face was undecipherable.

"I'm sorry about the vase, Thea."

"No problem. Leave it. I'll clear it away." Thea knelt and began picking up the pieces.

"I had a business meeting." Jo knew her words were lame but Thea didn't seem to notice as she picked up the carnations now out of their normal environment. "I'm sorry I'm late and didn't call."

Jo knew she was out of order and that it was nothing but an afterthought to be apologizing for being late. It hadn't occurred to her when she had agreed to having dinner with Lee or throughout the dinner. Only now looking at her friend cleaning up did it permeate her brain that maybe she should have.

"You didn't wait dinner for me, did you?"

This time Thea looked up at the expectant face of her friend, "No. If we'd had a dog I'd say your dinner was in the dog…" Thea stood and left for the kitchen.

Jo was bemusedly watching Thea walk away. "In the dog, what?" She tottered when she stood and realized that she'd had too much to drink. She wouldn't call herself drunk but she had enough that bed was a good place to be right now. Tomorrow she and Thea would talk. She'd come home early tomorrow night and they could go have a beer and play pool and float the manager problem with Thea.

At the kitchen, she dropped her head around the door. "I'll catch you in the morning, Thea. I'm tired and I have an early start.

See you at breakfast. Goodnight." When Thea didn't turn or acknowledge her words Jo shrugged and left for her room.

†

Thea gripped the sink and closed her eyes unable to prevent the tears that now trickled slowly down her cheeks. Bottom line as she saw it was that Joanna didn't care about her. It hurt so much she wished she didn't have to live under the same roof with Joanna. She shook her head because in her heart she knew that was the last thing she wanted. She'd take any morsel Joanna threw her way. Any at all.

She picked up the dustpan and broom and started back to the doorway to clean up Joanna's mess. As she did, she switched off the stove. Joanna's favorite dinner was ruined.

†

Calum watched Thea. She had said little since they arrived at the theater. The movie didn't start until seven but they had settled in their seats earlier than usual since it had rained heavily. He'd been pleasantly surprised when she had called him that morning to see if he still wanted to take in a movie. He jumped at the chance since he liked her. She was the first woman, other than his mother, that he'd taken seriously and wanted to get to know her better.

"How about I go buy our popcorn now?" He saw her give him a preoccupied smile. It was obvious she wasn't there with him but elsewhere.

"Thanks."

"See you in five."

†

Thea was pensive. The night before she had cleaned up after Joanna and cried herself silently to sleep. That caused her to be late waking and when she did, Joanna had already left for the studio.

Her anger with Joanna increased and before she knew it, she was dialing Calum's number and agreeing to go to the movie with him. She hadn't made any dinner for Joanna and insisted that Calum came to pick her up a few hours before the movie started. She didn't want to see Joanna if she bothered to come home at a reasonable time.

This attitude was out of her normal character. She hadn't even left a message. Joanna probably wouldn't even know she was gone. The new *businessperson* she had dinner with would no doubt want to take her out again and by the time she got home, Thea would be back and in the apartment. Thea knew she was behaving like a petulant, jealous child but she couldn't help herself. Then again, she wasn't a child was she? Bottom line, she was a jealous woman who was in love and she didn't have a clue what to do about it.

What was she doing with Calum? He was a nice guy and she knew she was using him. What would he think or say if he knew that her thoughts were all full of someone else and that someone was a woman. Damn. How had her life become so complicated? Daisy told her to follow her heart and she had. She was crazy to do that because it was hurting her more than her problems with George ever did.

"Hi, did you miss me?" Calum vaulted back into the chair beside her and handed her a large tub of popcorn.

Thea took it gratefully and began eating it in earnest. She was starving since all the emotional drama she was putting herself through had left her unable to eat anything all day. She could easily eat the tub of popcorn herself.

"What took you so long?" she asked around a mouthful.

"Long? You say I was long. Well, how would you like a giant chili dog with the popcorn?" He handed her a chilidog.

Thea smiled gratefully before biting into the chilidog relishing the taste. If nothing else, Calum was going to be good for her waistline. Or not. The feature began and Thea settled into her seat. She was going to enjoy the movie, regardless of her woes, for the reviews had been great.

†

"Okay fair's fair. I was late, and now Thea is making me pay for not calling. I can understand that but she's not like that. She's too polite and hasn't a spiteful bone in her body."

Jo deposited an empty can of beer in the trashcan and noticed a congealing meal inside. It was one of her favorites. Not that she had a particular favorite with Thea's culinary skills, for everything she made was wonderful tasting.

"Shit." Her mind remembered the brief conversation they'd had the night before. Thea said she hadn't kept dinner and if she had, it was in the dog. Well, now she knew who the dog was.

The hands on the wall clock inched toward six and Jo was worried. She'd called Alice but no one answered. Maybe they were together. Thea liked the younger woman and although she was a little too sensible for Jo, she would be okay for Thea as a friend. A safe one. Right?

With another beer in hand, she settled on the sofa pondering the problem of a manager. She'd never had a manager, so why change now. Then again, she wasn't up for all this negotiation stuff. All she wanted to do was make music and make people happy with her music. That had been the driving force that kept her on the road for so long. She'd been on the road for ten years without a break. Did she really like the break she was having now?

As she chewed that, the phone rang. It was probably Thea. In her rush to get the call, she kicked the can of beer, cursing as she looked at the mess. *Thea won't be happy with my messes two days in a row.* The machine kicked in and she heard a quick mumble before the phone went dead. *Damn.*

Jo was wriggling her toes in her socks that were soaked from beer but went to listen to the message. She selected play. "Hi, it's Thea. I've gone to the movies with a friend."

"That's it? What friend?"

As she considered that question, she was annoyed at how much she was hurt that Thea wasn't home. It was early and the movies usually meant people were home by ten. She'd go to the bar have a couple of beers, play a little pool, and would see Thea later. She had the day off tomorrow and maybe she and Thea would do something together.

†

"Who was that?"

Thea was astonished at the attack as soon as she stepped into the apartment. What business was it of Joanna's? "I don't know what you mean?"

"Yeah, you do. The leather clad boy you hitched a ride home with," Jo said in an agitated tone. "Where'd you pick him up?"

"Oh? Are you spying on me now? I never mentioned the guy you played lip sync with last night, did I?" Thea retaliated with the only information she had. What happened next she didn't expect.

Joanna laughed a loud and cheery sound that reverberated around the apartment. "Touché, my friend, touché. Does this mean we have secrets we want to share or not?"

Thea looked up into Joanna's dazzling blue eyes that shone with merriment and grinned. "Depends."

Joanna placed a friendly arm across Thea's shoulders. "I'll tell you about mine if you do yours?"

All of Thea's previous anger disappeared. "Okay, but I want to make a sandwich first. I'm starving."

"Oh. He couldn't afford to feed the beast then?"

Thea turned and gave her friend a scathing glance. "Whatever do you mean?"

"Nothing, nothing. Hey, Thea, I need to talk about a problem I have or at least I think I have. Want to help me out?"

"Sure, want something to eat or have you eaten?" A dark head descended toward her and for one heart stopping moment Thea thought Joanna was going to kiss her. She merely tapped her on the nose.

"I've eaten but I'd love a club if you want to take pity on me."

"You got it. So, what's the problem," Thea asked while pulling out the meat for the sandwiches.

"Apparently, I am in need of a manager."

"Really? Do you think you need one?"

"I don't know. Probably. I hate all the paperwork and stuff." Joanna chewed on her lip. "I guess if I want to do this right I'll have to take on a manager. Who in their right mind would work for pipe dreams? That's all I have to offer. I certainly can't afford to pay anyone."

"I thought that was what a good manager did," Thea said. "Hooked onto the potential and reaped the rewards later?"

"In your dreams, Thea. Everyone's out to make a buck. Now, if it was you as a manager, yeah, I'd go for that because you would but—"

Thea turned from what she was doing. "That's it," she shouted.

"What? What's it?"

"Me. I can be your manager. I believe in you and you pay me by letting me stay with you rent free and right now you pay for everything so it's the least I can do."

Joanna frowned. "I don't—"

"No, please, Joanna, what have you got to lose? If I fail, heck, you sack me and get someone else. It's easy and who knows, we might make a good team."

†

Jo considered the suggestion seriously for a moment wondering if it might work. If she failed, what the hell did it matter? It would be a way she could keep an eye on Thea, especially if she was succumbing to the charms of the biker. After all, wasn't she the protector here? "Okay, tomorrow we'll discuss what I want and I'll arrange a meeting for you with Jack."

Thea smiled at her. "No, I'll call Jack and arrange a meeting. You do your stuff and I'll do mine."

Grinning at the confidence that brimmed from the usually less than self-confident Thea, Jo nodded. "Okay, it's all yours, manager. Just remember one thing."

"Yeah, what's that?" Thea asked.

"Please don't give in to a sob story. Jack can be real persuasive when he sets his mind to it."

Thea laughed and slapped Jo's shoulder, "Yeah, and who else gets taken in by a sob story, hmm?"

Jo grinned at their banter. It was something she enjoyed and hoped would never disappear. "Come on, you can tell me more about biker boy and I'll give you the low down on a Brit and what he's like to kiss."

"You can't ask me that."

"I just did, didn't I?"

Thea looked away. "His name is Calum and there's nothing going on between us. He's a nice guy but he's too young for me. Besides I'd rather be kissing Alice than him."

Jo, shocked by the comment saw Thea's cheeks turn scarlet. "Really? A woman?" Jo eyed her friend. "Are you and Alice?"

"No. God, no. I just used her as an example."

For some reason that she didn't quite understand, a sense of relief washed over Jo. "Why didn't you tell me?"

"Maybe you wouldn't have wanted me to come with you if you knew."

"Nonsense. We're friends and friends don't judge." She pointed to her chest. "Besides, look at the life I've lived. I've dallied with the odd woman or two in the past. I find them better kissers."

Thea's eyes went wide and Jo softly chuckled before pulling her into a tight hug.

Chapter Fourteen

Jack looked at the shadow of the young woman in the outer office that had arranged the appointment to see him. She was supposedly Jo Lackerly's manager. He pressed the intercom. "Judy, send in Ms. Danvers."

As the door opened, the blonde woman who walked into his office surprised him. She didn't look like the confident bullshitter that usually came into his business. No, she looked nervous as if this was the first time she had ever been in this position.

"Ms. Danvers, nice to meet you. Please, take a seat." He held out his hand.

Thea took his hand and shook it.

Jack secretly smiled at the tremor he felt in the hand of the young woman. This should be interesting. Like leading a lamb to slaughter. Why did Jo send this child to do a job for her? Maybe it is some sort of ploy. "Do you want coffee or anything else to drink?"

"No. No, I'm fine. Thanks for asking."

"Then I guess my next line is what can I do for you, Ms. Danvers?"

†

Thea tugged at the hem of her skirt. She had bought a skirt suit the day before to make an impression, or so she'd told Joanna, who had grinned while paying for the addition to her wardrobe.

She considered that recollection before realizing that the man sitting before her had inadvertently paid for her clothes. What a strange world they lived in. For some reason that fact alone gave her the confidence that she had been lacking, sitting outside the office for the past fifteen minutes.

She knew she wasn't good at asserting herself and took a calming breath. *My friend's, no, the woman I love's, livelihood depends on my arriving at the best possible outcome.*

"I represent Ms. Lackerly and she tells me that you intend to send her on a three month tour. She does have certain requirements for such a tour."

"Well, you have my attention, Ms. Danvers. Please tell me what requirements Ms. Lackerly needs?"

An hour later Thea had a satisfied look on her face. Jack conceded a two-person entourage, an increase in salary—doubled actually—a personal transport of her choice and that was just for the tour, along with smart phones for both Joanna and herself.

Jack motioned to the door. "How would it be if we saw our girl in action?"

Thea jumped up and smiled warmly. "I'd love that. Thanks."

"Well, let's go then."

†

Thea had never been inside a recording studio and two guys who were doing something called mixing greeted her. However, her eyes were quickly pulled to the glass plate window. The sight of Joanna dressed casually in jeans and a pristine white, figure-hugging T-shirt talking animatedly with the piano player made the tempo of her heartbeat in triple time.

"How's it going, Joe?" Jack asked.

"So, so, Jack. Jo's attention span is nil today."

"Really, there's a surprise." Jack turned to Thea. "Would you shed any light on that part for us?"

Take Me As I Am

Thea shrugged. "Artists. You can never predict their moods."

Jack laughed before bending over the mixing station and speaking into a mic. "Quit the bickering, Jo, and give us a song. Your manager wouldn't thank you for going back to the table if you suddenly become difficult."

Thea's eyes sought Joanna who held her hands up in a gesture that indicated she wanted to know how things went. Smiling broadly, Thea gave her the thumbs up sign and watched as Jo jumped off the ground and shouted something indistinctly to the piano player.

Gentle strains sprang out and Jack pulled out a chair for Thea as Joanna strummed on her guitar and started to sing. *"I know I needed you like the soil needs the rain."*

The piano tinkled out a few bars more and the session ended. As it did, the two guys in the mixing room shouted out. "It's a wrap."

"That's my girl," Thea whispered.

The song mesmerized her. It was as if Joanna was singing to her, relaying a message for only her. It was a plaintive love song and Thea didn't know what to think, especially after her revelation two nights before.

Does it mean there's something between us? No. Joanna clearly is into guys. I bet she only mentioned she's been with women to make me relax.

†

Jack smiled. He suddenly appreciated something as he saw the look on Jo's face as she sang. There was no mistaking that she was singing to her manager and he found that interesting. The chemistry between them was evident and as he thought back, he realized that he had never heard Jo sing with such passion. There was definitely more to their arrangement than he'd first thought. Once, when they first met, Jo had jokingly—he thought—alluded to liking women more than men. Could the young woman who was her manager be the reason? Not only was it an interesting revelation but also a possible dilemma.

†

"We did it, Joanna, we did it." Thea was bouncing around the apartment like a kangaroo.

Jo chuckled as she watched. "You deserve all the credit, Thea. You might have thought you were a poor man's excuse for a manager but not to me. You are doing a great job. Want to celebrate?"

The laconic sexy voice seemed to cover Thea like a blanket and she stopped dancing before smiling at Joanna. *If only.* "Aren't you too tired?"

"No." Joanna squared her shoulders. "Let's go have...why don't you choose?"

"Me? You want me to choose where we go?"

"Sure. Am I that bad?"

Thea laughed and shook her head. "No. No, not at all but there are places you really don't like going to."

"Yeah, so. I'll get used to it." Joanna shrugged. "This is your night, Thea. You were wonderful as my manager. Thanks to you, I have a sweet deal for the tour."

The idea of going to a decent restaurant of her choosing was exciting but she'd rather spend the time alone with Joanna. "How about I send you out for a Chinese takeout and a bottle of wine?"

"Is that what you want, Thea?"

"Yeah, it's what I want. Once we've eaten, you can go to bed and get some sleep. You look all in."

"You got it." She grinned. "When I get back, I'll be all yours."

As Joanna left the apartment, Thea considered her last words. "I wish I did have you. I really do."

†

Thea listened as a DJ on one of Nashville's music stations was raving about Joanna and her successful tour and deservedly so. Joanna was returning home that night after being away for eleven weeks and four days. Yeah, she was counting even the hours. How pathetic was she? She originally hoped to go with Joanna but with the entourage of a make-up artist and a personal assistant, her going along wasn't in the budget.

After preparing one of the dishes that Joanna always enthused about, she waited anxiously for her return and the special night she hoped they would have together. Thea had missed Joanna's presence and the calls between them hadn't eased the loneliness she felt. Soon, very soon, Joanna would be coming through the door.

The phone rang and she practically ran to it expecting it to be Joanna. For a moment, she wondered why she was using the house phone and when she answered, disappointment filled her heart.

"Hi, Calum. No, I'm busy. Joanna's home tonight so I can't make it. How about I see you the day after tomorrow? You could come around for dinner. Yeah that sounds great, I'll see you then. Hey, take care on Rouser. I want you in one piece."

It was strange. She should be flattered that a young handsome man was courting her, but all she felt for him was friendship—a deep friendship—certainly nothing more. He had tried to kiss her a few times. In the end she had said friendship was all she had to offer and he had accepted that. They had been out on numerous occasions since Joanna had gone on tour and Alice had been envious. Thea thought that Alice was actually better suited for Calum. Who knew where Cupid's arrow would strike? Maybe she should do some matchmaking.

As she checked the roast, the door to the apartment opened and Thea's heart suddenly constricted as she hurried to see her friend. "Joanna, it's great to see you." Rushing forward, Thea flung her arms around the taller woman.

Jo laughed. "Love you, too, Thea. Now will you please stop strangling me?"

Thea's heart jumped at the expression and then settled as she scanned the woman before her. *She looks tired and in need of a good rest.*

She looks thin too. Don't they feed her on tour?

"Want to take a nap and then have dinner?"

"Love to, Thea, but I have another engagement."

"Where shall I dispose of your luggage, Jo?"

A tall figure, taller than Joanna, appeared at the doorway clutching several bags.

"Hey, Lee, come on in and I'll show you. First you need to meet my best buddy and manager, Thea."

The man with gentle gray eyes and a friendly expression smiled. "Hello, Thea. I've heard a great deal about you."

"Really? I haven't heard anything about you," Thea said acerbically.

"Hey, Thea, I told you about him remember? He's the love of my life." Joanna looked at her sheepishly. "So much so, we're engaged."

Silence filled the small area in front of the door. "Oh, *that* love of your life."

"Absolutely. Thea. So how's the stud in leather?"

"I told you that Calum was nothing more than a friend." Thea tried to gather her chaotic thoughts. "Congratulations to you both. When did this happen?" Her heart was breaking into a million pieces.

"Jo accepted my proposal two nights ago in Seattle. It was a surprise for us both," Lee said, smiling.

"I wish you well." Thea had to get out of the apartment and her eyes darted to the still open door.

"Thanks," Lee said.

"I'm going out. Dinner is in the oven if you want it. If not, I'll give it to the dog later."

"Can't we celebrate later?" Joanna asked in a pleading tone.

"Sure, but don't wait up for me. I might be out all night. Good evening to you both and congratulations, again."

Thea grabbed her coat from the closet, dashing as quickly as she could out of the apartment. Her body, drained of any energy, yet refused to stop for she was running as fast as she could away from the heartache. Joanna engaged. How could that be?

She never mentioned it yesterday when they spoke. Thea had thought she and Lee were friends.

†

Jo saw the devastated look on Thea's face and knew she was responsible. Why had she blurted out her engagement in such a horrible way? She had planned to tell Thea when they were alone. Thea was her only true friend and she thought she would understand. The hurt look on the beautiful face haunted her along with the comment about feeding the meal to the dog.

I really fucked it up this time.

Jo felt herself battling with her heart again. When she was on tour and away from Thea, she could do her own thing and think nothing of the consequences. With Thea in her midst, she felt that the attachment that had called to her originally now drew her like a spider's web.

I don't know if I can fix this. I've never seen her like that not even when she had to face George Andrews.

Deep down Jo knew her own heart was breaking and that was devastating to her.

Jo looked at Lee. "Do you want to eat here or go somewhere?"

"You have a dog?"

"Yeah. It's called a trashcan."

†

Alice sat at the kitchen table as Thea stood at the sink rinsing dishes.

"I think you should talk to her and let her know how you feel. It's been three weeks and she has her first television appearance tomorrow to promote the release of her record. You're part of that, Thea, and belong there."

Alice had been watching the gradual deterioration of her friend's mood since Joanna had arrived back home after her tour. The shocking announcement of her engagement to some businessman from New York had shaken her friend deeply.

Thea turned her anguished green eyes toward Alice. "I wish that were the truth but it isn't." She shrugged. "I've done nothing but sponge off Joanna ever since we got here. I need to get my act together and find a job."

Thea shook her head and swiped at an errant tear. "I tried to get a job but Joanna told me I should just enjoy seeing the sights and take a break from working."

"But you take care of the apartment and do all the cooking and laundry so Joanna can focus on her singing," Alice countered. "Besides, aren't you her manager? That certainly is a job."

"I'm not so sure about that. Joanna is gone all day at the studio, at venues, or out on the town with her new fiancé. She doesn't tell me about what's going on with Jack so I don't think I am her manager anymore."

"If she doesn't know how you feel, Thea, then she can't change anything."

"It won't matter. That man has all the right attributes making him the best possible choice for her. He appears to love her so what more can I ask for?" Thea turned to the sink.

"Are you going to sit around and mope or get off your butt and see to it that Joanna knows you're part of the team too?" Alice rolled her eyes. "She's too busy with the new career and her engagement to see that she is leaving you behind. It's up to you to show Joanna that for the moment, at least, you are part of her life. What the future holds for you will work out the way it should. Joanna will never abandon you." Alice gave her a sympathetic look. "All you need to look at is the way she acts around you, Thea. It is abundantly evident to everyone watching her with you."

"I'm not so sure of that, Alice." She took a seat across from her friend. "Right now it hurts so much that I can't risk any more pain to my heart."

Alice let out an exasperated sigh. "You know that in this town, managers are a dime a dozen and most would have snapped up the offer to represent her, Thea. Joanna is sharp as a razor and doesn't miss a trick and she chose you above all the rest. That should speak volumes to you."

From what Alice had heard from several people she knew at the recording studio, Thea had amazed Jack and he held her in the deepest of respect.

"She doesn't have time for me to be around now, Alice. Her life is going a totally different direction than mine."

"You can go along right with her. You're her manager."

"Joanna is big news now. She will want a more experienced manager." Thea hung her head in what looked like defeat. "It was only a temporary situation. I expect any day now for her to come home and announce that she has replaced me."

"That's ridiculous..."

The door opened, followed by a knapsack deposited on the floor before weary sounding steps came toward the kitchen. It wasn't long before the kitchen door opened and the dark familiar head popped around and gave them both a tired, slow grin.

"Hey, what are you two planning?" Jo came into the small kitchen.

"You know us, Jo, we're working on a couple of projects."

"Really, anything I can help with?"

"Well, as it happens..."

Thea gave Alice a sharp glare. "No. Nothing that you need to worry about, Joanna. Have you eaten?"

"Not today. Maybe not for two days. It's been kinda hectic. Jack said to go home and get some sleep once the television shoot is done since I might not get the chance of a peaceful six hours for some time to come."

Thea stood and walked to the fridge, pulled out a bottle of Joanna's favorite beer, and handed it to her.

"Thanks, you always know what I need." Joanna gave her a sleepy smile.

"After today your fridge will probably be filled with champagne," Thea said sarcastically.

"Well, I have to study," Alice said. "I have my finals next month and unless I buckle down, I'll be taking the semester again. I wouldn't care for that. Good luck with the show tomorrow, Jo. Thea, I'll catch up later okay. Think about what I said."

"Yeah, thanks."

†

"What'd she say?" Jo asked.

"Nothing that you'd care about." Thea took out a loaf of bread. "Do you want me to make you something to eat?"

"If it's not too much trouble."

Jo heard the inflection and hurt in Thea's voice, knowing she was the cause. The depression swirling around Thea ever since Jo had returned from tour broke her heart. At that moment, she was too tired to ponder how to make it right. Jo knew she owed her friend a decent explanation of the engagement and her reasons for accepting. She also needed to hear how she imagined Thea being a part of her life. It hadn't happened yet—she was just too damn busy. There was plenty of time. Thea was her manager, after all, and that was something she really needed to talk with her about.

†

Just as Alice was closing the door to the apartment, the elevator door opened and Calum walked out. As always, he was dressed in beautiful leather that made him look like he was modeling it for a fashion show. It looked so good on him. If only he were interested in her. She could dream, couldn't she?

"Hi, Calum. What brings you to this part of town on this lovely evening?"

"Hey, Alice. I just thought I'd see if my girl wants to go look at the sunset. She's been kinda down lately so I thought it might help."

Sometimes you meet people and you wish with every essence of your being that they would be saying things to you but they never did. Alice knew in her heart that Thea didn't appreciate Calum. Thea considered him a friend and her obsession with Jo might shed light on that if she were to ponder it more.

"How would it be if I invited you for coffee for say an hour and then you go see Thea? Jo's just arrived home and they are discussing stuff."

It wasn't exactly true. Alice didn't know if they were or not but at least she would give them a chance and she knew they both needed that.

"Sure. I can understand that, with Thea being Jo's manager and all. Makes me wonder why Thea doesn't spend more time with her though. I thought that's what managers did."

"Me too, but I think this may be a little different. Come on, we can walk. I'm the next floor up."

"Lead the way."

†

Jo watched Thea whiz around the kitchen and within twenty minutes, she was enjoying a wonderful omelet with a side salad and fries. As she munched on the fries and enjoyed her first forkful of omelet, Thea sat opposite her with a glass of soda in hand.

"I guess you ate earlier?" Jo spooned in another forkful of the delicious mixed omelet.

"I had a heavy lunch."

"This is delicious. I didn't realize how hungry I was until I started eating." Joanna polished off the remains of her meal and placed a hand over her stomach, smiling in satisfaction. "Thanks for the meal, Thea. I enjoyed it."

"Anytime, you know that. That's why I'm here, isn't it?"

Jo eyed Thea. Had she taken her for granted, making her feel like she was nothing more than the hired help? "You're more than that. You know that, right?"

"Sure thing." Thea looked away. "I can see you're tired. Go put your feet up on the sofa and watch a little television. It will do you good."

"Okay." She reached out and took Thea's hand. "Come with me and we can talk."

Jo watched the sad expression on Thea's face. Whatever it was that was happening between them needed to be resolved. Perhaps they could solve it now and start fresh. Tomorrow her life was going to take on a different direction.

†

When Joanna stood and stretched her lean, tall body, Thea had to stop herself from sighing at the sight. No matter what, Joanna would always be a welcome sight to her. Thea had missed that. The rare occasions that Joanna was there, she would settle on the sofa and fall asleep. That's what had been missing all these lonely weeks—Joanna's presence.

"I can do that. Want another beer?" Thea's heart tumbled as she met the blue eyes of her friend. This was what she had been yearning for—a small measure of contact. She didn't want much, just a little part of Joanna's time. This could be the last time. The thought made her heart break. All hell might break loose after today and she doubted they would get the chance to just sit and relax as they used to.

"Sure."

An hour later, they talked about the television show along with what Jack planned for Joanna next. Thea had agreed and given her opinion on a few of the things. The odd comment was news to her but generally, she knew of Jack's plans. She, after all, had agreed to them on behalf of Joanna.

A silence descended for a few moments and then Jo cleared her voice.

"We never did get the chance to talk about my engagement, Thea, and what it means."

Thea closed her eyes, steeling herself for what was to come next. Fear and sorrow gripped her heart. "No, we haven't. I guess we have both been too busy."

"Yeah, I guess." Joanna looked at her bottle of beer then smiled.

"Are you happy, Joanna?"

"I guess so. I wouldn't have said yes otherwise." She drank the last of the beer and put the bottle down on the coffee table.

That wasn't a definite yes. It was more of a sure, anything goes kind of statement that her friend often made. "That's all that matters and I'm happy for you. When's the wedding?"

Joanna laughed loudly and sat up on the sofa. "God only knows. I doubt this year if everything goes according to plan. I'm going to be touring for a year at least."

Thea's eyes flashed at the statement. Jack hadn't indicated anything of the sort in their discussions. "Really? I must have missed something in my discussions with Jack."

Joanna stood and stretched again. Thea watched her realizing that it was becoming too much of a burden to watch Joanna and know she could never be hers.

"It wasn't Jack's idea, it was mine." She walked to the apartment window, smiling.

"Why?"

Joanna turned toward her friend. "Because that's what it will take to make the big time and I'm going to make it this time, Thea. I know it, but I have to work for it." She looked out the window again. "Maybe my wish will come true and I'll finally get an apartment with a decent view. Overlooking a body of water sounds nice, don't you think?"

Thea rushed to the window and stood next to Joanna. She placed a gentle but insistent hand on her arm and blue eyes looked down at her hand.

Joanna moved, placed warm friendly arms around Thea, and pulled her closer.

"You already have made the big time in my eyes," Thea whispered.

"Yep, I know that and when we have that window view of the water everyone will know it as well."

Thea closed her eyes at the words. One word in particular *we*.

She must have forgotten she was going to share that view with her husband to be.

For an instant, it didn't matter. She would bask in the glow of knowing that at this moment in time, Joanna perhaps did mean her.

†

Jo looked into the clear innocent face of her friend. Was she still innocent? Jo didn't know because somewhere along the way, they had gone their own separate ways. She'd lost the connection that had made all the difference in her life since they'd met. She guessed it was a natural progression. Was it? Then why did she feel so hollow. Jo's goal was to succeed in country music and that dedication kept her from nourishing their friendship, as she should have. She didn't have an idea as to what Thea really wanted to do with her life because she never asked.

Normally, she wasn't much for personal contact but whenever she and Thea had any contact, it was good. It made her feel warm inside and she'd never had understood why she just accepted it as a part of their friendship. It was good to have a best friend and she felt that this woman in her arms was that, even if her way of acknowledging that to Thea was minimal.

Jo captured Thea's glance and stared into her eyes. She was drowning, mesmerized by the mellow conversation and the feeling of togetherness. It was so right and for a moment the puzzle pieces fell into place for her until the shrill sound of the doorbell broke the spell.

Jo felt bereft but managed to smile and released her hold on the smaller woman.

"Who can that be? I'm not expecting anyone this evening and don't want any other company," Thea said with a touch of anger.

"I'll go see." Jo left to answer the door.

Two minutes later Joanna walked back in and cleared her throat. "Did you say we didn't want any visitors this evening?"

Calum walked in behind her giving Thea, who now had rather red streaked cheeks, a long serious expression.

"I'll leave you two alone," Jo said. "I've got a heavy day tomorrow. Goodnight to you both."

†

"Joanna, please...." Thea said but she was too late. Joanna was already gone.

"If you want me to go, Thea, I will. I'm sorry to interrupt. I thought maybe you would like a little company." He turned to leave but Thea took hold of his arm.

"I'm sorry about the comment, Calum. We were having a good talk...the first for weeks. I wasn't expecting you."

It was another lame excuse but Calum apparently was buying into it as she saw the light return to the young man's eyes.

Whatever it is that he sees in me, I'm not worth it.

"Stay. Do you want a drink?" She moved toward the kitchen and was surprised when he pulled her toward him.

"I'd rather have a kiss."

She allowed the hug but turned away from the kiss.

"Calum, there's something you need to know."

Chapter Fifteen

This was Joanna's day and Thea didn't want anything to stop it from being a success. She knew that her miserable countenance wasn't going to help, so she opted to stay in bed until Joanna left. She could call her later and wish her luck.

A soft knock on the door heralded the dark head of the woman she had been thinking about peeping inside her bedroom. "Are you awake, Thea?"

What should she do? She could feign sleep and not answer or be honest and acknowledge Joanna's question.

"Hey, I thought you might be excited and want to come with me this morning," Joanna said softly.

Thea closed her eyes in dismay at the tentative words. Now she didn't know what to do. Everything was all crazy again.

"Asleep, huh, never mind. I'll call you later and tell you how it went."

Thea heard the words and her tears welled, picking up the disappointment in Joanna's voice. Rushing out of bed, she tangled herself up in the bedclothes, which delayed her getting out of the door. Joanna was closing the outer door behind her before she could catch her.

"Damn, I've missed her." She rushed out the door hoping to catch her before she got on the elevator. Now while standing in the cold hallway with her feet bare and in her flimsy nightdress, she couldn't stop trembling from the chill. She realized that for once, her friend might have needed her and she hadn't had the courage to face her. She had thought that she had overcome her timid ways but it was obvious that she hadn't. She shook her head in disgust. Once again her insecurities overshadowed all else and made her less than strong.

"I'm so sorry, Joanna." The words she whispered into the cold empty hallway, in many respects, reminded her of how her heart felt. Barren was the future she had in store once Joanna had moved on with her new life.

It was time to move on with hers, too, but where would she go? No way was Danvers an option. As soon as she set foot in that town, George would no doubt press her into marriage and she had no money or prospects to counter that.

Then like a bolt out of the blue, she realized she did have an option. It might be remote but something she had to try at least. It was her only hope.

†

"Are you nervous, darling?"

Jo looked at Lee and, for a moment, wondered who he was talking to before it dawned on her that he was actually speaking to her. "Me? No, why would I be nervous? I'm going to slay them." She refused to let this one chance slide by without attempting at least to make it happen.

"Want to tell me why you look so pensive if it's not the show?"

Hardly. Pensive isn't part of my makeup. "Hand me that mirror on the table, Lee."

Lee handed her the glass.

Jo frowned. Something wasn't right and it was evident on her face.

"I'll help you sort the problem out if you would allow me," Lee said.

"I guess I do look strange. I was thinking about Thea."

"Really? I was expecting her to be here since she's your manager and roommate, too. Couldn't make it?"

Jo didn't like the tone of his voice. It sounded like he'd already made up his mind that Thea was nothing but a hanger on and not worthy to be her manager. In the past few weeks, he'd even asked her to change to someone with more sophistication and experience. His excuse—Jack was a great man and very fair but others out there weren't as nice and Thea wouldn't be up for the job, if that were the case.

Jo let her blue eyes flash icily. "Thea is busy with a final request from me before the show. She must be stuck in traffic."

"Okay, while you go for the final practice session I'll look out for her and bring her to your room when she arrives."

Lee bent and kissed her passionately. Jo pulled away quickly, experiencing the emotion of familiarity and warmth, but the excitement she'd initially felt was missing. She knew then that she'd made a mistake in becoming engaged to Lee. The loneliness of the road made her take the easy option, just as she had in the past. Jo watched him leave her room and looked in the mirror again at her reflection. There was no doubt that she was changing and had been for some time. The change in many ways had been for the good.

What was the catalyst? The contract with Trigon Records? My bid for stardom? Age and experience tempering my old temper tantrums?

In a moment of clarity, she knew the answer. It was Thea.

"Ms. Lackerly, you're on in five minutes," some faceless person said, knocking on her door.

Jo picked up her guitar, wishing Thea were going to arrive. She hadn't really lied to Lee. Thea deserved to be there to see her win or lose the battle. After all, she was an integral part of it happening and it wasn't the same without her friend by her side. She needed her best friend, Thea. Together they could take on the world. Her heart told her the truth of the words. More than anything else, it reminded her that she had made a mistake in agreeing to Lee's proposal.

"I guess I was missing you, Thea, and let him sweep me away."

She stared at the mirror and shook her head.

†

"Where are you going, Thea?"

"I'm going to make my own way in the world as Joanna and I discussed last night."

Alice couldn't believe what she was seeing, never mind hearing. Thea was collecting her battered suitcase. "She didn't really say that, did she? The Jo I've met isn't cruel. It's not in her character. This is the biggest day of her life and you're walking out on her, now?"

"She didn't say it in so many words, but the meaning was clear. She's moving on, so should I, too. I'm not exactly without any skills, am I? I can cook, clean and work in a motel. I should get work easily." Thea looked away. "Look, all I want to do is be on my way, out of this town and on the next bus."

Alice wanted to wring Thea's neck. Even though she was older, Thea didn't have the sense she was born with if she was abandoning Jo now. It was cruel and the singer didn't deserve it. Okay, she might not have been that forthcoming about her engagement and she had left Thea alone for long periods too often. However, she had come home eventually and had paid for everything for the two of them from the time they had come to Nashville and more besides. Jo even gave Thea an allowance, enabling her to have money of her own. She'd heard the singer jovially tease Thea that now that she had her independence, maybe she would leave. Wasn't that what their mutual friend was doing, now?

"Does she know you're leaving today?"

"No, not exactly today."

"I think you should tell her that you're leaving and not allow her to find out when she arrives home exhausted and expecting to see you and not just a note. I take it you were going to leave a note?"

"Yes. Yes, of course I was…am. I've booked a ticket on the bus that leaves at five today. I won't have time to wait for her to come home. Lately, she's been coming home later than that. I'm sure she is spending her time with her fiancé."

"Then why not go and see her do the show. Then you can tell her and leave from there to the bus station. They're recording the session in an hour and that will give you plenty of time."

Alice saw the formulation of a negative response on Thea's face and immediately checked it. "I'll even give you a lift there and to the bus station."

"Okay. Just don't let me be late for the bus."

"Sure thing." Alice was grinning as she helped Thea pick up her possessions.

As they left the apartment, she noticed Thea give it a look much like a wistful longing, as though she didn't want to leave.

This really shouldn't be happening. What has gone so horribly wrong to make her want to run away from Jo? And just when she's on the brink of stardom.

She'd bet her next paycheck that Jo did not intend to leave Thea behind.

"By the way, how did Calum take you going away?"

"Oh, that's another story."

†

"Hi, Lee. I thought you'd be with our girl," Jack said.

"Her practice session went reasonably well, don't you think?"

Jack inclined his head. He noticed the reluctance of the businessman to answer his question fully. "Yes, it did. I know she's gonna take the country world by storm. Jason called and wants you to call back after you've finished here."

"Okay, that I can do. In fact, Jo doesn't need me at the moment so I'll go do it now." Lee turned to leave then turned back around. "Oh, and if you come across Jo's negligent manager, she wants to see her when she gets here."

The words hung in the air like a heavy mist as Lee left. Jack had to chuckle.
So it's Thea that's gotten under his skin. Interesting.
He shook his head and while walking toward Jo's dressing room, he saw Thea.
"Hey, are you looking for Jo?"
"Yes. It's like a rabbit warren here. I nearly didn't make it in time." Thea had the look of a deer caught in the headlight.
"Yeah, some studios are like that. Lee was waiting for you and had to leave, he said Jo was expecting you." Jack motioned toward a small corridor. "She's in the door to the left. Will you tell her I'll catch up with her after she's wowed them all? Oh, and, Thea, I'm glad you could make it. I know she'll be fine now."

†

"Will do, thanks." Thea watched a smiling Jack disappeared in the opposite direction. Thoughts whirled around in her brain. Why was Lee waiting for her? Joanna had expected her and Jack mentioned that Joanna would be fine now that she was here?
She knocked sharply on the door's blue fronted panel.
"Come in."
After taking a deep breath, Thea opened the door and went inside but didn't see Joanna. Jack said she was in here. Maybe she's busy and didn't have time to speak to her. "Joanna, it's me."
Joanna emerged from a screen with a beaming smile on her face. "You came!"
Thea did not intend to say anything that would stop her friend's buoyant spirit. She would need it for the performance. Her eyes were unable to stop moving across the scantily clad figure. Joanna was wearing a lace black bra that barely covered her breasts and a black matching thong. The sight was breathtaking and she could hardly breathe.

"I came. How could I miss your first television performance? I'm your manager aren't I?" Joanna hugged her, making her heart beat even more erratically.

"I'm glad. I thought you had taken to sleeping late these days."

The grin Thea received made her wonder why she was even contemplating leaving her friend and going away into the unknown. "No, not really. I'm sorry about this morning I was up late."

Joanna arched an eyebrow. "I thought you weren't interested in leather clad. Does he know that? It didn't look like that."

"He does now," Thea whispered.

"The thought of going out there without you here... well, let's just say I'm glad you're here."

There was a knock on the door. "Two minutes."

"This happens to us far too frequently don't you think?" Jo smiled broadly.

"Yeah, it does. We never complete a conversation these days. I do need to talk with you, Joanna."

"We will. I have two minutes and need to change into something a little more substantial." Joanna flipped her hand toward her state of undress and moved back behind the screen.

"Want me to leave you to it?"

"No, stay. We'll go out together. After all, we started this journey together didn't we?"

Everything was working out fine, wonderful, in fact. Jo knew she could do it now that Thea was there and they would do it together. When she emerged clad in a green cotton shirt and with black leather pants and boots, she saw Thea's face light up.

"What do you think?" Jo twirled.

"I...I...I'm lost for words. You look stunning. Really amazing. How can they not like you?"

"I think it's too low key but Lee and Jack think it looks the part. If you approve, then I'll go with the flow."

Jo selected a guitar from the two she brought with her. Holding out her hand, she opened the door. "Come on, manager, let's see what I can do out there shall we."

"Yeah, go slay them, Joanna."

†

Neither woman noticed the tall man standing in the shadows who watched them leave the room hand in hand. An acute stab of jealousy hit him as he watched them proceed to the recording area. *Shouldn't it be me by her side?* That surely was part of the deal when engaged and in love. Wasn't it?

†

From the wings of the studio, Thea watched the host of the show greet Joanna and ask her a few questions. She settled against a post to watch the interchange. For the moment, she was happy and content watching her friend go through the motions. A masculine voice speaking to her from behind her made her jump.

"She's quite something, isn't she?" Lee asked.

"Yes, yes, she is and she deserves this chance. She's worked so hard for it."

"Yes, I agree, which is why I wanted to speak to you about something."

"Really, what?"

"I think you should vacate as her manager and let someone more professional take her on."

Thea reeled at the comment feeling her anger rise.

Why would he say that? Everything I've done so far for Joanna met with her approval and I haven't faltered with Jack at all.

What could a professional do that she hadn't? "If Joanna asks me to step down I will."

"You're her friend. She won't do that. Nonetheless, you must see she has the potential to have the world at her feet. Would you want to screw that up for her if you make some inexperienced bad deals on her behalf?"

Thea turned, craning her neck upward to look into Lee's face. What she saw, she didn't like. There was no point denying it and blaming other factors, she didn't like Lee because he was engaged to Joanna and she wanted her. However, there was also his condescending attitude that made it seem as though he always knew best. How did he? How? Wasn't it up to Joanna? *Maybe she's been discussing it with him and was afraid to tell her.* Jealousy was eating at her and she knew the sooner she left, the better.

Thea's eyes trailed to Joanna who was now climbing on the stool to commence her song for the television cameras and the studio audience. Gentle strains of the tune carried to her.... *"Love is in my heart it needs you now don't you know…"*

Thea held back her tears. Was Lee right? Did Joanna want her to quit as her manager? Did it really matter? Isn't that the reason she was here anyway. To leave her friend so they could both move on with their lives, whatever and wherever that might be?

A second song was underway, her friend was enjoying herself, and she had never sounded as wonderful. Now was a good time to leave. Lee's comments made it obvious that was what he expected her to do. He'd made it abundantly clear that he was an integral part of Joanna's life and that they were going to share the rest of their lives together. How could she stay?

As the tune died away, the applause, including the technicians who were probably quite blasé about this type of performance, crashed around the studio.

Thea took it as her cue to leave.

†

Lee heard the ecstatic clapping. Not only was Joanna going to be a big star, but she was also going to be one on a record label that his company partly owned. Everyone was going to be

Take Me As I Am

happy. He remembered Thea and when he turned to speak to her again about being Jo's manager, he noticed she was gone. It didn't matter.

Thea Danvers wasn't necessary in Jo's adventure anymore. She had him now and he was sure she would be overjoyed that everything was falling into place. One lost friend along the way wasn't going to cause that much trouble. If he had his way, Jo was going to be a star. No, a superstar.

†

Alice sat with Thea at the bus station waiting for her Greyhound bus to announce boarding. She'd been shocked when Thea had rushed out of the television studio, obviously distressed but unable to communicate just why. Even now, an hour later, she still hadn't said a word, although sorrow and pain etched every line of her face. One thing she'd make certain of was when Jo arrived back at the apartment, she would give her a severe talking to even if the woman threw her out of the apartment.

"Do you have enough money for the journey, Thea?"

"Yes, thanks, Alice. I've enough to see me for a week or two." Thea glanced down at her purse held securely in her hands and drew in a breath.

"I don't mean to pry, but what about a place to stay?"

Where Thea was going, it would be expensive to stay for very long—even in some of the fleapits they called hotels. Maybe Thea had friends or relatives in the town that would help her. She hoped so. The woman beside her was far too caring and trusting to be out on her own in any city no matter the size.

"I'll manage." Thea looked at her friend. "Don't be concerned. I'll be all right."

"Will you call me when you get a place to stay and let me know you're safe? I'd appreciate it."

Thea placed a hand on Alice's arm and gave her a weak smile. "Yes, I will and, Alice, thank you for being such a good friend. Will you do something for me?"

"Sure anything."

Feeling the pain for her friend, Alice hugged her tight. "Everything will work out, Thea, it will. You see if it doesn't," she whispered.

†

Thea saw the concern mirrored in Alice's eyes. Did she always warrant the knight to come out of the trees to protect her? Tears stung the back of her eyes as her thought about Joanna and the role she played as her improbable protector.

Oh, God, how I wish success hadn't changed Joanna. If only we kept on that bus, and passed by Nashville and all it offered her. The words crashed around in her mind but she knew that it would crush her heart to prevent Joanna from succeeding in any way.

She pulled an envelope out of her pocket. "I intended to leave this at the apartment but I didn't." She handed it to Alice. "Please, give this to Joanna for me. She'll understand when she reads it."

"You didn't tell her, did you?"

"I couldn't. She was so happy and her performance was so marvelous. How could I burst her bubble by telling her I was leaving?"

"Greyhound bus number six seven nine for Knoxville and points east is now boarding on platform three," blared through the loud speaker.

"There it is." Thea broke away from Alice giving her a watery smile. "I'll miss you, Alice. If you get the chance, please, from time to time, check in on Joanna for me."

"Of course I will. Count on it."

Alice walked with Thea and they both handed the luggage to the driver for stowing underneath the bus. "Safe journey, my friend, and please, call me."

"I will. Goodbye, Alice." Thea, the last passenger to board the bus, climbed the steps before turning to her friend. "You know that Calum's a great guy. You should check out Sam's Bar on a Thursday one evening."

Thea entered the bus, took a seat by a window, and waved goodbye to her friend.

Chapter Sixteen

People packed into her dressing room as Jo fought to find Thea in the morass of bodies. She spotted Lee, who was smiling at everyone that came to shake his hand. The record producer was in his element. She finally gave up looking, realizing that Thea probably had already gone home. She hated fuss and this was definitely *fuss*.

She hoped the next four hours would roll by quickly so she could say goodbye. Goodbye to all of this and go home for a long bubble bath and good company. Lee was nothing else if not good company but she knew that wasn't enough. When she was feeling strung out, Thea would smooth it all away with her gentle chatter. Her friend had the gift and Jo knew above all else that she needed to have Thea in her life. That came to her clearly when Thea had arrived earlier at her dressing room. In that moment, she realized that Thea's unconditional understanding and faith ensured that she remain on the path to success.

"Jo, would you care for a glass of champagne?" Lee handed her a flute.

She looked at it and shook her head. "I'd rather have a beer. Is there any?" Jo looked around her small dressing room and wondered how so many could get into such a confined space. She didn't care for it that much herself, people were a little too close into her personal comfort zone.

"Darling, if you wanted a brewery, I suspect on the strength of your performance today Jack would be willing to buy you one."

"Yeah. One beer will do, thanks. Did you see Thea around or did she leave when the masses arrived?" Yesterday, she was nobody and today people were waving at her, grinning stupidly. It was what she had always wished for but now she hated it.

"I think she left when the masses arrived. I didn't actually see her go. I guess she'll be at the apartment waiting for you. I was kind of hoping you might want to spend the night with me. I have to go back to New York tomorrow."

Jo heard the slight disappointment in his charming tone. She had forgotten. "Lee, I'd love to spend the evening with you, but...."

"But?"

"Thea will be waiting for me. I said we'd talk and I want to share this with her, Lee. She's the reason I stuck around so long and kept up the long hours to get to this point. I owe her big time. Soon enough I won't have much free time. Will I?"

Lee placed his arms around her and hugged her close, "So very true, darling. When we get married, I promise you that what little free time you have I'll commandeer it." He kissed her lightly before releasing her to the fans bidding for her attention.

Jo slipped into the public eye once more and watched as Lee approached Jack with a slap on the back and a hearty handshake. For a moment, her gaze lingered on Lee and once again realized that the excitement was missing where he was concerned.

Moments later, Jack approached her. "You're on your way, now," he said.

"The icing would be Thea being here."

"Strange, I saw her speaking with Lee during your first song then she suddenly left." He lifted one shoulder. "I guess it was too overwhelming for her."

"Maybe so." Jo's eyes searched out Lee who was leaving the room.

†

Jo put her key in the door, sighing heavily. For several hours, she'd been plagued with a fluttering stomach she tried to rid herself of but failed. At first, she thought it was the telecast but once that was out of the way, it remained. She knew that Thea would have some tonic for her nerves. Who would have thought that nerves would strike hard, cynical Joanna 'Jo' Lackerly. Hadn't she seen enough in her lifetime thus far to rid herself of that emotional upset? Obviously not.

As she walked into the apartment, the darkness and absence of sound struck an irrational chord of fear in her. The place felt cold. Maybe there was a problem with the power?

"Thea, I'm home and am I glad to be here."

Her voice appeared to echo as she waited for a reply that never came. A puzzled expression crossed her face as she walked around the apartment. Thea wasn't in the kitchen and there was no evidence of cooking.

Then it dawned on her as she neared the living area and saw the closed door. *I bet she's having a celebration party for me. I'll walk through the door and there she'll be with candles, a cake, and a beer. I'd better school myself for the surprise.*

She turned the doorknob and opening the door gradually, noting the darkness. *Yep, sure thing, Thea is up to something.*

Jo expected to hear a shout from her friend or applause or something but there was nothing. She blinked several times in the darkness before running her hand to the switch to turn the lights on. As the area illuminated, she saw it was empty, too. What was going on?

After scanning the area quickly, her heart began beating erratically and she turned, rushing out of the room. Flinging open the door to Thea's bedroom, she switched on the light. The room was neat and tidy, however nothing represented that her friend was there. Usually Thea's nightgown was on the bed but it wasn't there, nor were any of her other knick-knacks. Jo moved automatically toward the closet and opened it. Empty hangers were forlornly waiting for clothes.

Jo looked around the room again and saw Thea's phone on the nightstand. She grabbed it and pressed the dimpled button at the bottom. "Shit, I need her passcode."

After pressing in various combinations of numbers including birthdates and failing she closed her eyes. "Fuck!" She tried one last combination 5656 and the screen opened—her passcode was Jo. A memo application was open. With trembling fingers, she pressed the play arrow...

"Joanna, by now you know that I have left. I appreciate that now that you are truly on your way to being a big star, you need someone with more...ah—I think sophistication is the right word—as your manager. The last thing I ever want to do is hold you back and now I've come to the realization that I'm doing just that. I wish only the best for you. I love you, Joanna, now and always. Be happy in your life with Lee."

"She's left me." Jo continued to hear Thea's words that were floating in the air all around her. She sank to the floor, placing her head in her hands while the tears of exhaustion and pain flooded her cheeks.

"This isn't happening. It can't be. It's all a dream. I've fallen asleep at the party and my worst nightmare is coming true. I need Thea in my life. I don't think I can make it without her." She wept harder. "It's all my fault for being so selfish and unthinking of Thea's needs. I brought her here only to abandon her and for what?"

For the first time since Jo could remember, she cried like a baby. Thea's leaving pierced her heart and soul. Thea was gone. What would she do now? Her eyes widened as she recalled Thea's words.

"Lee!" He'd used the word 'sophistication' on more than one occasion when he was trying to get her to change managers.

Hadn't Jack told her that Lee was talking to Thea before she suddenly left?

Jo snatched her phone from the back pocket of her jeans and pressed Lee's number.

"Hey, babe, did you change your mind and decide to spend the night with me instead?" Lee asked in an upbeat voice.

"What did you say to her?" Jo snarled.

"To who?"

"Don't you dare pretend innocence to me, Lee. I know you talked to Thea. Tell me what you said to her." Jo kept her voice controlled and even, while seething inside.

Silence filled the airwaves.

"Tell me, you bastard," Jo screamed.

"Babe, she's holding you back and you know it. You're on your way to being a mega star and you don't need the extra baggage of a hanger-on. She understood that."

"Fuck you. I never want to see or hear from you again." Jo ended the call. A few seconds later the phone began ringing and she held down the button until she saw *slide to power off* and swiped her finger across the screen.

†

Thea gazed unseeingly through the window of the bus as it traveled farther away from Nashville. She indulged in a few more tears that she had wanted desperately to shed while she waited with Alice for the bus to leave. She hadn't wanted to go, however her edifying conversation with Lee had summed it up—she wouldn't be needed in Joanna's life any more. Her friend was going into the stratosphere with her prospects and hangers-on like her were no longer needed. She was to be the first casualty on Jo's road to fame.

The last time she had traveled any distance on a bus, she had been running away from a fiancé, her hometown, and all that had meant. Once she'd met Joanna, she had felt that the singer was her home and she could face anything the world threw at her. Now she was alone and running away again. This time the reason—she no longer belonged in Joanna's life. Her heart was breaking into a thousand pieces. She hadn't wanted to leave her home behind because Joanna was her home and would always be regardless of the geography. Thea knew she would never truly be happy again. How could she? Joanna was her happiness.

Her eyes stung when she closed them. The pain in her chest threatened to engulf her in the morass she was feeling. This shouldn't be happening. She should be celebrating with Joanna and considering the next step in their futures. She'd run away from her friend without the decency of saying goodbye. She'd left the message on her phone not knowing whether Joanna would hear it or not.

What is it with me? Am I going to spend the rest of my life running away from my problems?

She didn't have enough of a backbone to stand up for herself and was destined always to need a protector.

Oh, God. Joanna, please, can't you see I want you as my improbable protector for the rest of my life? Please don't let me go forever. I love you and will always love you. I had to go, Joanna, I really did. Perhaps one day you will understand and find me again. I'm hoping you do because my life depends on it.

Thea looked out the window. Her impassioned words were echoing in her head.

How can she find me if she doesn't know where I am?

The bus steadily moved closer to its destination and Thea looked at the map resting in her lap. Once again, her tears fell on the paper and she wiped them away while contemplating what her life would be like in the small town in New York's Hudson Valley.

†

Fans screamed and shouted around her as Jo finished the concert performance in Atlanta. Tomorrow she would be back in Nashville and normality, although that wouldn't include Thea.

How could anything ever be normal again without her friend? Her life the past ten months had been surreal and crazy wild. She'd made the big time. That was what Jack told her every day when he contacted her.

The concert reviews and the record sales were phenomenal. The icing on the cake was the nomination by the Country Music Association for best new artist, song of the year, and album of the year. For a virtual newcomer that was unheard of. Eating, sleeping, and drinking music and more music consumed her. She didn't even allow herself the luxury of a day off. Her road crew was exhausted and would grumble at the exhausting schedule she put them on.

Tomorrow they could rest and perhaps go on to other projects. She hadn't really decided if she wanted to take on the road crew permanently, although Jack had asked her to consider it in the wake of her popularity.

With ten months, thousands of miles and numerous concerts under her belt, the trade papers referred to her as a workaholic and the hardest working performer in the industry. She was. Now, she had to go back to the apartment and face the despair of losing her friend once again.

It would be for the last time. Jack offered to have the apartment cleared out for her and move all her belongings to the new apartment she was renting in Nashville with a view of the river.

Her engagement to Lee ended after Thea left. Jo was holding him directly responsible for her friend's departure. Once she acknowledged that the only person important to her was Thea, she knew any other relationship would never work. She had been too selfish to realize how much Thea affected her life. What other reason would there be for Thea to leave? Thea was the only person Jo really cared about and it had broken her heart that she'd left without a trace.

She recalled the night that she'd discovered Thea gone and then the knock on the door. When she opened the door, Alice stood there glaring at her...

"Are you proud of yourself, Jo?" she'd sneered. "Thea is the sweetest kindest woman in the world and you treated her like shit."

Jo just hung her head. Alice hadn't said anything she hadn't said to herself. "Do you know where she is?"

"No. Even if I did, I wouldn't tell you. Do you even care how devastated she was? She loved you, Jo, and you threw her out."

"I didn't. I'd never do that."

"No, you sent your boyfriend to do your dirty work. How could you do that to her?"

"Alice, no! I never did that. I wouldn't. Please tell me where she went."

"Here," she shoved an envelope at her. "She asked me to give this to you." Alice shook her head. "I don't know how you live with yourself. You're pathetic," she snarled before turning and leaving.

Jo closed the door, clasping the letter to her heart. She ripped the envelope open hoping to find out where she was. She swallowed hard and with trembling fingers, she carefully opened the page.

Dear Joanna,

I know you are wondering what's going on and I can't blame you as I write this, I wonder, too.

Nevertheless, I've decided to break out on my own. It was time. I can't let you continue to fund everything for the rest of my life and it was beginning to feel like that. Please don't think me ungrateful because I'm far from it.

As I looked at our months together, I realized how much I'd grown up and could handle myself. I owe that to you, Joanna, and only you. Maybe one day in the future we can meet up again, talk about old times, and reminisce on how we have both fared in the world.

One thing I know for sure is that you are a star in my eyes and always will be. I wish you so much success, my friend. You deserve it. I, of course, won't tell you where I'm going because I know you too well. You will try to find me and I think it's time for us both to move on.

Wish me the same in your heart, Joanna, and know you will always be with me in my heart, wherever I travel.

Take care, my friend,
Thea

Jo traced her thumb across what she knew were teardrops. "What have I done?" she whispered.

After that, Jo threw herself into her work, numbing the pain she was feeling without Thea in her life. She had to admit that being the center of attention had done her ego a world of good but she still felt hollow inside. What did it all matter if she couldn't move on as Thea had decided to do? She didn't really blame her for leaving. She had been so engrossed in achieving her dream that she forgot that other people needed her—one person in particular. It had been her choice to bring Thea along and her friend didn't deserve abandonment and neglect. Many agonizing late night hours had her hoping that Thea had found a safe haven. If she knew for sure then maybe, she could settle down to a life, too.

She plastered a smile on her face for the people who asked for her autograph, duly complying with their eagerness for a memento of the concert and of her. As she made her way back to the dressing room, she slumped down in the leather chair and wiped away the perspiration from her brow before looking at herself in the mirror.

She saw an exhausted, unhappy, and lost woman who had no one to share her success and failures with. What seemed like a long time ago now, she had considered wealth and success her major goals in life. Now, she'd be happy playing a local bar if she had someone out in the audience who was happy with her as a person. Thea had once been that person. Jo had come close and had thrown it away.

Jo knew she was dreaming but with each concert, she hoped she'd look out and see Thea in the audience.

Chapter Seventeen

"Hey, Thea, a penny for them?"

A voice she recognized immediately pulled her out of her trance with a smile. "Oh, Mom, anything I was thinking about isn't even worth a penny."

"Really? You looked so intense. Have the Henderson's arrived yet?" Thea's mother's long tapering, well-manicured fingers swung around the guest register as she scanned the arrivals and departures.

"They called about an hour ago saying they were stuck in traffic near Albany and will be late. I said it wasn't a problem."

Karen Adams grinned at her daughter. Thea would make sure that she greeted new arrivals properly, even if they turned up at midnight. That was one of the wonderful bonuses when her daughter had arrived unexpectedly one morning almost ten months ago. Not only was it the perfect present for her birthday, but Thea had brought with her a flair for the business. Since she had taken on the role of assistant manager, the small hotel had gone from being an average place to an in demand upmarket place that was always full.

Whatever it was that brought her daughter back into her life, she was eternally grateful for it. Although at times, like now, when she saw her pensive features, she knew that it hadn't been a happy choice for her daughter to leave her old life behind. At first, she'd been inquisitive but the child hadn't given anything away other than she had lived in Nashville with a friend for a short time after leaving Danvers and then it became time to move on.

"Are you happy living here at the hotel, Thea? You could move in with us, you know?"

Thea nodded. "I love it here. I get to do what I enjoy and have my independence too. What more could I ask for?"

"How about having a social life other than coming to our house for dinner on Sundays? The only time you take off is the odd sightseeing tour during the afternoon or early evening."

†

Thea didn't make friends that easily and all she wanted to do was make her way in the hotel business, and maybe the social side could come later. The only friend she really wanted in her life didn't care enough to make any contact. She'd left messages on her machine for a couple of weeks after she left but she never heard back. Thea had to admit that the letter she left had been firm in that she wanted to make her own life but Joanna could have replied just once. Alice knew where she was, but Joanna hadn't asked. Thea couldn't blame her.

"Alice is coming to town soon and she's a friend. I promise to make the effort and go out and about with her while she's here."

Karen snorted, blinked, and then shook her head. "Your friend is in town for what, two days?"

"No. She's coming for four nights on her way to see relatives. She promised at Christmas she will stay longer, if she can."

As they were chatting, the swing door opened and in walked a short stocky man virtually bald with a ready smile and twinkling eyes. Alongside him was a taller younger man with a similar expression. "Now, what are you two ladies scheming? If I know you, Karen, it might not be in my best interests?"

Karen grinned and turned to hug the man. "Now, when have I not been in your best interests, Grayson?" The man held her close, whispering something into her ear, before lovingly kissing her.

"Oh, give it a rest can't you? Thea, tell them it's embarrassing."

"Bradley, I think our mom and your dad make one cute couple. How would you like to share some coffee while they continue to get to know one another again?"

The comment was ridiculous as they had seen one another at breakfast only three hours before but it made them all laugh.

Bradley Adams walked to his half-sister. "You should live in the house with us, Thea. Then you might consider I'm right." He placed a warm arm around his big sister's shoulders as they entered the back office.

†

"You look worried, my dear?" Grayson said. He stared at his wife with gentle eyes. He had fallen in love with Karen when he visited the Danvers area during his travels as a working salesman. He knew Karen was married, with a child, and kept his distance since his family had very devout ethics about the sanctity of marriage. However, the more he came to the town and got to know Karen, the more he couldn't help falling head over heels for her. Karen was caring, gentle, and loved her daughter. The husband, on the other hand, was a different matter. He was a drunk, gambler, and the town joke. It was clear that Daniel Danvers wasn't ever going to change.

One day, he'd come home after losing all their money from a cattle sale that was going to take them through the winter and had expected Karen to exist for months on no income. He would never forget the day he'd walked into the motel and found her crying inconsolably in the small lobby. That had been the final straw and he asked her to go away with him. She said no, as he expected. He remembered seeing Thea, who was as pretty as a picture, hugging her mother for comfort. Three months later, they had left town together with Karen leaving her only child behind. It had broken her heart but she couldn't have stayed after the bastard tried to sell her favors at the local bar. They had always intended to fight for Thea but Daniel Danvers had remarkably sobered up and caused such a stir about her running off, abandoning her child that they didn't stand a chance of winning.

During the years, Karen had tried to stay in touch, sending letters and presents to Thea, but now they knew Thea had never received anything. Daniel saw to that. Karen never stopped caring and had a friend in Danvers who provided regular updates to prevent her from going insane. When Daniel died, they'd considered going to talk with Thea but Bradley was gravely ill and by the time he recovered the chance was lost. Karen knew that Thea left Danvers and why. That was cause for concern until her friend told her it was the very best thing she could have done. The person she had gone with would look after her. Now reunited as a family, Karen had never been happier. That's all that mattered to Grayson.

"I don't think she's happy, Gray, there's something in her eyes that remains permanently sad. She won't talk about it, so how can I help her?"

"In time she will, Karen. She's finding her footing, that's all."

"Do you really think so? I wouldn't want to lose her again. Not after waiting all this time for her to be back in my life."

"Yeah, I do. Wherever she goes in the future she knows we are here for her and that must mean something, right?"

"I love you, Grayson. Did I ever tell you that?"

He chuckled before slipping his arms back around her and giving her a tender kiss. "Every day, my dear, every day. Shall we go see how our brood is doing?"

Hand in hand, they went behind the reception counter into the back office. As they opened the door, he heard laughter and it warmed his heart.

✝

Now standing in the apartment that she had shared with Thea, Jo surveyed the empty rooms, thinking that Thea would walk through the door and ask her what she was doing. Her friend would be aghast at the mess she was leaving behind and that mess only amounted to a couple of empty boxes and the dust that had accumulated during the time she had been touring. It hadn't had a proper cleaning since Thea left. Then again, she hadn't been in the apartment much since that time.

As she looked around one last time, she sighed heavily. This was the end of this particular journey. In the future, she would never have to live in a place like this again. She had bought a property in New York by the ocean and it belonged to her outright. It was something she never thought would happen in her life. For now, she was renting, with the option to buy, a super apartment in the most desirable area of Nashville. Once more her thoughts traveled to her friend. Thea would love all the labor saving gadgets and the décor in the new apartment. It was light and airy and Thea would have had a wonderful time filling the place with her plants and flowers.

Her bank balance was healthy, or so Jack said, and she had no reason to distrust him. She was due to tour Europe and Asia in three months' time. The world was literally at her feet yet she felt restless and didn't enjoy the accolades she was receiving. Jack indicated that he was worried about her schedule, afraid that she'd burn out before she could reap the rewards of her success. Maybe he was right. There was something eating at her insides, refusing to allow her to stop. If she did, she might not get up again.

"Hi." A voice she barely recognized hailed her from the open doorway.

"Alice."

The last time the two had spoken, it was antagonistic and Jo had been too shocked and unhappy to retaliate properly. She might be tired but she wouldn't put up with another tirade from the woman.

"I'm fine, you're looking…worn out but well," Alice said softly. "It's obvious you aren't happy to see me and that is understandable. I was angry and lashed out at you and I'm sorry for that." Alice shrugged. "I wasn't sure if you would ever return. I've seen the odd person come around who had a key but I didn't see you. I figured you'd given the place up. You're famous now, congrats."

"Thank you. I'm here now. I decided it wouldn't be right to leave everything to a stranger to pack. Besides, there are things that belong to Thea and I couldn't let anyone else deal with them."

"I miss her too." Alice's voice held a tinge of sadness.

"Look, I need to go. I have another appointment." Jo jangled her keys and looked around the doorway and the memory of her throwing her knapsack on the dainty table that always held welcoming blooms came to the forefront. It was a bittersweet recollection and how she wished she could do that again. She still could. The housekeeper could place the small table that she still had in her new apartment near the door with a vase of fresh flowers every day. In her heart, she knew it wouldn't be nearly the same.

"I won't keep you, I hope your career continues to shine and you and your husband are happy. See you around, Jo." Alice walked out into the hallway with Jo following behind. "I'll use the stairwell so you can use the elevator."

"Alice."

"Yes?" Alice turned back around.

"After Thea left, I broke the engagement. I never married." Jo thought that was common knowledge but apparently not. "Have you heard from Thea?" There was no way she would let Alice leave without asking that question. *Please, let it be good news.*

"She's fine, Jo. Working hard but she's well."

"Where is she?"

"I promised that I wouldn't tell anyone. I'm sorry but I have to honor her wishes."

"I see. Will you tell her that I asked about her?"

"Yes, of course I will. Maybe now that you are back in town, she'll call you. I know she tried to call several times and got no answer."

"I never received any calls or messages from her." Jo's heart thudded in her chest.

Alice shrugged. "That's what she told me."

Jo jabbed at the elevator button in irritation. How had she missed Thea's calls? The elevator doors opened and she got in. Alice was still standing there. "I'll see you around, Alice."

†

Alice watched the elevator doors close and knew that with the way Jo's lifestyle was taking off, there wasn't much chance of them meeting again. *Oh, well, I can always boast I knew Jo Lackerly before she became famous.*

Now, she'd go back to her apartment and call Thea. Her friend would want to know that Jo had been there and hear what she'd had to say. The question was how Thea would handle the news. Alice already knew that her friend probably wouldn't do anything for Jo's actions tarnished her well and truly.

Chapter Eighteen

"Hi, Stella. How are you doing today?"

"Hey, Thea, I'm good. What about yourself? I see your arms are full, as usual. Can I get you some help?"

"No, I'm good." Thea grinned while walking in step with the older sprightly woman who owned a seamstress business next to a bakery operated by her husband.

"You should get out more. I keep telling your mother just that and she says you will not listen. You young people are all the same...thinking you know best. We've already experienced it before so you should listen to us."

Thea grinned at the comment. "Bradley was going to help me but he has baseball practice."

"Oh, that boy is spoiled." The older woman chuckled. "Of course I spoiled my son and now my grandchildren.

"Yeah, but I never knew I had a brother, so I'm making up for lost time. He's a very caring young man and reminds me of someone I once knew."

"Ah, so our Thea has a secret love affair buried away, has she?"

Thea laughed nervously at the comment. It was so close to the mark but no one would ever know that, especially now Joanna was a star. "Nope, a friend. A good friend at the time. He was very caring like Bradley. We berate men but some of them are wonderful. Don't you think?"

Stella and her husband had been married for almost forty years and her mother was hosting a party at the hotel to mark the event.

When they entered the bakery, Thea breathed in the wonderful aroma of freshly baked bread. She loved to stand on the threshold and take in the distinctive aromas.

"Ah, two lovely ladies. What brings you in today?" asked a tall, strikingly handsome man with swarthy Mediterranean looks, twinkling brown eyes, and a sharp Grecian nose.

"Alex, you flatterer, you will be having me spying on all your customers in a calculating way if you carry on like that."

The man moved from around the counter and hugged the woman. "Stella, you are my one true love. No one can ever take your place."

Stella grinned in Thea's direction.

Ever since arriving in this part of the Hudson Valley Thea wondered if it wasn't magical. Everyone who was a couple seemed to thrive in this environment. She wondered if things would have been different between she and Joanna if they'd come here first.

"Thea, when you have this, don't give it away ever. No matter how absurd or impossible it may seem, it is too precious to lose," Stella said.

Thea shook her head, wondering if she would ever get the chance to feel like that. For a brief time she did have that. But it wasn't mutual.

"Leave the girl alone, Stella. She has plenty of time. Although I do know one or two eligible bachelors—"

"No. No. Please, Alex, I'd rather try to find the right person on my own. Thanks all the same."

The man released his wife with a wink and went back around the counter. "You should bring someone to our anniversary party, Thea. They would be most welcome."

"Thanks, but I'll be busy on Saturday."

Alex smiled broadly and set about putting together her order.

Thea's mind drifted to the conversation she'd had with Alice, saying that she'd spoken with Joanna. What a surprise that would be, if she invited the singer to the party and she turned up. Thea knew the older couple enjoyed Joanna's music since she'd seen the CD in both the bakery and at Stella's shop. It would probably make Joanna self-conscious to see the fan worship. Maybe it wouldn't. She was probably used to it by now.

The very CD she was thinking of flooded the room and Joanna's rich voice reverberated all around her. She smiled as she recalled the song. The one she had last heard at the television studio.

"Why do you look so sad, Thea?" Stella asked. "Don't you like our choice in music?" Stella looked at her husband.

"Oh, yes, I do. Very much. She has a wonderful voice, doesn't she?"

"Yeah, she does. A rags to riches story, I hear," Alex said. Thea noticed his miserable expression. "She was always rich, just never realized it."

Thea, wondering what he meant gave him a surprised gaze. "I don't understand."

"What he means is that with a voice like that and so much talent, how could one ever be poor," Stella said.

"Of course, that makes sense."

"I did read that her personal life is in tatters," Stella said. "Seems she was engaged and broke it off just before she hit it big."

In the background, Thea heard Joanna's voice gather strength as she hit a high note at the end of the song. She had purposefully avoided all the magazines and websites with items about Joanna, not wanting to know how happy she was with Lee.

So she ditched him right after I left. Hmm, I wonder why.

She recalled her phone call with Alice who'd said that Joanna told her she never got the phone calls Thea had made to her. She knew she had the right number for it was a number she'd never forget. Maybe she knew who it was and didn't want to answer.

No, Alice was certain she was sincere when she told her she didn't receive the calls. Should she try again? If she did and she didn't answer then she'd know what Joanna really thought. She just couldn't take that chance.

†

"I think you should reconsider, Jo. Your throat infection isn't clear yet and you need to give it another week or two. We can rearrange the concerts in France and Germany, start the tour in Italy instead, and reschedule them," Jack pleaded in earnest.

Jo had been ill for most of the month, reluctantly agreeing to a vacation before another grueling tour. This time it wouldn't be as arduous—only four months. The immense amount of traveling and jet lag would take its toll eventually, just as it had at the end of her last tour. Jo didn't seem to care one-way or another and that troubled him. If it hadn't been for the housekeeper informing him that Jo was ill, he wouldn't have known to send in one of the top doctors to help.

"No. I'll be fine. Trust me, I know my body, and it hates sitting around. Once I'm back on the road, everything will go like clockwork."

"I don't agree. This tour is too soon after the last one. It's your call of course. From a business point of view, it will help the new record release. Promise me if at any time you decide you've had enough, you'll let me know, and we will work it out. Okay?"

"How about I do the world tour and then take a three month vacation for real?"

Jack knew she needed more than a break. She needed to find the spark that was lacking in her life. He knew what that was. Thea Danvers. Jo needed to make her peace and have Thea back in her life no matter what the cost. He wouldn't tell her that, however, for she was too fragile right now, even if she wouldn't admit it.

"How about you go home and see what you feel like in the morning. Tomorrow is another day."

"I have the flight to New York tomorrow and that stands." Jo, walking to Jack, grinned before bending to kiss his cheek. "How come you're still free and single?"

"Away with you and that virus, I don't want it. Remember I'm older than you are and we aged types can't take the strain anymore. Anyway, who says I'm free and single?"

"We'll talk about that when I'm back."

"Yes, we will, when you want to talk about the true love of your life," he said with a wink.

They both laughed as she vacated the office. Jack continued to smile. Maybe it was time for her to know he loved a certain man just as she loved Thea—a fact he was pretty darned sure of.

†

"Thea, do you have a few minutes to spare?" Grayson asked, smiling.

"Yes, of course. What can I do for you?" Thea liked her mother's choice in a husband. When she was ten, she hadn't understood and throughout her teenage years, she'd hated him for taking her mother away from her. Now, she empathized or at least partially. She might never understand properly, since they refused to discuss the situation fully. There was something holding her mother back. Grayson was a decent man who loved his wife and family. He'd included her in the family immediately upon her arrival. It made her wonder at how he must have loved her mother to become embroiled in a situation which pitted him against the hatred of others.

"I know it's short notice, but I need someone I can trust to go out to Hartford."

"Why not send a courier?"

"I could but I wanted it to be personal. I can't go because Karen, knowing how I hate parties, will think I'm going to disappear and never return for the anniversary bash."

"Even so, why not a courier?"

"It's a special guest for Alex and Stella. They don't think she is going to come but if you can persuade her, I know she'll come."

"Grayson, why me?"

"Let me explain. This person is part of their family—estranged but still family—I'm afraid she won't bother. I need someone...no, the party needs someone of your caliber to get her onboard. Will you please do it, Thea?"

My caliber. What exactly would that be? Thea saw the pleading in his eyes and knew the only answer she could give. "Okay I'll do it. What's the address and who is it?"

"Ah, now you will be surprised, it's—"

†

The flight had been terrible. Jo was suffering from every attack of sinus problem imaginable. That, coupled with the fact that she had to evade a rather *delightful* pack of fans that had seen her board the plane, was almost more than she could handle. What she needed now was a protector.

As the word entered her brain, it triggered off the memory of her friend. Hadn't Thea once said that she would be her protector and then laughed at the outlandish suggestion? She sure could do with the help now. *Where are you, Thea? I need you.* She knew deep in her soul that she would always need Thea.

It was stupid to keep thinking that she'd come back. She wasn't ever going to.

That's the bottom line, Lackerly, so get used to it, she told herself.

Her grip on reality was leaving her to fantasies and it wasn't going to help her now or in the future. At the beginning of every concert, she silently dedicated it to Thea, just as she had on her latest album. *I have to move on, just like when I ditched Lee. It has to be the same with Thea. There's only going to be this one shot at fame and fortune and I need to prove all the old doubters that I can give it longevity.* All those people who said she would end up wasting her life, becoming nothing more than a drifter without a goal. *Well, I have a goal now.* It was just proving a little harder to remember what that was when she woke in the morning.

"Jo. Jo," voices shouted. Glancing around, she saw several fans rushing toward her and sucked in a breath. She wasn't up to the adoration today.

How did they recognize me or know I'd be here? I'm not that well known, am I?

Then she looked around at the newsstand and saw at least two magazines with her picture on the front. Perhaps she should have paid more attention to Jack when he extolled her new status in the music world.

Fifteen minutes and two security guards later, she was rushed into a VIP lounge and out of the airport without interference. This wouldn't have happened if she had taken Jack's advice and agreed to engage another manager who could take care of these situations for her. However, she had been her usual independent self and said she could do it all on her own. And, anyway, she still had a manager. Her words ended the discussion. She made sure that Jack knew that any mention of Thea was taboo. He didn't cross that line, ever.

Although she felt like shit, she had to be here. She'd made a promise that she refused to break. No one, not even Jack, knew why she refused to stay home and rest. Her flight to Europe was in two days but this was a family matter and no one else's business.

Security had hailed her a cab and she stepped into it. Exhausted, all she wanted was a soft bed to sleep in. With a hoarse voice, she gave the cabbie the address. She hoped it wasn't too far away and that a warm welcome was heading her way.

Chapter Nineteen

Thea muttered a few choice words as she negotiated another bend on her way to convince someone to attend Alex and Stella's anniversary party. How could she have refused? After all, they were wonderful people and if she could help them out in any way, she would. But it was only hours before the event. She was pushing for a miracle.

She glanced at the GPS screen and saw that she was on Apple Blossom Drive. "Now, to find number ten." Two minutes later she heard the GPS say 'you have arrived' and pulled up the short drive to the neat house.

Thea sucked in a nervous breath before knocking on the door. She hoped that the woman wasn't ferocious toward strangers. If truly estranged from her family, Thea couldn't understand the reason. Alex and Stella were always kind and friendly to everyone.

The door opened. A tall woman with gray, flowing hair that met her shoulders, and piercing blue eyes, looked at her. "Yes," she barked.

Thea drew back a fraction from the doorway as she once more surveyed the imposing woman. Something about her was drawing Thea to the woman. She was familiar.

"My name is Thea Danvers. I'm from New York—"

"New York? I hate that city. Far too claustrophobic. Why do I need to know anything about that place?" the older woman interrupted.

"No. No, I'm in the Hudson Valley and it isn't about New York City. It's about someone you know." Thea knew she was faltering. The woman was so forthright, with a hint of steel about her manner, that was intimidating.

"I don't know you or anyone from wherever you come from. You have the wrong address." The woman shut the door.

"Wait! I'm sorry. Are you, Mrs. Stephens?"

"Yes." There was arrogance about the woman that Thea recognized and she reckoned it had to do with her connection to Stella.

"Then I don't have the wrong address. I need to speak to you about your daughter."

Blue eyes surveyed Thea's and she thought she saw a twinkle in the depths. "Go on."

"Well, actually, I'm here to invite you to your daughter's diamond wedding anniversary."

"Really? You're too late. She invited me two months ago and I replied with a *no*."

Thea's compassionate nature kicked in and she knew her face-mirrored her disappointment. "Why?"

"Why? You're a stranger, why should I tell you?"

"You don't have to, of course, but Stella is so wonderful. How could you not want to go to her anniversary party?"

"I didn't approve the match forty years ago and I don't approve it, now. Is that reason enough for you?"

Green eyes flashed at the blue ones and suddenly it clicked where she had seen them before. Joanna.

"You remind me of a friend. She was stubborn, too."

"Then, my dear, you should be used to it. Why not go back to wherever you came from and enjoy your party."

"Doesn't forty years together count for something? That it was a good match and they love one another?"

A sharp laugh that bordered on cynical—another reminder of the singer—mocked her words. "It could also mean they didn't have any other choice and made the best of a bad choice."

"They didn't because they love one another very much."

"That's as you want to see it, but I know better." The woman shut the door again. "I have things to do."

"I'm sorry I bothered you, goodbye."

"Goodbye." The door shut before Thea could say anything else.

Why? Why had her stepfather assumed she could make the old hag see sense? It wasn't one of her talents obviously, never would be. She was too much a coward for the confrontational things in life.

With her head down, walking toward her car, she turned back, wondering if she should try again. In an upper window, she saw the shadows of two figures. They were probably talking about the foolish stranger who didn't know anything about them or the situation with the family. Thea climbed into her vehicle, wondering if she would ever have the courage to stand her ground instead of taking everything on the chin. Would she ever fight back for something she wanted?

A stray thought gathered momentum. *There's still time to fight for Joanna.*

†

"Who was that?" Jo asked.

"Oh, some annoying woman. She was trying to convince me to go to that anniversary party tonight for my daughter and that man." The older woman threw an envelope on a nearby table.

"Gran, why not go and bury the hatchet?"

"You ask me that? I thought you would have understood. I don't like your father, never have, and never will. He is a foreigner and not good enough for my only daughter. She could have done better."

A snort of laughter filled the room as the two women faced one another. Their similarities were only disguised by the aging process.

"Yep, my upstanding Gran, the racist. Do they know this at that church you attend?"

Skin, weathered with age, stretched across high cheekbones in a scowl. "You are not to mention this to anyone. Do you hear me? Why would you care? When was the last time you saw your parents?"

It was a good question and Jo tried desperately to find the answer. "Eight years ago but I stay in touch."

"In touch? You call a possible postcard from a town not even mentioned on any map, contact? You ask me about family loyalties? Take a break, and look at your own. For your information, my girl, it's been almost ten years since you last saw your family. Not that I can blame you, with a father like yours."

The laughter turned to a sneer as Jo walked across to her grandparent—the only one she had that she could recall. Gran didn't like her father—hated him was more accurate. That however didn't mean she did. Her father had been a wonderful role model.

"Guess it's time I made up for that and visited them. Better yet, it can be a surprise at the party. I'll take your invite." She picked up the envelope that the woman at the door left behind.

It had to take some courage for anyone to take on her grandmother and not go away unscathed. She had to make a point of meeting with the woman who was just there and apologize for her grandmother's rudeness. The invitation indicated that the party was in three hours. Now to get ready and call a cab, since she was going to be pushing it to be there on time. Better late than never might be the rule of the day.

"Who says you can have my invite?" her gran demanded.

"Are you going to need it?" Jo stood her ground and smiled as they traded sharp blue glances. Years ago, she would have dropped her gaze, but now she could and did stand up for herself. A nasty coughing bout raked Jo's body so she sat down heavily in the chair nearest to her. Bravado was her only asset because she didn't feel that well.

"You shouldn't be going. You're not fit enough." Her gran walked to her, placing a cool, leathery hand on her forehead. "You're burning up. You shouldn't go."

"I'll be fine. A hot bath and a shot of brandy to warm up the body will revive me. I'll come back early."

"We will see."

At those few words, Jo looked up and captured the worry that transmitted from the world-weary eyes. She winked at her. "Don't worry, Gran, I'm made of stern stuff. Remember who I take after."

"Humph, just as well you do. Now, go take that bath and I'll call you a cab for an hour from now."

Jo grinned and slowly stood, hugging the frail woman. Pity she still had such a ferocious tongue on her because she really was quite a caring woman. "Thanks, Gran."

As Jo mounted the stairs to her room, she heard her grandmother call her once more. "Don't use up all my best bath salts, Jo."

"Yeah, yeah, yeah." Smiling, Jo walked into her room to find something suitable to wear.

†

The party was in full swing and the guests of honor were amazed at the turnout. To them it looked like the whole village had decided to pay homage to their celebration.

"I'm sorry I couldn't do anything to help change Stella's mother's mind. She was one stubborn woman," Thea said.

Grayson grinned and hugged her close. "No problem. To tell you the truth, it was a long shot but worth a try. Who knows? Maybe the old crone might change her mind. There's time yet. Even if she doesn't, I think everyone is enjoying all the fuss. Don't you?"

They both looked at the laughing couple talking to their son and his wife. Their only grandchild was happily dancing nearby.

"Yeah, they are and there's no legislating for family, is there."

"Would you do me the honor of having this dance with me?" Her stepfather held out his hand and Thea took it with a smile as they joined the mass of people swaying to the music.

Karen was standing at the door, watching her husband and daughter dancing happily as Bradley munched on all the delectable food. Typical teenager, the boy was astounding her with his growth rate. At six foot, he towered above them all and was still growing like a weed. Someone in the family line must have been lanky, for neither Grayson nor she was very tall.

Her attention turned to the hotel entrance when it opened. A statuesque figure, almost as tall as Bradley, with midnight black hair cut to shoulder length, shone in the glare of the artificial lights of the foyer. The woman shook away the rain that had settled on her leather coat.

Karen walked toward the woman, who was looking around the room with a curious expression. She watched, as the stranger's eyes gazed at the fresh cut flowers that Thea insisted were a part of the hotel these days. An expensive addition but one that, strangely enough, she felt the guests appreciated in the often-unwelcoming harshness of day-to-day life.

"Can I help you? We're booked if you need a room," Karen said.

"I don't need a room but you can help me. Is this where the Xianthos wedding anniversary celebration is?"

Karen had seen this woman before, she was sure of it, Where? She probably was a cousin since she had the familiar Grecian complexion. "Yes, you're a little late. It's well underway, but you haven't missed the cutting of the cake. In fact, you're just in time. May I see your invitation?"

†

Jo felt as if she had come home here in the hotel. It had the hallmark of Thea stamped all over it—the use of the flowers, and the general friendly, cozy ambience of the place. But she couldn't be that lucky, could she? To see Thea here, of all places. It was probably a combination of wishful thinking and the medication her Gran had insisted she take before she left. She reached inside her jacket and drew out the invitation.

Silently watching the woman, Jo felt drawn to her. Her green eyes were identical to Thea's eyes. It was remarkable how, almost a year later, she could still see them so vividly, even in a stranger's eyes.

Karen's eyebrows rose, as she looked at the invitation. "I'm sorry but this invitation is made out…"

Jo smiled and lifted her hand to prevent the question.

"To my grandmother. My parents don't know I'm in town. I guess I wanted to surprise them. What better day, huh?"

Karen opened her eyes in astonishment. "I'm sorry for staring but it's rather a shock, I've heard so much about the long lost daughter. Is it true? Are you really Jo Xianthos?"

Jo nodded.

"Wow! Wait until they see you. It will make their day."

Jo smiled graciously as she inclined her head. The woman appeared genuine enough and her eyes were friendly. There was nothing false there…or was it the reaction to seeing the woman's eyes that were so like Thea's.

"Yeah, I guess it will be a shock for them, too." A wracking cough stopped Jo for several seconds.

"Oh, my dear, are you all right? I'll go fetch my daughter, she will find something dry for you to wear. Are you soaked from the rain?" Karen said with concern.

"No. No problem. I came by cab. The rain caught the jacket that's all. Can't seem to shake a cold I've had recently. It's nothing to worry about, but thanks for the offer. If you don't mind, I'd just rather see my parents."

"Of course. How stupid of me to delay you. Come with me." Karen walked to the door of the conference room that was now more like a concert room with the music and laughter emanating from it.

†

Jo sucked in a breath that hurt her chest. The damn virus wouldn't shift, no matter what she took or how much rest she'd had. She was here now and an hour with her parents today, of all days, was better than no hour at all.

She walked into the room behind the older woman, knowing that no one would notice her at first because the lights were dim and people were dancing. Then she scanned the place for her family and saw them at the longest table in the room. Her heart fluttered at the sight of her parents and her kid brother. Had it really been ten years?

"They're sitting there, Jo, why not go and join them?" The voice sounded so much like Thea that she glanced sharply at the woman by her side.

"Thanks, Mrs...?"

"Adams, Karen. I own the hotel and your parents are good friends of mine."

"Thanks, Karen."

While striding toward the long table, Jo received odd glances and heard whispers that floated around the room.

"It can't be. Can it?" echoed around the room.

†

Thea grinned at her stepfather as the song ended. "Grayson, I have to go check something in the office, I'll be back in half an hour for the cutting of the cake, I promise."

"I'll tell your mother and you know she won't be happy. She said you had to enjoy yourself tonight and she would take care of the hotel."

"I know she did and trust me, she can. This is personal business, Grayson. I have to make a call to someone I haven't seen in a while and it's long overdue."

Grayson smiled, then winked. "Half an hour or I send your mother after you. Go, I see she's heading in our direction."

Thea left the room by one of the service entrances quickly, rather than face her mother near the hotel foyer door.

"You'll never believe this Gray…." Thea heard as she left the room to make that call to Joanna.

Alice had given her the number Joanna left with her. After seeing people happy together and the love that they shared, she had to at least try to make contact again with her friend. She needed it, her heart hadn't stopped bleeding since she'd left the apartment they shared, and possibly, it never would. Somehow, she had to fight for this. It was too important to give up.

†

"Papa," Jo's husky voice said. Blue eyes sparkled with unshed tears as she looked at her father. He was still handsome and now with his hair liberally peppered with gray, he was very distinguished looking.

Alexander looked up and Stella put a hand to her mouth to stop herself sobbing.

"Joanna? My God, it is you!" The aged eyes now shimmered with tears as his head shook from side to side in astonishment.

"Yes, Papa, your black sheep has turned up at last." This time Jo rushed forward and her father engulfed her in a hug as fierce as any she had experienced in her lifetime. She listened to words her father spoke in his native language as he cried them into her hair, stroking it softly.

"Stella, Stella, our daughter has returned to us. Look, here she is and she's real, darling, she is."

Stella joined in the hug and they all dissolved into tears and laughter kissing one another repeatedly.

"Hey, Papa, I want to live to see another day, not be suffocated." Jo pulled away and smothered her laughter realizing that every eye in the room had turned to them.

Alexander laughed at the remark and drew her to arm's length as he looked at her closely. He shook his head and then placed a kiss on her cheek. "Thank you, Joanna, for making this evening even more special than it already is. Come, your brother will want to see you and so will his family. You have a niece you have never seen. Come, Joanna, come."

"Okay, okay, Papa, I'll come. I'm here for a while. I promise." Jo smiled at her father wondering why she had left coming home for so long. They loved her for nothing more than being their daughter. Why had she taken so long to realize that?

†

Thea couldn't stop the tears that drenched her cheeks as she let her cell phone fall from her dead fingers. Why, why was this happening to her? The number Joanna had given to Alice was being answered by a messenger service and they informed her that Ms. Lackerly had left the country for a tour and wouldn't be back for three months. They asked if she wanted to leave a forwarded message for the singer.

No. No, she needed to speak to Joanna, not leave some stupid message that might never get to her or if it did, it might not be for weeks. This wasn't fair, it really wasn't.

Her head fell toward the desk as she cried for the heartbreak she knew might never end. What should she do? She had thought she could live and start afresh without Joanna in her life but now a year later, the pain of the separation was as acute as the day she had left. No, now it was worse because she had to listen to her friend sing on the radio and in the shops she frequented, and even in the privacy of her own rooms. Now, to make it worse, posters of Joanna were everywhere and television ads were promoting her to the public. Soon Joanna would be the property of everyone and she would only ever see her through the anonymity of being a fan.

It was all her fault. She should never have left. She should have confronted Joanna with her fears and discussed the problems she perceived face-to-face and not run like a scared rabbit. She was no better off now than if she'd stayed in Danvers and married George Andrews.

The door to the office opened and she looked up with the ravages of her tears covering her face.

"Thea, darling, what's the matter?" Karen flew around the desk and pulled her daughter into her arms.

"Nothing, it's nothing, Mom. I promise it's—" Her tears belied her words as she sank her head into her mother's shoulder.

"You can tell me, Thea. It can't be that bad and if it is, I'll help you solve it, I promise you that."

"Mom, if only you could. It's impossible now. I can't contact her."

"Is it someone you knew before you came here, Thea? Perhaps she's just out of town?"

Thea looked into the green eyes that mirrored her own and saw compassion. How could she tell her mother how she felt about Joanna? Would she understand? "Yes, I knew her before, she was my friend. No, she was more than that. She was my protector, Mom. She looked after me when I left Danvers. Oh, Mom, you wouldn't understand. Even I find it hard to understand. She's out of the country and I really needed to speak with her one last time."

"Did she leave you alone, Thea? Is that why you had to find us? Did she abandon you alone in Nashville?"

"No. No, Mom, that's just it, I abandoned her. She did everything for me—looked after me, kept the roof over my head, fed me, and even paid me to help around the house. You wouldn't understand, Mom, she was perfect. I loved her."

Karen moved away and looked carefully at Thea before placing her arms back around her shoulders. "Now I understand the problem. Trust me. Everything will be fine, Thea, trust me. Now we have a cake to watch being cut by special friends of ours, are you up for that?"

"I'm sorry, Mom, I have a headache. Will you apologize to Alex and Stella for me and tell them I'll see them tomorrow. I really can't face people celebrating right now. I'm too miserable. Do you understand?"

Take Me As I Am

"Yes, darling, of course I do. They will be disappointed though, especially after the special surprise they had a little earlier."

"Mom, I just can't."

"I'll apologize and tell you all the gossip tomorrow. Now you go have a nice scented bath and have an early night. Tomorrow everything will be clearer, you see if it's not." Karen pushed Thea toward the private door to her rooms.

†

Karen heard the anguish and pain in Thea's words and the pathos behind them was hard to bear. It struck her heart and she wanted to strangle the woman who had hurt her so deeply. She had missed out for so many years on Thea's life and this was her chance to comfort her daughter and help her through the torment she was going through. Thea was in love with a woman, perhaps they had even been lovers, and she'd thought they wouldn't understand.

Love was love, no matter who it was. She would speak with the only person she knew who gave without judgement as he always had ever since she'd met him. Grayson. Yes, Grayson would know what to do for Thea. As a family, they would work it out together. Her daughter was no longer alone. She had them to help now.

The door to the office opened, the woman who had entered earlier and now she knew was a relative came inside. Karen put on her business smile. "Hi, how can I help you?"

"My parents insist I sing for them tonight. I wondered if you had a decent microphone."

"Why yes, of course we do. You will have to give me a few minutes to find it. My daughter runs all the equipment and she would go straight to it. However, I have to look around."

"Your daughter isn't here? She wouldn't be the lady who came to my Gran's home earlier today, would she? I wanted to apologize to her for my Gran's abruptness. "

"Actually, yes, she did. It was a foolish thought of my husband but well meant. Unfortunately, it's not possible to see her right now. She has a migraine and has retired for the night. You know how these things happen."

"Yeah, I do. A nice hot bath and an early night would be kinda welcome about now for me as well." Jo coughed again.

"Maybe after the song you can do just that and come back and see your parents tomorrow?"

"I wish I could. I'm afraid I'm going abroad tomorrow. This is my one and only chance for three months, although I'll be back in the fall to see them again and visit longer."

"Well, in that case, I'd better find the microphone for you, hadn't I."

Karen walked out of the room and switched off the light as she went out to find the equipment.

Tomorrow they would tackle Thea's problem and she was sure they would find a solution. There was always a solution to every problem. You had to find the key that was all, and in Thea's case, that key was an unknown woman.

Thea lay in her bed with her eyes closed as the morass that filled her life for the past year invaded the room, taunting her. It was so bad that, in the distance, she could hear the sounds of Joanna singing one of her signature songs. It sounded so real but she knew it was the same trick that her mind continually played on her.

Tears leaked out of the corner of her eyes and she wished once again that she could go back and make things right.

Chapter Twenty

The flight to Berlin was tedious but allowed Jo to reflect on her family situation. She'd spent all those years slipping in and out of small towns peddling her singing, making a meager living, all the while thinking that her parents wouldn't understand. When at the heart of it, they had. She was the one who hadn't recognized the value of a family connection. Her family's unconditional acceptance of her the night before had brought about the end of her time being a loner. It was something she had always thought had to be, if ever she was going to be a success in the music world. That wasn't the case at all. Her family would have happily supported her wandering ways and by default had for many years. Now all Jo wanted was for Thea to come back home and she would be complete and happy.

Complete and happy.

What a strangely innocuous phrase that packs an enormous punch for anyone whose life was just that. It was a feeling that she now knew she never wanted to end. She desperately wanted to be with Thea, to begin again and to continue indefinitely. Who would have thought a small woman with green eyes and a shy smile would come to mean life to her.

So why am I on a flight taking me thousands of miles away from that goal?

Jo, glancing out of the window, looked at the blue skies and the dashing white clouds realizing that what she wasn't doing, was facing up to her ultimate dream. To have someone who made her happy share her life. Here she was running away as she'd done time and time before. When would she finally come to terms with the fact that running wasn't going to solve her problems? It hadn't in the past and certainly wasn't in this instance.

Thea might have a wonderful new life and be so happy herself, that Jo turning up on her doorstep would wreck everything for her. She did not intend to do that.

Alice indicated that Thea tried to call me. I wonder why I never got the calls. She smacked her forehead. *I let Jack block all calls that weren't on my list. Damn this could have all been resolved by now.*

Maybe when she returned in three months Thea might have contacted her and they could meet up for coffee and talk about old times.

Yeah, and pigs might fly.

A wracking cough caught up with her and one of the cabin attendants in first class immediately came to her, enquiring if she needed anything. Accepting water, she drained it adding a couple of pills to help her sleep for a few hours before the flight landed. Swallowing the medication and settling her headrest back with a blanket curled around her like a cocoon, she closed her eyes as a couple of conversations floated around her from the previous evening.

†

"She's never going to let Dad be part of her family, Mom. Look, forty years later she hates the sight of him so much she wouldn't come tonight."

Jo's mother turned distressed eyes toward her. She knew she was the younger image of the woman they were discussing. Jacqueline Stephens had never approved of Stella falling for Alexander Xianthos. He was an upstart foreigner who was taking her only surviving child away. Added to the mix was the fact he wasn't American, couldn't speak the language properly, and was penniless.

A staunch American patriot, Jacqueline had lived through her husband Alfred's demise in World War II and her only son was killed in action in Korea. No one, especially a foreigner, was going to take her daughter away. They'd already taken enough from her to last a lifetime.

Not even Jo's birth had softened her attitude and when her brother Albert was born, named after her grandfather, nothing had changed. Jacqueline had refused to be any kind of maternal grandmother, except for always remembering birthdays and Christmas. There had been a glimmer of hope when Jacqueline had taken an interest in Jo in high school but that had only been because she was rebelling and it was Jacqueline's way of saying, 'I told you so'.

"You know that I felt betrayed because you were staying with my mother," Stella said. "Now, I'm thankful because otherwise you might never have come here this evening. The fates, as your father would say, are clearly on our side this evening. It would have been the icing on the cake if mother had for once buried the hatchet and come, too. I can always hope. However, one miracle is enough for anyone in one evening." She patted Jo's hand. "And this evening was ours."

"You can hope, Mom, but please don't hold your breath. In the forty years plus since you met Dad she hasn't thawed and you know what they say about the older generation."

"Oh, please, Jo." Stella hugged her daughter to her and laughed, "This feels so good. At times, I've wondered if we would ever see you again and now you're here for this special evening."

Jo chuckled before winking at her mother and turning her gaze around the room. "Seems like the whole town is here. Did you leave anyone out?"

"Really, Jo, how could we leave anyone out? You know how close knit we are and there would be sullen faces and petty feuds for months afterwards." Stella looked around at all the people.

Jo grinned and muttered, "More like years." Her eyes took in the room again. "I wish they wouldn't stare at me like that. I feel like something being inspected under a microscope."

Alexander placed a loving arm around his daughter while laughing at the comment. "They have never seen anyone they know so well become famous. Before long they will be asking for your autograph."

"Dad, don't be ridiculous." Jo smiled at a young woman who was staring intently at her before looking away in apparent embarrassment.

"Fans are everywhere, Joanna. You're the newest country music sensation taking the world by storm. Here you are in this small hotel and they don't have to pay for the appearance."

"Dad, you talk rubbish. You are always such a romantic." Of her parents, her dad was the one who would sing love songs to their mother on Valentine's Day and shower her with flowers and gifts, if he could afford it, on her birthdays. Most of all, he showed he loved her every day and that was something that Jo had forgotten until now.

"That's what the papers say." He kissed her cheek.

Jo smiled raising a skeptical eyebrow and was about to respond when her brother joined the fray. "He's right, sis, it's exactly what they say and Dad should know. He buys anything with your name in it."

A lump stuck in Jo's throat as her brother nodded his head, affirming his statement. Her dad bought everything that had her name on it and here she was thinking that they had never approved of her lifestyle or her obsession in continually pursuing her music career. She realized just how wrong she had been about so many things.

"How about in the future, I call you and tell you all my news from the horse's mouth so to speak?"

Alex, grinning with happiness, hugged his daughter to his broad frame and nodded. "You could also come see us more often. Your mother would like that and…"

"And?" Jo waited for the response with a gleam of mischief in her eyes.

"I would too. Now, are you going to sing for your parents this evening?"

"Sing? Oh, now if I'd known I was going to have to sing for my supper—" All her family's eyes were on her waiting for the reply.

"Alex, Jo isn't well and she shouldn't be taxing her voice."

"Mom, if I was on my deathbed and you wanted a song, you'd get it."

"Please, don't say things like that, darling. Although, I would love a song," Stella said.

"Then a song you shall have. I'll need a microphone."

"Karen is with her daughter in the office. I'm sure they will find one for you. Al, go ask for your sister."

Jo grinned at her kid brother and slapped him gently down. "I'll go. Al doesn't know what I need. I'll be right back to sing for you."

She sang more than one song and wowed yet another appreciative audience.

†

Jo opened her eyes a fraction and pulled down the blind to the window. She would get some sleep now that the pills were kicking in. She'd call her parents when she arrived at the hotel. She'd promised her dad updates and that was a promise she'd keep from now on. It gave a sense of belonging that she hadn't felt since Thea had left. Maybe this would fill the chasm of her friend's leaving.

†

Feeling guilty for leaving the party early, Thea tried to call Alex and Stella several times but they weren't home. It wasn't surprising. They had received a special surprise when their estranged daughter arrived unexpectedly to make their special evening even more extraordinary.

Her headache had been genuine, especially when she'd cried for an hour before she eventually succumbed to a restless sleep and endless dreams, not one of which she could recall. The party had been a marvelous success, not just for their friends, but also for the small hotel, which had been booked solid for the weekend. As people left today, they remarked on the excellent treatment they had received and promised that they would recommend the hotel to friends. If only a fraction of the platitudes came to anything remotely like a booking, they would be doing very well indeed.

Her mother had stayed on hotel duty until midnight and then joined the party as the night clerk worked until Thea came to work at seven. She felt better for admitting to her mother that she had a problem. Even though she wasn't entirely sure how her mother had taken it, since her mind was so upset at not connecting with Joanna, she could remember little else.

Now it was almost five and her mother was due to come in for the early evening shift. She hoped that her mother wouldn't decide it was time to discuss her problem. Thea wasn't up for it since she was still processing it all.

"You know, my mother always said if I frowned like that, the lines would never go away."

Thea turned and grinned at her mother. "You look like you could do with a strong cup of coffee."

Karen nodded. "I'm still feeling the effects of having drunk far more than I normally do. But, it has been a special occasion and you have to take them when you can."

"I'll get that coffee for you."

"Thanks. I need it to be black and strong to keep me awake. Can't have the guests arriving thinking I'm asleep on the job."

Thea placed a cup of steaming coffee in front of her mother, "I could take your shift for you and you could take the morning one from me one day this week?"

"Thea, you are way too good to me, but this was self-inflicted and therefore it shouldn't stop me working. I think if I'm a little slow it isn't going to be too much of a risk now, is it."

"Okay, but call me if you change your mind. I'm going to have dinner and then watch an old movie."

"I will and last night, Thea...."

"Mom, everything is cool, I promise. Last night I was tired and overreacting."

"Okay, darling, no problem. Go have dinner and I'll call you if I need you, otherwise have yourself a wonderful, relaxing evening." Karen bent to kiss her daughter.

"Good night, Mom, see you tomorrow."

†

Karen watched her daughter go. She had seen Thea's smile waver for a split second of sadness that shone out of her usually bright, green eyes. She didn't intend to discuss the revelation of the night before but wanted to tell her about Alex and Stella's famous daughter. She'd wait for Thea to broach the subject of her sexuality and knew she would when she was ready. Monday was their mother-daughter get together and would catch up on all the gossip during lunch.

†

Thea walked into the office and toward the door to her suite of rooms and wondered if this was all that life had to offer her. Was this it? Was she going to spend every evening leaving work and arriving back in her room alone to have a solitary meal and watch television by herself?

She needed to get on with her life and make a new one just as Joanna obviously had. But had she? She wasn't with Lee anymore but hadn't tried to contact her and that in itself spoke volumes. How could she contact her, since only Alice knew her phone number and where she was living? She couldn't find her if she didn't want to be found. But she did. She was in a self-imposed exile from the one person she longed for in her life. How did she let her life get to be such a mess? Alice would be there in a month and she'd tell her to let Joanna know how to contact her.

†

"Alice, great to see you."

"Great to see you too, Thea, you look wonderful." Alice held Thea away from her. "Look at you, all sophisticated looking. I love your new hair style, too."

"Thanks, you look stunning yourself." Thea hugged Alice again.

"Thanks. Guess what, I have a surprise for you." Alice pointed toward the entrance of the hotel.

For a few moments, Thea held her breath, hoping against hope that someone had answered her prayers. The doors opened and her heart sank as it had so many times before.

"Calum? Calum, how wonderful. What brings you here? Did you travel two together or just meet up?"

"Great to see you, Thea, you look marvelous." The young man grinned, swung Thea up in his arms, and gave her a resounding kiss on her cheek.

"Hey, hey put her down." Alice, laughing, came to them and placed a hand on the leather-clad arm.

Calum turned his gaze to her with what Thea could clearly see was love.

"Don't tell me, I'm being dense here. You two didn't meet up, you came together because you are together?"

"Well, yeah, that about sums it up. I wanted to tell you personally, not in an email or on the phone. This great lug wanted to come, too, so I hope that's okay with you, Thea. I know its short notice and all but—"

"No buts. Wow, this is fantastic news and it couldn't have happened to two better people. Do I get an invite to the wedding?"

"The wedding," Calum squeaked out.

"Where do I put him, Thea, so you and I can go out and catch up?"

Thea left them for a moment to go to reception and speak with her mother.

"Guys, I want you to meet my mother. Mom, this is Alice and Calum, the friends I've spoken about."

"Hi, Alice, Calum, I'm Karen. I hope you have a great time here in our little part of the world. Calum, do you enjoy baseball?"

"Sure, who doesn't?"

"Well, it's your lucky day. I've taken Thea's shift so she can spend time with you, I know you girls and your girl talk. It's normally what Thea and I do at lunch on a Monday. Calum, how would you like to go with my husband and son to see a game? As I'm working and can't go and we have a spare ticket," Karen said.

Thea flashed a grateful look in her mother's direction. Her mother was more of a fan then the men in the family and they had season tickets. It was very generous of her.

"Are you sure they won't mind?"

"No. They would welcome another male and if you are a friend of Thea's, even more so."

"Thanks."

†

Two hours later, Alice watched her friend order their coffee and some pastries from the small cozy café about a block from the hotel.

"Great ambience here, Thea. I can see why you enjoy living here. Your folks, by the way, are really nice people."

"Yes, it's very welcoming. It was little daunting at first, because everyone knows everyone else. I like the small town feel and working with my family is wonderful."

"I didn't think any place like this still existed."

"It exists, Alice, even if it's just in our mind."

The words were wistful and Alice knew Thea well enough to know that she was thinking about something else.

"Truthfully, you look great, Thea. Meeting your folks again and working at the hotel obviously agrees with you."

"Yeah, it does, but I miss you and…other stuff."

"I'm sorry I never told you about Calum, Thea. It happened by chance and I wanted to tell you face to face."

"Oh, God, don't be sorry. That's really wonderful news. I'm so happy for you. He's such a lovely man. Under all that show of brashness, he's like the rest of us, just trying to find a place in life."

"Have you found yours?"

Thea looked to the bakery across the road and Alice followed her eyes. A large bear of a man was talking to his customers with such ease, that she could almost hear his banter. A woman about his age was at his side smiling along with something he apparently said.

"I think maybe I have."

"If you need to think about it, Thea, I'd say there is doubt. Is it Jo?" Sharp eyes glanced at her.

"Of course not. Joanna and I went our separate ways and that's how it will stay, especially now."

Alice gazed into the café latte she had ordered as she pondered that remark. "What do you mean *especially now*?"

"Well, she's famous and wouldn't have time for someone as insignificant as me. Let's face it, she's gone onto better things and doesn't need me now."

"Did she ever say that?"

"No, of course she wouldn't say that. Joanna never said anything like that. It wasn't her way."

"No, it wasn't and you know that." Alice shook her head. "Stalemate, I guess. The both of you are as stubborn as mules," she said under her breath.

"I'm not stubborn. I called her last month but she had left for Europe."

"I take it she never returned your call?"

"She couldn't. I didn't leave a message with her answering service."

"Well, that'll keep the lines of communication open."

"I couldn't take the chance that she wouldn't return my call."

"I see. Maybe it's time you moved on. That's why you left her in the first place. Right?"

"Right."

"Are you trying to convince me or yourself?"

"Both." Thea laughed softly,

"Okay, I'll go with that. Now, tell me why you didn't mention you had a handsome brother?"

"Really, Alice, what would Calum say?"

"Oh, he would smile and say 'typical woman, never satisfied with the man she has'."

"Would he be right?" Thea sipped her cappuccino and smiled.

"No, he wouldn't. Not with me anyway. I think I loved him from the first time I ever saw him on that monster of a bike of his."

"You loved him then? Why didn't you tell me?" Thea's jaw dropped.

"You were my lucky charm, Thea. If he hadn't met you, he would never have noticed me. I tend to blend into the background."

"How can I be lucky for you? I was dating him. Not really, you know but—"

"Hey, don't worry. He told me it was more of a brother sister relationship. Although he did confess that he'd have taken it further if you had allowed it. We've found an understanding about that episode in his life and decided it was fate that led us to one another."

"Am I fate?"

"Yep. Got that in one, Thea. Perhaps for more than Calum and me."

Thea shrugged. "Maybe. We will never know that for sure."

Alice watched as Thea's eyes automatically scanned the street outside the café. "Is there a problem, Thea?"

"I don't know. Some friends have rushed out of their store and gone off like the very devil down the street. It's probably nothing to worry about. I'll ask my mother when we get back."

"If you want to go check it out, it's no problem for me."

"No, it'll wait. What won't wait are all the details of your romance with Calum. You have to tell me everything."

†

"I told her but would she listen? Oh no, stubborn, that's what she is as stubborn as a…mule." Jack paced his plush carpeted office waiting for another call from Antwerp where Jo had been due to go on stage.

"I'm sure she'll be fine, Jack, she's a young woman," said Belinda Orkney.

"How do you know she will? I should have insisted she stay behind until she was fit, not leave, and end up in the hospital. God knows what's wrong with her." Jack turned toward the woman who had run his private office diligently for five years. She rarely commented on anything to do with business dealings or the artists he handled but was always his sounding board.

"Could you have stopped her?" Belinda laid a hand on his arm.

Jack gave a rueful expression as he shook his head. "No. Jo is a loner. She wouldn't have anyone tell her what to do." He shrugged. "Well, maybe one person, but it certainly isn't me." Jack was feeling every one of his fifty-five years as he impatiently waited for a call from the European tour manager in Antwerp who was at the hospital where they had taken Jo.

"Have you contacted her parents? It might be wise if they knew before the media broadcasts it."

"I've informed them and they are on the next flight out of New York to Frankfurt then on to Antwerp."

"Do you want me to inform anyone else?"

Jack stared at the ground for a few moments and then turned to gaze unseeingly out of the window onto the busy street below. "I'd love to but I don't know how."

"Is it Ms. Danvers?

"Why do you say that?" Jack's shoulders stiffened as his personal assistant hit the nail on the head immediately.

"Sometimes you can see the chemistry between two people and believe me, sparks flew when they were together. I felt sorry for them both when I heard Ms. Danvers had left town. It must be scary to aim for the big time without at least a friend you can trust by your side. Jo lost both a friend and manager, not to mention a fiancé, all in the space of a week. Not surprising she's in this state now. The work load she had undertaken was going to tell on her eventually."

"I think she was working non-stop to forget the break-up of her personal life." Jack pursed his lips. "How could I complain? She's revived the company's fortunes single-handedly, but at what price?"

"Want me to try and locate Ms. Danvers and contact her as soon as I do?"

"You can try, but I doubt she wants to be found. Let me know if you do, I would like to inform her personally." He gave his assistant a sly look. "Why do you think it was Ms. Danvers she missed the most, and not Lee Weston?"

"That's easy. Lee works with you and she could have contacted him any time. But Thea hasn't been around since the television show a year ago."

"You're right on the money about that." Jack's phone rang and he rushed to his desk. "Wicklow. Yes, yes, I understand and she's in which hospital? Got that, her parents are on the way.

They'll get there. I'll charter them a flight, if necessary. Thanks, Andre, keep me informed."

Jack sank into his chair, leaned back, and wiped a weary hand across his eyes. "Double pneumonia, exhaustion, and possibly an unknown viral infection," he said. "God help us, what has she been doing to herself?"

"Did Andre say what the prognosis was?" Belinda asked.

"He said the doctors indicated the next forty-eight hours would be critical and that her family should be with her, if possible."

"Good thing you called them, then."

"Strange. Jo called me from the airport before she left and told me if anything happened to her, to call her parents." He snorted. "That was the first time I heard her mention family."

"If you give me their flight information, I'll arrange for someone to meet them there and get them booked on the earliest flight to Antwerp."

"I'll meet them personally," Jack said.

"Okay. I'll see if I can locate Thea."

"Thank you." Jack sat heavily in his chair, worry filling his mind. His gut told him that Thea was the key to Jo's wellbeing in the future. If there was a future for her.

Chapter Twenty-one

Thea returned to the hotel with Alice, saw Calum waiting in the foyer of the hotel, and thought it strange since the game couldn't be over yet.

"Let me check with my mother for a few minutes, Alice. Why don't you check on Calum since it looks like he didn't go to the game. I'll catch up with you two shortly."

Alice nodded and headed toward the young man who had a pensive look on his face. Thea ducked behind the reception desk and went into the office.

"Mom, I was in the café across from the bakery and saw Alex with Stella leaving hastily. Is there a problem that you know of?"

"You know they have a daughter and she surprised them the anniversary party?" Karen stared at her with sad eyes.

"Yes, you told me the night of the anniversary party. I didn't get to meet her because I left early."

"Appears she's critically ill and they've had to leave to be with her. I don't know any details other than that Alex said he would let me know when he knew the facts."

"Oh, no, they will be destroyed. I'm sorry to hear that. I'll pray for them. By the way, I saw Calum. Did he change his mind about going with Grayson and Bradley?"

"He said something came up and that he needed to see you and Alice. He looked kinda shocked. I hope he hasn't had bad news, too."

"I'd better go check." As she headed for the door, the phone pealed out and Karen answered. "Hello. May I ask who's calling? Just a minute." Karen placed her hand on the mouthpiece "Thea, do you know someone named Belinda Orkney? She sounds official?"

"Orkney? No, I don't think so. Orkney? It does ring a bell." Thea concentrated on the name. Where had she heard it before?

"She said it's urgent and wanted to know if you could spare a few minutes. Her boss would like a word with you."

"Her boss? Who's that?"

"Can you tell me the name of your boss? Okay, thank you." Karen placed her hand over the mouthpiece again. "A guy named Jack Wicklow."

Thea paled as she heard the name. Why would Jack want to speak with her?

"Shall I tell her you are out?"

Unable to decide for a moment what to do, Thea looked at her friends, saw shock, and upset mirrored in their eyes looking back at her. As if in slow motion, she turned back to her mother. "I'll take the call."

Thea waited, then heard Jack's voice.

"Thea, I can't believe Belinda found you. Something terrible has happened. Jo is in the hospital in Antwerp and it's critical."

"No, not Joanna," she whispered, her heart breaking. "Where exactly is she? I need to be there."

"I'll have Belinda get you on the next flight out from where you are now. She will email you with the details within a half hour. I'll meet you in Brussels. I'm glad we found you, Thea."

Thea gave him her email details and signed off with tears streaming down her cheeks. "Darling, what's the matter." Karen wrapped her arms around her daughter.

Thea, pulled away, picked up her purse, and then the keys to her mother's car. "I need to be alone for a while," she told her mother and her friends before rushing out of the hotel.

†

"I didn't know that Thea's Joanna was in fact my good friend's daughter and a famous singer. What a small world we live in? Who would have thought my little girl was a friend of Jo Lackerly," Karen said to Alice and Calum who were sharing supper with her.

"Well, Jo wasn't always famous, Mrs. Adams. She and Thea shared an apartment in Nashville and that was before anyone knew the name Jo Lackerly. They were very good friends though and they looked out for each other," Alice explained.

"When you say good friends…how good?" Karen gazed down at her half-eaten chili.

"Oh, they were good friends, Mrs. Adams, believe me," Calum said. "I would know. I courted Thea for a short time…."

Alice put a hand on Calum's sleeve to halt his ramblings. She knew what Thea's mother was asking. "They shared lots of things, Mrs. Adams. I think they had a history that they never talked about, at least not to Calum or me. Jo and Thea were…are very private people. If you are asking if there was a special friendship, then I think there could have been but other pressures got in the way."

Calum glanced first at Alice quizzically then Thea's mother and back to Alice. "I know I'm the token man here, but would someone let me in on what you mean by *special friendship*?"

Alice smiled. Calum was so lovable but so dense at times. When he got confused, he was just like a small boy. "What Mrs. Adams was actually asking, Calum, is did Thea and Jo *love* one another."

"Well, sure they did." Calum's brow knitted.

Karen spluttered a mouthful of coffee. "I see. Did they have a fight? Is that why they split up?"

"Calum, you don't understand," Alice interjected.

"Okay, what don't I understand?" Calum asked in an exasperated tone.

"She wanted to know if Joanna and Thea were lovers." Alice clutched Calum's hand as his face went pale. It was obvious to her that the thought had never crossed his mind.

"We dated, well, kind of. Wouldn't I have known?"

"Not necessarily, Cal. They were very private when it came to their life together. I think we should leave that particular question behind closed doors. If it ever gets answered, our friends will answer it themselves. Shall we all agree on that?" Alice kissed his cheek tenderly before laying her forehead against his.

"I agree," Karen said. "It's an invasion into my daughter's privacy and none of our business. Thea is old enough to have her own life and make her own mistakes and triumphs. Perhaps if I had stuck around when she was a child, I could have helped her understand what she is feeling." She blew out a breath.

"It is what it is, Mrs. Adams, and we can only go forward from here." Alice looked at the woman, who was obviously in distress, and squeezed her hand.

"I'm glad she has you for a friend. You are wise beyond your years."

†

Thea had driven several miles away to a small park where she could walk and settle her shattered emotions. Joanna, her Joanna was in Europe critically ill and she couldn't do anything to help her. No matter how mixed up their lives had become, they were friends and always would be. The connection they shared from the first day they met would last until they each drew their last breaths.

Now, as the tears streamed down her cheeks unchecked, she sank into a bench and gazed out over the park unable to see anything beyond her devastation. Joanna had never been one to dwell on fantasy or romantic notions, being quite hardheaded in that respect. Probably the life she had led in the past, especially with the guys she used to travel with, made her that way. Although with her, she felt that Joanna had started to dream again.

"Then I did a most unforgivable thing and threw it all in her face by leaving so abruptly," she whispered.

Now, I just want to be there. I hope Belinda sends me the information soon.

She'd heard a report on the radio as she drove saying that the singer was in a critical condition and that the next forty-eight hours would be crucial.

There is no guarantee when I do go that anyone will let me within a mile of her—I'm not family.

Would Jack arrange for her to see her friend? She certainly hoped so? Would Joanna survive to come back home? That thought shook her to the core.

Her heart bled for her friend's pain and her own, even if it was of her own making. At the end of the day, she blamed herself. The outcome—Joanna was sick and it was her fault. If she hadn't been so selfish with her own feelings and left her friend behind, none of this would have happened.

Bottom line was she loved—she was in love with Joanna. She had known it in Danvers and battled with it a year ago before leaving Joanna with her new life and love. Now, she was experiencing the same emotion even more profoundly. If all she could do were to say *hi, I'm sorry*, one last time, she would be thankful the rest of her days for that second chance. A year, month, week, day, hour, minute or a second spent with Joanna would be a cherished moment for the rest of her life.

She would go back to the hotel and talk with Alice, Calum and her mother. Her mother would want to know everything. She meant well but she was rather protective and at her age, it really wasn't necessary for anyone to protect her, unless the protector was Joanna. Thea looked up at the sky. It was a clear day without a cloud. Perhaps that was a good omen.

Joanna I love you, please come back to me and this time I promise not to leave you unless you tell me to go.

The email ringtone of her phone beeped.

†

The virtual silence of the sterile room persisted. Only the muted fans whirling inside the monitoring and oxygen machines gave any evidence that life stirred inside the white walled room. Jo's body encased in a summer blue-sky blanket, which topped a pristine white cotton sheet that needed changing every two hours because of her condition. She lay motionless, drugs ensuring that she didn't move any of the drips or other equipment attached to her body.

Nurses monitored the unconscious woman from a station, yards away, along with two other patients who were in the intensive care unit in critical condition.

Her pale features, drawn and haggard, could never be described as the same vibrant singer who days before had been singing to thousands of people at a concert in Hamburg. No one had known of her fatigue, or the number of painkillers she had taken to numb the pain, as the ever-increasing illness gripped her dangerously drained body.

"How is Ms. Lackerly?" Andre Kransky asked, watching Jo through the window.

"Holding her own, sir." The nurse smiled politely at the decidedly unkempt man.

"Thanks, can I go sit with her?" His gentle blue eyes gazed at the bed through the glass window.

"Yes, of course, sir."

"I'll keep an eye on her." Andre had brought her to the hospital and stayed by her side waiting for her family to arrive. He was a bit annoyed at how fast the tabloids found out about her illness. No doubt, someone at the hospital had leaked the information.

"I'm sure you will, sir." This time the nurse smiled.

Andre settled down in the armchair beside the motionless singer's bed and placed his head in his hands pushing distracted fingers through his hair. This had been his first European tour that he had managed on behalf of a named American artist.

"What a disaster." This was definitely not going to do his reputation any favors if people thought he couldn't take care of the star performer. Yet, anyone who knew this particular singer would know how difficult it was to care for her. She never let up or let anyone in. She'd looked so good in Hamburg, a shining star, when really she had been a comet exploding before it fragmented into thousands of tiny pieces.

Jack Wicklow had been shocked but thankfully, not accusing. Her parents were due to arrive in the next two hours and one of them would pick them up at the airport and bring them there personally.

He gazed at the singer, wondering why she hadn't allowed someone to know she was ill. They could have done something far earlier and she wouldn't be in the state she was in now. "Typical American, always thinking they know best." He knew Americans and he loved their work ethic and generosity so he instantly regretted his words.

The popular music world was at this woman's feet. Jo Lackerly had the looks, the voice, and the general manner to make it into super stardom and stay there if she wanted. The country fans were very loyal and she had the added talent of writing her own songs to make her great. If she had a death wish—and it would seem that she might—it wasn't going to be a long career. Funny how so many talented people go off the rails and never get back. These days it was usually drugs but exhausting yourself to the point of death worked equally as well. He'd seen it from time to time in the past fifteen years. When he'd met her, she certainly hadn't come across that way. Funny how people could be so deceptive and never really let anyone know them until it was too late.

It reminded him of a song she had sung three days before, silencing the crowd for a few moments before they burst out in thunderous applause. A good possibility for a record release he'd thought at the time. Now, he wondered how much of the song reflected what she was feeling. The words came back to him… *"A lifetime hidden with borrowed dreams waiting for a special chance."*

As he watched Jo's uneven breathing, he shook his head. Maybe he was being too harsh on the singer. Perhaps her illness came on suddenly. The doctors had indicated that perhaps she had an unknown virus along with pneumonia. He hoped the medications they were using would work.

He stood and placed a comforting hand on the pale skin of Jo's arm before leaving the room. He needed a shower and to change before going to the airport to meet Jack. He doubted Jo's parents would welcome some scruffy individual being in charge of their daughter's care in Europe. They might even blame him for all that had happened to her.

He knew he already did.

†

Thea paced the hotel lobby, a small travel bag ready at her feet. "Hi, Thea."

"Calum, hi. Where's Alice?"

"She's running late. I hoped I could talk you into having a drink with me before you leave and Alice catches up with us." He showed her his boyish smile and took her arm, leading her to the small hotel bar.

"I'll have a beer and a soda with lime for the lady," Calum told the bartender.

"You remembered?"

Calum blinked with a steady smile on his face. "Of course I did, Thea. I'll never forget anything about you."

A faint tinge of red streaked her cheeks at his genuine comment. "I was going to say how pleased I am that you and Alice are a couple. She's a really nice person."

"Yes, she is and a handful too. She has a lively intelligence that leaves me behind at times. Guess I'm going to be a lawyer's husband one day."

"Thanks for the drink." Thea grinned warmly at him. "What about your plans for a career? What are you doing now?"

"I decided that my dad needed a hand. He had a mild heart attack a couple of months back and I decided to give it a chance."

"I'm sorry to hear that, and…?"

"I love it. I think I'll be staying and anyway Alice will need to go to college full time if she wants to be a high flying lawyer."

"What do your parents think of Alice?" How could his parents not like the woman? She had a wonderful personality and worked hard to achieve what she wanted. It was good to hear the young man thinking in terms of Alice being in his life permanently. How love could change all preconceived ideas about what you want in life.

"They think she's marvelous. My mother is already planning the wedding. I haven't told Alice that yet, but I will."

"You love her very much, don't you, Calum?"

"Yes, I do. I confess I was falling for you, Thea, and thought Alice might be my rebound affair. However, the more we went out, the more I didn't want to let her leave. In the end, I realized that she's the woman for me and I'm glad she agrees."

Thea listened to the way he spoke. It was like listening to a poet narrating a love poem.

"What about yourself? Are you dating anyone?" he asked.

"No, too busy here at the hotel and somehow I'm just not interested." Thea glanced down at her drink before quickly placing it to her lips and taking a sip.

A silence stretched between them for a couple of minutes.

"Is it because of Jo?" Calum asked.

Green eyes full of sadness met his compassionate ones. Should she answer truthfully? He was her friend and now it was becoming harder and harder to disguise her feelings for Joanna. "Yes."

"We thought so."

"We?"

"Don't look so surprised, Thea. I think Alice has always known and she hasn't broken any confidences. Your mother and I speculated."

Thea didn't know if she should be mad, upset, or relieved. A fraction of all surged through her body. "You speculated?"

Calum held up a hand. "I'm not trying to upset you, Thea. We all care about you. Your mother started it and we just discussed—"

"My mother!" Now, Thea was mad. This was her personal business, not something for them to discuss behind her back.

"Well, yeah but it wasn't for long, we just—"

Thea got off her bar stool and stalked off toward the office.

Chapter Twenty-two

"Alex, look at our baby," Stella whispered, her throat thick as the tears trailed down her cheeks.

"They are looking after her, darling. She will come back to us. I know she will." The tall man's eyes were brimming with unshed tears.

A nurse busied herself with various tubes, leads, and oxygen.

"Will she?" Stella beseeched the nurse.

"I will have the doctor come in to answer your questions."

Stella closed her eyes as the tears flooded out. She didn't want to break down knowing Joanna would not approve. Her stoic child would frown and shake her head at the show of public emotion. This wasn't public. It was a hospital room where her child lay fighting for her life.

†

Alex stood behind his wife, who was sitting in the armchair clutching their daughter's hand hoping it would bring her back to them. How did she let herself become so ill? Surely others would have seen her condition and not allowed this to happen.

"Mr. and Mrs. Xianthos, I am Charles Dumont, your daughter's physician."

"What can you tell us about her, Doctor?" Alex asked while clutching Stella's hand.

"She isn't responding as well as I'd hoped. The added complication of a virus hasn't helped. We have identified the virus and we can now give her medication to help her body fight it. The next twenty-four hours are crucial. If she doesn't have the strength to fight, her body will soon find it difficult to pull back from the brink."

"She's always been a fighter, Doctor," Alex remarked absently. This wasn't like his Joanna.

"I'm afraid that at the moment, your daughter appears to have given up on the will to live. Now that you are here, I'm hoping that will change. Perhaps if you talked to her, it might help."

"Yes, yes, we will." Alex couldn't stop the tears from falling.

"I'll check back later." The doctor gave them a smile before leaving the ICU room.

"I know that Jo, for all her faults, has always been your favorite, darling." Stella sobbed. "We just found her again. We can't lose her." Stella hugged him close.

After sitting back down in the armchair, Stella took a breath and spoke. "Jo, do you remember when your dad fell into the pond trying to find your favorite fish? What were you, six at the time? My, it was funny wasn't it? I think you.…"

†

Grayson watched the flight take off as he turned to make his way home. Two hours before, both the women in his household had been crying. That wasn't a good sign. Thea's two friends had given him a general overview of what the situation was. Thea was accusing her mother of prying into her private life. A bewildered Karen was upset at the turn of events.

Once both Thea and Karen stopped crying, he managed to get them to talk. After calling an old friend at the airport, he was able to obtain a seat for Karen on the flight Thea was taking to

Brussels. A man named Jack Wicklow would meet them at the airport and escort them to the hospital.

What a day. He looked to the sky for the plane and smiled ruefully. Who would have known that Thea was such a dark horse? Or that the world was such a small place? The parents of Thea's friend were his and Karen's friends. Who would have given him odds on that one?

†

Alex watched Stella sleeping awkwardly beside their daughter. She had spent the past seven hours retelling every childhood story she could remember. Jo hadn't responded in any way. He had a great faith in lots of things and the fates were one of them. They surely haven't decided that the child he loved, lying like a pale shadow of her former self in a hospital bed, was now going to leave the earth for good. He couldn't believe it—wouldn't believe it. He knew that life was beckoning her to fight and fight she must.

He approached one of the nurses at the monitoring station after walking out of the room. "Hello, could you tell me where I might get coffee?"

"There's a machine at the end of the corridor but I'll order anything you require, sir."

Alex smiled briefly, realizing that at a private hospital, nothing was too much for the staff to do for the patients or their visitors.

"Perhaps later. Right now I'll find the machine so I can stretch my legs." He was about to walk away when he turned back. "If anything happens while I'm gone, please, find me."

The nurse smiled at him. "I will."

"Thanks." Waiting was so very hard to do, especially when it was waiting for someone you loved.

†

Karen watched as Thea talked with Jack, confirming their onward journey to Antwerp. It had been a very quiet six-hour flight to Brussels. There was occasional small talk but otherwise silence. Not that she blamed Thea. She didn't. Had it been her, she doubted she would have allowed her to go along. Thea was a very special individual who had keen insight into pain and hurt, along with happiness and love. That was a very rare attribute. Life may have been cruel to her, to have her fall in love with someone who was highly unlikely to return that love. Through it all, her child would be there for the woman regardless of the pain she felt inside.

Unrequited love. What a statement. There were numerous stories, movies, and poems written and screened on just that topic. They were all romantic overtones contrived with happily ever after the goal. With this particular story, would that be the outcome? Karen had her doubts. Once she learned it was Jo, her active research mind came into action.

The woman was a pinup figure for young and old alike and she recalled reading an article that indicated the woman had numerous affairs, all apparently with men. Her last was a broken engagement with a businessman from New York and the picture taken of them together made Karen wonder why. He had been a very handsome guy and they looked happy together in the photo.

How could her daughter expect a woman, who was by all accounts actively heterosexual, change? Then again, Thea didn't want her friend to change. Karen had finally realized why Thea left the singer. How could she live in the same apartment with a woman she loved who would never love her in the same way back? It was like having heartbreak thrown in her face twenty-four-seven.

"Hey, baby, are we set?"

"Yes, Mom. We will be going in a limo and it will take under an hour to get there."

"We'll be there soon, Thea, and you can talk to Joanna and tell her how you feel." Karen placed a comforting arm around her daughter's shoulders and smiled warmly.

Thea looked at her mother with surprise on her face. "I can't do that, Mom. Joanna doesn't care about me that way."

"We'll see, won't we? Faith, darling, faith. That's what it takes, and believe me, I know what I'm talking about."

"You never did tell me the truth about your affair with Grayson when you were with Dad."

"Nope, I never did. Maybe now is the time to tell you." Karen sucked in a breath and exhaled gradually.

"I think I deserve the truth, Mom. Dad's gone. It can't hurt him."

Karen glanced at her daughter in compassion. "No, it can't hurt him, darling, but it can still hurt you."

"Knowing the truth can't hurt any more than not knowing."

"Remember those words when you see Joanna." Karen grinned. "Now about your father...."

†

"You were sticking to your guns and stomped your little feet in a tantrum. We tried to explain to you why we couldn't have a pet since we lived in an apartment. You would have none of that telling us it could share your room—"

"I still want the pony," a groggy voice said.

"Jo? Oh Joanna, you've come back to us.

"Mom? Where am I?" Jo asked.

"You're in a hospital in Antwerp, Belgium," Alex said pressing the call button.

"Papa, why are you here?"

Stella ran a hand across Jo's forehead. "You were so sick and we came immediately."

"I feel like I was run over by a truck." Jo opened her eyes before closing them. "How long?"

"We've been here a day and a half," Alex said.

The door opened and both Stella and Alex looked at it, expecting the nurse.

"Thea, Karen, why are you here?" Stella asked with a confused look on her face.

Jo's eyes opened wide. "Thea? Is Thea here?"

Thea who had tears streaking her cheeks rushed to the bed.

"Why? Why are you here?" Stella asked.

"It's a long story," Karen replied.

Thea was kneeling at the side taking Joanna's hand into hers before placing it to her lips and kissing the palm. She looked lovingly at Joanna, before pushing away the dark bangs that always strayed across her face. "Joanna, what will I do with you?" Thea whispered.

"You're here. I've missed you so," Joanna whispered.

"I'm sorry I left you, but I'm here now and I'm here to stay. I promise."

Stella stood and gave a quizzical expression.

"Let's go outside and I'll explain everything," Karen took Stella's hand and led her and Alex out of the room.

Thea, unaware that the others had left, stared mesmerized at face of the woman she loved. "I love you, Joanna. Isn't it time you talked to me. It's been more than a year?"

She brushed away her tears. "A year when all I wished for was to see - you, speak to you, help you, and be with you. Do you know that every single minute since I left you, I've wanted to come back and be part of your life? I miss you so much, Joanna. Can we start again?"

Joanna just stared at her. "Are you real or am I hallucinating?"

"I'm real. You are all I'll ever want in life. I'm a shell without you, Joanna. Will you let me come home? I'll be your housekeeper, manager, whatever you want, I'll be." She looked at Joanna who had closed her eyes. Unable to stop herself, Thea began sobbing. With her head on the bed, she drenched the blanket with her tears.

Minutes or was it hours, passed before she felt a hand on her hair, stroking it.

"Thea," a croaky voice murmured.

Thea sucked in a breath and looked into the blue eyes watching her.

"You know I hate it when you cry."

"Joanna, I'm sorry."

"I am, too."

"I love you." Thea placed several kisses on Joanna's cheeks. Once the remembered reality that her friend was so very ill broke through her euphoric mist, she let go.

"I feel strange, though."

"Should I get the doctor?"

"I want something…you. I want to talk to you. I've missed you in my life, Thea, so very much. Want to fetch me a drink of water? My mouth feels like sandpaper."

Thea gasped and glanced around. On the side table was a paper cup the size of a large cupcake and a jug of water. Pouring the liquid, she brought a straw to Joanna's lips and smiled as her friend sipped. Thea felt the tears fall again but this time for a different reason. "I've missed you so much, too, Joanna. Will you come home with me and let me take care of you?"

†

Once, what seemed like another lifetime ago, Joanna remembered asking Thea to go with her…now, Thea was asking the same? It wouldn't be the same. How could it? I'm about to hit the top.

"Home?"

"Yes, home with me?"

"Where you are, is my home, Thea. Didn't I ever tell you that?"

"No, you never did." Thea watched as Joanna's eyes shut again.

At that moment, a nurse entered and checked Joanna.

"She's sleeping peacefully now. We called the doctor when she woke. He'll be here shortly."

Thea sighed heavily and then Alex entered the room and engulfed her in a hug that astounded her.

"Thank you, thank you, Thea, for coming. I had no idea you two were friends."

Thea was emotionally drained and laid her head on his broad shoulder and began crying like a baby. She had actually told Joanna she loved her and the singer hadn't flinched at all. Maybe there was hope for them yet.

Chapter Twenty-three

"She's my grandmother, not an ogre."

"Yeah, but she can be ogre like, if she doesn't approve of what she sees or hears."

"Remind you of anyone?"

Thea glanced at the woman by her side. Except for the fact that she tired easily in the evening, no one would know she'd been seriously ill. The doctors in Antwerp had discharged her to a doctor near her parent's home where she was living while convalescing. She was looking good.

"Yeah, both stubborn as mules."

"How can you say that?" Joanna asked in mock seriousness.

"Easy. I lived with you, remember?"

"Yeah, I remember," Joanna replied softly.

Thea negotiated the next bend before responding to the wistful note in the last comment. "When does Jack want you back?"

Jo looked at the houses that lined the suburban area.

"He has a television show lined up for next week and a couple of concerts in Nashville before I go back to Europe and finish the tour."

Thea screeched to a halt and turned to Joanna in astonishment. "You have all this already planned?"

"Well, yeah. I made commitments and gotta make good on them."

"You've been sick. How can they expect you to go back to such a heavy schedule?"

"Gran's place is next block."

"I know where your grandmother lives."

"Good." Jo smirked.

"You never answered me." Thea could feel her cheeks heat up, indicating her mounting anger.

"I'm not good at being my own manager."

"What do you mean? Lee told me that you would get the best."

"I knew he was instrumental in your leaving, Thea. He as much admitted it to me," Joanna growled. "I told him I already had the best."

"What? What do you mean by that? I was your manager." The driveway for Joanna's grandmother was in sight and Thea maneuvered toward it.

"Yeah, and your point would be?"

"You told him you had the best. I was a raw recruit. He told me so."

"His opinion never mattered to me, Thea. You were my manager. I didn't want anyone else. You only had my best interests at heart. I call that the best."

"I did. I would. Always."

"Love you, too, Thea." Joanna turned and winked. "Come on, Gran will be waiting."

Thea was flabbergasted as she watched her friend leave the vehicle. Had Joanna really said those special words? Or was it a flippant retort?

†

"She was wicked."

"Yep, and now you know where I get it from," Joanna said.

They were driving toward home after spending what turned out to be a rather enjoyable dinner with Joanna's grandmother.

"I do. I do. Wow, I never would have expected it."

"You doubt my American roots?"

"No. No, of course not. She's lovely, isn't she? It's a pity she doesn't get on with your dad."

"Yeah, but I don't stress myself about it. It is life, after all, and not everything can have the sugary happy ending. Can it?"

"Guess not."

As Thea drove, the rain pattered on the windshield and she concentrated on the road listening as Jo hummed a tune.

"Sing for me, please, Joanna."

"Sorry, I didn't realize I was humming." Jo smiled self-consciously. "You always make me feel relaxed and content with my lot in life. I'm glad we've had this time together to smooth the cracks in our relationship."

During the weeks of her recuperation, she'd hoped Thea might consider going back to Nashville with her when she went back. The scene was set for Thea to leave without causing a problem at the hotel. Karen had taken on another permanent member of staff to cover for Thea during the long periods of Jo's convalescence. All she had to do was convince Thea that it was the right choice, although she had a good idea that her friend wouldn't object. They hadn't discussed Thea's profession of love at the hospital because it had never seemed the time or place. Perhaps it was time they did.

For the moment, she was happy to sing, if that's what her best friend asked for… "Days are uncertain we don't know what to expect… How I love you each day. Come rain or shine, please be mine," she finished the song.

"That was beautiful, Joanna. Thank you. I haven't heard that one before."

"Just another ditty I wrote recently." She took Thea's hand. "I was thinking there's a club on the east side of town. Wanna go?"

"Are you sure you are well enough?"

"Sure, I am. Pop's not expecting me until midnight at least and it's only nine-thirty."

"Okay. I've never been to any club in town before. Where is it?"

†

Thea had heard about lesbian clubs but she had never been to one, Danvers wasn't exactly broadminded enough to have any club, never mind a lesbian one. Yet here she was with Joanna and it was both exciting and nerve wracking.

"How do you know about this place?"

"Thea, you forget I was brought up here."

"Joanna, this is a lesbian club."

"Yes, it is. Any objections?"

"No. No, of course not."

Joanna winked at her before holding out her hand. Thea took it shyly as they moved toward the bar.

"What do you want to drink?"

"I'll have a club soda. I'm driving, remember."

"We could get a cab later if you want a drink."

"Joanna, please don't forget you've been ill."

"How could I? You keep reminding me," Joanna muttered good-naturedly. "A scotch and a club soda," she told the bartender.

"What does that mean exactly?" Thea frowned, very conscious of the larger hand still holding hers.

Thea looked around and was amazed at the number of women in one room. It was a smorgasbord for the naïve and not so naïve lesbian. It was crowded with women laughing together, others stood watching the dancers, and there were some couples so close you couldn't make out where one woman ended and another began. Here she was with the woman of her dreams, in a place she never in her imagination expected to be, feeling inadequately prepared to deal with the challenge.

"There's a table in that corner." Thea motioned toward a tiny alcove away from the dance floor.

†

Jo's eyes surveyed the area with a sardonic expression.

It was a typical unobtrusive position for Thea. "You couldn't have found us a place any more discreet, I see."

"What do you mean?"

"Nothing. Let's sit and have our drinks."

After settling into the tiny booth, they both looked at the drinks in front of them rather than at one another.

"Where did Lackerly come from? I haven't heard anyone in your family with that last name."

Jo grinned. "I needed a stage name so I flipped opened the phone book, closed my eyes, and put my finger on a name. Lackerly is what came up."

Thea laughed. "What would you have done if it had been something like Butt?"

"Jo Butt, I like the sound of that." Jo's face turned serious. "Thea," she began.

"Jo Xianthos, or should I say, Jo Lackerly. Wow, what a coup in my club." A willowy woman with brown, wavy hair and a wonderful tan stood next to the table.

"You haven't changed, Liz. I see the place is still thriving."

"Why, of course, Jo, and why shouldn't it? Did you think it would nosedive once you stopped performing here?" Liz asked arrogantly.

"Nope, never considered it. I haven't your ego, Liz."

"I see you can still pick them. She's good looking but a little old, don't you think?"

Jo stood to confront the woman. Before she managed to say anything, Thea was suddenly between them.

"Joanna simply has taste," Thea said twinning her fingers with Joanna's fingers.

Jo smiled as she gently squeezed Thea's hand.

"I didn't know you needed anyone to speak for you. Then again, now you're some big shot, aren't you? Do they know about you and your association here, Jo? I think your country fans might be surprised. Even might cause a few raised eyebrows if they knew what I do."

"Are you threatening me?" Jo squared her shoulders. If Liz wanted a cat fight she was up for it. Just.

"Hardly think so. Liz, isn't it. Well, Liz, Joanna doesn't need to pretend anymore, she's earned her freedom in whatever she wants to do. Isn't that right, Joanna?" Thea turned her gaze to Jo.

"That's right." Jo nodded.

†

Joanna's slow seductive voice captured Thea and she lost herself completely in the smoldering eyes.

"Oh, I give up with you, Jo." Liz stalked off in a huff, half dragging the young woman who clutched her arm along with her.

Thea was lost in Joanna's hypnotic gaze as they both returned to their seats in the booth. Slowly, she cleared her throat and smiled. "She wasn't happy with you."

"Nope, she wasn't. Never has been since we were five and I accidentally pushed her off the swing in the park and she scraped her knees. Never has forgiven me."

"Five?" Seeing something from Joanna's childhood was a new facet for Thea. During the weeks of her convalescence, Joanna's parents had regaled her with various anecdotes of the singer's childhood, but this was different.

"Yep, Liz and I grew up in the same neighborhood. You might know her folks, Jim and Ellen Clancy. They own the grocery store. Or at least they did, last I recall."

Thea knew the name of the grocery store was Clancy's but a young couple worked there. "It's still called that but a young couple, Frank and Lisa, run it now."

"Frank? Really? He was so dumb in school."

"Joanna, that's not nice."

"Frank is the youngest son of the Clancy's kids. Dave probably went onto bigger and better things and as you can see…the only daughter wound up here." Joanna winked, slugged back her drink, and waved for another.

"Speaking of which, do I take it you used to perform here?"

"That can be taken in several ways you know," Joanna said laughing.

Thea flushed.

Joanna grinned and picked up Thea's hand.

Thea's blood sizzled at the contact. Maybe her wish wasn't so crazy after all. Joanna had been hugging her more since they came home and tonight there was all the handholding.

Besides, hadn't Liz said something about…?

"The band I was with was close to breaking up and I'd decided to try it on my own. Liz was opening this place and it was a good venue. The ladies appeared to enjoy the performances and I got paid along with fringe benefits."

"Fringe benefits?" *Now this really is getting interesting.*

"Plenty of ways to get hold of drugs and the company of the ladies wasn't bad either."

"Joanna."

"Come on, Thea, I was only messing with you. Look at my track record. It speaks for itself, doesn't it?"

Thea saw the glimmer of amusement in the blue eyes and she smiled. "Messing with me, huh? Well, it's time you settled down with someone you love. That's all I can say, regardless of gender, if they make you happy."

"You make me happy. Should I settle down with you?"

My God, this isn't happening. I'm in a dream. It has to be a dream.

Thea's heartbeat thumped rapidly in her chest as she stared wide-eyed at her friend.

"Drink your drink, Joanna. I need to go home soon, I have to work tomorrow."

†

Jo chuckled at the affronted and flustered expression on Thea's face. She downed the recently delivered drink and stood unsteadily.

Thea was right. I wasn't up to this yet and damn, I so wanted to explore this new relationship with her tonight.

Several women crowded around them, staring at her in disbelief.

"Jo Lackerly. It's Jo Lackerly!" The scream went up from several women and then before she knew it, a mass of bodies had surrounded them.

Thea watched wide-eyed at the crowd.

The screams increased and the number of women converging on the spot multiplied. Jo watched Thea using her smaller frame to sidle her way from around the table and across the huge line, managing to get next to her.

"Need any help?" Thea grabbed her hand.

Jo had never needed help more than she did at that moment. The next words that passed Thea's lips astounded her.

"Hey, ladies, she's mine. If you want her autograph, see the owner and maybe she might get Jo to perform one evening, if you let her alone, now."

A rousing cheer went up as the crowd turned toward Liz. A few remained but soon disappeared as Thea glared at them. Grasping Jo's hand tighter, she led her toward the exit.

Once outside the building, they both took in a gulp of air before glancing at one another and bursting out laughing.

"I was thinking that maybe when I went back to Nashville, I could rely on you being my manager again?"

Thea looked surprised and remained silent.

Jo assumed her invitation was unwanted and shrugged, feeling like the weight of the world was on her shoulders. "I guess that's selfish of me. You have a new life and you're catching up with your long lost family. I can't expect you to—"

"Joanna, shut up your babbling." Thea giggled.

Jo knew that her face showed astonishment at the comment.

"You do know that we made a great team. Right?"

Jo's face beamed as she saw the laughter and warmth filling Thea's features. She'd so missed this friendship and connection that had intensified during the past few weeks. A bubble inside her chest wanted to burst whenever she made Thea smile. How could she let her go now that she knew what she meant to her life?

"Yeah, we did and we can go onto greater things together in the future. What do you say?"

†

Thea knew that life with Joanna might not be all sunshine and roses, quite the opposite, probably. However, they had a bond that when broken bled them both to the point of soul death. Who knew what life held and how fate would mete out the years? All she knew was that, in the year that Joanna wasn't in her life, she'd merely existed and it had taken a near fatal illness to bring her to her senses. Now, she had a family and a home that she could come back to whenever she wanted.

Thea knew in her heart that the only place she wanted, no needed to be, was beside Joanna. The woman she loved with every fiber of her being. If all life offered her were a deep friendship, she would take it and be eternally grateful. After all, how many people could boast such a relationship in their lives and know it would stand the test of time.

"You need a protector," Thea stated.

"Me?" Joanna blinked rapidly at Thea.

"Yes, you." Thea had been relieved that her ruse in the club had gone as well as it had. Anything could have happened and Joanna was still frail, even if she didn't believe it.

"Don't I have one already? You?"

Their glances locked and they smiled simultaneously.

"I guess you have. You always did, as you are mine."

"Improbable protectors."

"Yep, improbable, but a wonderful team." Thea knew that they both felt the rightness of the situation. Smiling, she settled inside the car for the drive home. "Let's get you home."

†

Thea pulled the car to the sidewalk and looked at Joanna. She'd barely been able to keep her eyes open during the short journey.

"Joanna, we're here," Thea said, as she gently shook Joanna's arm.

"What? Here? Where…oh, right. Sorry. I must have dozed off. What a terrible companion I am," Joanna mumbled, as she ran her hand through her hair.

"Never terrible. Not with me, anyway." Thea took her hand away from Joanna's arm.

Joanna snaked out a hand and held their hands entwined in the air. "I do love you, Thea."

Thea gasped.

"Yeah, I know my timing, as always, sucks. I'm way too tired to have a meaningful conversation about us right now but I want to. In fact, I insist.

Chapter Twenty-four

Jack shook his graying head at the door that had been slammed hard behind the woman who had been rehearsing at the studio. He pulled at his chin in contemplation of what to do next before giving the sound mixer a rueful look.

"She never used to be this touchy about her stuff, Jack. This is the fourth session she's run out on us."

"You know Jo, she's a perfectionist. If it isn't right to her, she will go through it again and again until she's satisfied, Dave. I call that true professionalism. Has Steve finished with our new songbird?"

"Later today. Tandy is not only a great looking babe, but she's talented too. He told me she did everything top speed, with no rehearsal time."

The sigh from the man at the console made Jack smile. Their new signer was little more than a fresh-faced kid out of high school, but she could sure belt out a tune. When Jo was out of commission for months, they'd needed the new blood.

"Unlike our current songbird, huh? I'll talk with her and find out what the trouble is." Jack smiled at the sound mixer and left the small recording studio.

Jo was acting way out of character. She had been back in harness for a month now and still hadn't cut her first recording in the studio. At first, she'd wanted rehearsal after rehearsal then said she was as ready as she would ever be and they had planned to record at least three tracks for the new album. To date they hadn't managed to keep her in the studio to mix one track. At the rate it was going, it would be a year before they had sufficient tracks for a release. What puzzled him was what was wrong with her.

Yes, she'd been sick and the recovery had taken longer than he expected. He had only himself to blame for that. He'd insisted she take the time out for as long as she wanted. She had. He'd been supremely confident though that if she jumped right back on the horse that had thrown her, there wouldn't be a problem. Her only album release had gone platinum with great street appeal and had narrowly missed a top award. In this industry things moved on and he hated to say it, but the youngsters were piling up behind her to take her crown. Tandy being one of them.

Turning the corner along a short corridor, he saw the woman he'd been thinking about and smiled wryly. She had all the makings of a superstar who could remain indefinitely in the industry along with the guts and work ethic to see it through to the end. The question—did she want it badly enough? The first time he'd met her, he'd thought so. Now he wasn't so sure. She no longer had the drive she'd had the first year. Something else had become more important to her or maybe being near death had changed her. He didn't know what it was or how to find out. Jo wasn't exactly the most gregarious person when it came to her life.

"Hi, Jo, I was in the mixing room for that last session. It looked like things were going well." The attractive woman looked at him with a suspicious glint in her eyes.

"Yeah, so why did I leave? I want a new session man," Jo replied imperiously.

"Dave is one of the best, Jo, and you know it. Have you thought that perhaps—"

"Perhaps?" She lifted her eyes and stared at him.

"Perhaps it's you. It's been a while, you know, maybe you've become accustomed to the soft life. Not that I blame you, Jo. Hard work, especially the way you go about things, must take its toll. Look how sick it made you," Jack said, standing his ground.

Take Me As I Am

"Are you saying I've passed my best?" Jo asked caustically.

"Not me, Jo. Now others.... Want to prove them wrong?"

"Do I need to prove anything? The first album went platinum, didn't it?"

"Sure. However, you need at least two to ensure that the pundits out there don't think you're a one hit wonder. Anyway, don't you want to be singing to the grandkids and embarrassing the hell out of them?" Jack grinned, placing his arm about her shoulders in a friendly fashion.

"I'll do what's in my contract. If you want more you'll have to negotiate again." Jo's words were full of bravado.

Jack smiled. "I'll look forward to that. When do I get to meet your new manager? I take it you did finally decide to replace Ms. Danvers?"

†

"I didn't. Thea decided that she wanted to stay on the job. She will be here tomorrow to take up the role full time." Jo didn't care what people thought. It didn't matter to her. All that did matter was that Thea was on her way. She missed her so badly that it was affecting her recording sessions.

"I will have the pleasure of negotiating with Ms. Danvers again? Why, thank you, Jo, that's a wonderful gift."

Jo glanced at him sharply. What did that mean? Was he interested in Thea? He was too old. Then again, wasn't that bastard banker too old and he'd been downright ugly to boot.

She was once again deciding Thea's best interests. *Damn.* She'd spent too long with Thea when she was sick. That had to be the reason.

"I'll bring her here before tomorrow's session. But now, I'm going to call it a day. I have things to do. Do you mind?"

"No problem, Jo. Let's say we meet in the studio at...?"

Jo mulled the unsaid question for a moment. Thea was due in town in just a couple of hours. Tomorrow at ten would be good. "Ten okay with you, Jack?"

"Perfect if it's ten in the morning, otherwise, at night isn't an option. Not tomorrow anyway."

"Morning it is, Jack." Jo laughed for the first time since she left her hometown a month ago. "Will you apologize to Dave for me? Tell him I'll make up for my attitude tomorrow, I promise."

"Yeah. He'll forgive you, but I'd like to see a track completed, if you don't mind." Jack raised his eyebrows.

"How about two tracks or more?" All Jo heard was his chuckle of approval as she opened the door and hit the glare of the afternoon sunlight.

Things hadn't been going well, that was true. Not well at all. Her mind was back in her old hometown, where her family was, but more importantly, where Thea was. They'd both arranged to come back here together. Unfortunately, Bradley had a relapse of his earlier pneumonia and Thea had stayed behind to look after the family business, vowing to follow as soon as she could. True to her word, she was on her way. Bradley was finally out of the hospital and Thea's mother said everything was under control and that she should follow Joanna.

†

"I can't believe this, Joanna. It is spectacular."

"Yeah? See, I have the table here by the door for you. All you need do is fill it with flowers like you used to."

"You kept it?" Thea asked in amazement.

"Yes, of course I did."

Thea looked at Joanna's face. She was happy. The glow about her brightened the spacious hallway where they stood. At the same time, she felt an equal emotion. Joanna had always made her feel special, even if she never knew she did, by simply walking into the room. All that mattered was that they were together and the apartment was superb. Okay, not as friendly as the one they had originally, though they had a wonderful view of the Cumberland River to compensate.

"You do like it, don't you, Thea?" Joanna gave her friend a pensive look. "Okay, spit it out, what's wrong?"

"Nothing's wrong. Nothing at all. Everything is perfect. Come on, Joanna, and show me around the rest of the place." Thea unconsciously reached out and gently touched the lines of a frown that had appeared on Joanna's forehead.

A relieved expression replaced the frown and Joanna grinned happily. She took Thea's hand and literally dragged her around the massive apartment.

"Oh, Joanna, this place is fantastic."

†

Jo finally stopped outside one room smiling broadly before opening the door with a flourish, "Your very own boudoir, Madame. I hope you like it."

Thea moved forward with a tentative glance at the room.

"It won't bite you, Thea, I promise." Jo watched from the doorway, as Thea walked inside like a dreamer in a wonderland. Thea's awed expression engulfed Jo in a euphoria she'd never felt before.

"Look at all the carnations of every color." Thea held her hand to her mouth. "You remembered."

"Of course I did. I remember everything about you."

Thea smiled and ran her fingers over the coverlet on the bed that had a carnation embellished in the center.

"The furnishings are so unlike the rest of the house." She looked at Jo. "You picked it all out just for me, didn't you?"

Jo nodded. She'd spent hours deciding on the delicate, ornate furniture that reflected Thea in so many ways. It was her friend's domain and she hoped it would make her want to stay. Now she stood silently by the door, with a lump in her throat, watching Thea's every move.

Thea spun around, her face beaming with pleasure, "I don't know what to say, Joanna. It's incredible and the flowers... did you go to the market to select all these yourself?"

"Nope, didn't have the time, but I did ask for every single color possible." A sheepish look traveled across her face. "Do you like the room? I did choose the furniture myself and the salesperson thought I was crazy."

"What, did they think that you'd gone all delicately feminine on them?"

"Something like that." Jo pursed her lips. "Not that I cared. The only thing that matters to me is if you like it. Do you?" Jo asked anxiously.

A tender expression filled Thea's beautiful face. "I love it. You knew I would, that's what makes it so special. Thank you, Joanna, for being so thoughtful." She looked around the room again. "It feels like a home." Thea hugged her tight. "Anyone ever tell you that you are wonderful?"

Jo wrapped her arms around Thea and breathed in her clean, fresh scent. "Only you. I missed you, Thea. You don't know how glad I am that you're here. I need you."

"I missed you too. Have you been busy?"

"Oh, I think you should ask Jack and my sound man Dave about that." Jo released Thea, walked to the French doors that opened to a balcony, and went outside, settling against the railing, looking pensively out at the river.

"Do you want to talk about it?"

"Not really. Maybe another day." Jo let out a long sigh.

"That's cool. It's a beautiful view. Are you sure I haven't stolen the master bedroom from you?"

Jo smiled slowly. Thea was easing the tension she felt ever since arriving back in Nashville. She knew a great part of it had been the separation from Thea, but there was something more and she wasn't exactly sure what it was. Her recording sessions were disastrous, due mainly to her inability to concentrate.

"Well, it might be the master in some people's eyes, but to be honest I wanted the one next to this one. It has a different view—part water and part city. It helps the muse when I'm writing my songs."

"Ah, that means we can wave at one another from our balconies during breakfast." Thea giggled. "It will be like living in a hotel."

"I'd rather sit directly opposite you and bore you with my up and coming morning. Incidentally, do you want to accompany me to the studio tomorrow? Jack would like a word or two with you."

"I'd love to. I need to have a word or two with him, too. I can't have my girl working so hard that she gets sick again."

They stood side by side drinking in the beautiful tranquil view and the closeness of one another's company once more.

†

Jack entered the studio where Jo was working and prayed she was still there. The tired old expression *music to my ears* rang out when he heard her remarkable voice singing out as powerful as ever. He grinned as he looked around the studio, noticing that today the singer wasn't alone with the sound mixer.

Thea Danvers was standing at the back of the booth, watching every move Jo made with a gentle, awed expression on her face. *Bingo.* He now had his answer to the dilemma of why Jo had been so obstinate lately. Funny how the smallest packages always pack a tremendous punch.

He walked deeper into the studio, giving a thumb up sign to the technician before sitting down next to Thea.

"Great to see you again, T. I hear you are staying this time." He smiled warmly at the woman.

"Nice to see you again, Jack. I'll be around for as long as she needs me." Thea smiled at him before he saw her eyes track back to the singer. "This song is great, isn't it? Joanna hasn't lost her touch at all. She's marvelous."

"Yes, she is and this is a great song." Jack turned his attention to the singer behind the glass. "She's in great form. I'm glad you're back. She tended to be a lost soul since she's been back." He looked at Thea. "Actually she's been lost for a very long time," he said quietly. "I know all that will change, now that you are here. Whether she knows it or not she needs you here."

"Was she so bad?" As the strains of the music closed, Thea grinned before turning back to him. "Joanna said it was okay to ask about anything and this is a good place to start."

"Bad?" Jack shook his head. "Dave, was our Jo a bad girl during the last few weeks?"

Dave turned to them and gave a rueful look of agreement. "That word doesn't cover it, boss, as well you know. Mind, I don't know what you did coming back here, Thea, but it works. You should be part of the deal every time she steps into the studio."

He turned his attention back to the mixing controls.

"I see. What happened, Jack?" Thea asked.

"Nothing happened. That was the problem. She couldn't settle. You know Jo. She loves to do her sessions, but not this time. We couldn't get her to stay in the studio long enough. I think that's all in the past now, don't you?" He smiled before standing to go and talk to Jo from the console. "Lackerly, you're the star here again. Don't let me see you slacking, okay?"

Jo turned her expressive eyes that held a sliver of ice to the man before giving him a slight smile. "Yeah, yeah, until the next young star struck wonder comes through your door."

"I think you need to look in the mirror, Jo. I don't think you have ever been that young, even if you could prove it with an ID."

Thea listened to the banter between the two of them and smiled. This was looking great. She knew Joanna enjoyed working for the record company and particularly her relationship with Jack. She certainly wouldn't let him speak like that if she didn't. It was more a family affair at Trigon records than a multimillion-dollar business and she knew they were doing well or the large outfit in New York City wouldn't have a share in it. Lee Weston's face floated across her mind. The man had dealt her a body blow on their last conversation, one that cemented her decision to walk away from Joanna. In the end, she won out, for Joanna was here and wanted her in her life, not him.

"Thea, want to go to my office and talk turkey or better yet, have a cup of coffee and catch up?" Jack asked.

"I'm sorry, Jack, I was miles away. Sure, we can do that. I'd love some tea. Though I did promise Joanna I'd stay for the session." Her eyes traveled the singer strumming on her guitar, now in a world of her own as she concentrated on her performance.

"If I know that woman, she won't even know we've gone and I promise to have you back by lunch, in time to make her take a break. How does that sound to you?"

"Now I know why Joanna likes you so much." Thea was grinning, as she glanced once more at Joanna. She'd be back when the singer actually put the track down on tape.

"You do, do you, young lady? Well, don't think I'm not as sharp as a knife at the negotiating table just because I like her, too." He took her arm and led her out of the studio toward his office.

†

An hour later, the meeting with Jack was finished. It had gone surprisingly quickly and fruitfully. He appreciated that the grueling pace Joanna had set herself the year before shouldn't happen again. Not only for her, but also for the musicians who were her team. He told her that they had complained bitterly on the last leg of the American tour.

Now Thea was standing in the studio listening to the intro of Joanna's guitar. After entering the studio, she was surprised to see an additional man at the mixing board along with a very young woman—maybe child would be a better description—watching Joanna with an expression of concentration and devotion.

Thea sat on the sofa silently after Dave signaled her to be quiet when she entered the room. They were about to record and she knew better than to make a sound. Introductions to the girl could take place later. Her eyes traveled to Joanna, who was about to begin the cut. The plaintive words filled the room… "*I'll never doubt it when they say angels have wings.*"

For a few moments, after she finished, there was a marked silence in the room before a round of applause heralded another masterpiece completed. They had cut two songs and it was only lunch. Thea watched Joanna take in the recognition of her skills before seeing the young woman sitting at the mixer station room grab for one of the mixer's mics.

"You rock," she shouted. The kid sounded like she had a crush on Joanna and Thea speculated that she probably did.

The young man, who she vaguely recalled from her first time here in the studios with Joanna, stood and pushed the young woman away from the mic. "We got that wrapped. Great work, Jo. I'm glad to see you back in your best form. Let's take a break for lunch."

He waved and turned to the younger woman in the room then his eyes tracked to Thea smiling in her direction.

"Hi, Thea, isn't it?" The young man grinned holding out his hand that Thea shook returning his friendly smile.

"Yes, sorry forgive me, but..." Thea shrugged unable to recall his name.

"Steve, Steve Mitchell, we met about a year ago. However, I have the advantage, Jo talks about you all the time."

"Oh, you're Thea?"

The young woman in the studio stared at her arrogantly, or so Thea thought. Kids, brimming with confidence, did that these days. "Yes, I am. You would be?"

The girl looked at her and obviously had a few internal thoughts that she might or might not share. It all depended on how arrogant she was. Thea bemusedly watched the expression flitter across her face.

"Tandy Radnor. I'm the next queen of country. Isn't that right, boys?"

The two men in the room shrugged and smiled at Thea. Tandy was young, arrogant and probably equally talented, with the ego to go with it. Thea knew the men wouldn't say anything. Who knew, in the future she might be just that and that future could be tomorrow. This business was like that. Pondering what to say next, she was relieved when Joanna walked through the door and the atmosphere changed dramatically.

"Jo, that was fab. Are you going to let me have that song for my album? You promised me one. Remember? And I want that one."

Yep, she was a precocious kid, all right. Wonder if she is out of diapers yet.

Smiling at the talented woman-child, Jo tweaked her nose before winking at her. "Not that song, kid. I'll let you know tomorrow which one." Joanna was still smiling happily, as she turned to Thea. Her eyes shimmered with excitement. "Did you get back in time to hear the last one, Thea?"

So, she did notice I wasn't here. "Yeah I did. Your dad is going to love that one."

"You do know that my dad loves every song I sing, don't you. Always has, since I was a small girl. It comes with the territory. If I sang ten notes off key, he'd still love it." Joanna grinned. "He loves me."

Thea wanted so badly to say *I love you too*, but held back the emotion. It wasn't the right place or company. "Want to go out for lunch?"

"Absolutely," Jo responded, running a hand around her neck. "I feel all grimy and I really need a shower, but time is of the essence, now that I'm in the flow."

"Shall we all go to lunch?" Tandy broke into their conversation. "I'm at a loose end at the moment. Only a few bits and pieces to handle, and I can do that later. Right, Stevie?"

"Whatever you say, Tandy."

Thea wasn't happy at having to share her precious lunch hour time with Joanna with the young girl. If it was selfish to want Joanna to herself, she didn't care.

Joanna wiped a hand across her forehead. "Not today. Thea and I need to talk business since she's my manager too. I want a shower, so you go ahead and we'll have a rain check on lunch."

The pout on Tandy's lips told everyone that she wasn't happy. She gave them all a glare and childishly rushed out of the room, slamming the door behind her.

"I guess I get to calm down the prima donna, huh?" Steve muttered before leaving the room.

"Wow, she's got a temper. Glad Steve's on her control panel and not me," Dave remarked before turning his attention to the computer data blinking at him.

"Yeah, you probably were wishing it the other way around yesterday." Joanna was grinning as they left the room.

"Why don't you go ahead and take that shower and I'll find us some sandwiches and a cool drink. We can eat in today, if that is okay with you." Thea knew she'd said the right thing when Joanna turned to her nodding with a grateful smile on her face.

"Whatever would I do without you?" Joanna smiled indulgently.

"Probably get sick again, which isn't going to happen. I'll catch up with you in your room in half an hour tops."

"You got it. Don't get lost." The singer practically bounced down the corridor toward her room. Thea was happy indulging in all kinds of dreams as she went toward the exit in search of lunch.

†

Lounging on one of the large sofas in the main living area, Jo watched Thea arranging a display of flowers that, according to her, the florist totally ruined. Unable to control a wicked smile, Jo wondered how she'd explain to one of the most prestigious florists in Nashville that they had screwed up. "Have you ever thought of taking up arranging displays?"

Thea glanced over her shoulder, smiling. "Once, back at home when I thought we had the money."

Jo heard the wistful tone and it sparked a few ideas that might come into fruition in the future. Tomorrow, they were embarking on their first tour since her illness a year ago. The last three months had found her working in the studio to produce material for another album. They agreed on three months on the road prior to cutting the final tracks. That way it would whet the appetite of anyone with any doubt about Joanna having been an overnight sensation.

"Thought so. Well, who knows what you might achieve in the future. For now, I'm happy that you want to stick around as my manager." Jo gave Thea and infectious grin.

†

Thea felt the blood racing in her veins at the sight. Sometimes it took all her energy not to rush into Joanna's arms and confess her undying love, but she managed to hold back the stampeding emotions. "Good, because I have no intention of letting you to go off on tour alone again."

"That's my girl." Jo flashed another wonderful smile.

Thea's stomach was rushing up and down like a roller coaster. "Why don't you go to bed and have an early night, it will be the last you get for weeks. I'll prepare everything except your clothes for the morning." Thea smiled tenderly, watching Joanna stifle a yawn. She never let go even though she was exhausted.

"You are way too good to me, Thea, thanks. I must admit I'm rather tired. I'll see you in the morning. Are you excited?" Joanna studied her intently. "You know that a tour is hard work and not as glamorous as many think. For me it has its compensations in the adrenaline rush I get going out on the stage." She lifted one shoulder. "But you won't be going on stage so it might not be much fun for you."

Thea laughed. "I'm probably more excited than you are at the prospect. It's all new to me and is another adventure we can share." Thea wrapped her arms around her waist. "It is a part of your life that I've never shared with you so excited doesn't begin to cover it."

Thea walked to her and gave Joanna a light hug. "Now, go to bed and I'll see you in the morning."

Joanna stretched in a weary, but relaxed way before grinning. "Good night. Tomorrow our new journey will begin."

"Good night," Thea whispered as she watched Joanna leave. She blew out a large sigh wondering if Joanna knew how sexy she was when she stretched like that. The thought made Thea shiver in a wonderful way. She sat down at the desk and flicked over the tour dates and locations. Her eyes traveled across the pages to the final gig and it struck her that they would be within one-hundred-fifty miles of Danvers.

How ironic is that? She wondered if Joanna realized that.

Maybe she should send Lucy and John-Henry free tickets for the show. Better yet, she'd invite them to dinner and the show. After all, they had been the catalyst to them both being in such a fortunate situation. Thea smiled, recalling her mother telling her that Lucy had reported in on a regular basis during the years as she was growing up.

Her thoughts turned to Daisy, whom she knew wouldn't travel on her own. Maybe if the others were going, she would agree to attend the concert. Picking up her address book, she found the first of the three numbers and tapped the number on the dial pad.

It will be fun and I know Joanna won't mind. In fact, she will be happy to see them, especially John-Henry.

"Hi, Lucy, this is Thea...."

†

"How are we doing, Pete?" Thea asked the senior roadie who was arranging the final sound position of the band's equipment.

"Great, Thea. All we need now is Jo, for her sound check, and we will be right on the button tonight."

The large man had frightened Thea the first time she had seen him. Not only was he gigantic, but he was a mass of tattoos, some sinister in design. Her first thought had been that he was a Hell's Angel. Joanna had laughed at the thought and had vouched for the man, going so far as to say that if Thea was her improbable protector, Pete was certainly her credible one. True to her friend's prediction, he was a gentle giant to both she and Joanna. Others had a harder time especially those that tried to get too close to the singer when she was on stage.

"Ready, Pete?" Joanna asked, entering the stage area from the left wing.

Thea had found that Joanna was superstitious about which side she entered the stage. It had made her laugh at the absurdity of the situation. Who would have thought the singer would have those kinds of superstitions? She did and in a big way. That, along with sound checks, were the only things that made Joanna temperamental. Thea overheard Pete saying that Joanna was particularly ill tempered if they didn't adhere to her schedule. Woe to anyone who was late. Thea was certain he'd live to regret it if it happened more than once.

"Yep, want me to drag out the band?" He didn't wait for her nod, calling the band to the stage.

"Will you sit at the back for me, Thea, as I go through the paces?" Joanna asked absently. Though Thea thought it wouldn't matter if she were there or not, the sound mixer knew his profession very well, the fact that Joanna did that small courtesy made her feel wanted. That was all that mattered.

"Sure, break a leg."

An indulgent grin passed across Joanna's features and it made her heart soar.

Half an hour later they were finishing the last song and Thea gave thumbs up while returning to the stage where Joanna and the band stood talking about the various songs for that evening. Joanna was in her element and as Thea watched her, she knew that everything about the entertaining regime was in the singer's blood. There had been times when Thea wondered what Joanna would do if she hadn't been in a position to go back to her singing career.

The answer came immediately. She would make a great manager or better yet, songwriter. She rarely sang other people's compositions. Before they'd left, Joanna had given her newest song to the new kid on the block, as Thea was apt to call Tandy Radnor. There was no doubt in anyone's mind that the young woman would do it justice and Jack was predicting a hit. Joanna had given Thea a *who knows in this industry* shrug, admitting that she expected Tandy to push it up the charts if she chose to release it.

"Paul, slow the tempo down on the drums a little for Frank to cut in half way through that last song. I want the audience to hear the subtleness of the piano. He's worked hard on that difficult melody."

"You got it, Jo. Anything else?" Paul accepted the singer's change without a word.

Thea speculated that this was because Joanna knew her craft and didn't act like a bitchy superstar like some other singers she'd heard about.

Joanna grinned. "Be here by seven sharp. I know what you are like with the ladies, Paul." The man grinned back at her and winked.

Thea heard the tinkle of the piano keys and Frank signaled her to come and sit beside him.

"Excuse me, Jo. Do you have a minute? I'd like to discuss an idea I have for adding an extra two minutes to the instrumental part of 'Lonely' I've been working on it and I think it will add a whole new dimension to the song." Joanna looked at Lenny, the bass guitar player and scratched her head. "That would give me a little extra time to take a breather before I sing again and the three songs before it are intense. Let's hear what you have."

Thea knew that Joanna wouldn't let anything get by without her approval. The bass player ran his fingers cross the frets

Take Me As I Am

while Joanna listened with a smile on her face. "That's amazing and I know it will work. Okay, everyone, let's go through "Lonely" with this new arrangement. Don't want to get on the stage and look like we don't know what we are doing."

The band all nodded and took up their instruments again.

When they were finished and the band left, Joanna was concentrating on the sheaves of paper in her hand.

The two people, still sitting on the piano bench, looked at one another.

"I think she's forgotten us," Thea whispered conspiratorially to the lanky man at the piano.

"Could be, want to go for a coffee? I know a great place—"

"Frank, Lenny's new addition won't be a problem, will it?" Blue eyes captured the man's startled eyes.

"Not me, Jo. It sounded like you and the band nailed it in one. Do you want me to speak with him and get him to do a few more sessions before we go on tonight?"

"No, it's good."

Frank stood, smiling warmly at Thea and mouthing *rain check* as he left the stage.

Thea leaned on her elbows watching Joanna and a tender smile came to her lips.

Joanna lifted her head, catching Thea's unabashed smile and gave her a gentle indulgent look. "Hi there, want to share a light lunch with me?"

What a question. The singer's idea of a light lunch was a piece of rye bread and a gallon of coffee. Thea's, on the other hand, was a lovely colorful salad and a pot of aromatic tea.

"Do you need to ask if I'm hungry?"

Jo grinned and stuffed the music sheets in the back pocket of her jeans. "Thought so, let's go and you can tell me what you thought of the practice session."

"I will and thank you."

"For what?"

"For my not having to make up an excuse to not have coffee with Frank."

"I see the way he looks at you. I think he has a crush on you." Joanna shrugged. "Can't blame him."

Thea grinned, feeling a warmth course through her body at the softly spoken words.

Chapter Twenty-five

John-Henry grinned at the two women arguing in a controlled and quiet manner in the far corner of the café. He wondered why women always did that, bringing up all the reasons why they couldn't possibly do something when he knew they would do it anyway. Draining his coffee cup, he decided now was a good time to intervene, hoping he wouldn't get caught in any of the fallout.

"Lucy, I'd like a refill please." The low voice of the man had the owner of the café, Lucy, and her sparring partner, Daisy glancing at him.

"Sure." Lucy walked to the freshly made brew at the other end of the counter.

"How are you today, Daisy?" John-Henry asked Daisy.

The old woman scowled. "I'll be fine as soon as our stubborn friend there tells me why it's important I go to St Louis to see a concert when she won't tell me who it is performing." Daisy gave Lucy a hard glance.

John-Henry smiled. Thea had talked with him and Lucy and they all agreed that it would be better to surprise Daisy. There was no doubt in any of their minds that Daisy would bring up all kinds of excuses for not going, if she knew the truth. Daisy didn't have a kind word to say about Karen when Lucy inadvertently let it slip that Thea had been living with her once estranged mother.

"Will it help if I say I'm going too, as your chaperone?"

"Chaperone? Why would Lucy and I need one of those? We are both more than able to take care of ourselves. What is it with men who think women can't go into big cities and be safe? I'll have you know that I've been to Washington DC on my own, three times." Daisy's annoyance changed to focus entirely on him.

"Well, I wouldn't exactly—"

"Here you go, John-Henry. Now, Daisy, let's discuss this one more time, shall we? I have tickets for this concert and I want you to..."

"Yes, I know I'm coming. When are you picking me up?" Daisy asked.

John-Henry looked at Lucy and saw her shocked expression that he suspected mirrored his own.

"Yeah, no problem. I'll call for you around one, if that is okay. We need to go through security and our flight leaves at three thirty. It is a short flight and we will arrive in St. Louis in time for dinner at—"

"Spare me the details, Lucy, I have things to do. My hair, for one. I'll talk with you both later. Why couldn't you have told me earlier? I'll have to arrange something special now with Jenny...." Daisy was muttering to herself as she left the café.

Lucy stood behind the counter with her jaw dropping. "I spent the best part of an hour trying to talk her into going and now all of a sudden she has a change of heart. What did you say to her?"

"Me? Nothing, I swear. All I said was maybe she needed a chaperone or something along those lines."

"Oh, that's bad, John-Henry." Lucy chuckled. "You know how independent she is."

John-Henry nodded and winked.

"Thea said she'd meet us at the airport around five and take us to dinner. Jo will be too busy at that time, but after the concert, we're going backstage and then onto a late supper. She said Jo needs sustenance after a concert. Is that what she told you?" Lucy asked.

"Yep, pretty much. Although, Thea did say I could go backstage and watch from the right wing. She said it won't spoil the surprise for Jo since she never appears on stage from the right."

"Are you going to do that?"

"Hell, yes. It's been a long time since I've seen the behind the scenes action."

"Oh, no." Lucy's eyes widened. "That means you are leaving me with Daisy. I hope she's not going to be one of those unforgiving old women who do nothing but moan after she finds out we deceived her." Lucy pulled at her bottom lip.

"We haven't deceived her, Lucy, merely omitted all the facts. That sounds much better, don't you think?"

"You know exactly what to say, John-Henry. How about a piece of my apple pie? It's on the house."

"Now, that's something I won't turn down. Thank you, Lucy."

†

Jo, for the fifth time, flicked through her wardrobe and came up blank. Each time she thought she'd decided, she changed her mind. In the old days, it had never happened. She'd only possessed one decent change of clothes for her performances. Her eyes strayed to the well-worn jacket with 'Jo' on the back that she'd refused to retire. It was as much a part of her and her history as any of these outrageously expensive jackets, jeans and shirts she now owned would ever be.

"Damn, why do I have so many choices?" A tinkle of laughter brought her attention to Thea who was silently walking toward her.

"Joanna, there is no such thing as too many choices. Besides, if you'd let me hire a dresser for you, there wouldn't be a problem."

Thea's genuine smile was like a tonic to Jo and as always, when her friend was in the vicinity, she felt herself relax. When she was sick, the doctors told her she needed to slow down and give herself a chance to heal. At the time, she could tell they didn't believe she ever would. That all changed because she had Thea by her side. She thanked God every single day for that remarkable fact.

"Why would I need that when I have you?" Jo winked. "Want to help me decide?"

Half an hour later, both women looked at one another in exasperation.

"You have too many choices."

"Told you so," Jo replied smugly.

"Hmm, okay, close your eyes."

Jo complied. She was startled for a moment when a hand clasped hers and laid it gently on the rack.

"Choose, Joanna," Thea said.

A smile flickered across Jo's lips realizing what her friend wanted her to do. Her hand glided for a moment before dropping decisively on a hanger.

"Great choice, Joanna."

Blue eyes opened wide and a chuckle passed Jo's lips. "That's the first outfit I looked at when I started my search." The white silk shirt that was transparent enough to show off her black bra, along with black slacks, was understated elegance. "You know, there's something to be said for blind faith."

Jo began pulling the clothes from the wardrobe rail, laying them out on a chair in the room.

"I know what you mean. I was thinking that maybe after the show we could go to a club...."

Jo raised an eyebrow and had a slight frown.

"I know. Only if you can have a good, square meal. That's a given," Thea countered.

Jo could feel her smile crinkle in the corner of her eyes. "Hey, you eat almost as much as I do after a show," Jo teased.

Her highly charged performances helped to keep the late eating pounds off her lithe body. After the long lazy stay with her parents and their mollycoddling, she'd put on some extra weight.

Take Me As I Am

Most of that was due to her father, who daily made her break every one of her rules about not eating pastries when he baked them especially for her.

"Okay, I'll book somewhere for around midnight," Thea said.

"No problem with me. I'll eat anything." Jo was now refocusing on the upcoming performance this evening. She picked up her lyric sheets to study them again.

"Great. Now, I'll leave you to your own personal rehearsal and I'll catch up with you before you go on stage, as usual."

"Fine, thanks," Jo whispered absently.

†

Thea smiled tenderly at Joanna who was engrossed in her work. She really needed to be leaving for the airport. She knew Joanna would be surprised and pleased to see their old friends again.

Leaving the room, Thea looked around and smiled. It was going to be a great evening and in just more than an hour, her friends would be there with her, too. She was looking forward to seeing them again, especially Daisy. She'd missed the older woman greatly. Although she'd written and called her several times, Daisy had either not responded to her messages or was abrupt on the phone. *Today will be different, I know it.*

Once she'd arranged with Pete, the head roadie, to have Joanna's coffee arrive in her dressing room at the precise time they would have their ritual coffee before every performance, Thea turned to leave the building.

"I'll not be long. I promise to be back before she'll miss me," she told Pete with a smile.

With arms folded across his gigantic chest, Pete gave her a serious glance before a glint appeared in his eyes. "She'll miss you. She always does. Make sure you're back, Thea, before the show starts or we'll all be in trouble. Want to tell me where you're going, for safety's sake?"

Thea smiled warmly at the large man with an incredibly gentle tone. "Promise not to tell her?"

"You got it."

"I've invited some friends from where I used to live. Joanna knows them too and I want it to be a surprise. They arrive at the airport in half an hour and I'm taking them to dinner then bringing them here for the show. Joanna won't know until the end. Frank's going to see that one of our friends watches the show from the right hand side of the stage since she never goes to that side. I know he won't give away the surprise. What do you think?"

The giant of a man grinned. "I think she should be grateful she has you for a friend. You'd best be going. I'll personally make sure Jo doesn't know about the surprise."

"Thanks, Pete, and don't forget about her coffee." Thea was happy; everything was going to work out great.

"Never do." Pete walked with her out of the building and flagged a taxi for her.

†

"I can't see her, can you?" Lucy whispered, hurrying them purposely forward.

"The younger generation never knows when to walk slowly," Daisy muttered.

"Nope, she'll be here. Thea would never let us down," John-Henry remarked quietly. His eyes dove into the crowd of people waiting.

"I can see her! She's there. Look." Lucy flew forward and within seconds engulfed Thea into a warm hug. "Thea, you look wonderful. Traveling with Jo must be good for you."

Thea disengaged herself from the bear hug. "It's so wonderful to see you again, Lucy." Her eyes turned to John-Henry who gave her a wide smile before taking her in for a second warm hug.

"Where's Daisy?" Thea asked smiling excitedly. Her heart was full of happiness at seeing her friends again.

Lucy and John-Henry looked a little sheepish as they pointed toward Daisy, who was looking around agitatedly with a less than happy expression.

Thea grinned happily and shot off to greet her old friend.

"Do you think we should have told her about Daisy?" Lucy asked.

"Nope. That's up to the two of them and I think old grumpy will give in. In the end, she never could say no to Thea, could she?" John-Henry smiled.

"Too true, but she might be antsy."

"Well, we can put that down to a bad flight. It was kinda bumpy up there."

Thea walked up to Daisy and instinctively pulled her into a loving hug.

†

The sight of Thea made Daisy look twice, wondering why the younger woman was there. How did she know? Then it dawned on her. Why those two conniving no good so-called friends.

"Oh, Daisy, it's so good to see you. I'm so pleased you came. I have a wonderful dinner planned for us at a restaurant that I know you'll love. After that we'll go to Joanna's concert and then supper at a great club after that," Thea gushed.

"Humph, I wasn't...."

"Now, come on, Daisy, let's go. I'm starved," John-Henry said. "You be good and don't you go spoiling this for Thea," he whispered.

Daisy glared at the man.

"I've arranged for a car to take us to the restaurant," Thea said. "We can catch up as we go along."

Daisy recoiled when Thea hooked her arm in hers but heeded John-Henry's words. She'd make sure her two friends would know exactly how she felt about their deception. The four old friends left the terminal and a large black limousine whisked them away.

†

An hour later, Lucy gave Thea a sympathetic look in the restroom of the restaurant. "Sorry, Thea, we should have told you that Daisy wasn't that friendly toward you. We figured that she might change her tune once she saw you."

"I knew something wasn't sitting right with her. I've seen the look she gave me when she saw me and I knew I was in trouble."

"I should have known better. I let it slip that you were staying with your mother and she didn't take kindly to that."

Thea glanced at herself in the mirror. "You know, two years ago I would have been devastated that Daisy was upset with me. Now, I realize that people have opinions and that they don't always agree with others." She shrugged. "If Daisy wants me to disown my mother, she's barking up the wrong tree. It isn't ever going to happen. She doesn't know all the facts, Lucy."

Lucy chewed on her lip. "That's where you are wrong, Thea. Daisy knows all the facts. She has many redeeming qualities, except for one—her blind faith in your father. Your mother didn't stand a chance against that or the poison your father filled Daisy's mind with about her." Lucy hugged Thea. "Daisy is a little set in her ways but I'm sure she'll come around. Anyway, I'm real happy you asked us here and John-Henry can now boast even more about Jo."

"He boasts? Really? About what and to who?" Thea smiled at the change of subject. Daisy was going to feel however she wanted, and she could do nothing about that.

"Anyone who wants to know and some who don't. When one of her songs starts playing, he's there telling them that she used to play in the bar before her big break. Mind you, we are all proud of her and you, Thea. It wasn't easy leaving town and now, look at both of you now."

Thea felt the genuine warmth and sincerity in every word Lucy said. She knew that Joanna was going to be so embarrassed when she heard that John-Henry spoke so highly of her.

"We're doing well, now. We've had our moments, but somehow we can't stay apart for long," Thea whispered to herself.

"Your mother mentioned that Jo was quite ill for a time and that you helped to nurse her back to health?"

"Yes, it was a shock. She nearly killed herself with the workload and other things. Now she's more careful." She wondered if Joanna was being more careful or if she was on her behalf. Whichever it was really didn't matter, as long as the outcome was the same—Joanna remained healthy and happy.

†

Lucy heard the tenderness in Thea's voice and smiled inwardly. Karen was right when she said her daughter loved the singer. It was in every nuance of her speech and facial expressions when she mentioned Jo's name. It would be interesting to see her body language when she was around Jo.

"I'm glad for you both. Shall we get back to John-Henry? I'm sure by now he's had an earful from Daisy. Unless of course he went to the men's room, leaving her on her own. I'm not sure any one of us could take that." The two friends laughed and left the restroom.

"Oh," Lucy said, as they were making their way back to the table. "I completely forgot to tell you."

"What?"

"George Andrews was arrested this morning for fraud and embezzlement."

Thea laughed. "That is truly good news. Tell me all about it."

"Don't know much more than that. They were arresting him as we were leaving."

"I hope they take him to jail and throw away the key."

†

"Anyone seen Thea?" Jo asked sharply as she scanned the corridor outside her door. The usual coffee break had arrived on time except one very important aspect was missing. Thea. They would normally chat about insignificant items for an hour and then Thea would leave her to the final preparations for the evening performance. Where was she?

A young roadie, who she'd never seen before, shrugged then turned quickly, immediately running into Pete.

"Where's the fire?" Pete asked.

Jo watched with interest.

"She wants to know where the blonde is," the young man whispered.

Pete smiled. "Didn't take her long," he mumbled. "Get back to work."

Jo glanced at him before fixing him with a glare.

"Hi, Jo. I hear you're looking for Thea?" Pete swallowed hard.

"Yeah, have you seen her?"

"About three hours ago she went into town on an errand and said she'd be back before you missed her."

Jo frowned at the gentle giant of a man who appeared to be trying not to grin.

A sense of relief filled Jo's heart. "I think she mentioned something about seeing me later. I didn't realize she meant that much later."

She pursed her lips. Jo's mind was reliving the fragment of conversation she'd had with Thea earlier. Nothing about the conversation raised a red flag. Knowing Thea, she was probably tracking down a decent place for them to eat after the show. That was in keeping with her nature. That must be the reason she wasn't there. Still, not having her there was a bit unsettling.

"Since you're here, Pete, is everything going okay with the equipment?"

"Like a dream. The guys love working with you." Pete smiled.

Quirking an eyebrow at the comment, Jo gave him a sardonic look, "Bet they never said that a year or so ago."

Pete grinned before winking at her. "Things change. Go have your coffee and I'll tell Thea you were looking for her when she returns."

"Okay. Oh and, Pete?"

"Yep?"

"Are we employing younger roadies these days or is it that I'm getting old?" Jo asked absently as she opened the door to her room.

"A bit of both." Pete laughed while walking away.

Jo went back into her room and sank into a chair, poured herself some coffee, and sighed. The coffee smelled good and always did because Thea ensured that a particular brand always traveled with them. Pity her friend wasn't there with her. She enjoyed the peaceful hour before the show as they chatted. Sometimes she couldn't believe that life was so good and in the past, she would half expect her luck to change for the worse. Nowadays she didn't feel so negative about things, probably because Thea told her if she constantly thought on the black side, it was bound to happen. Thea often said, 'you have to make your own luck in this world'. Jo felt that together they were doing just that.

†

Thea, with a happy smile, glanced around the entrance for their car. She'd called the driver five minutes earlier and asked him to come back from wherever drivers go on such evenings. The limousine wasn't around, but she expected him any moment.

As she stepped closer to the curbside, her heel caught and she tripped and fell into the road. A silver sedan squealed to a halt to avoid missing her, but the side mirror collided with her cheek, stunning her.

John-Henry quickly came to her aid and pulled her to the sidewalk.

The driver of the vehicle got out and rushed to them. "I'm sorry! Are you hurt? Do you need to go to the emergency room? I can take you."

Thea looked dazedly at the middle-aged man. He appeared genuinely distressed at the incident. "I'm fine, thank you for the offer. Besides, it was my clumsy feet that caused the accident," Thea said.

"Well, if you're sure." The stranger shook his head and slowly made his way back to the vehicle and drove away.

"Thanks, John-Henry. I'd never hear the end of it from Joanna if I'd been knocked down on the eve of a show and not been there." Thea smiled and was shocked that her cheek still stung like hell.

"Oh, my, are you okay, Thea?" Lucy asked, her face concerned.

"I'm fine, just a silly accident. John-Henry came to my rescue."

"You need that taken care of." Daisy sidled up to Thea and touched her cheek.

Thea bit her lip at the pain and grimaced.

"I'll be just fine. I promise."

The limousine arrived. As the car stopped, the driver quickly exited and came around to help them inside the vehicle.

"Hey, what's happened?" He stared at Thea.

"I tripped and fell into the road and a hit a car's side mirror. I'm okay and ready to go back."

"Not on my watch," the driver said. "A visit to the hospital is in order."

Thea was about to protest but the throbbing on her face deepened and she was all of a sudden very weary.

"We won't be long. I know the doc who's on today."

A few minutes later, they were on the way to St Luke's Hospital, in the opposite direction from Joanna.

Chapter Twenty-six

"Where the fuck is she, Pete?" Jo turned scathing ice blue eyes in his direction. She knew her look was enough to wither the strongest spirit.

The giant of a man held up his arms, giving the irritated and upset singer a chagrined glance. "Truthfully, I don't know. However, I know the driver of the car she used, let me call him. Why not see the guys for your usual sound check and I'll get you an update when you finish the first set. Deal?"

"You know the driver, huh? Well, he'd better not be the reason she's not here or so help me God, Pete, you're a dead man." Jo's thoughts were churning away on every possible unfavorable scenario she could think of. It could be anything from a car accident, a mugging, or Thea being lost in a strange city at the mercy of some transient. After turning her back on Pete, she made for the stage and the waiting musicians.

"Any news, Jo?" Frank asked.

"No. Let's get this show on the road," Jo barked at the three men.

The lights in the concert hall went down and Jo's signature hit single played as the intro. Jo heaved a sigh, picked up her guitar, and ran out on stage to thunderous applause. The others followed closely on her heels and within minutes, the first song was in full swing.

†

"Damn you, Sonny, pick up your fucking cell." Pete spoke to the constant ringing tone of the cell in his hand. Just as he was about to give up and try again in a few minutes, a voice answered and he switched on the speaker.

"Sonny, God damn, man, where are you? More importantly where are your passengers?" Pete's words echoed down the deserted hall.

"Pete, slight change of venue. There was an accident."

"An accident! Thea?" Pete cast a worried glance toward the stage.

"Yeah, she tripped and fell into the road near the restaurant and a car almost hit her. Well actually she fell into the side mirror of an oncoming car."

Pete closed his eyes at the comment. A cold chill swept through him as if someone had just walked on his grave. "How bad? What about the people with her?"

A snort of laughter followed his inquiry, "She's in shock, but it will pass and she has a bruise on her cheek. The oldies are okay, but you could have warned me one of them talks constantly. She's driving me mad."

Pete heaved a sigh of relief. "Are you on your way back?"

A hearty laugh sounded. "Give me a minute."

Several moments later, a female voice spoke. "Pete?"

"Thea. Wow, am I glad that you are okay. You know she's gonna kill me." Pete couldn't help smiling. The sound of Thea's voice meant that he would keep his balls intact this time around.

"She doesn't know anything, does she, Pete?" Thea asked anxiously.

"Other than you're not here and she's worried sick about you. Will you be here for the interval?" That would ease the situation somewhat. No way was he going to tell the singer that Thea was at the hospital. He knew she would cancel the performance in a heartbeat and go wherever Thea was.

"I'm just waiting for some painkillers. Let me check on the progress. Joanna wasn't too anxious, was she? I know what she

Take Me As I Am

can be like if she's upset. The performance doesn't always go according to plan, does it?"

"Listen." He held the phone out and the echoes of the performance filled the phone. Pete heard her sigh.

"Good, I'll be right back," Thea said.

Pete shuffled around for a few minutes until he heard Thea's voice again.

"I have the drugs and a prescription so we can leave now," Thea said.

Pete heard Sonny's voice next.

"I'll have them back soon, Pete."

"Sonny, hey man, don't drive too fast and end up in another accident," Pete said.

"Got it, man. Catch you later."

Pete glanced down at the cell in his hand. Thea would be back before intermission. Thea needed to explain the situation to Jo. He knew she wouldn't take it well from him.

†

"Thank you for all your help." The driver helped Thea out of the limo, stopped by the side entrance of the concert hall.

Within seconds of entering the building, Pete greeted them.

"Hi, Pete, are we in time?"

Pete gave Thea a grin and unexpectedly hugged her close. "Yep, she's on her last song before the break. Why don't you go to the side stage? I know she'll want to know you're here."

Thea grinned at him. "But—" She turned to her friends.

"I'll take care of them," Pete said.

"Thea, you go on, I'm sure your friend here will see us to our seats. One thing I know is that I could do with a stiff drink after all this." John-Henry smiled warmly at Thea.

"Yes, Thea, go. I'm sure Jo wants to know you're in the building." Lucy hooked her arm in Daisy's and winked at John-Henry provocatively.

"Don't you let her bully you, Thea." Daisy said with a frown.

Thea chuckled. "Oh, she won't do that, Daisy. What an imagination you have. I'll catch up with you when she goes on for the second half. I promise." Thea smiled brightly at them all before going through the side door.

†

For a little while, she pushed the shock and fatigue from the accident into the background while walking as fast as she could toward the side stage. A wonderful sense of peace overwhelmed her when she saw Joanna with mic in hand, singing the last refrain of a poignant song reminding her how fragile life was. Her eyes glimmered with unshed tears as she watched the performance and the face of her beloved. Thea saw the cynical curve of Joanna's lips and knew she was responsible for it. The next session would be easier for them. She was there now.

As the applause rang out, Jo waved to the crowd and turned toward the stage. Her expression did a remarkable U-turn and flashed Thea a gigantic smile.

Rushing off the stage faster than she would normally, she tripped on a cable and Thea's hands went out to steady her—much as John-Henry had helped her—preventing her falling on her face. Were they mirroring one another?

"Hey, I didn't know you missed me that much." Thea grinned playfully. She experienced a stare that seared her soul and lit a flame inside her that would never perish. It always happened when Joanna looked at her in that way.

"You'll never know how much. Where have you been?"

"If I told you now, you'd never get back on stage. Come on, let's get you your fluids and then later at supper I'll explain."

Jo frowned and stared at her. Thea was so grateful that Lucy had done a great job at disguising the bruising on her face.

"Okay, let's go get those fluids. I have a feeling the next session is going to be more upbeat than the last one was." Jo grinned happily and slung an arm around Thea as they walked off to her dressing room.

†

The concert was a hit, if the playfully raucous crowd was anything to go by. Joanna certainly knew how to play to the crowd and get them involved. She had a confidence level that stuck her up there on a pedestal. It was probably why Jack predicted such great things for her if she wanted it badly enough. Funnily enough, it was hard to judge exactly what Joanna wanted to achieve these days.

"She's even better than she was back at the bar." Lucy spoke loud enough for them to hear above the noise below them. Having a personal box at the concert had been a great idea. John-Henry had given up the idea of the side stage area for the luxury of sitting with them and having a drink as he watched the performance. Thea had watched the pride move across his gnarly features as Joanna performed for the audience. He had every right to feel that way. More than anyone else, he was instrumental for her being on stage, performing to the masses, rather than in a small town bar.

"I'd say she would be wonderful any place she sang," John-Henry remarked as he hummed along to the song Joanna was singing.

Thea smiled. Did the bar owner have a crush on Jo, too? It wouldn't surprise her. She knew all too well how that worked. Grinning at Lucy, they both turned to Daisy and asked in unison. "What do you think, Daisy?"

Thea had watched the old woman tapping her feet to most of the songs. "I'm more of a Patsy Cline fan myself, but she'll do."

Lucy and Thea smiled. 'She'll do' sounded mighty fine to Thea.

As the song ended, there was a short silence while the singer pulled a stool forward, sat down and relaxed her body. "I wrote this song for some very special people in my life. We've never performed it before, so cut us a little slack if I forget the words."

Laughter greeted the words.

Thea smiled slowly. Joanna had never forgotten the words to any song as far as she knew. Fascinated, she listened as the gentle guitar strains heralded the start of the new song… "There was a life to live, places to be and people to meet. I did it all and didn't care how or who was hurt on the way "

The magic that called to Thea every time she heard Joanna sing sent out its tendrils and she was captivated once more. Was that song for her?

"That was a beautiful song. Is it someone you know of, Thea? Jo got a new beau?" Lucy asked, applauding the singer's performance vigorously.

"A beau? No, I don't think so. You can ask her later who she wrote it for," Thea answered absently.

"Thea, she's performing her last song. Are we going to surprise her by greeting her off stage?" Daisy asked.

"Oh, God yes, let's go, she's going to be so surprised."

Thea's mind turned back to her friends.

†

The small homey Italian restaurant that she'd chosen with Pete's help earlier that day was a bonus at this time of night. During the middle of the week, few people frequented the place. In fact, they'd arranged for all the roadies and other support staff to join them on this last night of the tour. Many of them would be going their separate ways tomorrow until the next tour, and there would definitely be a next time. Everyone was raving about the performance.

As predicted, Jo had been pleasantly surprised when she first saw John-Henry. Her heartfelt hug and genuine appreciation at his appearance near the stage was something you took pictures of and hung in your house to reflect on later in life as one of life's pleasurable memories. After that introduction, Lucy appeared from the wings then Daisy. Jo welcomed both of the overjoyed women at the same time before giving Thea a mock stern stare followed by a wink.

Within an hour, they were all out of the concert hall and ensconced in the friendly family run restaurant. Jo was visibly relaxing after the rigors of the concert and from her emotional upset when Thea hadn't been at the start of the show.

As they settled down at one end of the long table, made up especially for the group that was twenty strong, Jo looked at the three special people who had joined them. They made all the difference in her and Thea's friendship and for being where they were today. She knew that was no mean feat.

The waiter delivered the drinks everyone ordered. Jo picked up her glass of beer and raised it in the air. "Thanks to a marvelous team. I couldn't do it without you guys. Special thanks to Pete and the crew for making sure Lenny's equipment sounded so good, no one could notice if he was playing at the correct times or not."

The drummer gave her a long-suffering glance before raising his glass.

"Next tour…me and the boys are going back to take Europe. I'll gladly take anyone here who wants to travel with us."

Thea gave her a sharp glance.

"Oops, I forgot I arranged that."

"Does that include us?" John-Henry asked with a wicked grin.

"Anytime you want to join one of my tours, John-Henry, you got it. Wouldn't that bar of yours go to rack and ruin without you polishing the spots off the counter?"

John-Henry gave her a comical grimace. "That was uncalled for, young lady. I see they haven't drummed any manners into you since you left my place."

"My dad would love to meet you, John-Henry. He says the same." Happiness was bubbling in Jo as she teased the group around her.

When the first course arrived, everyone tucked into the food.

Thea gave a startled gasp as Jo leaned in and softly spoke to her in a tone so low only she could hear.

"Where did you get that bruise on your face?"

Thea covered her cheek with her hand and looked away.

Jo wouldn't give up. "Maybe if you tell me where you went this afternoon and why you were late, that might shed light on the issue?"

"Joanna, we're having supper, let's enjoy it with our friends and tomorrow I'll tell you all about it," Thea replied in a strangled voice.

"Do you promise?" Jo knew that if Thea promised it was a sure thing.

Thea gave her hand a quick squeeze. "I promise. Now tell me, how is that fiery pasta salad?"

Jo smiled at the change in mood, picked up her spoon, and filled it before placing it close to Thea's lips. "Try it and see."

"Damn that's hot, Joanna." Thea gulped down several mouthfuls of water as a burst of laughter from those who had seen what had happened emanated from the table.

Jo grinning devilishly turned to the others. "Anyone else want to try?" When no one took up the offer, she placed a spoonful of the fiery mixture in her mouth along with a piece of garlic bread.

The meal progressed at a rapid rate. The drinks flowed along with jokes and anecdotes making for a pleasantly rowdy atmosphere within the room. Even the restaurant owners had joined them.

"Are you two going to settle down anytime or are you going to drift indefinitely?" Daisy asked, stifling a yawn.

"We have settled down, Daisy. We share a house by the river and we both have a family home to go to when we travel to New York." Jo noticed Daisy's scowl.

The old woman looked toward Thea who was engrossed in conversation with Lucy and John-Henry. "Thea's a good woman and she needs to settle before it's too late."

Jo looked at the woman and quirked her eyebrows as she waited for Daisy to say more. When she didn't she asked, "As in settle, being married and having a family?"

"Well, she certainly can't find anyone if she's constantly moving from place to place with you."

"Maybe she doesn't mind traveling with me. Her priorities may have changed since she left Danvers. Not everyone wants the shackle of marriage and babies."

"Thea deserves a family life, Joanna. Didn't you go close to the line on that issue a year or so ago?"

The mention of her failed engagement to Lee Weston brought things starkly into focus. She was drifting with Thea toward a romance, never taking the final step. She couldn't deny that when they were together, other people faded into the background becoming important only on a secondary level. She was probably too shit scared to take the chance and lose Thea again.

"I did for a short time, but it didn't work out. I guess I'm one of those people who are not destined to have the so-called happy family routine. Thea has had her moments, Daisy. I don't think I'm the stumbling block to her finding a man if she wants a man," Jo added in a whisper. Jo knew men didn't figure in what Thea classed as being romantically happy. Did Daisy know that?

"Maybe what you always thought of as a normal family life can be different if you meet the right person."

Jo listened to the older woman's softly spoken words that also held a note of tenderness. It was an aspect of Daisy that she suspected only Thea experienced. Daisy was usually quite caustic in her everyday dealings with most people. As she glanced up from her vigil with her warming half empty glass of beer, she saw

Daisy wasn't looking in her direction but toward Thea. That would be right on the button. She didn't expect Daisy to be tender with her.

As if she knew what was being said, Thea turned toward them with a bright smile.

"Don't leave it too late to tell her, is all I'm saying," Daisy remarked.

Tell her, tell her what? Jo shook her head. No, she can't mean that, can she?

"How would it be if we called it a night, Joanna, and meet up for brunch tomorrow before we all go our separate ways?" Thea asked.

"Good idea. I'm beat, too," Daisy replied. "I could sleep for a week."

Jo stared closely at the four of them. They did look beat and tomorrow she would find out exactly what had happened. For now, they all needed sleep. Not that she was going to go just yet. It was only one a.m., and Pete had promised a trip to one of the underground nightclubs he knew in the city. Anyway, the adrenaline rush from the performance hadn't yet completed its journey through her body and going to bed now was not an option.

"Pete, want to get Thea and our friends a taxi to take them to the hotel."

"Sure, Jo." Pete grinned and pulled out his cell.

When they left the restaurant, Jo took Thea aside for a few moments as the others climbed into the car. She placed a gentle finger on the bruise on Thea's pale face. "Are you okay? If you want me to come back to the hotel now, I will." The concern she felt for her friend vied with her need to rid herself of the energy racing through her body.

"Joanna, I'm fine. I just need a decent night's sleep, that's all. Please don't stay up partying all morning or you won't make brunch at eleven in the hotel restaurant. If you're not there, I'll be shaking you in your bed."

Thea's gentle smile surrounded Jo with a calming feeling. She took a step away from Thea and thrust her hands in her jean pockets. "Duly warned. Sleep well, Thea." She watched Thea climb into the taxi before the car glided away from the sidewalk and she continued watching until it was totally out of sight.

A large hand settled on her shoulder. "Ready, boss?"

"Yeah. Did Thea tell you anything about her adventures today?" Jo asked absently as she walked quietly toward the minivan that was going to take them all to the nightclub.

"Nope. Now, come on, Jo. Time is a-wasting and I have a new band for you to listen to this evening."

Chapter Twenty-seven

Thea sank down on her bed. The crisp clean linen complimented the shower she'd quickly indulged in before sleep dragged her to bed. Her head was aching and she now really wished she hadn't drunk three glasses of wine because the medication wouldn't work properly. With that thought floating in her mind, she laid her head on the pillow and closed her eyes. Someone surely must be looking out for her because it had been a close call today.

Joanna was going to be livid at her incompetence and probably wouldn't let her out on her own again. Despite her throbbing head, she giggled at the thought. The thing that kept nagging at her was their growing closeness and what that was doing to her. Joanna was so cagey about her emotions, so it was like pulling teeth. She recalled the first time Joanna had said she loved her before promptly falling asleep on her. Thea rolled her eyes. Was this going to be all that ever happened between them? Innuendo. Her thoughts pulled and pushed her into a sleep heavily laden with confusing dreams.

†

Jo watched the band Pete had recommended, mixing blues and soul with an underground beat that was hard at first to follow, but gradually, as she listened, the music made more sense to her.

The band was not mainstream and hardly likely to become famous out there in today's music world. Maybe tomorrow.

"What do you think?" Pete dragged a chair across the floor and sat opposite her, hiding the tiny stage from her view.

Drinking heavily from the bottle of beer that she'd nursed for more than an hour, Jo knew her mind wasn't on the band. There were other more pressing matters than unwinding after the concert. "Okay, I guess."

"Want someone to talk to? You look preoccupied."

Jo shook her head. His idea of someone to talk to was a free male in any of the places they frequented. The choices he made for her didn't match hers in any way, shape, or form. Especially now.

"Nope." She yawned passing a hand across her face wearily. "I think I'll call it a day, Pete. Things to do in the morning and if I don't turn up on time, Thea will go psycho on me."

A loud rumble of laughter echoed around them as Pete laughed.

"I said something funny?"

"No, Jo. Well, sure, maybe. Thea wouldn't know how to be a psycho. You on the other hand—"

"Oh, I'm the type, huh? Never knew there was one." Jo stood and waved the server close so she could pay her meager bill. The tip was more than the drink she'd still hadn't finished.

"Jo, tomorrow—"

Curious at the change in Pete's tone, Jo refocused her attention on him. "Tomorrow?"

"Yeah, what time are you planning on leaving?"

Certain he was going to say something else, Jo gave him a shrewd glance. "Not sure, maybe around three. All depends on the flight back to the coast. Thea will know. Check with her in the morning."

Pete smiled slowly before nodding. "Want me to get you a cab?"

"No, I'll take my chances out there. Anyway, I noticed a taxi stand a couple of hundred yards up the street. See you tomorrow." Jo left the small club and walked out into the early morning sidewalk.

As she strolled toward the area of the taxis, she looked up at the sky. It was a midnight blue sprinkled with tiny stars twinkling high above, welcoming her under its night blanket. Lyrics buzzed in her head as she stood gazing up at the heavens. A small breeze pushed her hair across her forehead and after attempting to brush it away several times, she left it to the elements. Her eyes then looked down the virtually deserted road. Except for the odd taxi, there was little or no activity. Few lights shone from the apartment buildings that lined the street she traveled. As she came closer to a waiting taxi, her mind wandered. Maybe if she were lucky, Thea would have waited up for her. *Yeah, right.* Talk about selfish.

She opened the door of the taxi and climbed inside quickly advising the driver of her hotel. As it sped off into the night, she wondered if that wasn't her problem, full stop. Selfishness. Maybe Daisy was right. Thea needed a family life and she'd done nothing but take her away from it all. How could she be so inconsiderate? Tomorrow when they went home, they'd have a good old-fashioned one-on-one girl talk. Who knew what might happen after that. All she knew for sure was that she never wanted Thea to be anywhere but beside her. Selfishness be damned.

†

Lucy sat patiently in the hotel restaurant alone. Daisy had muttered that she needed a little more time and would be there eventually, John-Henry sounded half asleep when she called his room telling him that she'd be along shortly. The many years working the early shift in the café allowed her precious little time to indulge that luxury called sleeping in.

"Hi there, Luce, where's everyone else?" Jo, with a warm smile on her face, sat down next to her friend.

"Daisy and John-Henry sounded as if they were sleeping in. Can't blame them. It was a long day yesterday. I expected Thea would be with you." Lucy smiled at her young friend. She'd come a long way since their morning chats in the café when the singer had eaten her brunch there every morning.

"Thea's not here?" Jo's heartbeat rose fractionally, that wasn't like her. She pushed her chair back and stood. "Excuse me, I need to call Thea."

"Just a minute," Lucy said.

Jo turned and walked away when she literally collided with Thea. "Where's the fire?"

Thea, glancing up at Jo flushed. "You'll never believe this...I slept late."

Jo chuckled before grinning at her friend. "You did have a long exciting day yesterday, didn't you?"

Lucy watched her two friends and wondered if either of them knew the intense chemistry they were giving off.

"What do you mean?" Thea's body language screamed defensiveness with a touch of worry.

"Our friends, remember?" Jo placed a comforting arm around her shoulders. "Let's eat. I know you're never up to a decent conversation until you've blessed the hollow pit with its sacrifice of the day."

"Oh, Joanna." Thea smiled and relaxed visibly.

"Another latecomer, I see." Lucy grinned. "My, my, Thea, you've changed. I remember you were always the early bird. Funnily enough, I was thinking the very same about Jo."

"How?" they replied in unison.

"Sit down first and let's order at least coffee. And tea for you, Thea." Lucy tapped her forehead. "I remember."

Fifteen minutes and several gossipy stories later, Daisy and John-Henry arrived together having met up in the elevator area of the floor they all shared.

†

Jo looked at her watch. "It's now one p.m. and I hope no one minds, but I've taken the liberty of ordering a bottle of champagne to toast the future." She motioned for the server to bring the glasses and the magnum of champagne.

"This is...well, it's decadent," Lucy said readily, holding up her champagne flute.

"Of course it is, and when you do this kind of thing once in a while, it's wonderful, especially when you share it with good friends." Jo settled back in her chair, sipping on her drink.

"Joanna, you asked me how I received the bruise on my face." Thea gingerly touched the black and blue abrasion.

Jo immediately sat upright. "I did, are you ready to tell me now?"

Nodding slowly, Thea drew in a deep breath. She anxiously looked at their friends hoping that Joanna wouldn't cause a scene. There was a distinct possibility that she would. "Promise me that you won't get angry?"

"How can I promise that, Thea? I don't even know what the problem was, and now I'm getting antsy waiting."

"Steady there, Jo, girl, Thea knows what a temper you have. We all do. Let her tell you what happened." John-Henry reached out cautiously and touched her arm.

Jo's jaw twitched and she crossed her arms. Silence ensued until the sound of a chair scraping back signaled that Jo was rising. She scowled. "Enjoy your drink," she said before storming off.

Thea watched helplessly as her friend left. *What did I do?*

"Well, that went well." Daisy gulped down the remaining contents of her champagne and coughed. "Damn bubbles."

"Thea, why is it such a problem for you to tell her about the accident?" Lucy asked. "You should have told her last night."

Thea could feel tears welling in eyes.

John-Henry stood. "I'll go talk with her and tell her what happened, Thea. You're probably still in shock."

"No. No, John-Henry. Thank you, all the same. I'll go talk with her. Lucy was right, I should have told her last night. I don't know why I didn't." Thea's tone was plaintive. "Drink the rest of the champagne. Joanna and I will be back shortly." Thea stood and while she walked away, she listened to their conversation.

"Young love, you never know what's going to happen next." Daisy calmly took a sip of her drink.

"What?" John-Henry said.

Lucy chuckled and placed a hand on his. "We'll explain."

Thea's eyes flew open. "They know? How?"

†

Jo didn't want to go to her room as it would be too claustrophobic. Her thoughts were tumbling around in her head, unable to make sense of why Thea was being so cagey about her day. It didn't make sense unless there was something nefarious about it. But then surely the others were involved. The pool area outside of the hotel was empty as she had expected. She was sitting in a recliner, looking at the water rippling from the wind floating across the surface, without a jacket and only a skimpy t-shirt as protection against the whipping wind. The low temperature was taking a back seat to her emotional overload. Thea's reluctance to tell her something, which obviously must be terrible, begged the question of what kind of friendship did they have.

"Joanna?"

Thea's voice gently beseeched her to look in her direction and when she looked at her, she saw fear etched in Thea's face.

"Please, Joanna, I'm sorry."

"For what? You have every right to your own life and don't have to tell me anything you don't want to, Thea. I should be apologizing for being selfish." Jo shook her head.

"I should have told you immediately. I want to apolo—"

Jo held up her hand and stood to face Thea. "It's your life. What you do in your time away from me isn't my business. I forget you need your own space and…I'm sorry for being a jerk, especially in public." Jo moved until they were within an inch of one another.

A slow smile replaced the pensive expression on Thea's face as she reached out a hand to touch Joanna's chin. "I didn't want to spoil your performance by my stupidity of yesterday. That's why I've been reticent. After that I just figured it wasn't that important."

"Please tell me what happened and if you let me, I'll be the judge of your so called stupidity."

Thea sucked in a deep breath and related the story of her incident with a car. "Stupid, right?"

Jo, wanting to laugh, pursed her lips. It was a serious event and she held her mirth inside. "I'd say more klutzy, wouldn't you?"

"Are you calling me a klutz?" Thea grinned.

"Do you have a better word for it?" Jo reached out, pulled Thea close, and rested her chin lightly on Thea's head. "Does it hurt?"

"Not as much as yesterday. Thank you for asking."

"That's a given…asking about you, that is. I always want to do that, Thea."

"Yeah?" Thea moved and Jo lifted her chin and they looked at one another.

"Yes, if you will let me," Jo softly said.

"If you will let me reciprocate." Thea was blinking rapidly.

Jo smiled and bent her head closer and drifted her lips over Thea's mouth. "Wouldn't have it any other way."

Thea shivered.

"Are you cold?" The raw biting wind whipping through her t-shirt didn't feel that cold with Thea this close.

"A little. I think you and I really need to discuss what's happening between us. Our friends are still here, and as much as I want to just be with you, it would be impolite to abandon them." Thea placed her hand in Joanna's wrapping their fingers together. "Let's see them off and we can talk… or…." Thea grinned before dragging Joanna toward the hotel.

Take Me As I Am

"I like the sound of the 'or'." Jo shivered and looked down.

"Me, too." Thea smiled a seductive smile.

†

Thea hugged her arms around herself as she watched the limousine depart, taking her friends to the airport. Joanna, pulled away to a conference call from the studio, couldn't make it to their departure. As the vehicle disappeared, she ventured back inside the hotel deciding to go back to her room and wait for Joanna to call.

After getting out of the elevator, she walked slowly down the hallway sucking in the silence. A few moments later, she entered her room, placed her pocket book on the table, and smiled as she soaked up the opulence of the place. The small hotel rooms, including the bridal suite of the Danvers motel paled in comparison to the furnishings she was looking at.

She moved to the plush sofa, sank into its depths, and sighed before her thoughts began traversing the past couple of hours. When they returned to the others, strange looks, especially from John-Henry greeted them. As usual, Joanna didn't seem to notice anything amiss and began an easy conversation with an abject apology. It was agony and ecstasy to sit next to Joanna and not hold her hand or touch her. Their fleeting kiss had changed everything but she wondered if Joanna realized that.

Thea rubbed her hands against her temples gently.

"She calls herself selfish but it's me who is in the big picture. If we go down the path I want, she could lose everything that she's worked so hard to gain. Am I ready for that? Is she?"

She sighed and closed her eyes. "Jack might be good with us having a sexual relationship but her fans…God, I've heard that country fans aren't generally liberal. What'll I do?"

She stood, walked to the table, reached inside her pocket book, and removed her iPhone. Selecting a name, she pressed the call icon.

"Mom, hi, how are you?... Yeah that's wonderful. Bradley can visit next time for sure. He's going to die when I tell him who Joanna has been working with. Mom... No, I'm not in trouble. I just need some advice, that's all. Do you have time to talk?... No, it's okay. Wasn't important really just... oh, I don't know. Sometimes I feel so out of place... Joanna is great... She—no, not with her, the music business... I guess. It makes Joanna happy though and that's the most important... Oh, I muddle along and if Joanna is happy, so am I by default. It works like that doesn't it, when you love someone? ... Of course I do. Okay, give everyone my love. I'll try to come back for Easter. Love you, Mom. Bye."

The call ended and Thea looked down at her phone. It was the best on the market according to Joanna. Hers had a pink finish, Joanna's had gold. When Joanna had given it to her initially, she had looked at it in dread. Her basic flip phone that she bought when she moved in with her mom had been good enough. As Joanna had extolled all the apps, email and music it could do, she'd been nervous of using it. Now it was an invaluable part of her wardrobe.

The ring tone sounded.

"Hi, have you finished? You have to go today, but... No, don't worry. I'll arrange a flight for us... I'll call you back."

Thea shook her head as she stared at the caller ID. "There always seems to be an obstacle to us having that talk. Perhaps it just isn't meant to be. No! I refuse to believe that."

Take Me As I Am

Chapter Twenty-eight

Jack watched the two singers complete the duet that the studio insisted they practice. It was for the AMC awards the next day. At first, Jo hadn't been keen on the idea. Tandy's style was so different from hers, a pop diva if ever there was one. The compensation was that they'd sing one of Jo's songs and release the duet after the show. Both of the women had been riding high in the public awareness during the year. Tandy, for the younger audience, had traversed country to pop and the public loved it. Jo, whose tremendous comeback tour ended on a high note, had a new group of fans since Tandy used several of her songs on her first album. Jack, shaking his head ruefully, reflected on what he knew of Jo.

Every time she appeared to be on a high, something would suddenly come along to rock her boat and tip her back into the ocean of life's uncertainties. Now that Thea was beside her, things had been more on an even keel and he hoped that would continue. She'd been working non-stop for months now and he mentioned to Thea that Jo needed a vacation before she capsized like before. Thea had agreed and promised to make sure Joanna would take some extended time off.

When they stopped singing, Jack watched Tandy fling her arms around Jo, kissing her and shrieking with delight. He saw the strain on Jo's face and that worried him. "Great cut, ladies, I think you'll wow them tomorrow." His words stopped the squealing from the younger woman and he was glad.

"I know we will." Tandy grinned, whispered something to Jo, and left the studio.

"Want to go for coffee, Jo?"

"Yeah, I'd murder for coffee right about now." Jo placed her guitar carefully in a case and locked it. "Let's go."

"You look tired, Jo. Have you started staying out late again?" Jack made sure that his smile was warm and friendly.

"Nope, just can't seem to sleep very well. Thea tells me it's too much adrenaline."

They entered his office suite. "Will you send in some coffee and sandwiches?" Jack asked his secretary before going into his office and closing the door.

Ten minutes later, piping hot coffee and a delicious range of food arrived. "Thanks, Amy. Unless it's an emergency, I don't want to be disturbed until we're done here."

Once the secretary left, they both indulged until they couldn't eat any more.

Settling back on the sofa opposite Jo, Jack smiled. "Any news from Thea?"

"I talked with her last night. She's stopping on her way back to check out one of the venues on the next tour. She wasn't happy with the negotiations." Jo had a tender expression on her face as she spoke.

"Thea certainly looks out for you." Jack sipped his coffee. "Are Thea and the town of Danvers in Missouri related in any way?"

"Yep, how did you come up with that?" Jo laughed. "Her great, great grandfather founded the town way back, well, whenever it was founded. A family thing she was very proud of. By the time she'd grown up, it was all but a note in the local history books. She had few options when I came along at the wrong time or the right one, depending on your point of view."

"I'm sure it was the right time." Jack watched the singer closely. He saw her smile at a memory she obviously cherished.

"As am I. Where would I be without her?"

"I'll second that. What about Tandy?"

Take Me As I Am

"What about her?" Jo looked up sharply

Jack laughed at Jo's puzzled expression before pouring them the last dregs of the coffee. "You do know she has a crush on you, right?"

"What? Thea said the same thing when she first met her. She's a kid barely out of high school and other than being sometimes a little too overzealous at times, she's not interested in anything but getting to the top." Jo rolled her eyes.

"Mark my words, Jo, she has her eye set on you. I've seen it all before." Jack settled back in his chair with a wicked smile tracing his lips.

"I'm old enough to be her mother and I've never encouraged her."

"When a kid like that takes a fancy to an older person, it's hard to stop the force of nature."

"Jack, if Thea finds out about this she's going to go ballistic. I won't have anything upsetting her, especially not something like that." Jo stood and started pacing the room.

"Precisely why I wanted to point it out and make sure you understood the situation completely. If Thea already has mentioned it to you then she definitely is suspicious about Tandy's intentions." He screwed up his face. "I'd hate to see anything happen to—"

"Jack, Thea and I are friends." Her eyes danced around the room. "Really close friends. She knows that, other than wishing Tandy every success, I'm not attracted to her nor have any interest in a relationship with her. Hell, she's doing me a favor by singing my songs. The royalties are flooding in and soon I won't have to sing for my supper."

"You don't have to now, do you?" Jack let out a nervous laugh.

"Thanks to you, I don't. But it's in the blood now and I love to perform. Maybe when the next album goes platinum." Jo gave the man the full thrust of her dynamic personality. "I'll do something else."

"Hey, I was only teasing. You're not thinking of retiring, are you?"

"Nope. As I said, it's in my blood. Until the day you want to get rid of me or they put the lid on my coffin, I'm going to be singing like a canary." Jo was grinning. "I need to get going. Thea is due to arrive in a few hours. See you later." She made for the door and left the office.

Jack stared after her, his mind rehashing their conversation. It had been interesting. Especially the way she went on the defensive regarding Thea and his allegations about Tandy's intentions. Anyone who took the time to notice would see the obvious chemistry between Jo and Thea. It was electric and far more than just friendship. If you had talent—Jo certainly had that in abundance—being gay generally didn't matter in the music industry. Nevertheless, he'd seen firsthand how country artists who came out as lesbian or gay took meteoric falls that destroyed their careers. Perhaps he should do a few subtle changes toward a main stream audience potential.

"I'll have to speak with Thea and get her thoughts."

†

Karen Adams smiled as she made the phone connection to her daughter.

"How are you, darling?… I know. It's so exciting. Bradley is making sure everyone at the hotel knows about it and the big screen is going up in the dining room for the event. Are you excited? … You don't sound it… I know you aren't one for all that glamour and stuff but Joanna will need you by her side… Darling, you're her rock. Never forget that. Are we still on course to visit at Easter? … Excellent… I love you, too, darling, see you soon."

Karen sat in reflection for a few moments as she considered the short conversation she'd had with Thea. "It's time, my darling, to make the most important decision of your life. Living on the knife edge really can't work forever."

†

As the award ceremony ended, along with a lavish reception, many celebrants began adjourning to other venues. Trigon Records took three awards and many people were eager for them to visit their particular after-party event. Success always brought that to the forefront.

Jack stood at the table they were all sitting at with a wide grin. He turned to Ralph Burgess, a senior executive and major shareholder in Trigon Records, who was sitting next to him. "Ralph, I think we have cause to celebrate big time tonight. Especially our two stars here." He smiled at Tandy then winked in Jo's direction.

"I agree," Ralph said.

"Jack, do you mind if I call it a day? I have a migraine," Thea said apologetically.

"In that case I'll call it a day, too. We have a very early flight out tomorrow." Jo grinned at Thea.

Disappointed groans rumbled around the table.

"Wouldn't be a party without you, Jo," Jack interjected. "You deserve most of the praise. You wrote the best song and had a hand in many of the songs on Tandy's album." He knew that of the three awards—best single, album of the year, and new artist—Jo deserved much of the credit. Hers was the material Tandy sang which had propelled her to the top quickly and decisively.

Thea stood and shrugged. "Go have some fun, Joanna. You deserve it. Jack's right without you this would have been a very different awards story."

"Hey, I resent that, I sang them." Tandy scowled.

"Are you sure?" Jo, ignoring Tandy, frowned.

"Yes. I'll make sure you catch that plane in the morning. Good night, everyone." Thea walked the short distance to the exit and left.

Jo looked around. "I think I need to go and—"

Tandy pounced on Jo and flung her arms around the older woman. "Come on, Jo, let's party together. I'll see you have a good time."

Jack could see Jo's agitation with Tandy, wondering if she was thinking about their conversation regarding Tandy's crush. No, she was probably thinking about Thea.

"I'll go for an hour then I'm leaving. Okay?"

It was a night for celebration and Jack was glad Jo agreed to join them, even if it was only for a little while. He grinned and pointed toward the side exit where he had a car waiting to whisk them away to another party.

†

Jo watched the party from the fringes. It was now in full swing and all she wanted to do was go to the hotel, take a shower, and have a nap. After that, she and Thea would fly to New York for a long overdue break. Her eyes scanned the revelers and she realized that her heart definitely wasn't in the room, knowing that with this kind of function, it never would be again. She'd told herself enough times that people didn't change, but she knew she had in a big way and she owed it all to Thea.

Sometimes she just wished she could tell Thea exactly what she meant to her. It seemed that every time she attempted to strike up that type of conversation, fate stepped in and she tabled it for another time. How many more other times would there be? She had the feeling that Thea thought she was less than committed in their relationship, but that wasn't the case, far from it. She was just out of her depth. That didn't happen often.

"You look bored, Jo, want me to cheer you up?" Tandy grinned wildly and grabbed Jo's arm.

It was obvious that the girl had been drinking. This was all she needed—a tipsy kid who needed someone to look after her. "I'm tired, it's been a long day. I'm older and like my rest." Jo extracted her arm from Tandy's enthusiastic grip.

"Oh, come on, Jo, no way could anyone say you are old. You've been keeping company with the wrong types. Take that manager of yours…she's no fun. Anyone ever tell her she could smile once in a while?"

Jo, bristling at the unkind comments about Thea, turned an icicle glance toward Tandy. "You don't know Thea or you wouldn't say that, so stop your running at the mouth."

The girl grinned wickedly and winked. "You can keep her. I'd rather get to know you better. How about it?"

Jo rolled her eyes at the suggestion. It was comical. Tandy was a child who had a long way to go before she grew up.

"Jack," she shouted as the record producer shot past her.

Jack turned and grinned happily at her. Why wouldn't he, he was reaping the reward of the talent of the two singers he'd had the foresight to sign to his record label. "Great party, Jo. Aren't you glad you came?"

"Hmm, let me take a rain check on that question. Who's plying Tandy with booze?"

Jack gave her a sheepish glance and then turned his eyes to Tandy who had wrapped herself around Jo. "Sorry, Jo, private party and I can't keep up with what the kid does every second. Let me get Steve. He's supposed to be her escort today." Jack took off, leaving Jo to hold onto the drunken kid. She suddenly felt hot wet lips travel down her neck. "Stop!"

Tandy then kissed her passionately on the lips.

"What the fuck. Get off me!" Jo, prying herself from Tandy, forcibly took her to Steve who was looking perplexed. She dumped a scowling, whiny, drunken singing star in his lap.

"What am I supposed to do with her?" Steve asked.

"Not my problem." Jo waved her arm in the air and headed for the door.

"Jo, where're you going?" Jack was walking by her side. "Don't go. I won't let her bother you anymore."

"I'm outta here, Jack."

Once outside, Jo leaned against the wall sighing deeply. She needed to talk with Thea about the kiss before Tandy blabbed about it or someone from the studio mentioned it inadvertently. Why did it seem she was always apologizing for everything even when it wasn't her fault?

Jo was hoping that by the time she got to the hotel Thea's migraine had eased enough for them to talk. Damn. How did everything got so screwed up.

"I love you, Thea," she whispered before climbing into a cab.

†

Jo opened the door to the suite she was sharing with Thea and immediately heard soft moans. With quick strides, she went to Thea's room and pushed the partially opened door wider. Another moan had Jo kneeling beside the bed.

"Did you take your meds?"

"You came."

"Yes. Did you take your meds," she asked again.

"They aren't working." Thea reached up and held her head. "It's never been this bad."

"What can I do?"

"Hold me."

"Scoot." When Thea complied, Jo lay next to her and kissed her forehead before gently putting her arm around Thea.

"Thanks."

"Anytime."

"Stay with me."

"Always." Jo began making small circles on Thea's back, marveling how soft her skin was. "I know it is hard but try to relax. I'm here and I won't let you go."

"Promise."

"Yes." Jo knew the moment had come for her to declare her feelings for Thea but she was in pain. Jo didn't want to say something so important when Thea was in so much pain. She would tell her tomorrow. It wasn't long before she heard Thea's breathing even out. Jo yawned and just as sleep overtook her, she smiled.

Thea woke with a start. For the most part, the migraine was gone, although remnants were still playing on the edges of her head. What wasn't gone was Joanna, who had her arm wrapped protectively around her waist. This feeling was exactly what she'd hoped for all her life. Someone who cared for her, kept her safe, and watched over her.

"It's like a dream come true," she whispered.

Joanna snuggled closer. "For me, too," she whispered back.

With a happy smile, Thea closed her eyes and fell into a deep, restorative sleep.

Chapter Twenty-nine

The flight was uneventful and quiet—very quiet. Thea looked drawn as she slept fitfully in the seat next to hers. Her migraine was a humdinger but, as usual, Thea hadn't complained. Jo, looking at Thea, knew that by the afternoon that she would be her usual chirpy self again. How she hated to see her in so much pain. She wished she could take it away, but she couldn't. She smiled, recalling waking up that morning with Thea nestled in her arms. The rightness of that simple thing struck her in a way she'd never thought possible. Her body was thrumming with not only desire but a peace that she'd never known. The words 'it's like a dream come true' reverberated loudly in her mind, for she knew that being here with Thea was all she had ever wanted and more.

The sign to fasten their seat belts blinked on and she gently shook Thea. "Hey, sleepyhead, we're about to land. Time to wake up."

Thea moved in her seat and smiled before opening her eyes and looking at Jo. "It wasn't a dream. We're really here together on our way to having a vacation."

Jo ran a finger down Thea's cheek. "It wasn't a dream."

†

Jo flagged down a taxi and they climbed inside.
"How are you feeling now?" Jo asked.

"Better, thanks. Must have been all the excitement of the awards. I'm so proud of you, Joanna. Did you have a good time at the after party?"

Jo was about to answer when the cabbie spoke. "Hey, lady, mind me saying you look familiar?" The cab driver's eyes, watching her from his rear view mirror, held a quizzical expression. His features were blurred by day old stubble.

"Doubt it, unless you live in the neighborhood we're going to." Jo frowned thinking he might have seen her on TV last night.

"Nope, I'm from the other side of town. You must look like one of those actresses or something," he muttered and turned his attention back to the road.

"Why didn't you say you were a famous singer?" Thea chuckled.

Jo felt her whole body respond like magic to that sound and winked. "Oh, I figure we are on vacation and we don't need it. Right?"

"Right."

"Dad will be at work now. What do you say we brunch with my folks around ten?" Jo asked casually.

"Try to stop me." Thea squeezed her hand.

Jo felt a surge of pleasure go through her at the touch. "Never. I think this is my stop."

"Eleven, then. If my folks are free, shall I invite them too?"

Jo grinned and held herself back from the kiss she desperately wanted. "Absolutely. Call me when you get home so I know you're safe."

"Of course. Now go, your mom is going to be so happy to see you," Thea said.

Jo waved before turning to her family home.

†

Other than different drapes on the windows, the place looked the same as it had when she had been a child. Her eyes scanned the deserted street as memories of days playing ball regardless of the traffic, and other such games as a kid that had made growing up fun. They'd been happy times though. For a few moments, she could hear the laughter and see the scene, smell the fresh bread baking, and remember Mrs. Spencer who played the damn piano so loud and off key you could hear it no matter where you were in the street. Her mind vividly recalled Gary Thomas, her first boyfriend and the first to kiss her. They'd been six at the time. That evening he lost his tooth and vowed never to kiss a girl again. She wondered if he ever did. Something she wasn't likely to find out since the Thomas's had left for Texas when Gary was ten.

"Jo, how good to see you. Your parents never said you were coming home." Mrs. Riker, the neighborhood gossip who ran the post office, hugged her in a warm welcome. "I hope I see you later." The woman smiled warmly and waved goodbye as she went on her way to work.

Jo grinned at the familiarity. It was so like the neighborhood she remembered. Maybe things hadn't changed that much. She obviously had. With a smile etched across her lips, she buzzed her parent's apartment. One thing she knew for sure at this time in the morning was that both her parents—being early birds—would be out of bed. That hadn't changed when she'd been there last.

She pressed the intercom.

"Hello?" Jo's eyes crinkled as she heard her mother's voice. It felt good to be there. She missed family more and more each time she left them. She was getting older and needed to settle down. A vision of Thea came to mind and she smiled.

"Hi, Mom, it's me." A shriek had Jo taking a step away from the intercom. A grin filled her face as the door buzzed open and she stepped inside the familiar hallway. Within a couple of minutes, her mother was kissing and hugging her.

"Why didn't you tell us you were coming? We could have met you at the airport," her mother admonished even though she was smiling.

"Low key, Mom. You know I like it that way. Anyway, Dad needs his sleep since he has to get up so early. The regulars would never forgive him for having their orders late. Whatever would they do without his fresh bagels and rolls for breakfast." Jo held her mother away from her for the usual scrutiny.

"You look haggard, Joanna. What have you been doing to yourself? I told Thea to look after you." Her mother clucked and glanced over her shoulder. "Where is she?"

"Thea has done a great job of looking after me. Yesterday was awards night with parties and all that. I didn't get my usual six hours."

"We watched you last night. Your dad is so proud of you."

"And you're not?" Jo laughed.

"Yes, yes, I am. I'm not a big country music fan. You're the only one I listen to."

Jo hugged her mom. "No problem, Mom. Thea doesn't really like country music much either. She likes my new work with a new young singer though." She hated Tandy but she wasn't saying that.

"That girl has good taste. I've always told her so. I miss Thea. She's like a breath of fresh air in a room when she enters."

Jo's blood rushed to her head. Thea was exactly that and more, so very much more.

"Will you and Dad be able to meet me and possibly Thea's folks for brunch at ten?"

"What a question. We will make time. Now come in and tell me all about the awards you won last night.

†

Joanna's grandmother's house was beautifully maintained with obvious respect and love. The wood looked as good as the day the building was completed. Whenever Thea entered the house, she felt that the inside reflected the out. The carefully chosen furnishings complimented the polished wooden floors and immaculately preserved oak paneling in various rooms. It was a wonderful home and like one she hoped one day to discover and own.

"Thea, Gran tells me you've been Skyping her every week since we left. You never told me." Joanna was in the kitchen helping her grandmother make sandwiches.

Thea walked to the open doorway and grinned at the two of them together. They did look alike except that Joanna had a much darker complexion from her Greek heritage. "Ah, yes, but do I need your permission to communicate with such a lovely woman?"

Realizing what she said, Thea could feel her cheeks grow hot from embarrassment.

"No. I think your taste is perfect." Joanna softly kissed her Gran on the cheek.

Jacqueline tutted. "What have you two been up to since we last saw one another...no, maybe since you've been back home. Thea has told me everything else."

Joanna picked up a slice of cucumber from the dish and popped it into her mouth and her grandmother gave her a severe look. "We are having a break with family. Non music related."

"Now, that's something new. Thea, thank you for making her see the light."

Thea looked at the delicious assortment of sandwiches. Her stomach was aggressively growling and her mouth was watering. She looked at Joanna, threw her glance at the food, and sighed.

They both chuckled.

"Care to share what has amused you both? The sandwiches are ready. Let's take them into the parlor and we can talk there while we eat them.

Minutes later, they were munching on sandwiches. Joanna, as usual was gulping her coffee far too fast. Thea speculated on how long it would be before Joanna burned her mouth.

"The food is delicious, Gran. I wish you came on our tours." She looked at her friend and grinned. "Thea has a bottomless pit to fill."

"I do, not that I'm really admitting that, but you on a tour would be wonderful. I can arrange it, if you like," Thea said.

"Silly children. I'm way too old for all that traveling, but thank you."

"The offer stands if you change your mind." Thea smiled fondly at the woman.

"Now that we have that out of the way. When are you coming to stay with me, Joanna? Your parents can't hog all your time. I want to see you as well."

"Gran, why not come for dinner on Sunday? You know mom will be thrilled and all the family will be there. Come on, Gran, life is too short. Will you bury the hatchet with my dad, please?"

"I will not, Joanna, and that is my final word on the matter."

"Fine. I was only asking." Jo closed her eyes in what looked like defeat.

For the next two hours, they talked about the concert tour, the award ceremony, and general things. When they departed, Thea hugged the older woman and whispered in her ear, "Diner, the hotel, a mixed family affair. Will that work?"

"We'll see."

†

On the drive home, Jo watched the scenery flashing by. She had never felt as relaxed as she did at that moment. It was easy to be in Thea's company. As they neared her family home, Jo closed her eyes. "Thea, I was wondering if we could have some time alone and talk about stuff."

"We can talk anytime, Joanna, you know that. I thought we did."

Jo sat up from her slouched position and smiled. "We do. I guess what I wanted to say is that we need a serious talk. Privately. No interruptions from the family, phone, crisis, or even an earthquake."

"Hope we don't have one of those." Thea grinned.

"I'm serious. How does a trip to Canada sound? We could rent a cabin for a few days and have a holiday alone. I'm sure our parents won't mind." Jo waited for a reply.

Ever since she'd held Thea in her arms while she slept, she could think of little else. She wanted to go where they would have as much uninterrupted time as possible. Everything in her mind and body was screaming that the outcome of their time alone was incredibly important. The place had to be just right for she knew there would be no second chances. She had to get it right.

"Sounds good. You arrange it and I'll be there with bells on."

"Bells. Now, that sounds interesting." Jo laughed just as the car stopped outside her parent's home. "Right. I'll arrange everything and call you with the details."

With a happy smile, Thea turned. Jo took the opportunity and leaned closer until their lips met. The pressure and sensual bomb amplified every nerve in her body. As their lips touched, Jo placed her arms around Thea and dragged her closer. She asserted a gentle pressure and ran her tongue along Thea's lips. When her mouth opened and their tongues intertwined, Thea moaned.

Jo pulled away slowly and stared at Thea passionately. "My God, I'm so sorry, Thea." Jo placed her hands over her face.

†

Thea stared at her friend. This was brilliant. A miracle. It was everything she could have hoped for would happen and Joanna was apologizing. That was ridiculous. Unable to stop herself she chuckled softly.

Joanna's cheeks went pink. "I'm sorry, Thea," she said while opening the car's door.

Thea's hand snaked out at lightning speed and held Joanna's arm, preventing her from fleeing the vehicle, "Not so fast, Joanna." Thea smirked. She couldn't help it. For once, she felt like she had all the power if the incredulous look on Joanna's face was anything to go by.

"What?" Jo barked out harshly.

"Not exactly the tone I expected after that wonderful romantic interlude." Thea couldn't help but tease Joanna, who looked remarkably uncomfortable. Finally taking pity on her, Thea leaned across and kissed her again.

"We'll talk tomorrow. Oh, and I think we can share a room wherever you plan to take me. I love you," Thea said softly. Not wanting to let her go yet, Thea slid her hand onto Joanna's forearm, caressing it slowly. She could feel the trembling under her fingers and wondered if Joanna was going to collapse in a heap in the seat.

†

Jo felt like she was gliding out of the car before standing numbly on the sidewalk watching Thea wave as she pulled away. Certain her mouth was open in shock, Jo placed her fingers on her lips. The memory of their shared kisses brought a glow inside her that she had never felt before. Not even the brief kiss at the hotel pool the week before had made her feel this way.

Is this what everyone calls love?

She'd certainly never felt this way after kissing anyone.

She entered the apartment building and, when she found herself in front of the door to her family's apartment, she wondered how she got there. Her mind and body were floating with the feelings that were coursing through her. All she wanted to do was to stay awake and shout from the rooftops that she was in love with Thea. Most important—she knew that Thea loved her, too. She'd said so. Hadn't she always known that? That thought made her heart soar.

Jo opened the door quietly, knowing that her parents would already be in bed since it was after ten and they went to work early. For her, sleep wasn't an option. Her body was on fire. It was very similar to the adrenaline rush she always had after a performance but much more pleasurable. Maybe if she waited another twenty minutes, she could call Thea to make sure it wasn't all in her imagination. Yeah, she could do that and would.

She extracted a cold beer from the refrigerator and after removing the top, drank heavily from the bottle. "Thea. Wow. Thea." The name alone evoked all manner of emotions within her.

She said we can share a room. Don't we always? But it's separate beds. Does it mean what I think it does? My God.

Her mind was doing loops in every imaginable way while she was leaning against the breakfast table, grinning. As she did, the giddiness within her bubbled up and grew with such intensity that she was sure her cheeks would split wide open. She was kinda glad that no one else was up because she probably looked goofy. God, this was stupid. She wasn't a teenager. She was a grown woman with too many relationships behind her ever to think love would be part of her life. Yet, here she was, totally besotted and absolutely, irrevocably in love with Thea. That name again. She knew if she said the name a thousand times—no a million—it wouldn't be enough. It would never be enough.

After throwing the empty bottle in the recycle bin, she looked at her watch. Fifteen minutes. Thea would be back at the hotel now. Taking another cold beer, she went to her room, sat down on the bed, dialed the direct line to Thea's rooms, and pressed the speaker button. Several rings later the night clerk answered the phone.

"Is Ms. Danvers available?"

"Who's calling?"

She wasn't happy about giving out her name, but realized that the guy was only doing his job. "Joanna Lackerly."

"Thank you, Ms. Lackerly, Ms. Danvers is with her mother at the moment. Do you want me to have her call you back?"

For a few moments, Jo wanted that desperately. "No. No, that's okay. I'll catch her tomorrow. Please just let her know I called. Goodnight." She pressed the off switch on the phone and threw it on the bed.

"Thea has arrived home safely and that's the most important thing. Tomorrow we will embark on another journey together. I can't believe I'm saying that, and what it means." Jo picked up her guitar that she'd left on her bed and gently strummed a few notes. Before she knew it, she was writing a song. A song for Thea.

Chapter Thirty

Belinda Orkney watched her boss pace in his office. She could see his tall gait indistinctly through the frosted glass. Any minute he'd be asking her to do something on his behalf. Yep...here it comes.

The door to Jack's office opened and out stepped the man, a frown on his face as he homed in on his PA. "Belinda, the press blurb that came through yesterday, don't send it to Jo or Thea...especially Thea. I'll deal with it when they come back to Nashville."

Belinda looked at the man in consternation. "Jack, I already sent it out last night. Thought you'd want that since the review was fantastic."

"Can we retrieve them?"

"Sorry, they were sent by courier and are probably already there by now. Want me to call them and find out?"

"God, no. Let's see if we have any fall out, shall we? I'll have a brandy with my coffee." The man walked away, shutting the door behind him with a thud.

Belinda wondered about the brandy. It was, after all, only eight in the morning. Something big must be going on. Her hand strayed to the folder on her desk that she was ready to file and she gave it a second glance. The review was excellent and said they expected greater things from the two women who had performed a duet. Although praising Tandy because she won the awards

Take Me As I Am

technically, Jo had a glowing mention. Clearly the critic wanted to hear more from her on both the song writing and singing fronts.

Her eyes strayed to the photos, several of Tandy and the awards. A couple of others of the singers together singing and as she flicked through the ones left, she didn't see anything odd. Then she saw it and whistled softly. Now she knew why Jack was worried. She'd missed that one last night when she'd sent the packs to the two women. There, in a tight clinch indulging in a passionate kiss were unmistakably Jo and Tandy. From what she could see, both women appeared to be enjoying the kiss for all it was worth. She closed her eyes for a fraction of second realizing what Jack was worried about. Country music and lesbians rarely mixed. "I wonder if Thea knows Jo likes women." Jack's words echoed in her ears, 'Especially Thea'.

Belinda's eyes widened. "Oh, shit!"

†

A tender smile crossed her lips as Thea thought of Jo who had apologized for not seeing her for breakfast. Her grandmother had fallen in the yard earlier that morning and she was on her way there with her mom in tow.

The indications were that although severely shaken, her grandmother hadn't broken anything. They were going to check on her to see for themselves, even if the stubborn woman didn't want them there. She'd noticed many of Joanna's traits in her grandmother and that was probably why they got on so well. Both were confident in what they wanted and how to go about getting it.

That was until the past night. A warm sensual feeling began flooding her body at the kisses she'd enjoyed in Joanna's arms. So much so that she had to shake away the increasingly salacious thoughts or she would be unable to function.

Thea walked toward her old desk and flipped through the mail picking up an envelope that had arrived by courier from Trigon Records. It was the review of the awards ceremony. She and Joanna had talked briefly about the event but hadn't gone in depth. She expected that they would talk about it when they went away for a few days. At least she would have a heads up on what the critics thought. She knew her friend wouldn't tell her much since she had no conceit in that area. Not like Tandy who was so full of herself and her talent.

She ripped open the strip and photos along with a description of them landed on the desk. She picked up the blurb and glanced down at the first photos. They made her smile. She saw Joanna trying desperately not to be bored sitting at the table. Reading the leaflet, she grinned at the praise, especially the part about Joanna's contribution. The critic obviously admired Jo and with good reason.

The glow began again as she drifted into a sensual haze at the image of Joanna. Her fingers picked up the photos and flicked through them until finding the ones with Joanna in them. Her eyes caught on one that taken with Joanna and Tandy, presumably during the duet. She could see it in her expression that Joanna was happy as she strummed the guitar. Another when she was singing, when Joanna was involved in her music it spoke volumes as nothing else could about the woman and the real love of her life. Hard to compete with she knew, but she wasn't in there to compete with it. She was there to share it and watch her friend rise to the heady heights of success she deserved. The phone rang and the photos discarded on her desk and forgotten.

"Hi." Thea's breath caught in her mouth when she heard Joanna's husky voice.

"Hi, yourself, how's your Gran?"

There was a deep chuckle. "You know Gran, she's fine. A little shaken and Mom actually stood up to her for a change. It was awesome."

"I bet it was. How are you today?"

"Good, what about you?" Thea heard her voice dropping into a sexy drawl.

"Great, I just opened the pack from Trigon and you had some great reviews. Some of the pictures aren't bad either."

"We can look at them together later. Can you be ready to leave by lunchtime?"

Thea smiled stupidly as she hugged her phone closer. This was ridiculous. She felt like a teenager. "Yes, what do I need to pack?"

"We're going to a cabin in the hills. It's still reasonable weather, but you'll need a jacket for the evening. Do you like hiking?"

"Oh, yeah, I love it." Maybe she was being a little too enthusiastic. Hiking wasn't a pastime she'd ever really indulged in before. However, for Joanna, she'd climb Mount Everest if the woman asked her.

"Great, I'll pick you up at noon. Be ready."

"I'll be ready. I hope you are." Thea heard the sexy laughter at the other end. Oh yeah, was she ready.

"See you later. Thea, I love you." The phone went dead before Thea was able to collect her scattered thoughts. All other things became lost in the tornado her mind had churned up at the words.

Joanna loved her.

The door opened and Karen popped her head around the door, "Have you time to speak with the contractor?"

"Yeah, sure, I'll be right out." She picked up the discarded photos, slipped them back into the envelope, and dropped them onto the pile on her desk.

†

Their meeting at noon had been an anti-climax to the feeling they had both been experiencing during the morning in anticipation of the trip. As Jo arrived to collect Thea, she'd become embroiled in signing autographs for a few of the guys who were working on the renovations at the hotel. Thea had looked on with a smug expression on her face.

Jo finally extricated herself from the enthusiastic contractors, giving them a brilliant smile of farewell as she finally climbed into the four-wheel drive vehicle she'd rented for the trip, and with an apologetic grin, drove away from the hotel. For the next hour, while they fought the flow of traffic, they remained in a companionable silence until Jo turned to Thea and gave her a warm smile.

"I'm looking forward to this break, Thea. It seems like ages since we spent any time alone together."

"I know exactly what you mean. Where are we going, anyway?"

Jo winked, wagged her finger, and then chuckled. "If you don't mind, I thought you deserved a surprise."

"Not at all. Do you want me to drive? How long will it take?"

Smiling warmly at the offer, Jo shook her head. "No, you drive me around enough. I thought I'd show you another of my skills. I can drive. Oh, it'll take around five hours, maybe six if I get lost."

†

"Tell me about the party you went to after the awards," Thea said.

"Not much to tell really. It was loud and people were obnoxious," Jo said tentatively.

"Tandy must be riding on cloud nine at the moment with all those accolades," Thea said.

For a split second, Jo wondered if Thea knew anything about what had happened at the party afterward. No way. It hadn't gotten on Facebook since that was the first place she'd checked. Nor had it been on Instagram. For a change and with a bit of luck, no one saw the kiss. As a precaution, she had purposely gone to the nearest newsstand and looked at all the music and entertainment press. Anything, in fact, that had any reference to the award ceremony. Frank, who ran the stand, was about to strangle her for messing up his merchandise, but she'd known him all her life. She had bought her first comic from him when she was five years old. Anyway, she'd given him a handsome bonus for the privilege. "Yeah, I guess. Didn't really see much of her afterward."

"Didn't Jack make you spend time together so everyone could admire his two protégés?"

"You know Jack too well. Does he know that you can read his mind? He'd be even more worried when you discuss my next contract." Jo smiled as she negotiated a steep bend taking them toward the mountain ranges and the cabin she'd arranged for them.

"We shall keep that a secret between the two of us, I think. Can't have Jack getting the upper hand, can I? Remember, I do have your interests to look after."

"Oh, I know that and let me tell you, there isn't a day that goes by that I don't thank God that you are the one to look after my interests. Thank you, Thea."

†

An hour and a half later, they pulled up outside a beautifully restored log cabin. It had a wonderful deck that looked out onto the lake, which was teeming with various bird life and glorious vegetation.

"Oh, Joanna, it's beautiful." Thea breathed. She opened her door, jumping out of the vehicle stumbling, but not enough to fall.

Although Jo did smile indulgently at Thea's enthusiasm, she climbed out slowly, collecting their possessions. This was an excellent place to begin what she hoped would be the start of a wonderful new phase of their partnership for the rest of their lives.

"You like it?" Jo grinned.

Being suddenly engulfed in a suffocating hug gave her the answer she wanted. "I guess you do. I'm glad." Jo drank in the wondrous feelings of having Thea held tightly in her arms. It was so very right.

"I love you, Joanna. When I think you can't surprise me anymore, you do just that." Thea turned glittering eyes to Jo.

"I love you, too, Thea." Their whispered words floated between them as they continued to gaze deeply into one another's eyes. Lips hovered a fraction of an inch away from the kiss that they both wanted badly, but just as they were about to meet, they heard a clearing of a voice from the side of their vehicle.

"Sorry to disturb you, youngun's. I wanted to check that you have everything before I go?" A man of about fifty with a grizzled face covered in a brown beard with streaks of gray running through it looked at them.

Jo suddenly became protective of Thea and moved in front of her. "Who are you?"

The older man gave her long stare and pulled at his whiskers for a few seconds before he nodded. "You, Lackerly?"

"Yes."

"I'm Chandler. We talked on the phone. This is my cabin."

"Hi. Sorry. I wasn't sure if anyone would be here to greet us." Jo walked down the steps toward the man and held her hand out.

"No problem. I've set up the logs for the fire and if you don't want that, there is the modern heater on the wall."

From his tone, Jo surmised he preferred the traditional means of heat. "Great, thanks." She smiled at the man then turned back to Thea, who was peering inside the cabin.

"My goodness, Joanna, you should see this place." Thea had her hands cupped together as she peered into the window.

Jo chuckled. "Looks like your cabin pleased her and that's the main thing."

The man gave her an odd look before smiling slowly. "Yep, seems that way. My number is on the refrigerator if you get into any difficulties. I can be here within the hour." He turned and left as silently as he'd arrived.

"Thanks," Jo replied. She stepped up on the porch and opened the door. Thea quickly joined her. It had all the traditional adornments, but just as equally, modern conveniences to make it as luxuriously easy a weekend as anyone could want. That was exactly what Jo wanted. There were definitely better things to do with their time if they were lucky.

"Joanna, we have everything we could possibly want here. It's marvelous," Thea enthused as she opened the fridge. "There's champagne. Wow."

Jo stood beside Thea and peered inside, grinning at the thought of sharing champagne with her love. Not that she needed the intoxication. Being this close to Thea was making her feel drunk. Her nose picked up the faint traces of perfume as she rested her chin on Thea's shoulder. "Is it too early to open that?"

Thea turned so they were facing one another. Mesmerized once more by their closeness, Jo wasn't surprised when Thea reached up and kissed her. She lit up like a candle as their lips tangled together.

For the next few minutes they indulged in the wonder of the moment before Jo pulled away, resting her head on Thea's forehead. "I love you, Thea. I need you to know that."

A beautiful smile was initially her answer as they indulged in another long hot, passionate kiss, "I love you, Joanna. I always have, from the first moment I saw you."

Both women had tears of deep joy in their eyes. They kissed again before pulling apart.

"We need to talk," Jo said.

"Yes, I agree." Thea just smiled.

"We should put our bags away and then we can sit out on the deck. What do you say?"

"Sounds like a plan to me. I'll make us a snack."

Jo collected their belongings then hesitated when she opened one of the bedroom doors. Should she place them both here, or... Thea did say one bedroom. Maybe it's too early and we should talk first. Yeah, that's what they would do.

"You open the champagne," Thea called from the kitchen.

"Great idea, I'm starving." Jo left the suitcases by the door and went to join Thea. She could feel the easy camaraderie they always had no matter the tension between them. Even back when they had first met, it was uncanny, but wonderful all the same.

†

Fifteen minutes later, toasting the vacation and eating the snack Thea put together, they sat close together on the swing on the deck. Joanna placed her arm around Thea's shoulder and they settled together as close as possible.

Thea made the first breakthrough. "I've loved you for a long time now and you were the reason I left Danvers," she whispered.

Jo smiled tenderly. "I can't believe how blind I was. I was so blind that I almost made the biggest mistake of my life by marrying Lee."

"Did you love him, Joanna?" Thea asked.

Jo shuffled uncomfortably for a few moments before settling back and sighing heavily. "I'm not surprised that you're asking me that. I would if the tables were turned." She ran a hand over her face. "I've given it a lot of thought. I was attracted to his attraction for me. At first, it was wonderful but after a time, I realized I didn't care as much for him as he did for me. It certainly wasn't love. It couldn't have been," Jo admitted.

"Why?"

Jo tightened her hold on Thea's hand and dropped a tender kiss on the top of her head. "Because I know what it feels like to love you. Believe me, everything and every other emotion pales into insignificance. I now know what love is and I have you to thank for that, Thea. As God is my witness, I'll love you for the rest of my life."

"I'm honored you feel that way, Joanna, because I don't know what I'd do without you in my life. I loved you so much that it hurt when you were with him." Tears chose that moment to appear in Thea's eyes.

Jo kissed them gently away. "I love you, Thea. I realize that I never knew what love is until you showed me," she whispered. "I'm sorry if I hurt you. It breaks my heart to know that."

"I think we should take this inside."

Jo stood and scooped Thea up into her arms.

†

Their bodies, naked under the sheet, trembled as they touched.

Jo tenderly kissed Thea while running her fingers down the length of her body. "You are so beautiful, my love." She could feel the quivering body under her touch. In the past, sex for Jo had been nothing more than to satisfy a need, yet with Thea it was different. Thea was innocent and her first time needed to be special, and she would make sure that happened.

"Is it okay if I touch you here?" Jo skimmed her fingers on Thea's breast.

"Oh, God, yes," Thea moaned.

"Tell me if I hurt you or you don't like something."

"Joanna, you aren't going to hurt me."

With the gentlest of touches, Jo explored Thea's body. Her mouth took in an erect nipple and it sent pleasure coursing through her when Thea moaned. She wanted to melt into her new lover and become one with her.

The kisses began small then erupted into a passion that took Jo by surprise. Never before had she felt the all-consuming love welling inside her body for Thea. She wanted more…needed more, her body filled with electricity and desire.

"Make love with me," Thea whispered.

"Are you sure that is what you want?" Jo wanted to be certain because she knew that once they made love there would be no turning back. Thea was forever and always had been.

"Yes. Yes, I want that more than life itself."

For a moment, Jo gazed into the green eyes and she saw both love and desire only for her. She slid her naked body next to Thea's and softly ran her fingers across the trembling body. Soon she felt fingers running along her body, mirroring her movements. As she bent to kiss the waiting lips, Jo gloried in the absolute, overpowering love she was feeling. It wasn't long before she could feel their bodies begging for further exploration.

Jo lifted herself up and looked deep into Thea's eyes asking a question.

Thea smiled. "Yes, I want you more than I ever believed possible."

Jo took a hard, extended nipple in her mouth again and ran her tongue slowly across it.

Thea responded with low moans as she held Jo's head in place. When Jo lightly bit the nipple, she could feel Thea's body explode in a series of small, intense quivers. The only thing Jo wanted was to make Thea happy and show her how much she loved her. She moved to the other nipple as her hand glided downward to the inside of the trembling thighs. Once again nipping the nipple produced the ripples of pre-orgasm but this time they were stronger and longer.

Thea grabbed her head and pulled her up for a kiss.

The kiss was so passionate and long that Jo was gasping for breath before noticing tears. "Have I hurt you?" she asked, as she kissed the tear stained cheeks.

"No," Thea managed to say. "I have never felt like this before, it is so powerful. I want more, Jo. I want it all."

Gently brushing blonde locks, Jo smiled. "We have a lifetime." Then she kissed the waiting lips as her fingers stroked Thea's center lightly. She was very wet and ready but Jo waited, taking Thea higher and higher. Fingers slid inside easily and Thea instantly began moving in time.

Jo stopped her motion as she gently kissed Thea. Then she took the small hand and led it down her long body to her own center. For a moment, she closed her eyes and tried to control her overwhelming need as the fingers moved through her wetness. Soon they were moving as one in a dance as old as time.

Take Me As I Am

Jo could hear Thea panting as they both bore down on the other's fingers wanting and needing release. "Now, Thea, now," she cried, just before they came at the same time.

Lying in Thea's arms, spent, and incredibly happy, Jo kissed Thea tenderly. "I love you more than I ever thought possible. Never in my life did I think I could ever be this unbelievably happy." Jo shook her head. "You were there beside me, always loving me even when I was being a bitch."

Thea ran a finger down Jo's cheek. "It was a rough road sometimes, but we found our way to each other in the end." She giggled. "I never imagined that my body would react in such a primal way."

"You were not alone in that." Jo snuggled close and kissed Thea igniting their passion once again and their bodies danced once more.

†

"Anyone ever tell you that you are the sexiest woman in the world?"

"Hardly. Joanna, you are something else." Thea's laughter caused a tingling sensation in Jo's body as she watched Thea staring as several types of birds glided over the lake.

"I'm in love, indulge me." Placing her arms around Thea's waist, she pulled her close. This was like a fantastic dream that she didn't want ever to end. If they were lucky, it wouldn't. Not for them.

"Anytime, my love, anytime. What shall we do today?" Thea looked up and kissed her lover's chin.

"Whatever you want, I'm completely at your disposal."

Turning so that they faced each other, Thea grinned wolfishly, "Really? Completely?"

"Yeah, for the rest of my life, if you want."

The words spoken softly had that tone about them that meant exactly what Joanna was offering her. A total commitment. Thea was at a loss for words.

"Too much for you?" Jo asked at the startled, amazed look in her lover's eyes.

"I...I...want—"

Swooping in to take a light passionate kiss, Jo laughed heartily. "I...want. That's all you have to say, darling?"

Thea could feel her face heat up and knew it was bright red. "I want you, Joanna Lackerly Xianthos, forever."

They both lost themselves once more in kisses that had them sinking to the ground at the overwhelming sensations it created within them. Another word was insatiable, but who cared.

An hour later, sated for the moment, a larger hand trailed gentle caresses on small perfectly formed breasts, partially bared from their previous lovemaking. They enjoyed the sun and tranquility of the area and the feeling that for the moment the world was just for the two of them.

"Do you think it will always be like this?" Thea asked, her voice tremulous. She moved to rest her body invitingly on top of her lover's relishing the chance to stare, without embarrassment, at the ample breasts of the singer. She recalled doing the same thing back in Danvers a long, long time ago and the same emotions she felt then had now multiplied a thousand fold. Now she knew what it was. Her lips then gave the voluptuous globes her full attention.

A low moan escaped Jo as she felt the caress and then was lost in the reaction. Eventually strangling out a reply, "We'll make it so, Thea, I promise."

Unable to leave the delicious breasts that she feasted on, her hand trailed down to the singer's trousers, which she already unfastened. Fingers quickly found their mark, feeling the soft curls and Thea reveled in the moans from her lover at her touch. Before long, they were lost inside one another, conversation not required on this journey of discovery.

†

Jo watched Thea checking everything for the tenth time before being satisfied. Thea finally looked at her and smiled, announcing, "All tidy. Just as when we arrived."

Laughing at the comment, Jo shook her head at the woman. "Thea, trust me, no one will care how we leave it. It's the same as a hotel, you pay your fee and that's the end of it."

"You forget my first love is the hotel business." Thea had a scowl on her face.

Unable to stop herself, Jo felt her stomach heave in laughter. She tried desperately to stop it. Placing a hand on Thea's arm they stared at one another willing the other to give in, neither did. "Did anyone tell you that you were stubborn?"

"Would anyone dare?"

Giggling like a schoolgirl, Jo gently lifted her lover's face and snatched a kiss. "Never. I thought maybe I'd replaced your first love."

†

Thea knew Jo was teasing her as she glimpsed the devilment in Joanna's eyes. How she loved this woman and most importantly, how great it was that they could do this with only the boundaries of love as an obstacle. Love had no boundaries. Reaching up to caress the lines around Joanna's face, she smiled tenderly. "There's nothing that means as much to me as you do. You're a part of me for the rest of my life and I'm glad that you found me."

†

For a split second Jo considered the situation. Would she want it any other way? All the freedom and money she ever wanted, any person she wanted, too, nothing to stop her. Could she be faithful? Could she be the person who for the past four days had control of her life? Could she? For Thea, it was a no brainer. "I have only one thing to say. Please love me no matter what happens because I never want to let you go, ever."

Thea smiled and kissed Jo deeply. "I don't care what happened before. You're mine now and I know it."

"I'm glad because I'd die if you ever forgot."

"Never going to happen, Joanna, never. Trust me." They collapsed into an embrace that made everything pale in comparison. This was the truth. Nothing could change that, nothing.

Chapter Thirty-one

The hotel interior looked great and all the regular customers appeared to welcome the facelift of the old building. Strange what a little paint and tender loving care did to a place. Thea had to admit the time alone with Joanna had not only heightened her senses to the singer whenever she was around, but also made her realize that the love she felt for her could only strengthen if given time. They'd been back for a week and Jack was pressing Joanna to travel back to Nashville. He wanted her to cut the duet with Tandy as soon as possible. As usual, her lover had been less than enthusiastic…

"I'm not interested in Tandy or singing with her again," Joanna said vehemently.

"I know, sweetheart, but she's high on the charts and you need to get back out there for your fans. They've done so much for you. Just one more song. Okay?"

"Fine, I'll go but I'll be back on Friday. I don't want to be away from you any longer than that."

Thea had known that was a bravado statement. Once she was back in the studio, it would be hard to pry her away. Why would she want to? It was Joanna's passion, second to her—she hoped—or at least they held equal footing these days. She recalled the morning waking in Joanna's tender embrace. Joanna was wide-awake, watching the gentle breeze billow the filmy curtains at the window. Making love was a desire that both had been able to quench whenever they had the privacy. Lying in bed that morning was no different. A grin she was unable to prevent flashed across her face just as the door to the office opened.

"Dare I ask what you were thinking about, Thea?" Jo grinned wickedly. "Judging by that smirk on your face I have a pretty good idea." She gave a knowing look. "You know earlier this morning, when I was discussing with my mother about family and friends, she told me I had the dopiest expression on my face and wanted me to explain why Aunt Marge's gall bladder operation was something to laugh at."

"And why the dopey expression?" Thea asked.

Joanna laughed. "For the same reason you had one on your face a few minutes ago." Shutting the door behind her, she stood on the other side of the tidy desk winking suggestively at Thea.

"You're bad to the bone, Joanna. Have I told you that before?" Thea stood and quickly enfolded Jo in a loving welcome followed by a long indulgent kiss that made both catch their breaths.

"Nope, you never have, others might have, but…"

Giving the woman a close look, she tipped her head to one side. "But?"

"Never for the same reasons as you probably do." Jo grinned at the slowly dawning expression before Thea gently cuffed her on the chin for her teasing.

"Time for lunch, dear?" Joanna smiled broadly and wiggled her eyebrows.

"I can't right now. My mom will be calling about the renovations any minute now. She thinks that while she, Grayson and Bradley are on vacation, the place will grind to a halt."

"No worries. I just was hoping…" The phone rang.

Thea rushed around the desk to answer. "I'm sorry," she mouthed.

Jo smiled and, with a wave, left the room.

Fifteen minutes later, Thea had completed her call with her mom and then taken another from the main contractor who was asking about payment. Fortunately, she had the payment ready for him, but was disappointed that Joanna had left so hurriedly. Despondently she sank down to the chair, tidied the desk, and smiled when she saw the envelope that contained the award ceremony info.

"Joanna's going to laugh. I've found the stuff from the ceremony. I knew I left it somewhere easy to find." Thea chuckled as she recalled telling Joanna that she hadn't been able to find the packet for their trip.

Flicking through them, she smiled at several. Jack looked very handsome dressed up to the nines and she wondered if he had a wife or partner. The man was cagey about his personal life, though who wouldn't be in that business? She pulled a face when she saw one of Tandy smiling winningly for the camera. She was one confident and showy cookie that one. "God help anyone who ever gets involved—"

The rest of the photos splayed out like an unwanted deck of cards onto her desk as she lifelessly held one photo in her hand. Her mind falling like a pebble over a waterfall, knowing that what she was seeing must be a fake. It had to be. She knew that Joanna would never act like that in public, especially with Tandy. The picture screamed at her as she scrutinized it closely. Both women appeared to be enjoying the intimate moment. Why hadn't Joanna mentioned it to her, especially now that they were lovers? Didn't she think it was worth mentioning? Of course it was. It didn't look casual and it had far-reaching consequences if the media blew it out of proportion and started labeling Joanna.

"It didn't happen. It can't have. Someone photo shopped this or it would have been out publicly by now."

Is what I have with Joanna temporary? She'd always said that love wasn't for her and none of her relationships had ever worked. Could this be the reason why? Her inherent lack of faithfulness?

God, what a fool I was to believe that Joanna wanted me and only me in her life? I have, haven't I...I'm such a fool.

As her mind played scenarios with her fragile feelings and the insecurities of old resurfaced, the door to her office opened. Jo walked confidently back into the room, her arms full of sandwiches and snacks along with a couple of Starbucks coffees. Thea melted again as she came face to face with the woman who held her heart and had perhaps already crushed it.

Thea pushed the photo toward Jo when she placed what she had on the desk.

"You might want to see this one. It's in profile but a good shot." Thea could hardly contain her breaking heart.

There has to be a reason. Please, Joanna, give me a reason.

Joanna frowned and picked up the photo.

"Do you want to tell me what this is all about?" Thea crossed her arms and wished she were anywhere else as she waited for an answer. She would be unable to eat the delicious food in front of her until she knew one way or the other what she meant to Joanna.

"Do I need to explain anything? It was a party and people get carried away," Joanna retorted and sat in the chair opposite her.

Thea swallowed hard, not knowing what to say. Jealousy was driving her much like the first time she had left Joanna. Was she going to be predictable and do so again? "I guess not."

"Good, what's the deal with mom?"

Thea had heard that tone before and gave Joanna a long hard stare. It was her way of ending a conversation.

So, it was finished between them. But was it?

Dare she let it go and leave it to fester in the background?

No, not this time.

"Tell me one thing, please, Joanna. Do you love me?"

Joanna stood, walked toward her lover with a small smile on her face and an unfathomable expression in her eyes. "I love

Take Me As I Am

you, want you, need you, and most important of all, I will *not* ever cheat on you," she said, kneeling beside Thea.

Thea gulped back a sob of happiness before flinging her arms around Joanna and whispering incoherently. Joanna was off balance making her fall backward, dragging Thea with her, both collapsing on the floor in a heap. Both women were laughing at how ridiculous they looked.

Joanna's eyes filled with a dangerously smoldering look. "Have you ever thought about making out on the floor?"

Thea chuckled and knew her cheeks were beet red. "We can't, Joanna, not here. Someone might come in." Thea struggled to extricate herself from the strong, but loving arms that held her. After a few passionate kisses, Joanna released her.

Thea stood above Joanna and offered her a hand to get up.

"Someone might come, that's true. Another time perhaps, after we lock the door," Joanna said with a wide grin.

Unable to stop the flush from returning to her cheeks, Thea shook her head. "Perhaps."

"Can I interest you in a little light lunch instead?" Joanna gave an exaggerated wave toward the fare on the wooden table.

Thea was giggling at the gesture. "Light lunch. Joanna, there's enough there for five people not two."

"Got to keep my girl well fed, can't have anyone thinking I neglect her. Tell me how the vacation to Vegas is going. I really never suspected your parents of being closet Elvis impersonator fans."

They both laughed and started on the food.

Thea breathed deeply, allowing her destructive thoughts to dissipate for good. After all, she had the real thing and all Tandy had was a photo. It was no contest. After picking up the offending photo, she ran it through the shredder and brushed her hands together. "Next time you are going to be around Tandy, let me know and I will be there to protect you from her advances. Then she will know in no uncertain terms that you are mine."

"My protector." Jo grinned as she bit into a sandwich.

Thea wriggled her eyebrows. "Damn right."

†

Standing and watching Joanna perform her latest hit on stage from the sidelines, Thea couldn't help but feel enormously proud of her and all she had achieved since they met that incredible fateful day in Danvers more than four years earlier. They'd had their difficulties as most people do. Perhaps theirs wasn't exactly the conventional ones, but they'd seen the good and bad sides of one another's characters. Perhaps that was the wrong term, their human failings would be better and they both had those, as everyone did at times. Because of the business they were in, the situations took on an exaggerated feeling, but they would cope because they cared about one another on every possible level.

The first few weeks of their flourishing love for one another had been euphoric in many ways. At first, they decided to keep it private, not even telling their closest family. However, who could have kept it from Joanna's family, especially her grandmother? After her initial shock, she had become their staunchest supporter. Joanna let it slip that her father had doubts about them settling down as a family unit instead of always touring and roaming the world. She hadn't known if Joanna had sown that seed on purpose because she knew how her grandmother might react. Her own mother had welcomed Joanna into the family with open arms. She knew what it meant to be in love and have obstacles in the way of that love succeeding. Anyway, as she put it, there were more important issues in the world than petty squabbles about same gender love.

As the song on stage became wistful in melody, so did Thea's mind. She recalled lying in Joanna's arms that morning. Life couldn't get any richer for her. Of course, it had repercussions. Jack had been a pillar of strength when they admitted their love and agreed that for the moment they should take a private view on it. He was grateful that they told him, especially if the press caught hold of the story and decided to make a big thing of it. He assured them that if that case arose he had other avenues for Joanna to explore. The most interesting being her crossing the line from country music to pop. There had been numerous influential people asking about her writing songs for prominent pop personas.

Fortunately, for them, Tandy was making bigger waves in her own world. She had a whirlwind affair with a roadie on tour and ended up marrying him and divorcing him within the month. The kid was running at full throttle into every experience she could and although she knew, that Joanna probably had a soft spot for the girl even if she denied it. She speculated that Joanna had a desire to see the that girl didn't make the same mistakes she had when she had first started out. The evidence was that Tandy would make her own mistakes and Joanna was there if she needed her help.

Crashing applause followed the song as it ended and she smiled. Her lover would be finished in a few minutes and they could go home and indulge in making love. Joanna, always hyped up after a concert, had lots of restless energy to expunge.

"Hey, Thea, are you in a daydream? Our girl wants you on the stage." Pete pushed her toward the stage. "What's going on? I never go on stage...ever," she said to Pete who shoved her out onto the stage.

"Ah, there she is. Come on out here, Thea, the folks are dying to meet you." Jo grinned winningly at her.

Unable to do anything else but slip out on the stage, she was amazed as the crowd applauded and she heard wolf whistles.

Wait until Joanna gets home. She's in big trouble this time, she thought.

"Ladies and gentlemen, I met this lady a while back and she is the other half of what makes Jo Lackerly the woman she is today. If you will indulge me, I have a song especially for her."

Thea knew her eyes were bulging in surprise. Joanna's coaxing eyes that led her to sit on the stool next to her mesmerized her.

"I love you," Joanna whispered before a goofy smile filled her face.

God, what love does to you. She strummed her guitar and began to sing…

"From the tips of your ears, fingers and toes there's a map I have of you.

All of you with every breath and beat of your heart.

Watching you shake your head then that smile, this is just for me.

Someplace deep inside I'll be waiting and together we know.

No matter how long it takes, you will be mine completely, loving you for eternity, improbable protector of my heart.

Your clothes peel off as you take a shower.

My eyes wonder at the sight relishing every splash.

Deliciously exciting, demanding my attention.

I'm amazed at your power you take me ensnaring me in your tower.

No matter how long it takes, you will be mine completely, loving you for eternity, improbable protector of my heart.

Sometimes the road is rough it takes us to the far side.

Darkness might greet us on the way.

Love never leaves me behind now that you are part of my heart.

Luminosity invades like a brilliant star scorching me inside with your light.

No matter how long it takes, you will be mine completely, loving you for eternity, improbable protector of my heart.

Echoes of loneliness can invade recalling times and other ways.

Now I know for sure that you are here to accompany me through all my days.

No longer, lonely but filled with tender love to share.

No false promises can ever be good enough for you.

No matter how long it takes, you will be mine completely, loving you for eternity, improbable protector of my heart.

Take your time now darling as you watch me leave for a time.

Because you know, I'll be back.

No one can ever replace you in my heart and the love we share.

In every way in any way, I'll not let anyone take you away.

What I feel is real and will last eternally.

No matter how long it takes, you will be mine completely, loving you for eternity, improbable protector of my heart."

As the ending chord of Jo's guitar completed the segment, she bent toward Thea. "All yours, my love."

Thea was unable to do more than tremble. "Do you know what you're doing? That was a love song," she whispered. "I...I can't believe you did that. Are you mad?"

Joanna grinned wickedly. "Yeah, for you. Do you mind?"

Thea shook her head before dropping down from the stool and giving her partner a long-suffering look before leaving the stage.

"Did you know she was going to do that?" Pete asked. "Tell the world she loved you?"

She was embarrassed at the good-natured way Pete said what she was thinking.

"Nope. You didn't, did you? She sure pulled it off. Next best thing to a proposal in this business, I'd say." He grinned. "Listen to the audience cheering. Bet she does two encores at least."

Pete left and Thea bemusedly watched the love of her life give her final encore.

†

Snuggling into the well-muscled shoulder of her lover, Thea reflected on what had happened the past night. After the concert, reporters had plagued Joanna and Thea hadn't gotten away from the skirmish either. They repeatedly asked if anything was going on between them. Both had declined to comment, fueling the situation even more. They'd called Jack to tell him what had happened and he had said not to worry, that he'd handle the press.

Thea stood and watched Joanna pour them a drink, snatch a few sandwiches from the refrigerator, and settle onto the large sofa. Then Joanna looked directly at her with a puzzled expression on her face.

"Am I in trouble? Last time you looked like that it was about that photo of me and Tandy." Joanna bit ravenously into a sandwich.

Thea sometimes wondered about her friend. She didn't always see past what she thought was okay and gave little regard to what others felt. "I was surprised that's all. I hate being made a public fool." There she'd said it and it was out.

"What?" Joanna pushed the food and drink away before standing and walking to Thea.

"Joanna, I'm not like you. I hate the limelight and you know that." Thea stood her ground because she knew if Joanna kissed her, she would lose her powers of reasoning and go to pieces. Sensual pieces. Incredibly pleasurable pieces. But pieces all the same.

"I wanted the world to know I love you. I'm sorry it didn't sit right with you, Thea. I won't take it back. How can I? It's how I feel."

The words tinged with sadness sent a simple yet powerful message to her heart. "Was this your way of proposing to me?"

The glum expression on Joanna's face cleared as she smiled brilliantly, "I couldn't have put it better myself. Do you have an answer for me?"

Thea stepped toward Joanna and tenderly traced the lines around her lips that the smile created. "I love you no matter what and if you need an answer, then there can only be one. Yes." Flinging her arms around Joanna, she kissed her deeply, igniting their passion.

Several minutes later, they parted breathlessly. Joanna swung Thea up into her arms and strode purposefully toward their bedroom.

"Don't you want to eat first?" Thea asked.

"Hmmm, sure. I have a wonderful appetizer in my arms right now that is waiting for me."

A gurgle of sexual pleasure left Thea's throat, as she knew exactly what that meant. "And?" Thea began teasing her lover by placing delicate tiny kisses along her collarbone and neck.

"And eating her might be an option." They both laughed as they landed on the bed and made love until dawn.

†

Now, as she felt the tender stroking of Joanna's hand on her abdomen, she marveled at how life could change, bringing so much happiness into it. She was happy, so very much so that sometimes it was hard to take and her heart felt like bursting.

"Want to share what you're thinking?" Joanna's voice rumbled against her.

"How did you know I was awake?"

"Easy, your breathing changed. You forget, my love, I have sensitive ears and they are very, very sensitive with regard to you." The hand that had been doing a circular movement on her stomach now teased her by caressing the underside of her breast. Damn it, but Joanna could turn her on in a second.

"Oh, I was thinking about us and how happy I am." Thea moved so that she could partially see Joanna's face.

"I'm glad you're happy because I know I sure am and it's all because of you."

"No, please, it's all because of you." Thea giggled.

"Oh, no, please, it's all because of you, my love." For several minutes, they traded like for like until the passion that they held in check bubbled and they found that making love was far better than trading words.

As their passion ignited to a flame, the improbable protectors went about their work by protecting and nourishing a love that had grown from an improbable meeting.

Anything in life was possible.

The End

Take Me As I Am

Jo Lackerly's Songbook

Traveling Girl

I'm a traveling girl.
I travel the world to find you.
One day I will
You and I will be together forever.

When you walked away, you didn't know,
How much you'd come to mean to me.
It wasn't easy then to tell you
Now that you're gone I can't find you.

I watched you go, never thinking
I'd never see you again.
It would never be the same when you went away
It would never be the same until you're home.

I'm a traveling girl.
I travel the world to find you.
One day I will
You and I will be together forever.

Experience tells me that
You will never come back to me,
But I'll search for eternity.
There's always the chance

That I will see you looking out for me
And when you do,
I'll be there to tell you,
I love you.

I'm a traveling girl.
I travel the world to find you.
One day I will
You and I will be together forever.

As I sit here singing this song for you
I look upon the sea of faces.
The only face I want to see staring at me
Is you and I will;

I will one day and have you back to stay.
I live to love you again
I will never fail to seek you out.
And one day soon you will know
How much I miss your smiling face.

I'm a traveling girl.
I travel the world to find you.
One day I will
You and I will be together forever.

Invaluable Friend

When you said you would be there for me,
I believed you.
When the darkness came
No one was around to shed the light
You brought a torch

You support me,
You have faith in me,

Take Me As I Am

You hold my hand,
You will cry with me.
And when the time comes
You will provide a smile for me.
You are my invaluable friend.

When you saw me fail,
You picked me up,
Dusted me off
Told me to try again.

You never talked
You just grinned
Made me smile all over again.

You support me,
You have faith in me,
You hold my hand,
You will cry with me.

You support me,
You have faith in me,
You hold my hand,
You will cry with me.
And when the time comes
You will provide a smile for me.
You are my invaluable friend.

As I grow older,
I know that no matter where in the world you are,
You will always be the shoulder that I cry on,
The shoulder that I laugh on,
The shoulder that I rely on.
You will be the one thing that remains constant;
You will be simply my friend.

You support me,
You have faith in me,
You hold my hand,
You will cry with me.
And when the time comes
You will provide a smile for me.
You are my invaluable friend.

What Made You Change Your Mind?
What made you change your mind?

I can't believe it you said you're leaving with me.
Was it something I said?
Something I did?
Tell me please I need you so.
What made you change your mind?

You said you would come with me
Let me protect you no matter what.
I know I'm not the best that the world has to offer,
I would be there regardless the cost.

What made you change your mind?

When you accepted my offer you made my life come on fire.
My heart, it was singing,
My body was ringing
With the happiness, you were bringing.

What made you change your mind?

As I step out the door,
I wait to hear you take your place at my side.
As I leave this place my heart will ache
If you're not here with me.

Take Me As I Am

What made you change your mind?

How many roads will I travel alone?
What dreams will I shed now that you stay away from me?
Whatever will it take for you to come home to me?
For you are my home no matter the place?
You are where my dreams come my thoughts are true.

What made you change your mind?

What Do I See
I know I needed you like the soil needs the rain.
You are my love the one that makes me yearn
I feel no pain
In time, you will see you are meant for me

Who will care
Who will share my life
If you don't stay beside me?

I look around what do I see?
My life spirals around me
No one to tell,
No one to share,
No one to wonder if I'm there.

You were so small
So insignificant
Something called.
I cannot say if you will stay
Why should you play my game?
Know only this I'm there for you
Until the end of time they say

I look around what do I see?
My life spirals around me

No one to tell,
No one to share,
No one to wonder if I'm there.

I know as I look in your eyes
It might be the last time, who knows
You gave me love and I'm thankful of
No devotion can you give that means so much as you do to me
Yet through it all I've never said what you mean to me

I look around what do I see?
My life spirals around me
No one to tell,
No one to share,
No one to wonder if I'm there.

I know as time goes by we might never be
I'll always know you love me
Who can take away the pleasure that gives
No one here on earth I think

I look around what do I see?
My life spirals around me
No one to tell,
No one to share,
No one to wonder if I'm there.

Don't Despair

Love is in my heart it needs you now don't you know
Life brought us burdens that we shared and shed along the way
Who will know but us what brings us to this tryst
There can be no one for me but you and I know you know it too

Don't despair

Take Me As I Am

Let me repair that need in you
That calls to my heart
That binds our souls for eternity

I've never expected to be this secure usually always the one who's bored
It doesn't matter to my heart that you might never feel you take the part
I know that deep inside of me I'm calling out your name you see
Foolish people often say intelligence left that day
The very day you entered my life to stay

Don't despair
Let me repair that need in you
That calls to my heart
That binds our souls for eternity

The stars will shine the heavens awake to my cry
I want you in my life again,
It doesn't hurt you see anymore
Because I know, you will return to me if you go away
Your heart is mine if only you could see

Don't despair
Let me repair that need in you
That calls to my heart
That binds our souls for eternity

My love will grow with endless energy
Make no mistake I'm here for you and if your tears flow
I'll wipe them away and make you smile
Tomorrow will be ours for all time
Our souls guarantee that above all

Don't despair
Let me repair that need in you

That calls to my heart
That binds our souls for eternity

Borrowed Dreams
A lifetime hidden with borrowed dreams
Waiting for a special chance
To create for real the happiness and love
I know exists deep inside me

You take a chance at times
Never knowing if it could be your last
Or if it will bear fruit along the way
So you go away

How we learn in this life
With the chances we take
Or those we mistake
We may simply forget

Break them apart before they arrive.
A lifetime hidden with borrowed dreams
Waiting for a special chance
To create for real the happiness and love

I know exists deep inside me.
I never realized you were my chance
Now I know and things have changed
Knowing that you're out there

My life will never be the same
Yet a lifetime of fears
Disillusionment keeps us apart
A lifetime hidden with borrowed dreams

Waiting for a special chance
To create for real the happiness and love

I know exists deep inside me
For as we ducked and dived

Creating a shallow life
We both thought we were happy
Never taking the time to say how we feel
Letting it slip away

The chance to be with you
Allowing us to be free
Now we walk alone
Never to experience the warmth we gave

Losing you has changed my way
Allowing only despair to remain
A lifetime hidden with borrowed dreams
Waiting for a special chance

To create for real the happiness and love
I know exists deep inside me
If one day a second chance comes my way
I'll take it in my hands and to my heart for all to see

That you are my chance to be free inside of me
Where happiness blooms and dreams come true
You will see it too, my love
Once we take the chance forever more

A lifetime hidden with borrowed dreams
Waiting for a special chance
To create for real the happiness and love
I know exists deep inside me.

Be Mine

Days are uncertain we don't know what to expect
Will we know what to do will we ever know who

JM Dragon & Erin O'Reilly

There's a place in our heart that knows the answer
Can we recall it and know for sure what saves our souls
In my heart, I'll give you the sun though it may rain
As I walk the day, I'll follow the road you take
The night crosses our path and I'll be there
Holding your hand and yearning for you to take me inside
Thoughts of you flood my mind
As always, I'm putty in your hand
Foolish that may seem to you
Yet you smile and allow me to follow blindly
I'd give anything to know you love me for what I am
Stars shine above and give me the confidence to say
How I love you each day.
Come rain or shine please be mine

No Longer Alone

I'll never doubt it when they say angels have wings
Maybe because I need you to fly right down beside me
For in dreams I loved you for eternity
Will you be mine in reality?

When I close my eyes
I'm on top of the world
With you close in my arms
No longer alone
I have you sharing our souls

All I have to offer is my love
No fortune can I bring only me
With an offer to stay with you each day
Caring, proud, tenderly sharing our lives

You are my one and only treasure
When I close my eyes, I'm on top of the world
With you close in my arms
No longer alone, I have you sharing our souls

Forever devoted I'll wait
Who knows when that heavenly burden will cross my path?
To heal those wounds each moment alone continues to ooze
God speed you here my darling don't make me wait another minute, hour or a day

When I close my eyes
I'm on top of the world
With you close in my arms
No longer alone
I have you sharing our souls

My Mama Told Me

My Mama told me you got to be good in life;
My Papa said you have to try
I didn't believe them going out on my own;
Being good wasn't part of my life's mysteries

There was a life to live, places to be and people to meet
I did it all and didn't care how or who was hurt on the way
Telling myself being good wasn't part of the deal
Years took their toll, as I split from town to town never knowing you see

That you had to want to be good to be allowed to stay free
I floundered and cried, I'd even sadly tried
To end it all one day
Until I met you and all I could feel was you inside me

Telling me the darkness was nothing at all
To break away and live to be free be good that's all it takes
Being good wasn't an option in me or so I tried to tell myself frequently
However, with you by my side, I gladly surrendered to all that you taught

For good was in you to lighten my way and I'll never fail
Because you showed me the way allowing good in my life, sharing and caring
Eventually reaping the rewards you thought lost in your life

My Mama was right my Papa too but it took me a while
To find what was missing and see the real me
That thankfully others saw and faithfully stand by me today
I found out all you need do is care and it will be returned a thousand fold

For I'm prepared to break down the best fences built
And ask nothing in return because the greatest reward
Is the goodness that friendship helped build.

Improbable Protector

From the tips of your ears, fingers and toes
There's a map I have of you
All of you with every breath and beat of your heart
Watching you shake your head
Then that smile,
This is just for me
Some place deep inside
I'll be waiting and together we know

No matter how long it takes,
You will be mine completely,
Loving you for eternity,
Improbable protector of my heart

Your clothes peel off as you take a shower
My eyes wonder at the sight relishing every splash
Deliciously exciting, demanding my attention
I'm amazed at your power you take me ensnaring me in your tower

Take Me As I Am

No matter how long it takes,
You will be mine completely,
Loving you for eternity,
Improbable protector of my heart

Sometimes the road is rough
It takes us to the far side
Darkness might greet us on the way
Love never leaves me behind now
That you are part of my heart
Luminosity invades like a brilliant star
Scorching me inside with your light

No matter how long it takes,
You will be mine completely,
Loving you for eternity,
Improbable protector of my heart

Echoes of loneliness can invade
Recalling times and other ways
Now I know for sure that you are here
To accompany me through all my days
No longer lonely but filled with tender love to share
No false promises can ever be good enough for you

No matter how long it takes,
You will be mine completely,
Loving you for eternity,
Improbable protector of my heart

Take your time now darling
As you watch me leave for a time
Because you know, I'll be back
No one can ever replace you in my heart and the love we share
In every way in any way, I'll not let anyone take you away
What I feel is real and will last eternally

JM Dragon & Erin O'Reilly

No matter how long it takes,
You will be mine completely,
Loving you for eternity,
Improbable protector of my heart

About the Authors

JM Dragon

JM Dragon is a New Zealand citizen, living in the beautiful Canterbury countryside. JM Dragon loves to garden, travel, write, take care of her animals, family, and pursue her business interests—Affinity eBook Press. She is a keen reader of sci-fi, crime/mystery, classic and romance, which helps to feed the imagination for her own stories.

Currently published by Affinity eBook Press NZ LTD, her books include *Do Dreams come True*, *Fix It Girl*, *In Name Only*, *The Destiny Series*, *Circus*, and 2015 GCLS winner *The One*.

Contact her at jm1dragon@yahoo.com or on Facebook at http://www.facebook.com/julie.dragon.

Erin O'Reilly

Erin O'Reilly resides in Texas. She is an accomplished author with twenty-three published works, including her newest collaboration with JM Dragon *Take Me as I Am* and soon to be released *No Other Love*. She was the Sapphic Readers Award winner for her book *Deception*. Her focus as a writer is to develop strong characters that make a dramatic impact on her story lines.

When not writing she is the technical Director and CEO of Affinity eBook Press.Contact Erin at erinoreilly@affinityebooks.com

Other Books from Affinity eBook Press

Carved in Stone by Jen Silver Join the characters from *Starting Over* and *Arc Over Time* in this final book from the Starling Hill trilogy. *Carved in Stone* has romance, adventure, a treasure hunt, and happy endings for all, living and dead.

Anywhere, Everywhere by Renee MacKenzie Gwen Martin's life in the Ten Thousand Islands area changes irrevocably when Piper Jackson comes into her life. Without trust, can the budding relationship between Gwen and Piper survive? Or will the answers to the questions continue to haunt them?

Venus Rising by Ali Spooner Levi Johnson arrives at Venus Rising, an exclusive lesbian only tropical resort in the Virgin Islands and finds more than she expected—a sizzling hot love triangle. Torn between her attraction to both women struggles to choose the right woman to share her life.

The Devil's Tree by Ali Spooner Torn between her love for the pack and her need to find what's missing in her life Devin Benoit travels to New Orleans. Will the previous happenings at the Devil's Tree help or hinder Devin in the fight of her life, and the life of Tia, the woman who now owns her heart?

The Case of the Beggars' Coppice by Erica Lawson Edda Case is a woman in crisis who discovers that things are not as they seem. Is it truly a message for her from beyond the grave or is something more sinister taking place? Can Edda solve the mystery of *The Beggars' Coppice*?

Locked Inside by Annette Mori   How much does the power of love matter to someone who must overcome obstacles far greater than most people face in a lifetime.

Line of Sight by Ali Spooner   Sasha and her lover Kara are back. Continue the thrilling adventures of this couple from the Sasha Thibodaux series.

Requiem for Vukovar by Angela Koenig   Requiem for Vukovar continues the Refraction series and the exploits of Jeri O'Donnell and her partner, Kelly Corcoran. In an epic siege largely ignored by the wider world, Kelly, who was prepared to give up comforts and certainties when she became part of Jeri's nomadic life, encounters more than physical danger. Her ability to maintain her core integrity is assaulted by the inevitable ugliness of war. For Jeri, the true battle is confronting her attraction to violence as she struggles against losing herself in the exhilaration of combat.

Against All Odds by JM Dragon   From award winning and bestselling author JM Dragon, with significant updates by, Erin O'Reilly comes an original tale of romance where everything seems to be stacked against two women whose destinies bring them together. Life however takes a twisted path setting both Steph and Louise in directions they never thought possible. Will love win out against all odds or will love be forever lost?

The Settlement by Ali Spooner   The outpouring of love and friendship toward Cadin helps her on her path to healing and learning to trust her heart to love once again. Join bestselling author Ali Spooner on this sensational journey that ends with a heartwarming romance.

Once Upon a Time by Alane Hotchkin   Raven only wanted to escape the blows that life had dealt her. She longed to be on the open sea and free. When she came upon a beautiful young girl sitting alone in the middle of a meadow, little did she know that her destiny would be changed forever. Will they become the pawns of the ancient vision or will both paths lead to the same port of destiny? Find out it in this exciting high seas adventure that will capture your imagination.

Asset Management by Annette Mori Follow the twists and turns to the explosive conclusion. Not everything is black and white. There are many shades of gray and sometimes it's difficult to decipher who is good and who is evil. No one is all virtue or all malevolence, but sometimes love helps us rise above.

Do Dreams Come True? by JM Dragon How do two people who really shouldn't get on end up in a relationship? Find out in this deliciously ordinary romance.

Return to Me by Erin O'Reilly Will Salvation bring just that to Ellie, allowing her to find peace and happiness again, or will it have her questioning all that she believes in? A wonderful romance cloaked within an intriguing mystery.

Arc Over Time by Jen Silver This wonderful romantic continuation with the characters from *Starting Over* ties up loose ends. But the question is—does everyone have a happy ending? A must read.

The Presence by Charlene Neal Can Rebecca and Kayleigh overcome ghosts from the past and their own insecurities, or will a presence from the past tear them apart?

A Walk Away by Lacey Schmidt Sometimes chance brings you to the right person to help you resolve some of your baggage, and you learn to like yourself a little more. Kat and Rand are smart enough to recognize this chance in each other, but they also find that there is a catch to every opportunity—walking toward something is always walking away from something else.

Possessing Morgan by Erica Lawson The investigation has barely begun when Andrea becomes the target of a nearly fatal hit-and-run. But was it really aimed at her? Can she and Morgan find the common ground they need to solve the case and stop the attacks, or are the gaps just too wide to bridge?

Twenty-three Miles by Renee MacKenzie This is a story about community, and how it comes together in dangerous and devastating times. When you don't know who to trust, you better have friends who will rally around you. Will Talia and Shay find the answers they need to the mystery of the murders on the parkway, or will justice be elusive? Will they survive their quest for the truth?

Reece's Star by TJ Vertigo Under Faith's guiding, loving hand, will Reece successfully traverse the rocky road of emotion and embrace the positive changes in her life? Or will she panic and be unable to control that Animal part of herself? Will she take that next step to declare herself fully capable of love and devotion? This third installment in the popular series that began with *Private Dancer* continues the passionate and often hilarious romance of Reece and Faith as they both grow in love and in trust.

Confined Spaces by Renee MacKenzie Corporate politics, complicated romance, and long distances conspire to keep Andie and Kara all boxed in. Can love triumph despite the Confined Spaces?

Cowgirl Up by Ali Spooner Ride along with the MC2, for boot scootin', butt kickin', dirt eatin', rodeo adventures, with a love story thrown into the mix.

If I Were a Boy by Erin O'Reilly Will Katie and Helen be able to make a life together work or succumb to doubts and the pressures of family? This story will fill you with the thrill of passion and the tenderness of love.

The Chronicles of Ratha: Book 2 A Lion Among the Lambs by Erica Lawson Can Jordana believe in herself like her Noorthi sisters do? Only then can she fulfill her destiny as The Chosen One. Follow the colorful cast of characters in this action-packed adventure sequel as they traverse the galaxy. Of course, nothing ever goes smoothly when Jordana is involved.

Terminal Event by Ali Spooner Will the killer be caught or continue to evade authorities? Can Tally and Blair's budding romance survive the possibility? Read this intense murder mystery romance and find out.

Love Forever, Live Forever by Annette Mori Fate intervenes and puts Nicky directly back into the path of her first love, Sara, and the corresponding events send her into a tailspin. Now she must decide—who will be the person she ends up living with and loving forever?

The One by JM Dragon *2015 GCLS Winner for Romance, Intrigue, and Adventure. The One* is a romance with everything, love, intrigue, misunderstandings with a happy conclusion—the only question—who gets the girl?

Flight by Renee Mackenzie Some lives will be lost and others changed forever when the sisters' lives intersect. Will they be consumed by the wreckage, or will they be able to pick themselves up and take flight?

Affinity
eBook Press
NZ

E-Books, Print, Free e-books

Visit our website for more publications available online.

www.affinityebooks.com

Published by Affinity E-Book Press NZ LTD
Canterbury, New Zealand

Registered Company 2517228

Made in the USA
San Bernardino, CA
04 March 2016